Copyright

Manhunt: Chasing The Fox
© 2025 Toshibooks

All rights reserved. No part of this publication may be reproduced, distributed, or transmitted in any form or by any means, including photocopying, recording, or other electronic or mechanical methods, without the prior written permission of the publisher, except in the case of brief quotations embodied in critical reviews and certain other non-commercial uses permitted by copyright law.

This is a work of fiction. Names, characters, places, and incidents are either the product of the author's imagination or used fictitiously. Any resemblance to actual persons, living or dead, or actual events is purely coincidental.

Published by Toshibooks

First Edition: November 2025
ISBN (paperback): 9798301260179
Printed in United Kingdom

For permissions or inquiries, please contact us on our social media accounts:
Gmail: Toshibooks2024@gmail.com
Instagram: @toshibooks_
Tik Tok: @toshibooks
X: @Toshibooks_

Dedication

To all other first-time authors hoping to make a breakthrough.

Content warning

This novel contains graphic depictions of violence and explores challenging themes, including physical and mental assault. It may be distressing to some readers.

Prologue

The summer of 1984 had descended upon England with a gentle grace. Life in Leighton Buzzard, Dunstable, and Tring, three small, provincial English towns, was placid and uneventful. Nestled in the embrace of the Chiltern Hills, these scattered towns that formed a quaint triangle seemed to exist in a different world - one where time moved slowly, and the summer days stretched luxuriously, inviting residents to linger on their porches, swap stories over fences, and savour the lingering warmth of the evening sun. It was an area where everyone knew everyone, and the night, soft and warm, was something to be trusted.

Hardly the setting for major crime - or so it seemed.

Part One: The Terror Begins

Chapter 1

The tranquil façade of these sleepy towns masked a sinister reality. High above in the Ivinghoe Hills, a lone man clad from head to toe in black stood atop Ivinghoe Beacon, a popular spot for hikers, dog walkers and model aeroplane enthusiasts. His silhouette was unadorned against the early evening sky, a stark contrast to the idyllic scene below. He was motionless, peering through binoculars with a cold intensity, his eyes narrowing as he surveyed the homes scattered around the region below him. The scene unfolding in the streets was of little concern to him; his focus was singular, his purpose darker than the shade of his outfit. He was observing a home that stood alone, bordered by open land, offering the perfect route for a swift, unseen escape.

As the final light of dusk began to pierce the horizon, the area beneath him was stirring. The daily routine of the townsfolk unfurled with the predictability of a well-rehearsed play: doors were locked, curtains drawn, children tucked away in their beds. There was a comforting rhythm to it all - an unspoken agreement that each day would pass as the last had. But today, that routine was about to be interrupted.

The lone man was about to execute his plan with a chilling precision. With Leighton Buzzard's inhabitants blissfully unaware of the danger lurking so close to home, he slipped into the Chambers' cottage while Lizzie and Alan Chambers were out at a friend's house having dinner. The back door lock popped open with relative ease. The lock was old and no match for the man's trusty screwdriver. He knew that as he had been watching and observing the property for several days.

The cottage, a quintessential representation of country charm, was quaint and well-loved, its floral sofa a testament to the comfort of home. The man had chosen this particular home with care; it was perfect for his purposes.

He moved with the precision of a surgeon. His hands gloved and steady, he grabbed food from the fridge, poured a glass of water and took his stash into the living room. There he worked a thin blade through the fabric of the sofa's back, carefully slicing it open. Sweat beaded on his forehead, but he was methodical, thorough. The room was silent, save for the slow rip of fabric giving way. He pulled at the foam, hollowing out a space big enough for his wiry frame. He removed the evidence, hiding it in an outside bin. Then he wriggled inside the sofa, pulling the fabric back into place, sealing himself in like a spider waiting in its web.

And then, he waited.

Time stretched on, the only sound his own shallow breathing. The man knew how to make himself disappear. How to become part of the furniture. He focused on each breath, his body tense but still, like a lion crouched in the tall grass, waiting for the perfect moment to pounce on its prey.

He could feel the stiffness settling in his muscles, the ache creeping up his spine. Still, he didn't move. His eyes stayed wide open, staring into the darkness of his makeshift hiding spot.

The couple returned home just after ten o'clock, the front door creaking open, and slamming shut, the sound echoing through the quiet house. The man's heart quickened, but his breath remained even. He listened carefully to the soft thud of bags hitting the kitchen counter, the rustle of paper, and the murmur of their voices. He imagined the scene in his mind's eye - Lizzie laughing as Alan tried to juggle too many things at once.

They had no idea. No idea that their cosy, little home had been breached. No idea that a stranger lay coiled like a snake, hidden right beneath their noses.

"Do you want tea, love?" Lizzie's voice carried from the kitchen, light and pleasant, blissfully unaware.

"Yeah, that'd be good. I'll get the milk," Alan replied. The man could hear the refrigerator door opening, the clink of bottles. He imagined the couple, so comfortable in their routine, so assured in their safety. They were wrong. So, so wrong.

The man felt a twisted thrill deep in his gut as he listened to them go about their lives, his pulse a steady thrum in his ears. The ordinary sounds of domesticity – teacups clinking, the faint hiss of the kettle, soft laughter - became a symphony of ignorance. They were living their lives, clueless that a stranger was hiding inside their sofa, listening, waiting.

Alan eventually settled into his sofa, the familiar rustle of the newspaper folding open. The man's ears pricked up at every sound, every word exchanged between them. His breathing was measured, his body numb and sweaty from hours in the cramped hollow of the sofa, but his mind was razor sharp. Lizzie hummed softly as she moved about, her footsteps light, her movements graceful.

The man imagined her delicate hands making tea, pouring milk, unaware that they could so easily be turned into instruments of something far darker. His fingers twitched involuntarily. The thought of it - the power he held - sent a shiver of excitement through him. He was in control. They were his to toy with, to decide their fates.

Minutes ticked by and still, he remained hidden. Lizzie's laughter bubbled up from the kitchen, mixing with the clinking of dishes. She was telling Alan a story, something about an old school friend. The man didn't care about the details; he focused on her voice, its rise and fall, the way it wove a sense of normalcy around the room.

Alan muttered something in response, his voice a low rumble. The man's body tensed, his fingers curled tighter around the blade in his hand, just in case.

"Do you hear that?" Alan's voice broke the rhythm of the evening. The man's pulse quickened. For a moment, his breath hitched, his eyes widening in the dark.

"Hear what?" Lizzie asked, her voice distant, still in the kitchen.

Alan paused; he was sat directly above the man's hiding place. "I don't know. Thought I heard something, that's all."

A moment of silence hung in the air. The man could hear his own heart pounding in his ears, the tension crackling around him. He pressed his body even flatter against the hollowed-out sofa, barely daring to breathe. Sweat trickled down his spine.

"You're always hearing things, love," Lizzie chuckled. The sound of water running in the sink drowned out the stress for a moment. "Probably the house settling or something."

Alan hesitated, then muttered, "Yeah, must be." The friction ebbed, and he settled back into his sofa with a soft groan. Oblivious to the danger, he picked up his newspaper once more.

Meanwhile, the man exhaled silently, his lips bending into a slight, twisted smile. How easy it would be to reach out, to make them know he was there. To make them see. But that wasn't his plan - not yet.

He needed more. More time, more control.

Midnight approached, and the cottage was darkened, albeit for a lamp in the living room, its soft, yellow glow barely reaching the man's hiding spot. Alan yawned loudly, his body sinking further into his sofa. "Must be time for bed" he conceded.

Alan stood up and turned off the television, while Lizzie switched off the lamp. The couple started their nightly routine, brushing their teeth, whispering in hushed tones. The man listened to every word, every breath.

Lizzie, always cautious, checked the front door lock with her usual ritualistic accuracy. She glanced toward the living room with a hint of unease. "You think I'm paranoid, but I'd rather be safe than sorry," she muttered to herself, her fingers lingering on the latch. Lizzie was a woman in her sixties, her life a blend of practicality and affection. Tonight, something about the quiet felt off, a prickling discomfort that she couldn't quite shake.

Alan, dismissive as ever, grumbled from the bathroom. "Nothing ever happens around here, Lizzie. We're in the middle of nowhere, for God's sake."

But something *was* happening. Inside his hiding place, the man was a coiled spring, every nerve ending attuned to the subtle shifts in the atmosphere.

When Alan and Lizzie had finally retired in their bed, the man waited - counting the seconds, then minutes. The house settled into a deep silence, the only sounds now the distant hum of the refrigerator and the occasional creak of the building.

Upstairs, Lizzie had left her bedside lamp on. Her unease grew with the quiet of the house, an unsettling feeling that gnawed at her. She pulled the blankets up to her chin, and slowly her eyes began to rest. Alan had sunk into the mattress with a sigh, his weariness quickly overcoming him. Within minutes, his soft snores filled the room, a regular counterpoint to Lizzie's anxious thoughts.

The man's body ached as he slowly manoeuvred himself out of the hollowed sofa, each movement calculated, every shift of weight deliberate. He slipped out silently, like a phantom emerging from the shadows.

The room was dark, but his eyes had adjusted. He could see the silhouettes of the furniture, the glint of a knife left carelessly on the counter. He crept through the living room, his footsteps silent, his breath steady.

He pulled out a balaclava from his pocket and slipped it on. He was ready. He stood at the bottom of the stairs, listening to the soft snores coming from above. His hand tightened around the handle of his blade. The man smiled in the dark, feeling the cold thrill of terror simmering just beneath the surface, and he waited a few more minutes.

He crept up the stairs, each step measured and cautious. He avoided the squeaky spots with practiced ease, the darkened house now his domain. At the top of the stairs, he paused, listening intently. His heartbeat was steady, his breath slow and controlled. The thrill of the hunt, the invasion of their personal space, was an intoxicating rush. He pushed the bedroom door open just enough to slip inside, his gloved hand brushing against the cool metal of the door handle.

The bedroom was bathed in the pale, wan glow of the lamp. Lizzie lay in bed, her back turned, her face partially hidden by the pillow. Alan was snoring softly beside her, oblivious to the danger that was now inches away. The man moved closer, each step calculated, until he was standing directly over Lizzie's side of the bed. His gloved fingers reached out, brushing gently against her cheek.

Lizzie's eyes snapped open, terror flooding her features as she registered the figure looming over her. Before she could scream, the man's hand clamped over her mouth, his touch cold and unyielding. "Not a word," he whispered, his voice a chilling whisper that sent shivers down her spine.

Alan stirred, sensing the disturbance, his eyes fluttering open to see the dark figure towering over his wife. Panic surged through him as he bolted upright, but the man was quicker. In a swift, practiced motion, he brandished his knife, its handle catching the dim lamplight and casting a menacing gleam.

"Stay quiet, both of you," the man hissed, his voice low and threatening. "Or it gets worse."

Alan's hands trembled as he raised them in a gesture of surrender, his voice a trembling whisper. "Please...we don't have much. Take whatever you want."

The man's lips curved into a malevolent smile beneath his balaclava. He savoured the fear, the trembling of their bodies, the wide, terrified eyes. It was a perverse pleasure, seeing them so vulnerable. But just as he was about to escalate his threats, a noise cut through the oppressive silence.

Two late night dog walkers, Victor and Philippa Smith stood chatting outside the cottage while their dog did its business against the white picket fence running along the front of the garden.

The man's eyes darted to the open window, his expression darkening with a mixture of frustration and alarm. As he opened the curtain and peered out of the window, Victor looked up. Their eyes met catching Victor by surprise.

"Hey, why's there a man wearing a balaclava in Lizzie's bedroom?" he quizzed.

"A what?" replied a surprised Philippa.

The man quickly stepped away from the curtain. This wasn't part of the plan. The sudden interference, the unexpected scrutiny - it was too risky. Without a second thought, he bolted down the stairs, his movements frantic as he dashed through the kitchen and out the back door, over the back fence and into the dark of the fields.

Lizzie, her face pale and her hands trembling, burst out crying, her mind racing with fear. "Alan are you alright?" she gasped, her voice barely more than a whisper.

Alan, his breath ragged and his mind still in shock, nodded weakly. "He had a knife…I thought…"

Lizzie's steady voice cut through the panic. "Stay calm," she said urgently. "We need to call the police. Now."
By dawn, the quiet town was wide awake, the fear spreading like wildfire. The man had breached the sanctity of one of their homes, hiding inside a sofa, and the sense of security that had once blanketed the town was shattered. The Chamber's cottage, once a symbol of peaceful domesticity, had become the scene of an intrusion that would forever alter their perception of safety.

The community gathered, whispers of the intruder's presence mingling with the rising sun. The man had been among them, watching, waiting, hidden in their very midst. As the sun rose over the Chiltern Hills, the townsfolk faced a new reality: an evil buzzard was flying high, and no one knew if or where he would strike next. The once unassuming tranquillity of their lives had been disrupted, leaving behind a lingering sense of unease that would take more than just time to heal.

Chapter 2

Two days later, the warm afternoon sun gently filtered through the lace curtains of a small, secluded bungalow, on the outskirts of Tring, casting intricate patterns of light and darkness that danced across the room. The air was heavy with the comforting scents of old wood and lavender, blending with the faint aroma of blooming roses that drifted in through the open window. Donna Rutland, a seventy-four-year-old woman with a graceful air and a face etched with the lines of a life well-lived, moved around the cosy living room humming softly to herself. She adjusted a stack of books on a small, round table, straightened a framed photograph on the mantelpiece, and dusted off a ceramic figurine with tender care.

Her husband, Arthur, sat in his favourite armchair by the window, his head tilted back slightly, and eyes closed. His newspaper, which he had been reading only moments before, was now draped across his chest. The corners of his mouth twitched upward, perhaps in response to a pleasant dream or simply the contentment that comes with a peaceful afternoon nap. His thinning white hair caught the sunlight, giving it a soft, almost angelic glow. A light breeze fluttered the lace curtains, and the room was filled with the sounds of birds chirping in the distance and the faint chatter of neighbours from down the lane.

It was a scene that could be painted on a canvas, a moment of pure, tranquil domesticity. But inside this serene little bungalow, something was terribly wrong. Lurking within the cosy confines of their living room, hidden away deep within the back of the old leather sofa, an intruder lay in wait, his presence unseen and his intentions unknown.

Earlier that day, the man had slipped into the bungalow with the stealth and precision of a seasoned criminal. He had observed the occupants' comings and goings from his vantage point in the Chiltern Hills. Nobody had suspected him, he was just another naturist, gazing at the wildlife through his binoculars.

He was a man of lithe build, his movements almost unnatural in their quietness, a shadow in the daylight. With the quick flick of his blade, he had sliced open the back of the sofa, creating a hollow space just big enough for him to crawl into and hide. He had chosen his hiding spot well. From there, he could hear every movement without being seen himself, concealed within the very fabric of the Rutland's' everyday life.

He listened intently to the tempo of the couple's day: the soft drone of Donna's song, the rustle of Arthur's newspaper, the faint clink of teacups as they enjoyed their afternoon tea. He lay still, waiting for the right moment to strike.

As the hours crept by, the sun began its slow descent in the sky, and the day transformed into early evening. The golden hues of the afternoon light gradually gave way to the muted tones of dusk, casting longer, softer shadows throughout the room. Donna, her energy seemingly endless, moved into the kitchen to prepare dinner, the comforting clatter of pots and pans adding a homely background noise to the evening. Arthur, now awake and stretching the stiffness from his limbs, switched on the radio, and the gentle strains of a classical symphony filled the bungalow, soothing and melodic.

The man remained perfectly still, his body cramped from the tight confines of his hiding place, but his mind was focused, his senses heightened. He was accustomed to discomfort; in fact, he thrived on it. Each muscle that ached, each cramp that seized his body, only sharpened his resolve. He knew he had to bide his time. Tonight, he was going to strike. He had decided that much already, and he was a man who always saw his plans through. The Rutland's dinner time passed slowly, and the couple began to wind down, their routine practiced and predictable. Donna glanced at the clock on the wall, a simple piece with a soft, rhythmic tick that marked the passing of time. She yawned softly, stretching her arms above her head, and turned to Arthur with a gentle smile. "Time for bed, love," she said softly, her voice warm and tender as she placed a comforting hand on his shoulder. They loved an early night.

Arthur nodded, his eyes crinkling at the corners as he smiled back at her. He folded his newspaper neatly and set it aside, the rustling of the paper breaking the calm stillness of the room. The two of them shuffled slowly toward their bedroom, their movements slow and tired but full of a quiet contentment. The living room fell into darkness as they left, save for the dim glow of the streetlight outside that seeped through the window, casting faint lines of light on the walls.

For a moment, an almost tangible silence settled over the bungalow. All that could be heard was the soft ticking of the clock and the distant buzz of the world outside. Then, like a wild bear emerging from hibernation, the man began to move. He slipped out from his hiding place, emerging from the darkness of the sofa with a smooth, almost feline grace. He stretched his limbs carefully, feeling the pressure ease from his muscles, but his eyes remained concentrated, his mind alert. He put on his balaclava and gripped his knife tight.

Each step he took was slow and calculated. He knew the layout of the cottage well, having observed the Rutland's conversation and movements. He moved like a silhouette, gliding silently across the floorboards, making his way down the hallway toward the bedroom where Arthur and Donna now lay. Inside, Arthur was already asleep, his breathing steady and deep, while Donna, with her back to the door, was still drifting in and out of consciousness.

The man reached the doorway and paused, his breath steady and controlled. His eyes gleamed with malice, cold and calculating. This was it - the moment he had been waiting for. He took another careful step forward, his hand tightening around the handle of his knife.
A floorboard screeched under his weight, the sound piercing the silence like a needle through cloth.

Donna stirred, her instincts pricking at her sleep-dulled senses. "Arthur, did you hear that?" she whispered, her voice barely a breath as she turned slightly toward him.

The man reacted instantly. He lunged forward, his movements swift and menacing, his voice low and threatening. "Not a word," he hissed, brandishing his knife. The blade caught the faint light from the window, gleaming with a cold, deadly promise.

Donna froze, her heart pounding in her chest like a drumbeat. She could see his masked face, partially shrouded in shadiness, and her breath caught in her throat. There was a darkness in his eyes, a malice that sent a shiver down her spine.

Arthur jolted awake, his eyes snapping open as he tried to comprehend what was happening. "What...who are you?" he croaked, his voice hoarse and trembling with fear.

"Shut up," the man growled, his tone dripping with danger. "You make a sound, and I swear-"

He stepped around to Arthur's side of the bed, moving with a chilling calm. In one swift motion, he pulled a length of coarse rope from his pocket and tied Arthur's hands together, his grip firm and unyielding. "Don't move, or she gets it," he snarled, his eyes never leaving Arthur's face.

Arthur's breath came in shallow, panicked gasps, his eyes wide with terror. He nodded slowly, understanding the gravity of the situation, his heart pounding in his chest.

Without breaking his gaze from Arthur, the man moved back to Donna's side of the bed, his demeanour shifting. There was a new glint in his eyes, one of cruel intent. He reached down and pulled back the duvet covers, revealing Donna's legs beneath her light nightgown.

Donna's breath hitched in her throat, her eyes darting to Arthur, who lay helpless beside her. She was paralysed with fear, her body stiff and trembling. Tears welled up in her eyes, spilling down her cheeks in silent streams.

The man ran his left hand slowly up Donna's leg, his touch cold and invasive. "Ssh, don't make a sound," he whispered, his voice a soft, sinister murmur in the darkness. Donna's body was rigid with terror, her heart beating so loudly she was sure he could hear it. She squeezed her eyes shut, trying to block out the reality of what was happening, her tears falling faster now.

As the man's hand reached inside her underwear, Donna sobbed uncontrollably. The man showed no remorse, he smiled from underneath his mask. The assault lasted only a few minutes before the sound of a car's engine approached from the distance, its headlights suddenly sweeping across the bedroom window. Bright beams of light cut through the darkness, casting sharp, moving shades across the room. The man's eyes flicked toward the window, his grip on the knife tightening instinctively. For a moment, panic flashed across his face. Another disturbance.

In that split second, Donna saw an opportunity. Summoning every ounce of courage she had, she acted.

"Arthur!" she shouted, her voice breaking the strain like a lightning strike. It was louder than she intended, but it was enough. The sudden burst of noise startled the man, his head snapping back toward her, eyes wide with surprise.

Outside, a dog began barking, its frantic yaps growing closer and more insistent. The man's eyes darted to the window again, calculating his options. The risk was too high now. Too many variables. Too much noise. He wasn't here to get caught.

"Damn it," he muttered under his breath, taking a step back, his gaze shifting rapidly between Arthur and Donna. "You got lucky tonight," he spat, his voice filled with frustration and anger.
And then, just as quickly as he had appeared, he turned and bolted out of the bedroom. His footsteps were hefty and rapid as they pounded down the hallway, a stark contrast to his earlier stealth. Arthur and Donna could hear the back door slam open, and a gust of warm night air swept into the bungalow, bringing with it an unexpected chill as their intruder fled into the darkness of the nearby fields.

For a moment, the bungalow was engulfed in silence once more, broken only by Donna's shaky, uneven breaths and Arthur's stunned murmurs. The fear still lingered, deep and suffocating, as the reality of what had just happened began to sink in.

"Donna are you-" Arthur started, his voice a trembling whisper, his eyes wide with concern.

"I'm fine," she interrupted, her voice barely audible, her body still trembling. "We're fine. But he...he was in our home, Arthur."

Donna untied Arthur and pulled him in close. His heart raced with a mixture of relief and horror, his mind struggling to process the events that had unfolded.

After a few minutes, Donna plucked up the courage to call the police, while Arthur surveyed the crime scene.

They both stared in disbelief as they noticed the torn back of the sofa, the leather sliced open, revealing the hollow where the man had hidden for hours.

The terrible truth settled over them like a dark, oppressive cloud. They hadn't just been visited by the man; he had been with them all day, lurking in the corners of their own home, waiting for the right moment to strike.

The realisation left them cold, a deep, unsettling chill settling into their bones. But as they held each other in the dim light of their living room, they knew one thing for certain: they were alive. And sometimes, in the face of darkness, that was enough.

Chapter 3

The following evening, the sun began to set over the small village of Cheddington, its low arc painting the quaint streets with a warm, golden hue. The last of the spring flowers bobbed gently in the breeze, their colours vivid against the backdrop of a serene evening. The village, accustomed to its cadenced quiet, seemed to have settled into its habitual lull. In a place where little ever happened, the pervasive sense of calm was both a comfort and a façade.

Beneath this veneer of peace, a sinister reality was taking shape.

The man, an outline in the twilight, moved silently through the creeping dusk. All day he had been observing the cottage on the corner of Tring Road, his keen eyes tracking its every movement. He was a meticulous predator; he knew the owner's routines and vulnerabilities. Tonight, Benjamin Young, the owner of the cottage - a solitary bachelor in his mid-thirties - was out for the evening, leaving behind an opportunity the man was determined to seize.

"Time to move," he muttered to himself, the words barely more than a hiss in the growing darkness. He approached the back of the cottage with the stealth of a practiced infiltrator. The window he had selected days before, now weathered and worn, yielded to his touch. The lock, old and feeble, surrendered with a soft click that barely disturbed the stillness of the night.

Inside, the man paused, letting his senses adjust to the dim interior. The cottage was enveloped in darkness, its silence profound and almost oppressive. It was perfect.

He slipped through the small kitchen, his eyes scanning every detail with a rapacious focus - the hum of the fridge, the faint clink of a loose floor tile beneath his boot. His gloved fingers brushed over the countertop, grazing a pile of unopened mail. He glanced into the living room; it was empty. He moved down the narrow hall, his steps silent and calculated. He passed a closed door and halted, sensing something behind it. With a slight twist of the handle, he pushed the door open, revealing a tidy bedroom. The room was modest, with a narrow bed neatly made, but it was the gleam of metal propped against the wall that drew his attention - a twelve-bore shotgun. His heart quickened with a dark thrill.

"Well, well," he whispered, a twisted smile creeping across his face. He picked up the gun, feeling its weight, the power it represented. Moments later, he found gun shells, and some cash stashed in a drawer, hidden beneath some clothes. "Won't be needing those anymore, mate," he uttered.

Pocketing the shells, he moved back into the living room, his eyes now fixed on the small television set. Next to it, a collection of pornographic tapes lay scattered. He leaned in, tracing the crude handwriting on one of the labels *'Debbie Does Dallas'*. An aggressive grin spread across his face as he selected it. He slipped the tape into the VCR player, turned on the television, and watched as the screen flickered to life, bathing the room in a ghostly glow.

The man grabbed some dining room chairs, some nearby blankets and made himself a den. He then had the audacity to make a cup of tea and a sandwich from the contents of the fridge.

Time passed slowly, each minute stretching into an eternity as the video played. The man lounged in his den, the shotgun resting on his lap, the £300 cash he had found stuffed into his coat pocket. His breathing was controlled, his eyes fixed on the screen, anticipation building with each passing moment. He checked his watch; the man would be home soon.

Just after ten o'clock, the soft glow of headlights swept across the front window. The man's pulse quickened, a rush of adrenaline sharpening his focus. He rose slowly from his den, the television's glow casting an eeriness across the room. He turned off the television, slipped on his balaclava and melted into the darkness, his senses acutely tuned to the sounds outside. He heard the soft crunch of gravel, the jingle of keys. The front door creaked open.

"Bloody hell, another late one," came Benjamin's weary voice, oblivious to the danger that lurked inside. The door closed behind him. The man tensed, listening to the approach of footsteps growing closer, each step a harbinger of what was to come.

As Benjamin stepped into the living room, the man struck. He lunged out of the darkness, smashing the cold barrel of the shotgun into Benjmain's ribs, drooping him to his knees.

"Don't move," the man hissed, his breath hot and rancid. Benjamin's eyes widened in shock, his mouth opening in a wordless gasp of terror.

"Wh-what do you want?" he gasped, his hands trembling uncontrollably.

"Take whatever you need, just-"

"Shut up," the man cut him off, his voice a sharp, harsh whisper. He picked Benjamin up and shoved him toward a dining room chair. "Sit. Now."

Benjamin, his breath coming in short, ragged bursts, complied, collapsing into the chair. The man kept the shotgun levelled at him, the weapon a constant, menacing presence. Reaching into his pocket, he pulled out a tie, one from Benjamin's collection. Benjamin's eyes widened even further in fear.

"Please...please don't do this," he begged, his voice breaking as he tried to offer anything to delay the inevitable. "I have money. I can-"

"Quiet," the man snapped, his patience wearing thin. He moved behind Benjamin, looping the tie around his wrists and pulling it tight. Benjamin whimpered as the tie dug into his skin, the fear evident in every shuddering breath.

The man tied the knots efficiently, securing Benjamin to the chair. His face twisted into a grotesque smile, a twisted semblance of friendliness. "There now. We're just going to have a little chat," he said, his tone almost playful. He walked back to the television, turned it on again, and resumed the tape. The screen flickered with grainy, explicit images that cast a sickly glow across the room. The man undid his jeans, slid down his underpants, and slowly caressed himself.

Benjamin's face drained of colour as he realised what was playing. "Oh God," he whispered, the gravity of his situation sinking in.

"Like to watch, do you?" The man asked, his voice a low growl. He crouched down in front of his captive, their faces inches apart. "Well, tonight's your lucky night. Because so do I."

Benjamin twisted in the chair, his eyes darting around the room, desperately searching for something, anything, to help him. "Please...whatever you're thinking...you don't have to do this."

The man's expression darkened behind his balaclava. Without warning, he slapped Benjamin hard across the face, the sound echoing sharply through the small room. "Did I say you could speak?"

Benjamin went silent, his lip trembling as a thin line of blood trickled from where his teeth had cut the inside of his cheek. The man straightened, pacing slowly around the room. The shotgun, now casually slung over his shoulder, seemed almost an extension of him.

"I've been watching you," the man murmured, more to himself than to his captive. "Watching this place. Studying it. Studying you. And I know your type. Thinks he's safe out here in his little village, locked up in his little cottage. But no one's ever really safe, are they?"

He stopped in front of the television again, his eyes fixed on the screen. "You just never know what might be lying in wait."

The minutes stretched on, each second a slow, torturous tick of the clock. Benjamin tried to control his breathing, to avoid looking at the screen, to steel himself against the horrors he could only imagine. But he could feel the man's gaze on him, a substantial, oppressive presence that seemed to suffocate the room.

Without warning, the man moved closer, his lips brushing against Benjamin's ear as he whispered, "Time to have some fun."

Benjamin closed his eyes, bracing himself for the worst. The man's cold, low chuckle was the last sound he heard before the terror that was to follow.

The man knelt before Benjamin; his gaze fixated on the young man's tear-streaked face. His left-hand moved with a disturbing intimacy, pressing against Benjamin's body, an act laced with menace. Benjamin's sobs grew louder, trembling under the weight of his fear, but the man remained unmoved, his tongue darting out to wet his lips as he savoured the fear in his captive's eyes.

As the man toyed with the fabric of Benjamin 's clothing, methodically undoing his trousers, the atmosphere grew increasingly charged. Benjamin's silent sobs echoed through the room. The man was focused, driven by a dark intent that consumed the moment, indifferent to the terror etched in Benjamin's eyes.

The sexual assault that followed was ferocious and forceful. Benjamin stared up at the ceiling as the man attacked him with his hands and his mouth. With every intimate stroke, the man let out a groan of grotesque pleasure.

The assault continued all night, each touch from the man followed by the sound of Benjamin's pain and anguish. The man revelled in the power he wielded, drawing out the suffering with a perverse satisfaction. The cottage, once a symbol of quiet domesticity, was now a stage for an unspeakable horror.

By the time the man had ended Benjamin's torture, the first light of dawn was breaking. Benjamin lay bound to the chair, shaking uncontrollably, his breath ragged and uneven. His face was a mask of trauma.

The echoes of the man's footsteps faded into the early morning mist, as he made his escape through nearby woodlands. The darkness that had invaded the cottage would linger long after the man had disappeared, leaving behind a haunting presence that would overshadow the village's peaceful façade for years to come.

The man knelt in the dense woodland; his hands caked with dirt as he carefully buried the shotgun beneath a thick tangle of roots. The soft earth gave way easily, swallowing the weapon that had served him well on this occasion, but it was too dangerous to keep close. He patted the soil down, his eyes scanning the area to mark the spot in his memory - a fallen log, a cluster of ferns. Confident that the shotgun was hidden from prying eyes, he continued his getaway.

Three days later, when he returned to retrieve it, a cold panic gripped him. The familiar landmarks blurred together, and no matter how much he dug or searched, the shotgun seemed to have vanished, lost to the very earth he'd thought would keep it safe.

Chapter 4

The following day, the first light of dawn crept slowly over the newly dubbed 'Triangle of Terror' - Leighton Buzzard, Dunstable, and Tring - its pale fingers stretching across the quiet streets and casting long, skeletal shadows. The early morning calm, usually a comfort, was now steeped in a tangible sense of unease. Curtains remained tightly drawn, and inside their homes, residents spoke in hushed, anxious tones. The news of the sexual assault on Benjamin Young had travelled fast. And now, another assault had occurred.

Detective Inspector Peter Hargreaves, a twenty-two-year veteran of the Leighton Buzzard police force, stood at the back door of a small cottage; his gaze fixed on a set of footprints half-hidden in the dewy grass. They trailed off toward the back fence and the woods, disappearing into the dense undergrowth like a bad memory that refused to be forgotten. He glanced back at his partner, Detective Sergeant Linda Collins, who had served alongside him for nearly a decade, who was speaking with the homeowner - a frail, elderly man, named Mike Cox, whose hands shook uncontrollably as he recounted the horrors of the night before.

"He was in my bedroom," Mike murmured, his voice breaking with the weight of his fear. "Didn't hear him come in. Didn't even see him until he was right there… standing over my bed."

Collins leaned in closer, her expression a mix of professional concern and personal empathy. "What did he look like? Anything specific?"

"Just… just his eyes," Mike whispered, his voice trembling. "Cold. Like he was looking right through me. He was wearing a mask and didn't say a word, just… stood there. Then he attacked me and was gone, like he was never there."

Hargreaves scanned the scene with a growing sense of frustration. Four houses had been hit, all in different locations but close enough to establish a connection.

Collins walked over to Hargreaves; her face lined with tension. "This is the fourth incident now. Similar description: masked intruder, broke in, made a den inside their home, had a cup of tea, ate food, looked through photo albums, watched videos, laid out belts and ties, attacked them, in and out like a ghost."

"Bloody hell," Hargreaves muttered under his breath, more to himself than to Collins. He glanced at the old man's back door, which still swung loosely on its hinges, then back at the fading footprints. "He's got a taste for fear. That's what he wants."

Collins nodded, her eyes scanning the surrounding area. "What's our next move?"

Hargreaves, his jaw set with determination, turned to face her. "It's probably just a homeless person, hungry and needing some respite from the outside world. Albeit with a sick and twisted mind. Let's search the area for homeless people. See if anyone matches the description."

Collins flipped open her notebook, her expression resolute. "The press has nicknamed him 'The Fox'." A name that suited him well. Known for his cunning and stealth, The Fox was an expert in building dens and attacking at night.

"They can call him what they want," Hargreaves said, his eyes drifting toward the woods where the footprints had disappeared. "If they contact us, tell them whatever you like. Let them run wild with it. Maybe it'll draw him out."

As he spoke, Hargreaves felt the weight of the task ahead. Whoever this intruder was, he thrived on the chaos and fright he spread. The darkness that had settled over the area was not just a physical absence of light but a creeping, pervasive menace that left everyone on edge. And Hargreaves worried that the worst was yet to come.

Across the 'Triangle of Terror', phones rang incessantly as concerned voices filled the airwaves. The quiet towns and villages were abuzz with rumours and whispered fears. "Did you hear about the break-in last night? And the sexual assault the night before?". In her modest kitchen, Mary Whitfield clutched the receiver tightly, her voice wavering as she spoke with her neighbour. "Yes, I've heard," she said, her tone anxious. "No, I don't know where he'll strike next, but I'm keeping the lights on tonight. All of them. And I'm checking my sofas, twice if I must."

Mary's hands trembled as she hung up, her mind racing with dark thoughts. The idea of someone slipping into homes without a trace and hiding inside sofas, was enough to make her feel vulnerable in her own space. She moved through her house with heightened vigilance, her gaze darting to every window, every door. The Fox could come through any of them.

Two streets away from where Benjamin Young lived, Tom Bridger, a retired constable, sat on his porch, his weathered face etched with concern. His old instincts had kicked in, the hairs on the back of his neck prickling with a sense of impending danger. He gripped his baseball bat like a lifeline, his eyes scanning the street with a mixture of hope and dread. "He'll be back," Bridger muttered to himself, his voice a low rumble. "Foxes always come back."

The day passed in a blur of activity as Hargreaves and Collins continued their canvassing efforts. Each door they knocked on, each person they interviewed, offered no real clues as to who The Fox might be.

The sun climbed higher in the sky, casting an uneasy light over the towns and villages. The chatter of frightened residents and the buzz of rumours filled the atmosphere, creating a pressure that seemed almost physical.

As their shift ended, Hargreaves and Collins had worked their way through the neighbourhoods, their every step marked by the weight of their responsibility. When they eventually returned to their car, Collins opened the passenger door and slid into her seat, her face lined with worry. "We've got a difficult task ahead of us," she said, her voice tired but resolute.

Hargreaves nodded; his eyes fixed on the horizon. "We do. And we need to be ready for whatever comes next. This Fox character is out there, watching, waiting. We've got to find a way to outsmart him."

Hargreaves words carried a weighty sense of foreboding. The Fox had demonstrated an unsettling ability to remain one step ahead, exploiting the townspeople's fears to his advantage. Each new break-in was not just a crime but a statement - a declaration of his dominance over the frightened communities.

In the newsroom of the Leighton Buzzard Observer newspaper, local journalist Claire Milford was immersed in her work, surrounded by the clacking of typewriters and the haze of cigarette smoke. She was new to the area, having been transferred from London, and the pace of life in Leighton Buzzard was a stark contrast to the hustle and bustle she had been accustomed to. But now, a story with real bite had emerged - a story that had quickly become the focal point of her reporting.

Claire's pen tapped rhythmically against her notepad as she reviewed police reports and witness statements. The picture that was emerging was one of a crafty figure who moved with a chilling precision, leaving behind only fear and confusion. She scribbled a headline on her pad: "The Fox Strikes Again." The idea of this elusive raider capturing the imagination of the public was both thrilling and terrifying.

As she envisioned the morning edition flying off the stands, Claire's excitement was tempered by a growing sense of unease. She had covered crime in major cities before, witnessed firsthand the way fear could tear communities apart, turning neighbours against each other and projecting deep-seated doubts. In these quiet rural areas, the stakes seemed even higher. The fear of the unknown was like a wildfire, spreading quickly and consuming everything in its path.

The evening brought a chill to the atmosphere, despite the blazing heat of the summer. The towns and villages, once buzzing with anxious chatter, now seemed subdued, as if holding their breath in anticipation of what might come next. The Fox had become a spectre haunting their every thought, a dark presence that lurked just beyond the edge of their comfort.

As night fell, the fear that had gripped the locals only seemed to deepen. In their homes, residents checked and rechecked their locks, their hearts pounding with a mixture of dread and helplessness. The sky outside seemed darker, the noises of the night more ominous. Despite the hot, sticky night, they were too scared to chance leaving a window open.

Hargreaves and Collins had returned to their office to review the day's findings before heading home. The frustration was evident in their voices, a sharp edge to their words as they discussed their next steps.

"We're missing something," Collins said, her frustration evident. "There's got to be a pattern, a clue we're overlooking."

Hargreaves rubbed his temples, trying to focus through the haze of exhaustion. "We need to think like him. What drives someone to do this? What's his end game?". "Let's go home and get some rest. I'll see you bright and early in the morning."

The words lingered, dark questions that neither of them could easily answer. The Fox had proven himself to be a master of evasion, who slipped through their grasp with a chilling ease.

The Fox was not just a criminal; he was a harbinger of terror; he had turned the area into a maze of anxiety and suspicion. The hunt was on, and The Fox loomed large, a dark and enigmatic force that seemed to defy comprehension.

Chapter 5

The once tranquil region encompassing Hertfordshire, Bedfordshire, and Buckinghamshire had been transformed into a realm of fear and paranoia. Windows, once left open to catch a refreshing breeze, were now bolted shut. Doors with old, rusty locks were upgraded to modern, heavy-duty versions. The change in the area was not just a reaction to the series of break-ins and assaults; it was a response to something far more unsettling.

Conversations at local pubs, hairdressers and newsagents were dominated by talk of The Fox - an intruder who seemed to slip through the night like a wisp of smoke, unseen and unstoppable. What had started as a series of seemingly random burglaries had escalated into a dark, almost mythical terror. The usual inane chatter had been replaced by fearful whispers and speculation. The Fox was no longer just a name; he had become an entity of dread.

Detective Inspector Peter Hargreaves sat at his desk in the Leighton Buzzard police station, the dim light casting clouds over the map of Herts, Beds, and Bucks spread before him. The map was a collage of red pins marking the sites of The Fox's crimes. But despite the glaring visual representation of his spree, Hargreaves couldn't distinguish any discernible pattern. No rhythm to the madness, no clue as to what drove this criminal's decisions.

"What kind of person thinks to hide inside a sofa all day, let alone actually does it," Hargreaves muttered, his voice a low growl of frustration. The walls of his office seemed to close in, laden with the weight of the investigation's mounting pressure. His eyes, bloodshot from working late into the night, flicked over the scatter of pins, each one representing a piece of a puzzle that refused to fit together.

Across from him, Detective Sergeant Linda Collins leaned back in her chair, her eyes sharp but tired. She rubbed her temples, trying to stave off the headache that came with long hours and mounting stress. "Psychological terror," she said, her voice carrying the burdensome weight of her own exhaustion. "That's what this is. Maximum fear factor."

Hargreaves nodded; his gaze fixed on the map as if willing it to reveal some hidden truth. "Last night's attack proves it. He's getting bolder. He's enjoying it."

The night before, The Fox had gone further than before, sexually assaulting an elderly couple, Michael and Louise Stamp. They lived in an isolated farmhouse in Tring, an easy target with an easy escape route.

Hargreaves and Collins set off to visit the victims, which was becoming an all too familiar occurrence.

The Fox had chosen to break in during the day when the occupants were out, a calculated move that showed his confidence and control. He had removed all the light bulbs from the property, ensuring that when the couple returned, they would be plunged into an all-encompassing darkness. The act of removing the bulbs was more than just a crime; it was a deliberate act of psychological torment.

He had stolen money and, more significantly, he had found another shotgun and gun shells. A huge stroke of luck.

Michael Stamp and his wife had lived on the farm for over thirty years. Michael, a greying man with hands weathered by decades of hard work, sat at the kitchen table, his eyes hollow and haunted. The trauma was visible in every tremor of his hands, every haunted glance.

"He was just…there," Michael whispered, his voice cracking with the weight of his terror. "I was looking for candles when the power didn't work. I didn't see him until he was standing in the doorway."

The memory seemed to choke him, his words faltering as he continued. "He just...he just stared. And then he laughed." His voice broke entirely, and he looked down, unable to continue.

Collins exchanged a glance with Hargreaves, the look on Michael's face a stark reminder of the psychological damage inflicted by their elusive adversary. It was the look of someone who had stared into the eyes of a monster and found themselves forever changed.

"Can you describe him to us, any distinguishing features?" asked Collins.

"It was hard to tell due to the darkness, but the moonlight helped a bit. I'd say he was erm, he was around five feet nine or ten inches tall, and he had a slim frame. He was wearing a mask, but I saw curly hair, and his accent-" replied Michael.

"Yes, go on-" asked Collins.

"It was northern. Soft but sounded Geordie," responded Louise.

"And did he smell, erm, like he hadn't showered in days?" Collins queried.

"Oh no, he smelled fresh." Michael retorted.

"Well then. I think we can rule out this perpetrator sleeping rough on the streets. Thank you for your help, it has been very useful." Hargreaves said, his voice firm but tinged with an undercurrent of frustration. "We will find him; I promise you that."

But as they left the farmhouse, Collins could see the doubt etched on Hargreaves's face. The weight of the case was beginning to show, and the fear that had taken root in the community seemed to be seeping into the detectives themselves.

"So, he's not homeless," Collins said, breaking the silence that had settled between them. "He's hidden in amongst us."

Hargreaves's face hardened, a mixture of determination and grim resignation. "Yeah," he replied. "And he's enjoying every bloody minute of it."

Back in Leighton Buzzard, Claire Milford, the journalist who had first dubbed the intruder 'The Fox', was feeling the pressure of the growing panic. The headlines were selling papers and fuelling the fear, but the responsibility of covering such a chilling story was taking its toll. Claire sat in her cramped office, surrounded by the clutter of police reports and half-empty coffee cups, her fingers tapping nervously on her desk as she reviewed the latest updates.

She picked up the phone and dialled Tom Bridger, the retired constable who had been keeping a close eye on the developments. "Tom, it's Claire Milford. I wanted to ask about the other night. Did you see or hear anything?"

Bridger's voice came through the line, gravelly and tense. "You mean apart from the entire town locking themselves in their houses despite the boiling hot summer? No, I didn't see or hear anything. But I heard about that poor couple in Tring. We're dealing with something different here, Claire. This isn't just some common thief."

Claire's brow furrowed, her concern deepening. "I know. It's like he wants to be seen now. He's pushing people to their limits." Bridger sighed heavily. "Fear makes people do strange things. Makes them see things that aren't there. Or miss things that are." There was a pause, a moment of grim realisation. "We need to be careful. He's playing a game, and he's winning."

The words weighed heavily on them; a chilling reminder of the stakes involved. The Fox was not just a criminal; he was a master manipulator, an umbra that danced just out of reach, feeding off the fear and uncertainty he created.

After committing three more burglaries, The Fox struck again, this time breaking into another house in Tring. The home was empty which The Fox knew having studied it for many days. The occupants informed the police the intruder had carefully removed clothing from drawers and photographs from albums The crimes were linked to The Fox, as the meticulousness spoke volumes about his intent to cause psychological damage, not just material loss.

The following night, in Wingrave, the moon hung low in the sky, a dull, misty orb barely piercing the darkness that enveloped the village. A welcome faint drizzle began to fall from the sky, coating the rooftops and streets in a slick, cold sheen. Somewhere on the outskirts, in a neighbourhood where the streetlights flickered weakly against the encroaching night, a soul destroyer crept through the alleyways. He moved with sleek elegance, disappearing smoothly into the dim surroundings.

The Fox, no one knew his real name - only the reputation that preceded him, was a silent hunter with a reputation for brutal efficiency. Tonight, he was out hunting again.

The target was a two-story house, dark and still except for a single light flickering in an upstairs window. The Fox crouched beneath the cover of an overgrown hedge, his breath steady and measured. His eyes, cold and calculating, he scanned the perimeter. He saw the slightest tremble of a curtain in an upstairs room. Someone was home.

He moved swiftly, silent as death itself. With a gloved hand, he tested the window on the side of the house. With a gentle push, it gave way. Sliding it open, he slipped inside, crouching low to let his eyes adjust to the dim interior. The house smelled of mildew and something sour - unwashed clothes, maybe. He could hear the faint ticking of a clock coming from the living room.

The Fox didn't need a weapon; but he carried his stolen shotgun for maximum fear effect. His senses were sharp, ears attuned to the smallest sounds. He crept forward, listening.

Low whispers came from upstairs. A man and a woman's voice - nervous, on edge. The Fox felt a faint smile tug at his lips. He took the stairs slowly, avoiding the spots where the wood might rasp. Each step was calculated, his weight carefully distributed to remain silent. At the top of the stairs, he paused, listening again. The voices had fallen silent.

He was close now. He could hear their breaths, smell the fear sweating off their skin. The Fox took a moment, his gloved hand slowly reaching for the doorknob. In one fluid motion, he twisted and kicked the door open with a force that sent it crashing against the wall.

Chaos erupted. The man who had been whispering, Markus Longman, a thin, wiry figure, staggered backward, eyes wide with terror. He regained his composure and charged forward, bellowing like an enraged animal. The Fox reacted quickly - too quickly for Markus. He sidestepped Markus, his movement almost lazy, letting Markus crash into the wall. Before he could recover, The Fox struck - a swift elbow to the back of the skull. Markus let out a grunt and staggered, but he wasn't down. He turned, swinging a wild haymaker. The Fox ducked under it, came up, and delivered a vicious uppercut to his jaw. There was a sickening crack, and Markus's eyes rolled back as he slumped to the floor.

Markus sat frozen, back against the wall. His eyes darted around, looking for something, anything to use as a weapon. His hand found a lamp on a nearby table. He grabbed it and swung it in desperation. The Fox caught his wrist mid-swing, twisted it sharply, and the lamp fell to the floor with a dull thud.

A single, fluid movement brought The Fox's knee into Markus's face. He doubled over, gasping for air, and then a sharp, snapping kick to the side of his head flattened him to the floor.

Silence filled the room, broken only by the heavy breathing of the two men, and the sobbing of Sara, Markus's wife. The Fox stood over them, his face unreadable. He knelt, grabbing Markus by the collar and pulling him close. His voice, when he spoke, was low and calm - a voice devoid of mercy.

"Tell the world," he said. "You just got outboxed and outfoxed."

He released Markus, letting him drop back to the floor, semi-conscious. The Fox took one last glance at the wreckage, then quietly slipped away, vanishing as silently as he had appeared.

Chapter 6

The atmosphere was dense with the smell of warm rain-soaked earth, and the village of Heath and Reach sat in an unsettling stillness, the kind that settles just before something breaks. The Fox had returned, slipping through the night like a bat on the prowl. This time, his target was a quaint little house, the kind with flowerpots on the windowsills and a white picket fence. A place of warmth and safety. A place he would turn into his lair.

The Fox moved with a cold, calculated confidence, slipping past locks and bolts as if they were mere inconveniences. The occupants of the house were out for the evening, unaware of the creeping terror that had chosen them. As he crept through the back door, he removed each light bulb, leaving the home shrouded in an impenetrable darkness, a void where light had no purchase. He rearranged the furniture with the accuracy of a chess player setting the board. Every chair, every table was moved, covered with blankets and sheets, twisted into a camouflaged nest in the centre of the living room.

The Fox's movements were fluid, purposeful. He worked in silence, as if darkness itself was his ally. In the main bedroom, he opened drawers with a calm hand, selecting dressing gown cords like a connoisseur, tucking them into his coat with a clinical grace. He reached for the telephone and cut the wires with a swift motion - one less connection to the outside world. His fingertips brushed against the buttons of the answering machine, hovering over them for a moment as if contemplating something, before he withdrew.

He moved with a cat-like agility, his senses heightened, his pulse steady. The house was his now, a temporary kingdom he had claimed for himself. He ransacked the fridge with a sense of entitlement, taking what he wanted - slices of ham, a half-eaten apple, and a carton of milk. The sound of the kettle boiling broke the silence, its whistle cutting through the darkness like a scream. He made himself a cup of tea, stirred it slowly, and savoured it. The audacity of it all - the invasion, the reordering of a life that wasn't his - was not lost on him. It was an act of psychological warfare, a game of dominance and terror.

Hours passed, and with them, a stillness that could make the skin crawl. The Fox's lair, cloaked in darkness, became a living thing - a place where the walls had eyes, and every creak of the floorboards whispered his presence. He waited in his constructed den, the silence so thick it felt as if the walls themselves were holding their breath. His heartbeat was the only rhythm in this symphony of dread. Time stretched, distorted, a trick played by the darkness.

At one o'clock in the morning, the crunch of gravel under tyres signalled the return of the homeowners. The Fox tensed, his muscles coiling like a spring. Keys rattled in the front door, and the lock clicked open. His breathing slowed, his pulse quickened, and his eyes narrowed into slits, peering through the gaps in his makeshift hideout. The door screeched open, and the couple, Antony and Antoinette Bednarek stepped inside, they were oblivious, tired, and unsuspecting.

But something must have changed in the air - a scent, a sound - Antony paused. He turned his head as if sensing the shift in the atmosphere, a subtle but undeniable wrongness. The Fox's heart drummed faster; he could feel it in his throat. A single misstep, a clang of the floor beneath him, broke the spell. The couple froze. Antony's eyes widened in horror, and in that instant, The Fox bolted from his hiding place, a swift blur of motion.

"Oi, come back here you bastard," shouted Antony.

For once The Fox had lost his cool. Panic surged through his veins as he burst through the back door. The heat of the night hit him like a hot flannel. He sprinted through the garden, vaulting over the hedges, and melted into the darkness beyond. Behind him, the shrieks of terror rose into the night like a wailing siren. He didn't look back; he didn't need to.

Antony and Antoinette shaking from the experience, called the police.

"He's been here," shouted Antony. "The Fox, he's been in my house."

The police arrived within minutes, flooding the quiet street with flashing lights and the murmur of radios. In the house, the police surveyed the crime scene. They found his lair - a still-warm cup of tea sat ominously inside his den, a chilling testament to his unsettling presence. The Fox, in his haste to leave, had also left behind £130 in stolen cash, an anorak, and a packet of peanuts, spilled on the floor like a breadcrumb trail of madness.

For Antony and Antoinette, it was as if a spirit had invaded their sanctuary, a phantasm that had sipped tea where they dined, watched them from the darkness where they once felt safe.

But The Fox wasn't done. The hunger for fear, for chaos, pulled him onward. The anger grew inside him, he rarely lost his cool. He needed to strike back instantly; prove to himself he was still in control.

He moved across the fields on foot, the darkness swallowing him whole. He emerged on the Planets estate in Leighton Buzzard. Here, another house, another life, would be drawn into his web of terror.

Ashton and Zarah Hartwig slept soundly, wrapped in the comfort of ignorance. They had locked their doors and windows, never imagining that a nightmare would manifest in their home. But nightmares have a way of seeping through cracks, of slipping under doors and through windows. The Fox crept through the blackness, his breath controlled, his footsteps silent. He prized open the back door lock with ease and snuck into the house.

Inside their bedroom, the dim glow of a night-light cast a faint halo around their sleeping. The Fox stood in the doorway, his presence filling the room with a chilling malevolence. He wore a different mask than usual - a grotesque thing fashioned from a trouser leg with jagged cut-out eye holes. It was both absurd and terrifying, like something born from a fevered mind.

Ashton stirred first, his eyes opening slowly, adjusting to the darkness. At first, he thought he was dreaming, but the dream solidified into reality as his gaze fixed on the figure standing in the doorway. His breath caught in his throat, and he let out a guttural shout, instinct taking over.

The Fox reacted instantly, raising his shotgun. Whether by intent or accident, a deafening blast shattered the silence, and a spray of wood splinters flew across the room as the bullet struck the doorframe. Ashton screamed in pain, clutching his hand, blood dripping onto the floor. An index finger had been blown off. But adrenaline is a powerful thing. Even with the injury, he lunged from his bed, charging at The Fox with a primal roar.

The Fox turned and fled. He sprinted down the stairs, out the back door, over the back fence and through the night, his breath coming in ragged bursts, his feet pounding the ground like the rapid-fire beats of a drum. He was a phantom, a creature of the night, leaving behind only fear in his wake.

Ashton didn't give chase, his eyes were wide with panic, his heart racing as blood poured from his mangled hand. The pain was excruciating, but it was the shock that truly began to sink in, numbing his thoughts. Zarah, frantic and barely able to think straight, rushed into the bathroom, yanking open the cupboard and grabbing every towel she could find. Her mind raced as she ran back to Ashton's side. He was now sitting on the edge of their bed, his face pale, breathing uneven, as if his body was still trying to catch up to what had happened.

She knelt beside him, wrapping his hand as tightly as she could, though her own fingers trembled violently. Blood seeped through the fabric, staining it almost instantly. Tears welled in her eyes, but she forced herself to stay focused. She couldn't lose control now.

"My finger... it's by the door," Ashton muttered, his voice hoarse from the adrenaline surging through him. "Go to the freezer, get some ice. Hurry." He winced, struggling to stay coherent through the waves of pain. "And grab a freezer bag too - we'll need to preserve it."

Zarah, her face stricken with fear, nodded and hurried toward the stairs. Her mind spun in a thousand directions - she couldn't believe what was happening. Their home, once a safe haven, had been violated in the worst possible way.

With a deep breath, Ashton forced himself to focus. His good hand fumbled as he reached over to the telephone. His fingers trembled as he dialled nine-nine-nine.

"Hello," he rasped into the receiver. "Yes, I need the police and an ambulance. I've been shot. By The Fox." The words sounded surreal even to him. He had read about The Fox, heard the stories, but never imagined he would be a victim in his own home.

Within minutes, the once-quiet street was alight with flashing blue lights. Police cars and an ambulance arrived at the scene, their flashing lights illuminating the front of the house with an unsettling shine. The warm summer air was punctuated by the sound of sirens and urgent footsteps.
Detective Inspector Peter Hargreaves arrived swiftly; his eyes sharp as he surveyed the scene. He knew the sight too well - The Fox was becoming bolder, more violent. Inside the house, he found Zarah pale and shaking, and Ashton gripping his bandaged hand as paramedics worked around him. Blood still pooled on the floor near the door, a chilling reminder of what had transpired just minutes before.

Ashton recounted the horrifying moment in broken sentences, struggling to piece together the terror of it all. Zarah sat by his side, her face drawn and hollow. They could barely believe it themselves - The Fox had been inside their home. He had aimed, fired, and left them scarred, both physically and emotionally.
The Fox had stolen more than a finger that night - he had taken their sense of security, their peace of mind. And as Ashton stared out the window of the ambulance, he knew that this wound, like the one on his hand, would take far longer to heal than anyone could imagine.

Ashton and Zarah's lives would never be the same. From that night forward, they lived in constant fear, haunted by the thought that The Fox could return. The lingering threat cast a shadow over their once peaceful lives. Ashton, a landscape gardener, was now out of work, not only because of the physical damage to his hand but because of the psychological trauma he faced daily. Every sound made them jump. Every night they wondered if he was out there, watching, waiting.

The morning after, Hargreaves sat in his office reading a report of the previous night's events, his jaw clenched, eyes burning with frustration. The Fox was out of control and becoming more violent with each attack.

The atmosphere in Herts, Beds and Bucks had turned electric. The Fox was no longer a mere criminal; he had become something else - an entity, a force of nature. Stories of his exploits spread like wildfire, each tale more terrifying than the last. He was the bogeyman, lurking in the nearby fields, hiding in every street corner.

The hunt for The Fox had transformed into something primal. It was no longer about justice or law - it was a battle of wills, a struggle to regain control over a fear that had gripped the 'Triangle of Terror' by the throat. Hargreaves knew the stakes were escalating with every passing day. This wasn't just a hunt for a man - it was a hunt for a legend, a spectre who thrived in the darkness, who revelled in the terror he sowed.

The weight of it all settled on Hargreaves' shoulders. He stared out into the hot summer sky, knowing that somewhere out there, The Fox was walking free. His presence was a dark stain on the fabric of their lives, a constant, gnawing dread that refused to fade.

The hunt was far from over, and with no new leads, a chilling realisation gripped Hargreaves. They were chasing a man who had become a myth. The Fox was out there, always one step ahead, a dark and enigmatic presence that defied capture. And so, the game continued, a game drenched in darkness, fear, and the unending echo of a shotgun blast in the night.

Chapter 7

The Fox had terrorised communities for weeks now, slipping in and out of homes leaving a trail of destruction in his wake. Each crime, a violation of both physical space and personal security, adding another layer of horror to the ever-growing mystery. His methods were unpredictable yet precise. He attacked homes that seemed vulnerable - ones where the locks were weak, the windows left open, or the inhabitants complacent.

But now, the police were fighting back, determined to put an end to his spree. Flyers appeared in neighbourhoods across the region, posted on telephone poles, in shop windows, and through letterboxes. The bold black letters screamed the urgent warning: **Beware of The Fox.** Beneath that headline, there were instructions - practical advice aimed at protecting the public.

"Do not leave windows or doors unlocked, even during the heat of the summer. If you notice anything suspicious - no matter how small - report it to the police immediately."

The message struck at the heart of the fear that had already gripped the three counties. People double-checked their doors at night, hesitated before leaving a window ajar, and scrutinised every unusual movement in the street. The sense of safety had been shattered, and the police wanted to make sure no one underestimated the threat The Fox posed.

Yet behind the public warnings, a more critical effort was underway. Deep in the heart of the police forensic labs, the case against The Fox was being built piece by painstaking piece, evidence that could one day tie this elusive criminal to his growing list of crimes. Detective Inspector Peter Hargreaves led his team with a grim determination. He knew they had to be thorough, patient, and methodical, but time was not on their side. The Fox was still out there, and every day that passed without an arrest was another opportunity for him to strike again.

A small breakthrough had come when forensic officers working at several of the crime scenes began to notice patterns - subtle ones, but patterns, nonetheless. At first, the scenes had appeared to be isolated incidents, unrelated in any obvious way. There were no clear fingerprints, no easily recognisable patterns of entry or exit. The Fox was careful, methodical. He left very little behind, and that was what made him so dangerous.

But crime scene investigators were trained to look beyond the obvious, to find the details that most would overlook. And it was in these details that they began to piece together the puzzle. One of the first clues came in the form of the forced locks. While The Fox's entry points varied - sometimes a back door, sometimes a window, other times through side entrances - the way he broke in had a consistency to it.

Using a fast-setting plastic, a specially designed material that could capture minute details quickly, forensic teams had taken impressions of the locks that had been forced open. They compared these impressions from multiple crime scenes and discovered a striking similarity. The tool used to pry open the locks left marks that matched across multiple properties.

After careful analysis, they deduced that an 8mm-wide flat screwdriver had been used. This wasn't just any screwdriver. The markings on the tool were unusual, indicating either that the blade had been modified or that it was an older, perhaps custom-made, piece of equipment. This was their first concrete link - the same tool, used again and again, leaving its unmistakable signature behind.

But that wasn't all. As they scoured the crime scenes, meticulously gathering any trace of physical evidence, they unearthed something even more useful.

Human beings shed fibres just as animals shed fur, but these fibres were so small that they can only be seen under a microscope. At one of the homes where The Fox had attacked, the forensic team had collected fibres from a bedroom, a painstaking process that required patience and expertise. When these fibres were analysed, they made a remarkable discovery: white rabbit hairs had been found on the knots tied around the victim's hands.

It was a clue that seemed almost bizarre at first. Why would there be rabbit hairs at the scene? As they delved deeper into the analysis, two possibilities emerged. Either The Fox had handled a white rabbit at some point, or he had worn gloves lined with angora wool - an expensive, rare material made from rabbit fur.

This single piece of evidence, seemingly so minor, opened up new avenues of investigation. The presence of the rabbit hair tied The Fox directly to the crimes. No matter how careful he had been, he hadn't anticipated the forensic teams discovering such a minute detail.

But they weren't done yet.

In addition to the rabbit hair, forensic officers also collected other fibres - tiny, almost invisible to the naked eye - scattered throughout the scenes. The fibres were found in odd places: on carpets, under furniture, and even embedded in the victims' clothing. It was the kind of detail that could easily be dismissed if not for the dedication of the team working the case. They analysed these fibres and found something striking.

Fibres from one of the crime scenes matched fibres from another scene, despite the two locations being miles apart and the victims having no known connection to each other. The fibres appeared to come from a woollen jumper, likely worn by The Fox. Further tests were conducted, examining the chemical composition of the fibres and the dye mixtures used in their production. The results were conclusive - the fibres were identical. The Fox had worn the same clothing during both attacks.

This was a significant find. While fibres were far from the kind of smoking gun that could directly lead to an arrest, they were another brick in the growing wall of evidence linking these crimes together. The Fox, who had worked so hard to cover his tracks, was starting to leave behind a trail that was becoming harder and harder to erase.

By now, the police had gathered enough evidence to definitively link multiple crimes to the same perpetrator. The screwdriver marks, the rabbit hairs, and the fibres from the jumper all pointed to one person - The Fox. There was no longer any doubt. These were not isolated incidents. They were all the work of the same man, moving stealthily from one home to another, leaving behind traces of his presence that, piece by piece, were building a case against him.

The scientific proof was undeniable. Each time The Fox broke into a house, he inadvertently left behind clues, no matter how meticulous he thought he had been. The crime scenes were now telling a story, and it was one the police were eager to read.

"We're closing in," Hargreaves said quietly to Collins one evening, as he reviewed the latest reports.

"Yes sir. He is starting to slip up. It won't be long before he makes a big mistake, and we get him," replied a chirpy Collins.

The team was energised by the progress. They had the evidence, and now they just needed the man. With the forensic evidence tying the crimes together, they had moved past the point of speculation. The Fox had a distinct modus operandi, one that was revealed in the fibres from his clothing, the hairs from his gloves, and the marks left by his screwdriver. He was methodical, yes, but human. And like all humans, he was leaving behind traces of his presence.

With the forensic evidence mounting, the hunt for The Fox grew more intense. The police now had a description - based on the fibres, they knew he likely wore a wool jumper, possibly grey or blue. The rabbit hair suggested he may have worn angora-lined gloves at some point. And the specific tool he used to break into homes, the 8mm flat screwdriver with unusual markings, provided another clue to his habits.

But despite these breakthroughs, The Fox was still at large. Hargreaves and his team knew that it was only a matter of time before he struck again, and the pressure was mounting. Public anxiety was growing, especially with the police's warnings plastered across towns and villages. Everyone was on edge, and every clank in the night or rustle outside a window made people jump.

Hargreaves ordered increased patrols in the areas where The Fox had been known to strike. Officers were briefed on the new evidence, and a dedicated unit was tasked with scouring pawnshops, hardware stores, and markets, looking for any sign of someone selling or buying a distinctive screwdriver or angora-lined gloves.

The team worked tirelessly; their focus sharpened by the weight of the evidence they had collected. They knew The Fox couldn't hide forever. He had grown too comfortable, too reckless. Each crime left behind another piece of the puzzle, and soon, Hargreaves was sure, they would have enough to identify him.

Chapter 8

Five years earlier, in the winter of 1979, fear had gripped the north of England. For five years, the elusive killer known as the Yorkshire Ripper had terrorised women across the region, leaving a trail of brutality and unanswered questions. The police, stretched thin by the mounting number of attacks and public pressure, were struggling to make headway. Thirteen women had been murdered, their bodies found in public spaces, all victims of horrific violence. Investigations had been plagued by missteps, false leads, and a growing mistrust from the public. The police force needed fresh leadership, someone with a reputation for methodical work and a history of successful cases. That person was Detective Chief Superintendent Mark Talbot.

Talbot, already a highly respected officer within British law enforcement circles, had earned his stripes in solving several high-profile cases, most notably bringing down notorious criminals with cunning, patience, and precision. When the Yorkshire Ripper investigation was handed to him, he took it as both a challenge and a moral duty. To him, this was not just about catching a killer but about restoring public faith in the police and protecting vulnerable women paralysed by fear.

When Talbot first assumed control of the investigation in early 1980, he was stepping into a quagmire. The case files were immense - thousands of witness statements, mountains of forensic reports, and more than two hundred thousand pieces of evidence had already been gathered. However, despite the wealth of information, the police were no closer to identifying the killer. The previous task force, overwhelmed and under pressure, had become bogged down by dead-end leads and miscommunication between various departments.

One of Talbot's first actions was to review the entire case from the beginning. He realised that the investigation had been too reactive, with the police chasing tips and suspects without a cohesive strategy. Moreover, the investigative team had been plagued by internal issues: competing egos, jurisdictional disputes, and an overwhelming sense of frustration. Talbot knew he had to centralise the investigation and bring a fresh perspective.

He set about reorganising the investigative team, bringing in officers he trusted and restructuring how information was handled. A new incident room was created where all incoming leads would be managed more efficiently. He appointed senior officers to review and re-interview key witnesses and reanalyse evidence. His goal was to establish a clear timeline of events, focusing on the most solid clues and discarding the red herrings that had derailed the investigation.

In Talbot's mind, the first major problem was the noise surrounding the case. There had been too much information, much of it irrelevant. He told his team: "We need to go back to basics. Look at the facts. The killer is out there, and the truth is hidden in these files. We just have to find it."

Unlike previous investigators who had been swayed by the emotional weight of the case, Talbot was known for his logical, methodical approach. He believed that the key to capturing the Yorkshire Ripper lay in identifying patterns in the killer's behaviour, locations, and victimology. He also understood that they had to out-think the Yorkshire Ripper, who had shown a disturbing ability to evade capture, despite being seen by witnesses' multiple times.

One of the early mistakes made by the initial investigative team was their reliance on a hoax recording and letters purportedly sent by the Yorkshire Ripper. The man in the recording, nicknamed "Wearside Jack" due to his Sunderland accent, had misled investigators, directing them away from the real killer. Talbot immediately expressed scepticism about the authenticity of the recording. He pushed for the team to focus on physical evidence and witness testimonies rather than speculative leads from unverified sources.

Talbot's sharp eye for detail led to a breakthrough when he revisited the forensic evidence from the various crime scenes. Though the Yorkshire Ripper's attacks had varied somewhat in location and time, Talbot noticed that the areas were linked by proximity to transportation hubs - particularly lorry routes and service stations. This suggested that the killer might be a travelling worker, someone who could move easily between towns and cities without drawing too much attention.

Furthermore, Talbot brought in criminal psychologists to build a more refined profile of the killer. The Yorkshire Ripper's crimes were marked by extreme violence toward his victims, most of whom were vulnerable women - either sex workers or women alone in the streets late at night. This indicated a deep-seated misogyny and a desire for power and control. The psychologists worked with Talbot to analyse the escalation in violence, theorising that the killer might be an unassuming man in public but deeply troubled in his private life, someone capable of hiding in plain sight.

As the months wore on, Talbot's commitment to the case became a personal mission. The pressure from the public and the media was immense. The public's frustration with the lack of progress was palpable, and every day the killer remained at large was a blow to the morale of the Yorkshire police. Newspapers ran scathing editorials criticising the police, while politicians made public statements calling for accountability. As the face of the investigation, Talbot bore the brunt of this pressure, but he remained resolute, never allowing the media frenzy to distract him from the task at hand.

Behind the scenes, Talbot's health and personal life began to suffer. His wife, aware of the weight her husband carried, worried about the toll it was taking on him. Friends noticed how gaunt and exhausted he looked. Talbot's sleep became more fitful as the weeks dragged on without any significant breakthroughs. However, he remained a constant presence at the investigation headquarters, rarely taking time off. The Yorkshire Ripper's victims haunted him. He often revisited the crime scene photographs, mentally placing himself in the moments leading up to the murders, trying to think as the killer might.

By December 1980, Talbot's team had narrowed their suspect list to a few hundred individuals. Among them was Peter Sutcliffe, a lorry driver from Bradford, who had been interviewed several times by the police but had slipped through the net due to a series of unfortunate administrative errors and miscommunications.

Sutcliffe's arrest came almost by accident. On the night of January second, 1981, Sutcliffe was spotted by two police officers in Sheffield acting suspiciously in a parked car with a sex worker. When questioned, he gave a false name, and the officers noted discrepancies in his story. It was only after they checked his license plate, which was found to be fake, that they decided to take him into custody. During the routine search, they discovered tools in his car that raised alarm bells: a hammer and a knife, eerily like the instruments used in the Yorkshire Ripper murders.

Talbot was immediately notified of the arrest. Although Sutcliffe initially denied any involvement in the killings, further searches of his property and vehicle uncovered additional damning evidence, including a second set of clothing hidden in a nearby yard. Under intense interrogation, Sutcliffe finally cracked, confessing to the murders with chilling detachment.

Sutcliffe's confession detailed his methodical approach to the killings, how he would choose his victims, and the psychological compulsion that drove him to kill. He admitted to hearing voices commanding him to murder women, and his confessions matched with the forensic evidence and witness statements the police had gathered over the years.

The arrest of Peter Sutcliffe was a moment of both triumph and sombre reflection for Talbot and his team. While they had finally captured the man responsible for the horrific crimes, it was not without a sense of regret that Sutcliffe had been able to evade justice for so long. Thirteen women had died, and several more had been attacked, their lives forever altered.

In the days following Sutcliffe's arrest, Talbot worked closely with the Crown Prosecution Service to ensure that the evidence was airtight. Sutcliffe was charged with multiple counts of murder and attempted murder, and the trial that followed was one of the most high-profile in British legal history. He was found guilty and sentenced to life imprisonment without the possibility of parole.

For Talbot, the end of the case brought little personal satisfaction. The investigation had consumed him for over a year, and while justice had been served, the cost had been hefty. After the trial, he gave a series of interviews to the press, expressing his admiration for the resilience of the victims' families and acknowledging the failings of the investigation in its earlier stages. "We got him in the end," he said in one interview, "but it should have been sooner."

Talbot's leadership during the Yorkshire Ripper investigation cemented his legacy as one of Britain's most skilled and dedicated detectives. His methodical approach, his insistence on revisiting evidence, and his reliance on psychological profiling were pivotal in finally capturing Peter Sutcliffe. Talbot's techniques were later studied by law enforcement agencies around the world and became standard practice in complex, multi-victim investigations.

The Yorkshire Ripper case also sparked significant changes within British policing. The failings of the initial investigation led to reforms in how large-scale investigations were managed, particularly in the handling of forensic evidence and witness statements. More resources were allocated to tracking serial offenders, and inter-agency communication was improved to prevent future breakdowns in the sharing of critical information.

In the years following Sutcliffe's capture, Talbot would often reflect on the case in private. He remained haunted by the knowledge that, had things been done differently in the early days of the investigation, lives could have been saved. He was proud of his work, but the weight of those lost lives stayed with him.

Chapter 9

The Fox's crimes had escalated to an unprecedented level, forcing law enforcement to expand their efforts to catch him. As the crimes were committed in three different police force areas, and due to their serious nature, the investigation took on the status of a national enquiry under the new command of Detective Chief Superintendent Mark Talbot. Operations were moved to Dunstable police station.

Due to the similarities of the cases, Talbot's expertise was needed to help capture The Fox. He had learned from the Yorkshire Ripper case the importance of sharing information and recording it properly.

The search team swelled to over two hundred officers, all working tirelessly to track down the elusive criminal. The police were receiving over three hundred calls a day from the public, all leads needed to be followed up. The growing scope of the investigation demanded a larger operations room to accommodate the influx of personnel and resources needed to bring The Fox to justice.

The operations room at Dunstable police station was awash in a haze of stale coffee and underlying stress. The usual murmur of low conversation was absent, replaced by the sporadic squeak of leather chairs and the occasional clatter of a pen dropping on the floor. The room was charged with an unmistakable sense of dread. This wasn't just another case - it was an insidious infection that had seeped into the very bones of the town, tightening its grip with every new attack.

Detective Chief Superintendent Mark Talbot from West Yorkshire entered the room, his presence immediately commanding attention. He carried a stack of folders under one arm, and as he stepped in, the room fell silent. Talbot's reputation preceded him - he was the man who had brought down the notorious Yorkshire Ripper, Peter Sutcliffe. Yet even he knew that this case, with its elusiveness and psychological torment, was a different beast entirely. His sharp eyes took in the faces around him, reading the fear, frustration, and simmering anger that marked his audience.

"Alright, listen up," Talbot began, his voice steady and authoritative. The weight of his words seemed to press down on the room, accentuating the gravity of the situation. "I've been brought in to lead Operation Peanut. This task force's sole mission is to catch The Fox. I know you've all been working this case tirelessly for weeks, and you have uncovered some useful forensic evidence, but it's clear that what we've been doing isn't working. We need to change tactics."

Detective Sergeant Linda Collins, who had been deeply involved in the case from the outset, spoke up. "We've got no fingerprints, no clear descriptions. He's like a ghost - he comes and goes without leaving a trace."

Talbot nodded in acknowledgment. "That's because he's smart. Methodical. He's not just breaking into homes; he's breaking into their minds. He wants people to be afraid, and he's damn good at it."

He set down the folders on the central table, spreading out a series of crime scene photos that painted a chilling narrative. Each image depicted the same unsettling scenario: open doors and windows, broken locks, rooms upended, and disturbing makeshift dens created within the victims' homes. Yet, in every photo, there was no clear image of the intruder. It was as if The Fox had deliberately blurred the lines between reality and nightmare.

"This guy knows what he's doing," Talbot said, his voice carrying the weight of grim recognition. "No pattern to his targets. No obvious motive beyond scaring the hell out of people. We're dealing with someone who understands fear, who thrives on it."

Detective Sergeant Jake Miller, known for his grizzled demeanour and sharp temper, leaned back in his chair, his scepticism evident. "So, what's the plan, boss? Are we just supposed to sit around and wait for him to strike again?"

Talbot fixed Jake with a steely gaze, his patience wearing thin. "No, Jake. We're going to get inside his head. We need to think like him. This isn't a normal investigation. We're hunting a sociopath."

The plan began to take shape as Talbot outlined the new strategy. "We are stationing officers in barns and houses around the area known as the 'Triangle of Terror' to attempt to catch the attacker. I want a psychological profile - something to help us build a picture of The Fox's character traits."

He continued with specifics. "What we know so far: The Fox is between twenty and thirty years old. He's always masked, so the exact details of his appearance are elusive. He's approximately five foot eight to ten inches tall, with a slim, athletic build, weighing between ten and eleven stones. He has long fingers and appears to be left-handed. Witnesses have suggested a northern accent, possibly 'Geordie.'"

Detective Sergeant Linda Collins nodded, her face set with determination. "We need to profile him and figure out what makes him tick."

Talbot's eyes met hers with a shared sense of urgency. "Exactly. I want every detail, no matter how small. We're going to piece together who this guy is and how he thinks. I want a list of every burglary, every break-in, every sexual assault, every reported prowler in the region for the last ten years. He didn't just appear out of nowhere."

The room erupted into a flurry of activity. Officers began rifling through files, pulling out statements and organising evidence. Talbot's energy had ignited a spark of urgency among the team, pushing them into action. But as the meeting concluded, Collins lingered behind, her gaze locked on the crime scene photos laid out on the table.
"He's changing, you know," Collins said quietly, her voice carrying the weight of her growing concern.

Talbot turned to her; eyebrows raised in curiosity. "What do you mean?"

Collin's expression was troubled. "He's evolving. The first few break-ins were simple burglaries, almost like he was testing the waters. Now he's targeting more vulnerable people and isolated homes. It's not just about getting in and out unnoticed anymore. He's breaking people."

Talbot absorbed her words, his face reflecting a grim realisation. "He's getting more confident. More dangerous. And that means he'll make a mistake eventually."

Collins looked sceptical; her eyes shadowed with doubt. "You really think so?"

Talbot offered a small, grim smile. "They all do. It's part of the nature of sociopaths. They believe they're invincible until they're not."

Later that evening, Talbot found himself alone in his dimly lit office, the walls adorned with maps of Herts, Beds, and Bucks, and numerous crime scene photos. Talbot leaned back in his chair, closing his eyes as he tried to immerse himself in the mindset of The Fox.

"He's clever," he muttered to himself, grappling with the enigma before him. "He's careful. But he's not invincible."

In his mind's eye, Talbot pictured The Fox as a cold, calculating individual - someone who meticulously observed his prey for days, perhaps weeks, before making his move. A man who thrived on the adrenaline rush and the sense of control. But Talbot knew every criminal had a weakness. His challenge was to uncover it.

His thoughts were abruptly interrupted by the shrill ring of his phone. It was Claire Milford, the journalist who had coined the moniker 'The Fox.'
"DCS Talbot," Claire's voice came through with a sense of urgency, "I've got something you might want to see. A letter arrived at the paper this afternoon. I think it's from him."

Talbot's heart raced with a surge of adrenaline. "You're sure?"

Claire hesitated. "I can't be absolutely certain, but it's addressed to me directly and mentions the nickname I gave him. No one else knew that before it went to print."

"I'm on my way," Talbot said, abruptly ending the call and grabbing his coat.

At the Leighton Buzzard Observer office, Claire handed him the letter with a tremor in her hand. The paper was cheap, and the handwriting uneven, betraying an unsettlingly casual tone. Talbot's eyes scanned the message, his face hardening into a mask of concentration as he read:

"TO THE ONE WHO NAMED ME THE FOX, YOU AIN'T SEEN NOTHING YET. I AM EVERYWHERE AND NOWHERE. I CAN SEE YOU, EVEN IF YOU CAN'T SEE ME. WHEN THE TIME COMES, YOU'LL KNOW IT'S ME. I PROMISE."

The words seemed to vibrate with an ominous energy, and Talbot's expression darkened. "If this isn't a hoax, he's taunting us," he said finally, his voice low and intense. "He's trying to get inside our heads."

Claire's face was pale, her eyes wide with a mix of fear and curiosity. "How do we know if it is a hoax or not?"

Talbot took a deep breath, his mind racing through the implications. "Well, we wait. And if he contacts you again, make sure I am the first person you call. We are going to catch him."

Milford nodded her head, while Talbot gathered his things and left the room.

The weight of Talbot's words settled heavily in the room, the promise of an imminent confrontation lingering. But deep down, Talbot knew the truth: catching The Fox wouldn't be simple. The Fox was more than just a criminal; he was an enigma, forever one step ahead. To capture him, Talbot would need to embrace the elusive nature of his quarry, becoming an evil exploiter himself in the relentless pursuit of justice. The hunt was on, and the stakes had never been higher.

The face of British law enforcement was about to change forever. It was a time of transformation, not only for society but also for the way police tackled the rising tide of crime. The United Kingdom had seen a dramatic rise in criminal activity, and with it, the complexities of policing were becoming more apparent. The traditional methods of investigation were reaching their limits. Criminal cases were becoming more intricate, with offenders leaving fewer clues behind, and the sheer volume of information officers had to sift through was overwhelming.

Detective Chief Superintendent Mark Talbot, known for his sharp instincts and dedication, was at the forefront of a revolution in policing. His career had been built on hard work, persistence, and old-fashioned investigative legwork. But now, with the advancements in technology, he was about to lead his team into uncharted territory. For the first time in British law enforcement history, detectives would use a computer to assist in solving a major case. This machine affectionately nicknamed Metal Mickey would become a silent partner in one of the most important investigations of Talbot's career.

Talbot stood in a large room inside Dunstable police station, staring at the blinking lights and whirling of Metal Mickey, a room-sized computer that looked like something out of a science fiction movie. It was massive, a monstrosity of wires, switches, and blinking screens, but to Talbot, it represented the future. This machine had the potential to do what no human could - process and organise the vast amounts of data that were pouring in from across the 'Triangle of Terror'. In the age before modern databases, this was a monumental leap forward.

The police were faced with a monumental challenge: crime was evolving, and the criminals were becoming smarter. Serial offenders moved across jurisdictions, making it difficult for local forces to link crimes. Eye-witness reports, forensic evidence, and crime scene details had to be logged manually, and any connections between cases were often lost in the deluge of paperwork. Detectives worked tirelessly, but human limitations meant that critical leads were sometimes missed.

Talbot had seen this firsthand. His team was often buried under stacks of reports and witness statements. They could only do so much, and every officer had their breaking point. Solving a case often came down to luck - whether the right officer happened to remember the right detail at the right time. Talbot knew they needed something more.

And that something was Metal Mickey.

The machine had been brought in to assist the force in sifting through criminal records, compiling data, and searching for patterns that could link The Fox's crimes across different areas. For the first time, detectives could use technology to narrow down suspects based on witness accounts, crime scene details, and known offender profiles. It wasn't perfect, and it certainly wasn't fast, but Metal Mickey could process thousands of pieces of data in a fraction of the time it would take a human team to do the same.

Talbot oversaw this new initiative, a job that came with both excitement and pressure. This wasn't just an experiment - it was a test of whether the police could evolve and meet the challenges of the future.

At first, some of his team were sceptical. After all, policing had always been about gut instinct, about knocking on doors, interviewing suspects, and following leads. The idea that a machine - a cold, unfeeling piece of metal - could somehow help them catch The Fox seemed far-fetched to many.

But Talbot, ever the pragmatist, knew they had to adapt. He called a meeting in the operations room, standing in front of his team with a sense of purpose.

"Look, I know we've all got our doubts about this thing," Talbot said, gesturing toward Metal Mickey, visible through the glass window of the adjacent room. "But we're drowning in data. We've got thousands of names, addresses, witness reports, and we're just not getting anywhere fast enough. This machine can help us cut through that. It can process information in a way we can't - not this fast, not this accurately."

There was silence in the room, some officers shifting uncomfortably in their seats. Detective Sergeant Jake Miller, one of Talbot's most trusted men, raised an eyebrow and leaned back in his chair.

"Boss, I get what you're saying, but can a machine really catch a criminal? I mean, we've always done this the hard way - talking to people, making connections."

Talbot nodded. He understood the concern. He had the same questions himself. But he also knew that times were changing.

"It's not about replacing the work we do," Talbot explained. "It's about helping us do it better. Metal Mickey's not going to interview suspects or walk the beat. That's still our job. But what it can do is help us see the patterns we're missing - connections between crimes, suspects who match The Fox's description but live in different jurisdictions. It's a tool, and if we use it right, it could make all the difference."
The room was quiet for a moment before Miller finally nodded.

"Alright, let's give it a go."

Within days, the team began feeding information into Metal Mickey. Every detail from every crime scene - addresses, times of the break-ins and assaults, descriptions of The Fox, even the types of tools used to force entry - was meticulously logged. The machine hummed and whirred, its internal systems processing the data faster than any human team could have hoped to do.

As the days went by, Metal Mickey began to spit out potential leads. The computer's algorithms analysed the data, looking for matches in known offender profiles, cross-referencing witness descriptions, and identifying similarities between seemingly unrelated incidents.

Metal Mickey provided the names of over five thousand potential suspects. It was a painstaking and time-consuming list of people for the police to work through.

Talbot and his team were astonished. The machine had done in days what would have taken them months to piece together.

Metal Mickey became a permanent fixture in the investigation. But while technology was becoming an essential part of policing, Talbot never lost sight of the human element. He knew that computers, no matter how advanced, could never replace the instincts and dedication of a detective on the ground. Metal Mickey was a tool - an important one - but it was still the men and women of the force who would ultimately bring justice to the victims.

And so, as the sun set on another long day of policing, Detective Chief Superintendent Mark Talbot stood in his office, watching the lights of the town twinkle in the distance. The world was changing, and the police force was changing with it. But one thing would never change: the fight against crime was a human endeavour, built on the backs of those who were willing to dedicate their lives to protecting others.

For Talbot, the future was bright - and he was ready to lead his team into it.

Chapter 10

Since relocating from the north of England, The Fox had lodged with his brother. His domain was a grimy, unremarkable house in Leighton Buzzard. From the outside, it was a rundown semi-detached dwelling on a nondescript street - a place that seemed to blend seamlessly into its surroundings, almost as if its very ordinariness served to obscure the sinister presence within. To the casual observer, it was just another residence in a sea of similar homes, but for The Fox, it was the perfect hiding spot. A sanctuary for someone who thrived in the shady crevices of society, it was here that he found solace in his own darkness.

It was another balmy warm summer's evening, the moonlight trickled through the bare branches of the trees outside, casting fleeting shadows that danced across the worn walls of the living room. The Fox reclined in a creaking wooden chair, a faint smile curving his lips as he contemplated the scene before him. The room was sparsely furnished, yet meticulously organised. A sense of order prevailed amid the chaos - a reflection of the man himself.

He traced his fingers along the jagged scar on his cheek, a mark of his past. The scar was more than a physical reminder; it was a symbol of the deep-seated anger and resentment that fuelled his every move. His father's voice echoed in his mind, sharp and unforgiving. "Useless boy. Can't do anything right." Those words had been seared into his memory, defining his early life and shaping his path. But those days were long gone. Now, The Fox had carved out his own existence - a stalker operating on a higher plane.

"A clever fox outsmarting the hounds," he muttered to himself, his eyes glinting with a manic light. The name the media had given him - The Fox - was more than a moniker; it was an identity he had embraced. He wasn't just a thief or a thug; he was a master of his craft. A manipulator who thrived on the fear he instilled in others. The police, the newspapers, the public - they were all merely players in his elaborate game.

The small wooden table beside him was cluttered with trophies from his conquests. A man's silk tie, a woman's leather belt, a faded photograph of a smiling couple. Each item was a piece of his legacy, a testament to his power. He picked up the tie, letting it slip through his fingers like liquid. The faint scent of perfume lingered, a poltergeist of the past. "Antoinette something," he whispered with a twisted smile. "Pretty little thing. Screamed so nicely."

His eyes darkened, and the smile faded. It wasn't about the things he took or the chaos he created. No, it was about control. He decided who lived in fear and who slept soundly at night. He dictated the rhythm of terror. With each invasion, each shattered life, he felt a deep-seated satisfaction. The police, the newspapers, the public were all dancing to his tune - and they didn't even know it.

A distant, haunting voice cut through his reverie - the voice of his mother. "You'll never be anything but trouble." She had never understood him, never recognised the potential in his cunning. But he didn't need her approval. Not anymore. "Look at me now, Mum," he said softly, a cruel twist to his words. "Look at what I've become."

A sudden rustling from outside jerked him back to reality. He peered through the grimy window, his eyes narrowing as he scanned the nighttime. A fox - an actual fox - emerged from the underbrush, its eyes glowing with an eerie luminescence. The Fox regarded the creature with a strange, reflective gaze. "Ah, my brother," he murmured. "Out hunting tonight, too?"

He rose from his chair, his movements deliberate and measured. The thrill of the hunt was something he relished - the anticipation, the creeping silence before the storm. His childhood had been spent hiding in the evenings, evading the blows of a drunken father and the cold indifference of his mother. He had learned early on that the world belonged to those who could seize it. Now, he was the one calling the shots. The hunters had become the hunted, and the hounds hadn't even begun to catch on.

He picked up a crumpled clipping from the table, smoothing it out with a rough hand. Leighton Buzzard Observer, first of May 1984: 'The Fox Strikes Again.' He couldn't read, but he could tell from the photos in the article, it was about him.

"Keep chasing your own tail, Detective Chief Superintendent Mark Talbot," he said, his voice a low, mocking whisper. He had observed Talbot from a distance, noting the way the detective barked orders and tried to project confidence. But The Fox saw through the façade - the weariness in Talbot's eyes, the subtle hesitation in his step. Talbot was close, but not close enough. "You're not ready for me," he said, almost pitying the man. "Not yet."

The thought of Talbot lying awake at night, consumed by thoughts of him, brought The Fox a perverse pleasure. It was a game - a dance of cat and mouse, or rather, fox and hound. But Talbot didn't yet grasp the rules. The Fox knew them all too well. He understood the delicate balance of pushing boundaries and retreating, the art of timing and precision. He was the master of his own clock.

"Soon," he muttered to himself, his eyes glinting with a dark promise as he sketched a crude outline of a house in his notebook. "Soon, they'll understand the full extent of my craft."

The thrill of the next break-in pulsed through him like an electric current. He envisioned the meticulous planning, the careful execution - the fear, the screams, the whispered terror that would ripple through the towns and villages. They'd see him, but they wouldn't catch him.

"Good night," he whispered to the encroaching darkness. "Sleep tight. The Fox is watching."

The Fox gathered his things and slipped out of the house while his brother slept. Tonight, he didn't have to travel far. He moved silently through the back streets of Linslade, his form a ghostly silhouette against the night. Clad in a mask fashioned from a trouser leg and armed with a shotgun that felt solid in his gloved hands, he experienced a heady mixture of fear and exhilaration. Each time he performed his dark ritual, the hunger within him grew stronger.

He approached a modest two-story house, its curtains drawn tight against the night. The soft glow of a streetlight bathed the lawn in a gentle light. The Fox's keen eyes noted the outline of a car in the driveway - evidence of a couple inside, asleep and vulnerable. He could almost taste their fear, his pulse quickening with anticipation.

"No turning back," he muttered to himself, his voice barely more than a whisper.

He slipped around to the side of the house, where a small kitchen window was left ajar. He pried it open with ease and slid inside, landing silently on the cool linoleum floor. Every sound, every grind of the house seemed amplified in the silence. His heartbeat echoed in his ears as he moved stealthily through the darkened hallway.

Upstairs, he could hear the recurring breathing of the sleeping couple. He ascended the stairs slowly, each crackle of the wood beneath him a sharp reminder of the stakes. Reaching the top, he moved swiftly toward the bedroom, where the door stood agape. The darkness of the room swallowed him whole as he stepped inside, the vague outline of the bed coming into view. He raised the shotgun, the barrel gleaming ominously in the faint moonlight filtering through the window.

"Wake up," he commanded, his voice low and menacing.

A sleepy murmur, followed by a wave of panic. The husband, groggy and disoriented, was the first to sit up. His eyes expanded in dread as they focused on the dark figure in the doorway, the glint of moonlight reflecting off the barrel of the gun. The wife's breathing quickened as she awoke, her eyes spreading in horror.

"Out of bed," The Fox ordered, his voice cold and unyielding. "Now."

The elderly couple, Mick and Liza Brierley, hesitated, fear paralysing them momentarily. The Fox's eyes narrowed behind his mask, his grip on the shotgun tightening.

"I said, get up!" he barked, his tone leaving no room for argument. The couple scrambled from the bed, their hands trembling nonstop.

He tossed a pair of shoelaces at the woman's feet. "Tie him up. Do it tight."

With shaking hands, Liza complied, her fingers fumbling as she wrapped the laces around her husband's wrists. Her breaths came in short, panicked bursts. When the knots were secure, The Fox yanked on them, ensuring they were tight. He then grabbed a belt from the closet and bound her hands behind her back.

The room was warm and stuffy, each second stretching into what felt like an eternity. Mick's eyes darted between his wife and The Fox, his voice a strangled whisper. "Please...don't hurt her. Don't hurt us."

The Fox ignored the plea, his gaze locked on Liza. His breath was hot and shallow beneath the mask. He reached out with a gloved hand, brushing her cheek. She recoiled, but he seized her hair, jerking her head back.

"Stop it!" she screamed, her voice shattering the suffocating silence of the room.

Annoyed by her resistance, The Fox slammed the butt of his shotgun into the back of Liza's head. She slumped forward. Three additional brutal blows cracked her skull open, and blood gushed from the wound. Liza, barely conscious, stopped moving. No more resistance from her – it was pure control for The Fox.

"Any noise from you, and you get the same," he growled at Mick, who sat helpless on the bedroom floor, sobbing.

Empowered by his dominance, The Fox flipped Liza onto her back and yanked down her pyjama bottoms. With no mercy, he forced her legs apart and sexually assaulted her, all while keeping the shotgun aimed at Mick. Each violent thrust was answered by Mick's choked sobs.

The Fox's heart pounded with a sickening blend of dread and satisfaction. Once the physical torture was over, he pulled up his trousers and walked out of the bedroom and the house, leaving behind another scene of utter desolation - a couple bound, broken, and terrified.

Four days later, he struck again.

This time, the bungalow in Wing was isolated, surrounded by tall hedges that obscured it from prying eyes. Inside, a husband and wife, Jimmy and Selena King lay asleep, their two children in the room next door, blissfully unaware of the nightmare approaching. But The Fox had other plans.

He eased the back door open, his senses sharpened and his mind focused. He moved through the kitchen and into the hallway, his movements precise and calculated. The flicker of a small nightlight from the children's room served as a reminder of the delicate balance he had to maintain. He preferred not to have an audience.

He pushed the main bedroom door open and stepped inside. Selena stirred first, her eyes blinking in the darkness until she saw him - a slim figure in a black balaclava, a shotgun aimed directly at her husband's head.

"Don't scream," The Fox said calmly. "Or your children will wake up without a mother."
Selena's breath hitched, her eyes wide with fear. Jimmy was already awake, his face a mask of terror. "What do you want?" he asked, his voice trembling.

"Tie him up," The Fox replied, tossing a cord to Selena. Her hands trembled nonstop as she wrapped the rope around Jimmy's wrists, the cord biting into his skin. The Fox's eyes burned through the mask, his gaze a vulture's scrutiny.

Once she had finished, The Fox pushed her onto the bed and leaned in close to Jimmy. "Don't move," he warned, his voice grim and hostile. Jimmy's face twisted in helpless rage as he struggled against his bonds.

"Leave her alone!" he shouted; his voice hoarse with desperation. The Fox responded by swinging the shotgun like a club, striking him across the face. Blood splattered onto the sheets as Jimmy collapsed, dazed and bleeding.

Selena's scream was a strangled, terror-filled cry as The Fox leaned over her. His breath was hot and menacing against her skin.

"Open your mouth." he demanded.

Selena shook her head at first. A swift blow to the face from The Fox's shotgun ensured she soon changed her mind. A solitary trickle of blood seeped from her cut eyebrow down her cheek and onto her neck.

"I said open your mouth." The Fox demanded again.

Selena, unsure as to what his demands would lead to, slowly complied. The Fox, staring deadpan at Selena, moved his shotgun towards her mouth.

"Wider. Open wider." He requested, as he slowly forced the barrel of the shotgun into her mouth.

The sexual violence that followed was ferocious and lasted what felt like a lifetime, the shotgun never leaving her mouth. Selena, her tears now combining with the blood streaming down her face, struggled to breath, struggled to comprehend how her life was being turned upside down by such a wicked act of brutality.

When he was done, without another word, The Fox pulled up his trousers, turned around, and slipped back into the night, leaving behind a nightmare that would haunt the family forever - a shattered existence, irrevocably scarred.

The Fox's hunger was insatiable, and as he disappeared into the nighttime, he knew that he would strike again. The thrill of the hunt, the power he wielded - these were his driving forces.

Chapter 11

The Fox's neighbours saw him as a quiet man, polite but distant. He didn't socialise much, but he wasn't rude either. He was the type of man people forgot about minutes after a conversation. This anonymity was his greatest weapon.

Each day, he woke up early - before the sun had risen - to get a head start on his day. He'd pack his tools into the back of his van, a battered white Ford Transit that had seen better days, and drive to wherever the next job took him. Some days he'd be cutting hedges for an elderly couple, other days he'd be fixing a broken gate for a young family. His work was spread across the three counties - Hertfordshire, Bedfordshire, and Buckinghamshire - which gave him a wide range of areas to scout for potential targets.

He had learned early on that it was in the mundane details of life where people were most vulnerable. He listened intently as clients talked about their upcoming holidays, mentioned which neighbours they trusted to water the plants or when they expected delivery of an expensive item. They never thought twice about telling him such things. After all, he was just a labourer - a working man, like so many others. Harmless. Reliable. That was his secret: people saw only what he allowed them to see.

One particularly warm summer morning, The Fox was tasked with repairing a stone wall at a large estate in Hertfordshire. The owners, a wealthy couple in their fifties, were planning a three-week holiday to the south of France. As he worked, the wife, Carol, brought him a glass of water and chatted about the trip, casually mentioning that the house would be left empty during that time. Her husband, Quentin, had state-of-the-art window and door locks installed, but she was still worried about leaving it unattended.
"Don't worry," The Fox had said with a reassuring smile. "These new locks are top-notch. You'll be fine."

But even as he said the words, his mind was working out the details. He'd already noticed the flaws in the locks when he walked past the front and back doors. He had also noted the positioning of the neighbour's house, slightly obscured by a dense line of trees. A perfect setup for a job.

Carol smiled, reassured by his calm demeanour, and left him to his work. To her, he was just another nameless tradesman who would be gone by the end of the day. She had no idea that in just a few weeks, after their departure, The Fox would return to her home in the dead of night to strip it of its valuables. He didn't rush jobs like these. Planning was key.

The times between his crimes were just as important to The Fox as the actual acts themselves. He was methodical, careful not to act too soon after finishing a job. If he broke into a house the same week he worked on it, suspicions would naturally point in his direction. Instead, he played the long game. Weeks might pass before he returned to a property. By then, the connection between him and the crime was buried under the passage of time and memory.

When he wasn't working on jobs or scouting out potential targets, The Fox kept to himself. He had no real friends, only his brother to keep him company. He floated through the everyday world without leaving a trace. On occasion, he'd visit a local pub, nursing a pint and listening to the idle gossip of the locals. Pubs were great places for gathering information. People talked freely, especially after a few drinks. He'd hear stories of neighbours who had just bought new cars or gone on shopping sprees, boasting about their latest purchases.

There were moments when the monotony of his cover life wore on him. Moving from job to job, always pretending, always watching, it could be tiring. But he knew it was necessary. To slip up now - to give in to impatience - would risk everything. So, he played the part of the hard-working labourer, putting in long hours and doing quality work. If people liked him, they wouldn't suspect him.

Occasionally, his clients would recommend him to their friends and neighbours. These referrals were pure gold. It meant more access, more opportunities. The tight-knit communities in Hertfordshire, Bedfordshire, and Buckinghamshire were built on trust, and once you were in, you were in for good. The Fox used this to his advantage, becoming a familiar face in the area without drawing any unwanted attention.

It wasn't just homes The Fox targeted. Vulnerable people were often the easiest prey. He learned to identify them quickly: the elderly, living alone; women who had recently lost their husbands and were struggling to cope; young couples with children who left their doors unlocked, thinking nothing bad would ever happen to them. These were the people he could exploit without a second thought.

One job took him to the home of an elderly woman named Maeve Harrington in Newport Pagnell. She had recently lost her husband and was struggling to keep up with the maintenance of her large, old house. The Fox had been hired to fix a broken gutter, but as he worked, he took note of everything. Maeve was frail, her movements slow and unsteady. She lived alone, relying on a local care worker who visited twice a week to help with the shopping and cleaning. The house itself was a goldmine - old, with original fixtures that could fetch a small fortune if sold to the right buyers.

He'd bide his time with this one. It would be too easy to take advantage of her vulnerability immediately. No, he'd wait until the care worker was away on holiday, or until Maeve mentioned some other detail that would ensure there were no unexpected visitors. For now, he played the role of the helpful handyman, coming back every few weeks to do small jobs and build her trust.

One day, when the timing was perfect, The Fox would return, and no one would ever suspect him. After all, Maeve had spoken so highly of him to her neighbours - had even recommended him to a few of them. He was just a friendly local labourer, doing his bit to help those who couldn't help themselves. The perfect cover.

As much as The Fox enjoyed the actual work of breaking into homes and stealing from the vulnerable, he got an equal thrill from the hunt. The planning, the watching, the waiting - it was all part of the game. His jobs gave him unparalleled access to people's lives. He saw how they lived, where they kept their valuables, and when they left their homes unattended. But he also paid attention to the little things: who had dogs, who had old locks, who left their windows unlocked at night.

His labour jobs often took him to affluent areas, where people were more trusting and less guarded. These were the perfect targets. Wealthy enough to have things worth stealing, but too comfortable in their surroundings to suspect that the man fixing their fence or trimming their hedges was silently plotting their downfall.

In Aylesbury, he worked for a middle-aged couple who ran a small antiques business out of their home. They had hired him to help clear out their garden, which had become overgrown and difficult to manage. As he worked, he couldn't help but notice the various pieces of valuable furniture and art they had stored in their home. The wife, a chatty woman named Sylvia, proudly gave him a tour of their collection, pointing out the more valuable items and telling him how much they were worth.

"We've been collecting for years," she said with a smile. "Some of these pieces are worth more than the house itself."

The Fox nodded, his mind already working. He knew he would be back for these items, but not yet. He'd wait until they trusted him completely. Maybe even take on a few more jobs for them. The longer he worked for someone, the less they questioned his presence around their home. People had a way of letting their guard down once they thought they knew you. That was their mistake, and The Fox was always ready to exploit it.

When the time finally came to commit a crime, The Fox was meticulous in his preparation. He'd never act on impulse; every burglary was carefully planned and executed with precision. His labour jobs were not just a cover - they were a way to gather all the information he needed to carry out the perfect crime.

In the weeks leading up to a job, The Fox would stake out the property, watching from a distance, and making a mental note of every detail. He'd observe the comings and goings of the household, learning their routines. He knew when the house would be empty, when the neighbours were most likely to be away, and how long it would take for someone to notice if something was amiss.

He had no remorse for his actions. To him, it was just another job. A means to an end. And as long as he maintained his cover, no one would ever suspect the quiet, hardworking labourer who lived in their midst. He was The Fox, and he would continue to hunt, always one step ahead of the law, always hidden in plain sight.

And so, The Fox lived his life between two worlds: by day, a simple labourer, fixing fences and painting walls, and by night, a nocturnal animal, stalking his prey, waiting for the perfect moment to strike. It was an ordinary life, but only on the surface. Beneath that thin veneer of normalcy, there lurked a dangerous and calculating criminal, always watching, always waiting for his next opportunity. And for the people of Hertfordshire, Bedfordshire, and Buckinghamshire, that danger was closer than they could ever imagine.

Part Two: The Hunt Intensifies

Chapter 12

The summer of 1984 was unbearably hot, but it wasn't just the oppressive heat making everyone sweat. It was anxiety. The Fox was still out there, flickering in and out of the night like a wavering lampshade. The news was everywhere - on TV, in the papers, on the lips of every person up and down the country. With every new headline, with every whispered story, fear turned into anger, and anger began to fester.

At first, it was a quiet rebellion. People started buying extra locks for their doors and windows, spending money they didn't have for a sense of security that felt increasingly like an illusion. Hardware stores couldn't keep up with the demand. In Berkhamsted, the owner of Smith's Security & Ironmongery stood behind his counter, wiping his forehead with a rag as he tried to calm the frantic customers.

"I'm telling you, Mrs Hopkins, this is the last set of window bars I've got," he said, his voice strained. "You're lucky to be getting them."

People nodded, grumbled, but mostly they understood. Demand had skyrocketed. No one felt safe anymore. They were sleeping with windows shut tight, despite the sweltering heat, or barring them altogether. And for those who lived in single-story homes or had bedrooms on the ground floor, every rasp, every groan of the old beams in their houses, sounded like a footstep.

"More locks won't stop him," muttered a tall man with a bushy moustache and a face weathered from years of working under the sun. "Not if he's already inside your sofa when you lock up."

A murmur of agreement spread through the shop. The story of The Fox hiding inside people's homes, creating his dens, was the kind of nightmare that kept the whole town awake. A woman near the back, clutching a pair of heavy-duty padlocks, crossed herself.

Gun shops too saw a steady stream of nervous customers. In Hemel Hempstead, Trent's Firearms & Outdoor Supplies had a line of people out the door and halfway down the street. The owner, Arthur Trent, a tired looking old man who'd been in the business since his army days, stared at the queue with a mix of disbelief and concern.

"Listen up, folks!" he shouted. "If you don't have a proper license, you're not leaving here with a firearm, you hear me?"

But it wasn't just guns they wanted. Knives, baseball bats, metal rods - anything that could be turned into a weapon was disappearing from the shelves faster than Trent could restock. People were desperate, and desperation had a way of clouding judgement.

News reports filled the airwaves with stories of residents forming vigilante groups, ordinary men and women turning into self-appointed defenders of their streets. The police were stretched thin, and the sense of vulnerability had become suffocating. In small towns like Leighton Buzzard and Linslade, whispers turned into meetings, and meetings turned into patrols.

"We'll take turns," said Allen James, a stout man with a strong jaw and a face lined with age. He was a landscape gardener by trade but had emerged as a leader among his neighbours. They'd gathered in his garage, a motley crew of men and women, some young and strong, others old but no less determined. "We watch out for each other. If we see anything - anyone who doesn't belong - we handle it."

"Handle it how?" asked Toni Rimm, a middle-aged woman with a determined glint in her eye. She was holding a flashlight in one hand, a kitchen knife in the other. "We're not the bloody police."

Allen set his jaw. "No, we're not. But we're not helpless, either. If we see him, we alert the authorities. But if it comes to it...we do what we have to do to protect our own."

There were nods, murmurs of agreement. Fear had forged a new kind of community here - a collective resolve born out of desperation. The police couldn't be everywhere, and The Fox had proven he could slip through their fingers. If The Fox was going to play his games, then they would play theirs.

Still, there were some who hesitated. "We can't take the law into our own hands, Allen," warned Paula Taylor, a retired estate agent who'd always been a voice of reason. "What if we get the wrong person? What if we hurt someone innocent?"

Allen's eyes darkened. "Better to make that mistake than to be another victim."

The room fell silent. No one wanted to say it, but they all knew the truth: the police were overwhelmed, and The Fox was getting bolder. There was no room for half-measures now.

In the small village of Aston Clinton, a group calling themselves 'The Night Watch' had already begun patrolling the streets. They were a mix of local farmers, shop owners, and factory workers, all united by a single purpose: keep their families safe from The Fox.

Jonny Reid, a former soldier with a scar running down his cheek, was their de facto leader. He stood in the middle of a dimly lit garage, surrounded by a dozen men and women. Each of them held some form of weapon - a bat, a crowbar, even an antique hunting rifle.

"You heard the copper on the telly," Reid said, his voice low but commanding. "He says don't take the law into our own hands. But what's he gonna do if The Fox comes knocking? By the time the coppers get here, it'll be too late."

There were nods of agreement, murmurs of approval. "We've got to protect ourselves," someone muttered.

Reid continued, "We stay off the beaten track. We don't go looking for trouble, but if trouble comes, we're ready. If anyone sees anything, we alert the group. We move fast, we move quiet. And if we catch him..." He paused, letting the weight of his words sink in. "We make sure he can't hurt anyone ever again."

The room was silent, the tension plain for all to see. They were ordinary people, turned into something else by an intruder. And if they caught The Fox, God help him - or them.

It wasn't long before things began to spiral. The reports came in daily - mistaken identities, false alarms, frightened neighbours turning on each other. A man in Hemel Hempstead was nearly beaten to death because he'd been walking home late at night and fitted the vague description of The Fox. In Tring, an elderly woman fired a shotgun through her front door at what turned out to be a stray cat.

Detective Chief Superintendent Mark Talbot felt the pressure mounting. His worst concerns were coming true. The community was on the brink of tearing itself apart, and still, The Fox remained elusive.

One night, as Talbot sat in his office, a call came through. It was his Press Officer, Katie McGee, her voice urgent.

"Mark, you need to see this," she said. "It's spreading."

"What is?" he asked, already dreading the answer.

"The vigilantes. There's talk of them organising into a proper militia. Some are even saying they want to march on the police station, demand more action."

Talbot ran a hand through his hair, feeling the weight of it all crushing down on him. "Damn it. We're losing control."

He slammed down the phone, rubbed his face in frustration and stared up at the ceiling. Instead of pursuing a single threat, they were facing a pack of threats - desperate, scared, and increasingly armed.

He picked up the phone and dialled the number for Detective Sergeant Sarah Kendrick. "We need more officers on the ground," he said as soon as the line clicked open. "And we need them now. We can't let the locals take matters into their own hands."

In the quiet village of Wingrave, a group of locals huddled in a small, dimly lit barn. The scent of hay and sweat overpowered their senses. They were scared, desperate. Glen Davies, now considered a leader of sorts, spoke to them with a steady voice.

"If we don't protect our own, who will?" he asked. "The police are too slow, too scattered. But we know our streets, our neighbours. We've got eyes everywhere."

Helena Coombes, still gripping her flashlight and kitchen knife, nodded in agreement. "We won't let him take another one of us."

From the back of the room, a younger man named Stevie Stathers stood up. "I say we set traps," he suggested. "Like they do for foxes in the countryside. If he's lurking around, he's bound to trip one sooner or later."

The idea sparked a murmur of approval. Fear had turned their hearts hard, their minds sharp with the thirst for justice - or revenge.

Davies nodded. "Alright, we start setting traps tomorrow. But remember, if you see him, you call for help. Don't try to be a hero."

The barn was filled with a dark, determined energy. They were ready. But as the nights stretched on and their patrols became more frequent, the danger only seemed to escalate. And all the while, The Fox watched through his binoculars in the Chiltern Hills, a twisted smile on his face. He knew they were hunting him, but he also knew they weren't smart enough to catch him.

And soon, the hunters would find themselves hunted, caught in a game they didn't fully understand - a game where the only rule was survival, and the price of failure was blood.

Detective Chief Superintendent Mark Talbot knew things were spiralling. Each day brought another report of a vigilante group forming, another case of someone taking the law into their own hands. It was only a matter of time before things got out of control. He sat at his desk, his face drawn and tired.

"Bloody hell," he muttered under his breath. His eyes were bloodshot, dark circles etched beneath them. He hadn't slept properly in weeks. Every day, he felt the pressure mounting - on him, on his team, on the entire community. And every day, the fear and anger seemed to deepen.

Katie McGee stepped into the room, her face taut with worry. "Mark, we've got to address this vigilante thing before it blows up in our faces. They're scared, and they're armed. We're looking at a potential disaster here."

Talbot nodded. "I know. I know. But they're scared for a reason, Katie. We've got a bloody madman out there, and we're no closer to catching him. People are losing faith."

"Then we need to restore it," she said firmly. "Get ahead of this before it turns into a bloodbath."

Talbot took a deep breath. "Alright. Set up a press conference. I want every local paper, every radio station, every TV crew we can get. They need to hear from me directly."

McGee nodded, already reaching for the phone. "I'll get on it."

Chapter 13

Detective Chief Superintendent Mark Talbot stood in the dimly lit hallway of the Dunstable police station, staring at his reflection in a grimy window. He looked like death warmed up, he felt it too. It had been weeks since he'd rested properly, and it showed. The Fox was running him ragged - running them all ragged.

Today, he would face the press.

He adjusted his tie in the window's faint reflection, feeling the weight of what was coming. The press conference had been called hastily, but it was necessary. The public's fear had reached a fever pitch, and if they didn't address it soon, the whole region could descend into chaos. He had to give them something - reassurance, hope, anything to cling to in this endless nightmare.

Katie McGee, his Press Officer, appeared beside him, her face just as tired and worn. She gave him a brief nod. "They're ready for you, Mark," she said, her voice low.

Talbot took a deep breath. "How bad is it out there?"

"Packed," McGee replied. "Journalists from every major outlet. Local and national. Even some international. They smell blood in the water."

Talbot exhaled slowly. "And they're expecting answers we don't have yet."

McGee nodded, her expression grim. "Just be honest. Let them know we're doing everything we can."

"Honest," Talbot muttered. "Not sure they want honesty, Katie. They want a monster in chains. And right now, we've got a monster on the run."

Talbot took a final deep breath, steadied himself, and moved toward the doors leading into the conference room. As he pushed them open, a wall of flashing cameras and murmuring voices hit him like a wave.

The room was packed - dozens of reporters, cameras, and microphones crowded together in a sea of faces.

He walked to the podium at the front, his every step echoing in the silence that fell over the room. As he stood behind the microphone, he could feel the eyes of every person in the room bearing down on him, waiting for him to say something – anything - that could make sense of the terror that had gripped their lives.

"Good afternoon," Talbot began, his voice steady despite the tightness in his chest. "Thank you all for being here today. I know there's a lot of fear and uncertainty in our community right now, and I want to address that directly."

The room was silent except for the clicking of cameras and the scribbling of pens on notepads. Talbot could feel the pressure, the anticipation evident in the way the reporters leaned forward, hanging on his every word.

"As many of you are aware, we are currently investigating a series of violent home invasions and assaults across Hertfordshire, Bedfordshire, and Buckinghamshire, committed by an individual we are referring to as 'The Fox.' Over the past several weeks, The Fox has targeted multiple homes, often breaking in and creating dens within the properties, where he waits until his victims are at their most vulnerable."

A murmur rippled through the crowd, a mix of shock and horror. Talbot continued, his eyes scanning the room, making contact with the faces before him. "These crimes have been methodical, calculated, and brutal. The victims have been left traumatised; their sense of safety shattered. We understand the fear that this has caused in our community, and we are doing everything in our power to bring this individual to justice."

A reporter in the front row raised her hand, not waiting to be called on. "Detective Chief Superintendent Mark Talbot, can you confirm whether The Fox has left any messages or clues at the crime scenes? Is he trying to communicate with the police or the public?"

Talbot took a moment to consider his response. "At this time, we cannot disclose specific details regarding evidence found at the scenes, as it is part of an ongoing investigation. However, we can say that The Fox's actions suggest a pattern of control and psychological manipulation. He is careful, precise, and seems to take pleasure in the fear he creates."

Another reporter jumped in; her voice tinged with impatience. "How close are you to catching him? Are there any suspects?" Talbot's expression hardened slightly. "I understand the urgency, believe me. But investigations of this nature are complex. We are pursuing every lead, examining every piece of evidence, and dedicating all necessary resources to this case. But this individual is highly elusive. He knows how to cover his tracks."

"Is it true that people are forming vigilante groups in response to the attacks?" another journalist asked, his voice rising above the others.

Talbot's jaw compressed. "Yes, we are aware of community groups organising patrols. While we understand the frustration that has led to this, we strongly advise against taking the law into your own hands. These actions, while well-intentioned, can complicate our investigation and potentially put more lives at risk. We ask the public to remain vigilant, but to trust the police to do our job."

The room erupted into more questions, voices overlapping as reporters tried to get their next inquiry in. "Detective Chief Superintendent Mark Talbot, how can you ask the public to trust you when The Fox is still out there?" one shouted.

Talbot held up a hand, his gaze steady. "Because trust is our most powerful tool right now. Trust between the police and the public, trust in our process. We understand the anger. We feel it too. But we need to work together to end this."

A reporter from a major network pushed forward, his voice loud and demanding. "Do you have any message for The Fox himself?"

The room fell deathly silent, every eye trained on Talbot, waiting for his response. He leaned slightly into the microphone, his eyes dark and unyielding.

"To The Fox, I say this: we will not rest until you are caught. You may think you're untouchable, hidden in amongst us, but your time is running out. This community is stronger than the fear you've created. And you will face justice."

The words lingered, charged with a tense energy. Talbot could see the headlines forming in the reporters' eyes, the way they scribbled furiously in their notepads, and the clicking of camera shutters intensified. He knew his words were bold, but they needed to be. The public needed to hear it, and The Fox needed to feel it.

Another reporter, one from a local paper, raised his voice with a more measured question. "DCS Talbot, you've been at the forefront of this investigation for several weeks. Can you give us an insight into what your team is feeling right now, working day and night to track down someone like The Fox?"

Talbot looked at him, and for a moment, the hardness in his eyes softened. "My team is exhausted, but they're also relentless. We've been working around the clock, following every lead, examining every detail. We're dealing with an adversary who thrives on chaos, and that weighs heavily on all of us. But I promise you, and I promise the public, we will not stop. We will not let him win." The room fell silent again, a ponderous quiet that felt almost oppressive. Talbot could see the dread in the eyes of the journalists, the same worry that had gripped the community for weeks. He knew that nothing he could say would truly alleviate it until The Fox was caught, but he hoped he had at least given them some sense of direction, some belief that the darkness would not last forever.

As the press conference drew to a close, the questions continued to come, but Talbot's answers remained consistent - measured but firm. He would not give in to the hysteria. He would not allow The Fox to dictate the narrative.

"Thank you for your time," Talbot said finally, stepping away from the podium. "We will provide updates as they become available. In the meantime, please stay safe, stay cautious, and know that we are doing everything we can."

He turned and walked off the stage, the camera flashes bursting behind him like fireworks, the questions still flying. He could hear Katie McGee's voice behind him, trying to corral the press, but he needed a moment away from it all. He slipped through a side door into a quiet hallway, the noise of the conference room fading behind him.

He leaned against the wall, his head falling back as he closed his eyes. The weight of the last few weeks pressed down on him, and for a moment, he allowed himself to feel it - the exhaustion, the frustration, the distress. He knew the road ahead was going to be long, and he knew the press conference was only a small part of the battle. But it was a necessary one.

The door opened, and McGee slipped in beside him, her expression as tired as his own. "You did good out there, Mark," she said softly.

"Did I?" Talbot asked, his voice low. "It feels like shouting into the wind."

McGee nodded. "Maybe. But sometimes that's all we can do until the storm passes."
Talbot gave her a faint, tired smile. "Let's just hope we find this bastard before then."

McGee nodded, her expression hardening. "We will. We have to."
Talbot took a deep breath, pushing himself off the wall. "Back to work, then. The clock's ticking."

As they walked back toward the operations room, the weight of the task ahead settled back onto his shoulders. The Fox was still out there, still lurking in the background. But so was he, and he wasn't going to let up. Not now. Not ever.

Chapter 14

The village of Slapton was simmering with a nervous hostility that had been building for weeks. Whispers of The Fox floated through the air like an invisible toxin, infecting every conversation, every cautious glance between neighbours. The local news was relentless, broadcasting reports of his assaults and burglaries across the area. The headlines were becoming more frequent, the crimes more brazen, and fear more widespread. No one felt safe. Even in broad daylight, windows were shut, doors double-locked. A sense of paranoia was taking root, twisting its way into every household.

For Claire Mathers, a single mother of a ten-year-old boy, life had already been full of unease. Her ex-partner, Ray, was unpredictable - sometimes sweet, sometimes volatile - and their split had only increased her anxiety. Living alone was not easy.

It was a warm Sunday afternoon when Claire returned home after lunch, her son Jake still with Ray for the weekend. She turned the corner onto her quiet cul-de-sac and pulled into the driveway. She sighed, grateful for a few hours of calm in the middle of the chaos that had become her life.

As she stepped out of her car, the late afternoon sun beamed down on the small, modest houses lining the street. She noticed nothing unusual - until she reached her back door. Her breath stalled in her chest. The door, which she distinctly remembered locking that morning, was slightly ajar. She froze, her heart hammering in her ribs. She knew she hadn't left it like that. She always checked. Twice. Her mind raced with images of the masked intruder known as The Fox, his cold eyes staring from beneath a balaclava, the shotgun gleaming in his hands. She had seen his masked face on the news a hundred times over.

She inched closer, peering through the kitchen window. Her eyes widened as she saw it - someone had made a makeshift den in her utility room. The towels and laundry piled up in a corner, an empty plate and glass on the floor, and the unmistakable indentation of someone having been there.

It was as if the oxygen had been sucked out of her lungs.

"Oh my God…" she whispered. Panic surged through her veins, but she knew better than to enter. She backed away. Slowly. Taking great care not to make a noise.

As she tiptoed away her mind was racing, which neighbour would be home. She needed to use their house phone.

"Mrs Hipwell, number twelve, she is always home," she quietly muttered to herself.

Once she was a safe distance away, Claire ran as fast as her legs could take her to number twelve. She knocked on the door. Once. Twice. A third time. "Come on, come on," she gasped. And as she was about to knock a fourth time, an elderly lady opened the door.

"Hi Mrs Hipwell," Claire gulped. "It's him. He's in my house. I need your phone".

"It's who dear?" replied Mrs Hipwell.

"The Fox. He's in my house". And without taking another breath, Claire burst into the house.

She dialled for the police, her fingers trembling, and brought the phone to her ear. It rang once, then again. She could hardly breathe.

"Emergency services. What service do you require?"

"Police," Claire stuttered. "It's… it's my house. Someone's been inside. I think it's him. I think it's The Fox."

The operator's tone changed instantly. "Stay calm, ma'am. Are you safe right now?"

"Yes, I'm at a neighbour's house> My house is number twelve, Emu Close in Slapton. Please, hurry."

"We're dispatching units to your location. Armed police are on their way. Stay where you are, do not enter the house. Officers will be with you shortly."

Claire hung up, her breath coming in shallow bursts. She sat down on a sofa. Her hands shuddered.

"Would you like a cup of tea, dear? You look like you've had an awful fright." Mrs Hipwell disappeared into her kitchen.

Claire, meanwhile, stood up again, walked to the living room window and stared across the street at her house. She scanned the windows, half-expecting to see a masked face peering back at her. She imagined the intruder inside, maybe watching her right now, deciding what to do next. She wished Ray was there, wished she wasn't alone. The minutes ticked by, feeling like hours.

Inside the operations room in Dunstable police station, Detective Chief Superintendent Mark Talbot was hunched over his desk, his team buzzing around him like a hive. A report had come in only a day earlier of another assault. Talbot was studying it with intent.

His radio crackled to life. "Control to DCS Talbot. We've got a call - possible sighting of The Fox in Slapton. A lady came home, found her back door open and there are signs someone is inside. Armed units are on route."

Talbot's head shot up, his eyes alight with urgency. "This could be it," he said, grabbing his jacket from the back of his chair. "Everyone, listen up! We have a possible sighting of The Fox in Slapton. Armed units are rolling out. This could be the break we've been waiting for."

The room erupted into a frenzy of activity. Officers grabbed gear, shouted orders, and relayed instructions. Talbot could feel the energy in the air; they'd been chasing The Fox for weeks, and now they finally had a chance to corner him. He turned to his right-hand, Detective Sergeant Sarah Kendrick, who was already strapping on her bulletproof vest.

"Sarah, you're with me," Talbot said. "Tell the team to expect resistance. This guy's dangerous, and we're not taking any chances."

Kendrick nodded, her face a mask of grim determination. "Got it, boss. We're ready."

The convoy of marked and unmarked police cars tore through the streets, sirens wailing, blue lights flashing against the blue sky. The armed response units followed close behind in tactical vehicles, officers checking their weapons and preparing for a confrontation. The atmosphere was electric with anticipation - this wasn't just another false alarm. It was a real possibility that they could end The Fox's reign of terror right here, right now.

When the first squad car screeched to a halt outside Claire's house, she nearly jumped out of her skin. Within moments, the street was filled with armed officers, their black uniforms stark against the calm suburban setting. Claire could only watch as they swarmed her property with military precision, weapons raised, ready to breach.

Talbot arrived on the scene moments later, stepping out of his car and surveying the area with a sharp eye. He saw Claire standing on the lawn of Mrs Hipwell's home, pale and visibly shaken.

"Are you Claire Mathers?" he asked, his tone firm but reassuring.

"Yes, that's me," she replied, her voice shaky. "Please, is it really him? Is he in there?"

"We're going to find out," Talbot said. He signalled to the armed units. "On my command. Prepare to breach."

The officers moved swiftly, taking up positions around the house, covering all exits. One of them held a battering ram, ready to break down the door. Talbot's heart thudded in his chest. This was it - the moment they'd all been waiting for.

"Breach!" Talbot commanded.

The door burst open with a deafening crash. Officers flooded into the house, shouting orders. "Armed police! Show yourself! Hands where we can see them!"

The strain was unmistakable, every second stretched taut like a wire about to snap.

Inside, the house was still. The officers moved room by room, clearing each one with quick, efficient movements. The kitchen was empty. The living room, empty. The bedrooms, empty. Then, they reached the utility room. There it was - a makeshift den, just as Claire had described. Officers surrounded it, guns trained, ready for anything.

"Police! Come out now!" an officer shouted. No response. Only silence.

Talbot pushed through the throng of officers, his eyes narrowing. Something felt off. He glanced at the den - at the hastily made bed of towels, the half-eaten plate of food. Then he spotted something that made his heart sink. A small backpack with a Spider-Man logo, a teddy bear and a colouring book.

"Stand down," he said softly, lowering his gun. "It's not him."

The officers exchanged confused glances. "Sir?"

"I said, stand down!" Talbot barked. "It's not The Fox."

Just then, the back door slid open, and a voice called out hesitantly, "Hello? Claire?"

Everyone turned, guns raised again, adrenaline still pumping. A man stepped into the kitchen, holding a young boy's hand. "Who are you?" demanded Talbot.

"I'm - I'm Ray. Claire's ex-partner. What on earth is going on?" stuttered a very nervous Ray.

"There's been a mistake," replied a very disappointed Talbot.

Ray looked around at the swarm of armed police, his face a mixture of fear and bewilderment. "I - I brought Jake home early. He wasn't feeling well, so I let us in with my old key. Thought I'd wait until Claire got back. We were just in the garage looking for something."

Silence fell over the house, the dread dissipating in an instant. Talbot lowered his gun completely, a sigh escaping his lips as he shook his head. "You've got to be kidding me…"

As the armed police vacated the house, Claire called out to them "is it him, is he in there?"

"No," replied one of the officers. "But your ex-partner Ray is in there."

The colour from Claire's face drained once again. She ran to her house, entering via the smashed in front door. Her concerns had quickly turned to embarrassment. "I…I'm so sorry. I didn't know. I thought…I thought it was…"

"Never mind, ma'am," Talbot said, his voice calm but carrying an edge of frustration. "You did the right thing by calling us. It's better to be safe than sorry."

The remaining officers began to disperse, the worry draining away as the reality of the situation sank in. As the crowd thinned, Talbot turned to Kendrick, a wry smile tugging at his lips.

"Well, I guess that's one way to spend a Sunday afternoon," he said.

Kendrick chuckled, shaking her head. "Can't believe it. All that buildup…for nothing."
"Not for nothing," Talbot replied, his tone suddenly serious. "We're still on the hunt. The Fox is out there, and next time, it won't be a false alarm. We have to be ready."

As the police packed up their gear and prepared to leave, Claire stood by, holding Jake close. She could feel the stares of her neighbours from behind their curtains, could feel the weight of her mistake settling over her like a heavy cold. But more than anything, she felt a renewed sense of fear - because The Fox was still out there.

And with that thought, Claire's heart sank, knowing this was far from over.

Chapter 15

Detective Chief Superintendent Mark Talbot and his team were once again working into the night. Talbot leaned over the evidence spread out on desks in the operations room. The pieces of paper all connected in some way, forming a grotesque, spider-like web. It sprawled across the room, a chilling testament to The Fox's reign of terror. Talbot's brow was furrowed, his mind churning with half-formed thoughts and gut instincts. The chaotic web of paperwork was supposed to reveal something, but all it did was deepen the mystery.

"What's the latest with the names Metal Mickey has provided?" asked Detective Inspector Elaine Carter, stepping up beside Talbot. Carter was one of the sharpest on the team, a woman whose keen observational skills often pierced through the haze of complex cases. She held a stack of files close to her chest; her dark eyes fixed on the same piece of paper Talbot was studying.

Talbot sighed, pushing a hand through his short, greying hair. He straightened his back, casting a quick glance around the room where officers scribbled notes and sipped lukewarm coffee, their eyes tired but determined.

"We've cross-checked over one thousand names which Metal Mickey fed us," Talbot began, his voice a rumble of frustration. "Half of them were ghosts - aliases, identities that exist only on paper. The other half, well, they're either petty criminals with airtight alibis or people who vanished off the map years ago. It's like trying to grab smoke."

Carter's brows knitted in a mixture of disappointment and thoughtfulness. "And the contact we had in Aylesbury? Anything there?"

"Nothing," Talbot said, shaking his head. "The local force said the lead was stale before we even got to it. The name 'Robert Smith' is as common as it gets, and their records turned up nothing that matched our intel."

Carter glanced down at the spread of documents, eyes scanning names and numbers as if willing them to yield secrets. The harsh fluorescent lights cast deep shadows across her face. "Only another four thousand names to go."

"Not entirely," Talbot muttered, tapping a report that sat alone on a corner of the desk. "This one, Carter – Simon Petura. His name keeps showing up. Numerous calls on him, fits the description, bit of a weirdo. He's a small-time crook, but we need more intel on him."

Carter nodded, the fire of determination sparking in her eyes. "Then maybe it's time we rattle his cage."

Talbot's expression softened for a moment, admiration mixing with weariness. "That's the plan. Let's hope we can nail him before he strikes again."

The room fell into silence again, except for the faint rustling of papers and the ticking clock that marked the minutes toward midnight. Every second without a breakthrough felt like an eternity, but Talbot knew they couldn't stop. Not until The Fox was caught, and the web of terror was torn apart at last.

Meanwhile, in the quiet village of Markyate, the night was unnervingly still - a deceptive calm that belied the terror creeping through its streets. The Fox prowled through the darkness, moving with quiet, deliberate intent. He knew the layout of the bungalow ahead as if it were etched into his mind. The building was set back from the road, obscured by a deep row of overgrown hedges. Inside, an eighteen-year-old girl - Clare, her younger brother - Nigel, and her boyfriend - Stewart were nestled in a false sense of security, their lives hanging by a thread.

The Fox's balaclava was pulled snugly over his face, the fabric clinging to his breath. He gripped the shotgun tightly in his gloved hands, his movements accurate and prepared. As he rounded the back of the building, he addressed the flimsy lock on the kitchen door. It posed no challenge; within seconds, it was bypassed, and he slipped inside.

The bungalow was dimly lit, a single light casting a wan light in the hallway. The Fox soon saw to that. Treading on the floor lamp, he yanked the electrical cable until it became free. The Fox paused, letting the silence envelop him. The faint crackle of a vinyl record drifted through the air, a soft, tinny melody that contrasted starkly with the dark purpose of his visit. He crept forward, his sense heightened. In the living room, Nigel swayed to the music, his back turned, oblivious to the encroaching danger.

The Fox's steps were deliberate as he continued down the hallway toward the bedrooms. Clare was in the room at the end. He could hear the low, steady murmur of her sleep, a sound that quickened his pulse with twisted anticipation.

Suddenly, a door creaked open. The Fox spun around; shotgun raised. Stewart emerged from the bathroom; his eyes sprung wide with shock as they met the dark silhouette of The Fox. Stewart's mouth opened, but no words escaped.

"What the hell-" he began, his voice cracking with disbelief.

"Not another word," The Fox cut him off, his voice as cold as steel. "In the bedroom room. Now."

Stewart's face went pale. He raised his hands slowly, eyes darting nervously between The Fox and the living room, where the music still played. "Is that a real gun?" he asked, his voice a whisper of fear.

The Fox took a step closer, his finger brushing the trigger. "You want to find out?" he asked, his tone lethal.

Swallowing hard, Stewart turned into the bedroom, his movements rigid with terror. The Fox followed, the blackness swallowing them both. Clare, asleep, stirred as the door opened. She blinked; her eyes looked confused as they fell on the intruder.

"What's going on?" she asked, her voice groggy and laced with dread.

"Get up," The Fox ordered, jabbing the shotgun toward her.

Stewart moved immediately, but Clare hesitated, her eyes flickering between the gun and her boyfriend's anxious face. "Please, just do what he says," Stewart whispered urgently.

Clare's resolve crumbled. Trembling, she slid off the bed. The Fox marched them back into the hallway, where Nigel had finally emerged, drawn by the commotion. His eyes expanded in horror as he saw his sister and her boyfriend at gunpoint, the black-clad intruder behind them.

"What the-" he began, but The Fox silenced him with a piercing glare.

"All of you, back in the bedroom. Now!" The Fox's voice was unyielding, a command etched in menace. "Don't make a sound."

Fright and disbelief spread across their faces as they shuffled back into the bedroom. The Fox kept the gun trained on them as he pulled the lamp cable from his pocket, along with a silk tie.

"On the floor," he barked. "Face down. Hands behind your backs."

Stewart and Nigel exchanged a look of helpless dread before slowly complying. They lay flat on the carpet, their faces pressed against the rough fibres. The Fox moved with swift efficiency, tying their hands with rough, merciless jerks. The cable cut into Nigel's skin as he bound his wrists tightly, the pressure leaving red indentations.

Clare watched in horror, her breaths coming in rapid, shallow bursts. "Please...please, just take what you want and go," she pleaded, tears streaming down her face.
The Fox turned his gaze to her, his eyes narrowing behind the mask. "You don't get to make demands," he said, his voice devoid of empathy. "On the bed."

Clare hesitated, but the cold steel of the shotgun pressing against her shoulder forced her into compliance. She climbed onto the bed, her entire body trembling. The Fox grabbed a dressing gown cord hanging on the back of the door and bound her wrists to the headboard. He placed a pillow over her head, muffling her sobs.

The Fox, lifted up Clare's nightdress, ripped off her underwear, whilst sliding down his trousers and his underpants. All the while his eyes fixed on the two boys and his shotgun pointing at Clare. The room filled with the sound of Clare's distress and the muffled groans of the two boys, struggling against their restraints, as The Fox claimed yet another victim. His eyes darted around the room, surveying his handiwork. He pulled up his underwear and trousers. Then, without a word, he slipped out into the hallway, leaving the wreckage behind him.

The seconds dragged on like hours. The boys could hear The Fox's movements in the bungalow - opening cupboards, the squeak of the fridge door, boiling the kettle. Their hearts raced, each beat a drum of fear and desperation. They prayed he would simply take what he wanted and leave. Instead, he was refuelling with coffee and a sandwich.

Minutes later, they heard his footsteps returning. The door creaked open, and the room seemed to shrink with his presence. Clare couldn't see him through the pillow, but she could feel him there, looming over her.

She whimpered, her voice a faint, muffled plea. "Please...don't..."

The sexual assault that followed was ferocious and rapid, a ruthless display of power that left her shaking, broken and bleeding heavily. The boys could only listen, their own cries choked back by their restraints.
And then it was their turn.

The Fox walked over to Stewart, slipped his left hand into his pants and groped him. He licked his lips, and he watched the tears stream down Stewart's ashen face. With every stroke, there was a wince of pain. The Fox enjoying and savouring every moment. Stewart, frozen to the spot, praying his torture would soon end.

And then it was Nigel's turn. The same fate awaited him. The same pain was inflicted. And when it was over, The Fox stood up, breathing heavily, smiling to himself.

The three victims were hoping it was the end of their ordeal, but The Fox was already contemplating his next move. He untied Clare. "Get up, move over here." The Fox pushed her towards Nigel.

"Put your hands in his pants," ordered The Fox.

"But – but I can't." Clare sobbed.

"You can and you will." The Fox demanded. He was losing his temper.

"I can't, he's my, he's, my brother." sobbed Clare.

"Well just pretend he isn't then." The Fox snapped back. And without a moment's hesitation he grabbed Clare's hand and forced her to grope Nigel.

The Fox wasn't done. His final act was to force Nigel to reciprocate the horror on his own sister. Nigel froze to the spot, paralysed with shock. Stewart vomited onto the carpet, while Clare squeezed her eyes shut and turned away. The Fox watched, grinning with twisted satisfaction.

Finally, The Fox decided he had inflicted enough pain. He stood up, rifled through the room, grabbing a stack of videotapes from a shelf. He cast a final, lingering glance at his victims before sliding out into the night, leaving behind a trail of utter devastation. All three victims would be traumatised for the rest of their lives.

As the news of the latest attack began to filter through, Detective Constable Tom Hughes burst into the operations room in Dunstable police station, his face flushed and tie askew. "Guv, we've got another one. Just came in over the wire."

Detective Chief Superintendent Mark Talbot turned sharply, his eyes meeting Hughes's with a sharp, focused intensity. "Where?"

"Little village called Markyate," Hughes said, his voice taut with urgency. "About four miles out. Same MO - masked intruder, shotgun, no prints. Tied up a brother, a sister, her boyfriend, and sexually assaulted all three of them. Multiple times."

"Markyate?" Talbot snapped, his gaze fixing on the map on the wall. He located the village and marked it with a fresh pin. "Damn it. So much for our pattern."

"He's moving around," Carter interjected, her voice edged with anxiety. "He's impossible to trace."

Talbot's eyes located the new pin, the web of strings on the map converging toward a point he couldn't yet identify. "What's he doing, Elaine?" he murmured. "What's he after?"

"Control," she replied without hesitation. "He wants to control us, the towns, the villages, our thoughts. He's playing a game, and right now, we're just chasing our tails."

"Then we need to change the game," Talbot said, his voice hardening with resolve. He turned to Hughes. "Get more boots on the ground in these target areas. I want every road covered, every back alley watched. Get more plainclothes officers mingling with the locals. If he's working to some kind of twisted schedule, we need to be ready."

"Right away, Guv," Hughes nodded, already moving toward the door.

Carter stepped closer to Talbot, her voice dropping to a whisper. "Guv, we're running the team ragged. And The Fox...he's not just ahead of us; he's taunting us."

"I know," Talbot said, his face set in grim determination. "But there must be a pattern here, and if we find it, we find him."

She gave him a wary look. "And what if he's baiting us? Drawing us in like all the others?"

"Then we take the bait," Talbot replied. "But we'll be ready."

By midnight, every town and village within the reach of The Fox's terror was crawling with undercover officers. Cars were discreetly parked on the outskirts, and officers on foot patrolled the streets, their eyes scanning every alleyway, every potential hiding place.

Talbot arrived at the small bungalow, the scene of the latest crime, where three shaken occupants were being questioned. He moved quickly, asking for any details or descriptions they could provide.

Stewart, pointed to a floor lamp that had been knocked over. "He stood on this to rip out the electrical cord," Stewart explained.

Talbot examined the lamp before ordering forensics to analyse it for prints or any other trace evidence.

Nigel offered a description: "He was about five feet nine inches tall, wearing a blue and white stripey jumper, beige shoes, brown hair. He had a mask on, but I noticed he was left-handed - his wristwatch was on his right wrist."

Talbot nodded thoughtfully, thanking them for their help. He then instructed the forensic team to prioritise the analysis of the lamp, and the items used to tie the victims up.

On his way home, Talbot listened to his police radio crackling with intermittent updates, each silence stretching the nerves taut. "Any sign?" he barked into the radio.

"Nothing yet, Guv," came the reply from one of the units.

Talbot's grip tightened on the radio. He could almost sense The Fox lurking out there, hiding from them. The thought gnawed at him, an almost tangible presence that left him restless.

"Come on, you bastard," Talbot muttered under his breath, his eyes fixed on the road ahead. "Let's see how clever you really are."

The next day, the results came back from the Forensics team - confirming the footprint on the lamp was consistent with those found at other crime scenes, further linking the crime to The Fox.

Chapter 16

The late afternoon sun stretched across the quiet streets of Buckinghamshire, bathing the quaint homes in a golden hue. The village of Haddenham, known for its picturesque charm and serene atmosphere, seemed to be slumbering under the gentle warmth of the sunshine. Little did anyone know, a malevolent force was threading its way into their midst, drawn to the serenity like a hunter homing in on their target.

The Fox, dressed casually, moved silently through the leafy streets. His wiry figure slipping between the houses with an almost supernatural grace. He was methodical, his eyes constantly darting, scanning for the perfect opportunity to strike. Today, he had chosen a modest bungalow on Thistledown Road - a place that, from his observations, seemed to offer the perfect mix of vulnerability and isolation.

Emma Harcourt, the woman who lived there, had left her home an hour earlier, heading to the local shops for what was supposed to be a routine outing. Unbeknownst to her, her seemingly mundane errands were playing into The Fox's meticulously orchestrated plan. He had watched her leave her home from his vantage point in the Chiltern Hills. He knew she would be several hours, and he had time on his hands.

The Fox approached the bungalow, a nondescript building set back from the road behind a neat row of hedges. He crouched beside the back door, inspecting it with the keen eye of an expert. The lock was old and rusted, barely a challenge for someone with his skills. With a few deft movements, he popped it open and entered, leaving no trace of his entry.

Inside, the bungalow was calm, bathed in the soft afternoon light filtering through the lace curtains. It was an invitingly ordinary space - warm and homely. The Fox's eyes scanned the rooms, taking in the layout with care. The living room was decorated with cheerful floral prints, and family photos lined the mantelpiece. The master bedroom was neat and tidy, the smell of fresh flowers filled the air.

The Fox knew exactly what he wanted. He had a plan - one that required both patience and precision. He set to work, stripping the light bulbs from their sockets and locating belts from a cupboard. He located the phone lines and severed them, cutting off any chance of a call for help.

Next, he searched for materials to build his den - a place of concealment and control. The spare bedroom, filled with old furniture and dusty boxes, would serve his purpose well. He dragged an old wardrobe into the centre of the room, using it as a makeshift barrier. He then arranged the remaining furniture around it, creating a dark, claustrophobic nook where he could wait in silence.

The bungalow began to feel less like a home and more like a horror movie set for his grim performance.

Satisfied with his work, The Fox took a moment to ensure everything was in place. He stocked up on food and drink from the fridge and then positioned himself in the den, hidden from view, and waited.

Emma's day was turning out to be longer than expected. The shopping had taken more time, and she had bumped into an old school friend who offered to buy her a coffee. As she finally loaded her bags into the boot of her car several hours later than she had intended, she felt a sense of relief. But little did she know, her sanctuary had been violated, and a nightmare was unfolding within her own walls.

When she finally arrived home, the sun was dipping low on the horizon, casting an eerie twilight across the neighbourhood. Emma's footsteps were light as she approached her front door, her mind still preoccupied with mundane thoughts of groceries and dinner. As she unlocked the door and stepped inside, she felt an unsettling chill in the air. The usual hum of domesticity was conspicuously absent.

"Hello?" she called out, her voice echoing in the silence. The bungalow greeted her with a foreboding stillness. She stepped into the living room, the soft glow of twilight creeping through the lace curtains. "Hello? Is someone there?"

There was no response.

Emma's heart began to race, an instinctual alarm flaring up as she moved cautiously through the bungalow. The absence of light in the hallway was unnerving. She flicked the light switch. Nothing happened. A sense of dread washed over her as she reached the master bedroom. The door was slightly ajar, and she pushed it open with trembling fingers. The room was dark, the only light coming from the dying remnants of the day. Her eyes scanned the space, trying to make sense of everything.

She turned around, pushed open the door to the spare bedroom, and that's when she saw it – the wardrobe, its position unnatural. Emma hesitated, her mind racing with the possibility of an intruder. She turned on her heels and grabbed the phone, only to realise it was dead.

Panic surged through her as she fumbled around in the dark, her hands shaking uncontrollably. She turned to run, her instincts screaming at her to escape. But before she could make it to the front door, a noise from the hallway froze her in place - a deliberate, measured step.

The Fox emerged from out of nowhere, his balaclava concealing his face, his eyes cold and unfeeling. He was brandishing a shotgun, its metal gleaming ominously in the dim light.

"Emma Harcourt," he said, his voice muffled but menacing. "I've been waiting for you."

Emma's blood ran cold. She raised a hand instinctively, her voice trembling as she spoke. "Please...please, just take what you want and leave."

The Fox's eyes were emotionless as he took a step closer, the shotgun's barrel pointed directly at her. "It's not about what I want," he said calmly. "It's about what I'm going to do."

Emma's breath quickened, each inhale coming in short, panicked bursts. The room seemed to close in around her, the walls pressing in as she stumbled backward. The Fox moved with deliberate steps, his presence an overwhelming force.

"On the floor," he commanded, his voice cold and authoritative. "Face down."

Tears streamed down Emma's face as she sank to her knees, her body trembling wildly. She could barely see through the stream of tears as she complied, her heart pounding so loudly it felt like it might burst from her chest. The Fox moved swiftly, his movements exact as he grabbed belts from his pocket and bound her hands and feet.

Emma's mind was racing, trying to come up with a plan, a way to escape. But every attempt to think clearly was overshadowed by the overwhelming terror she felt and the reality of her situation. The sound of a car passing by her bungalow reached her, somebody inside could help her, but there was nothing she could do. She was utterly helpless.

The Fox didn't waste time. He dragged her toward the spare bedroom, his grip unyielding. The room had become a chamber of horror. Emma could barely make out the makeshift den within.

As The Fox positioned her in the centre of the room, he took a moment to savour the control he wielded. Emma's pleas fell on deaf ears, her sobs barely audible over the oppressive silence. The Fox's eyes were cold, his face obscured by the balaclava, but his presence was overwhelming. He moved with a calculated cruelty, placing her on the bed and securing her to the headboard with rough, tight knots.

Emma's terror was evident as she felt the pressure of the restraints cutting into her skin. The fear of what was to come was almost unbearable. She could hear his footsteps retreating, leaving her alone with her dread.

Moments stretched into eternity as she lay bound on the bed, the silence broken only by her ragged breaths. She could hear the faintest sounds - the creak of floorboards, the rustling of fabric. Each noise heightened her anxiety, a cruel reminder that The Fox was still in control.

The Fox returned, his footsteps purposeful and slow. He was carrying an assortment of items - a glass of water, a flashlight, and a few other objects that he set down with deliberate care. Emma's heart pounded as she heard the distinct click of the flashlight being turned on, the beam slicing through the darkness and illuminating The Fox's mask.

His eyes met hers, cold and impassive. "You see, Emma," he said, his voice smooth and devoid of empathy, "this is just the beginning."

Emma's pleas became more frantic as she struggled against her restraints, her body shaking uncontrollably. The Fox's calm demeanour contrasted starkly with her escalating terror. He methodically prepared himself, his actions precise and deliberate, a stark contrast to the chaos unfolding in Emma's mind.

The Fox took his time, savouring the fear he had instilled. He seemed to relish in the control he held, a sadistic pleasure evident in the way he moved. Emma's sobs filled the room, a haunting accompaniment to the tense silence.

As The Fox approached, Emma's pleas became more desperate. "Please...please, just let me go..."

The Fox's response was cold and unyielding. "You're not in a position to make demands," he said. And with that, he ripped at her clothes until she was naked from the waist down. An evil smile formed under his mask. He was in control, not her.

The onslaught that followed was cruel and cold blooded. The Fox showed no mercy. His actions a chilling display of dominance. Emma's screams were muffled, her body wracked with violent shudders as she endured the violation. The Fox's presence was a dark, unrelenting force, leaving her broken and shattered.

When the ordeal was finally over, The Fox stood over her, breathing heavily. He stood up, pulled his clothes up around his waist, and with a final, cold look at Emma, he turned and casually walked out the room and the bungalow.

The Fox had left his mark once again, another life had been ruined.

Chapter 17

It was a warm, quiet evening in Edlesborough. The small village nestled within the rolling hills of Buckinghamshire had seen very little crime over the years, its peaceful streets lined with modest homes and well-kept gardens. But on this night, an unseen destroyer stalked the streets, planning his next move. The Fox - Britain's most notorious and elusive criminal - had already left a trail of panic and turmoil in his wake. And now, he had his eyes set on number forty Meadow Lane.

The house stood at the end of a quiet cul-de-sac; its occupants blissfully unaware of the threat creeping ever closer. Inside, a couple slept soundly in their bedroom upstairs, tired from the day's activities and the seasonably warm night. Downstairs, The Fox broke in via the back door thanks to his trusty screwdriver making light work of the lock. Once inside, he moved carefully, trying his best not to disturb the peacefulness of the home as he searched for anything of value.

He rifled through drawers in the living room and kitchen. His hands moved with the confidence of someone who had done this countless times before, pulling out papers and small items without making a sound. After several minutes of searching, he found some cash tucked away in an envelope inside a drawer in the living room.

He picked up the envelope, his heart racing with the thrill of the theft. But as he bent down to retrieve his shotgun, which he had placed against a side table for easy access, disaster struck. The gun slipped from its precarious position and crashed to the floor with a loud, metallic thud.

The noise shattered the stillness of the house.

Upstairs, the muffled sound of voices reached his ears. The Fox froze, every muscle in his body tensing as he listened. The couple had been woken by the noise, and it didn't take long for them to realise that something wasn't right. Panicked, they reached for the phone and called the police.

The Fox cursed under his breath. He had been too careless, too rushed. But it wasn't in his nature to panic. He grabbed the cash, hoisted the shotgun over his shoulder, and headed for the back door. Years of practice had taught him that the key to escaping was speed and precision. Within seconds, he was out of the house and into the warm night air, disappearing across back gardens before anyone could see him.

He knew the police would arrive soon, but he also knew the area well. He had scouted it for weeks, noting every pathway, every alley, and every possible hiding spot. The police must have been in the area as he could hear sirens fast approaching. He needed a place to lie low, just for a few hours, until the heat died down.

The police, led by Detective Chief Superintendent Mark Talbot, arrived at Meadow Lane within minutes of the call. Sirens blared as officers poured out of their cars and surrounded the area. The couple, Marco and Sasha Hazell, still shaken, met them at the door and explained what had happened: a loud noise downstairs, followed by the discovery that drawers had been rifled through and some cash was missing.

Officers immediately began to search the area. The Fox had left signs of forced entry on the back door, his usual calling card, so they knew it was highly likely to be him. They swept the street, knocking on doors and questioning neighbours. One by one, the occupants of Meadow Lane opened their doors and provided what little information they had. Most had heard nothing; it was too late, and the night had been its usual calm self.

When the officers knocked on the door of number twenty-two, just a few houses down from the scene of the crime, there was no answer. They shone their torches through the windows, peering inside. The house looked empty - no lights, no movement, nothing to suggest anyone was home.

A quick conversation with one of the neighbours confirmed it: the family who lived at number twenty-two was on holiday. They had been gone for nearly a week, and no one expected them back for several more days.

Satisfied, the officers moved on, never suspecting that the man they were searching for was already inside.

The Fox watched from behind a sofa as the police officers swept past the house. His heart pounded in his chest, but he remained still, hidden in the darkness. The irony wasn't lost on him - the very people hunting him were just a few feet away, completely unaware that their quarry had already taken refuge inside the house they had dismissed as empty.

He had slipped into number twenty-two not long after fleeing from number forty. The house had been an easy target; he knew the occupants would be on holiday having fixed a back garden panel for them a week earlier. It provided the perfect place to lay low for a few hours. Once inside, he had quickly set to work creating a makeshift den in the living room, using blankets and cushions he found around the house. He draped one of the blankets over himself and the television to prevent any light from being seen outside.

The Fox knew he needed to be cautious. The police would be searching the area, and if they thought he was still nearby, they would lock down the village. But he had time. They wouldn't suspect that he had chosen to hide so close to the scene of the crime.

As he settled into his makeshift hideout, he began to rifle through the homeowners' belongings. In a cabinet by the television, he found a small collection of VHS tapes. One title caught his eye: *Gregory's Girl*, a British comedy about a teenager navigating the awkwardness of adolescence and love.

Smirking to himself, The Fox loaded the tape into the VCR player and pressed play. He had never seen the film before, and despite the absurdity of the situation - him, a wanted man, hiding from the police and watching a light-hearted comedy - he couldn't help but be drawn in. For a while, he forgot about the chase, the police, and the danger. He let himself disappear into the world of the film, the soft glow of the television illuminating his face as he sat beneath his blanket fort.

Outside, the police were growing increasingly frustrated. They had combed the neighbourhood, searched the surrounding streets, and even called in a helicopter to scan the area from above. But there was no sign of The Fox. It was as if he had vanished into thin air.

Detective Chief Superintendent Mark Talbot walked up and down the street, his face set in a bleak expression. The Fox had slipped through their fingers once again, and Talbot knew the media would be all over the story by morning. His superiors would want answers, and the public would be demanding to know how a single man could continue to evade capture so effectively.

"Anything?" Talbot asked one of the officers as he walked by. "Nothing, sir," the officer replied, shaking his head. "We've checked the area, knocked on all the doors. No one's seen or heard anything out of the ordinary."

Talbot cursed under his breath. "What about number twenty-two? I heard the families on holiday."

"We checked sir. Looks empty. No signs of anyone inside."

"Double-check," Talbot ordered. "I don't want any mistakes. If he's holed up in there, we need to know."

The officers did as they were told, shining their torches through the windows once again. But the house remained dark and silent, just as it had before. Talbot, now pacing the street, glanced up at the helicopter circling overhead. They were running out of options. The Fox was out there, somewhere, but the more time passed, the colder the trail would grow.

Inside number twenty-two, The Fox waited. He had turned off the television and now sat in the dark, listening to the faint buzzing of the helicopter above. It wouldn't be long before they gave up the search, he knew. They couldn't stay out there all night, and eventually, they would move on.

He glanced at his watch. It was nearly midnight. The village would soon fall back into its usual quiet tempo, and when it did, he would make his escape. He had no intention of staying in Edlesborough any longer than necessary. The cash he had taken from number forty was stuffed into his pocket, and his shotgun was slung over his shoulder. All he needed was an opportunity.

Another hour passed, before the helicopter eventually moved on, and the number of police officers in the area began to dwindle. The Fox, ever patient, waited until he was sure the coast was clear. When he finally moved, it was with the same precision and caution that had kept him one step ahead of the law for so long.

He slipped out the back door of number twenty-two, moving like a stray cat through the garden and over the back fence. The village was quiet now, with only the occasional distant sound of a car passing on the main road. He knew the area well, and within minutes, he had disappeared into the surrounding countryside, vanishing once again.

The next morning, the residents of Edlesborough awoke to the news that The Fox had struck again. Meadow Lane had been cordoned off, and police officers were once again combing the area for any clues that might lead them to the elusive criminal. But there was nothing. No prints, no witnesses, no sign of where he had gone.

Detective Chief Superintendent Mark Talbot stood outside number forty, his frustration evident in the look on his face. He had underestimated The Fox, and now the village was on edge, knowing that the man responsible for a string of burglaries and violent attacks had been right under their noses.

As Talbot made his way back to his car, he couldn't help but glance toward number twenty-two. It was still quiet, still empty, but something about it gnawed at him. He shook his head, trying to dismiss the thought. They had checked it twice, after all.

But little did Talbot know, The Fox had been there all along, hiding in plain sight.

Chapter 18

"Nine-nine-nine, what's your emergency."

"Yes, hello, police. I think I just saw The Fox," the man said, his voice urgent and breathless.

"Sir, can you provide your exact location and explain why you believe it was The Fox?" the operator asked, her tone steady and precise.

"He was wearing a balaclava, dressed head-to-toe in black, and moving quickly across the fields toward the woods in Little Gaddesden," the man replied, panic edging his words.

"Understood, sir. A police unit is being dispatched immediately." The woods in Little Gaddesden were a labyrinth of shadows and whispers. As twilight surrendered to the darkness of the late summer evening, Detective Chief Superintendent Mark Talbot led his team through the dense underbrush, the eerie quiet punctuated only by the occasional snap of a twig underfoot. The sky was filled with the earthy scent of damp soil and decaying leaves, a lingering reminder of recent rain.

The team were responding to yet another sighting. This time, they had picked up a trail.

"Stay sharp," Talbot commanded, his voice cutting through the oppressive silence of the woods. "The Fox might still be here, and he will know these woods better than we do. He's turned this into his own private hunting ground."

Detective Inspector Elaine Carter, her face illuminated by the beam of her flashlight, checked her watch. "It's nearly eleven p.m.," she said, sweat trickling down the sides of her face. "He's had time to set up traps or hideouts. This could turn into a wild goose chase if we're not careful."

Detective Sergeant Jake Miller, his face streaked with grime and sweat, glanced up from a map laid out on a makeshift table. "According to this, there's an old hunting cabin around here. It's not far from where we picked up his trail. It's worth checking out."

Talbot's eyes narrowed as he considered the suggestion. "Agreed. If he's trying to stay hidden, that cabin could be his base of operations. Let's move."

The team pressed deeper into the woods, their boots squelching in the muddy undergrowth. The canopy overhead was a dense tapestry of leaves, allowing only slivers of moonlight to seep through, casting an eerie glow on the floor. Every rustle of leaves, every snap of a twig seemed magnified in the stillness, heightening the sense of unease that clung to the night.

"Keep your eyes peeled," Talbot instructed. "And be mindful of the terrain. It's rough, and The Fox is counting on that."

As they traversed through the tangled thicket, Carter's flashlight beam fell upon an old, gnarled tree, its bark twisted and cracked. "Guv, look at this," she said, her voice low. "Fresh footprints. They're not ours."

Talbot crouched beside the muddy prints, his heart quickening. The footprints were distinct - shoes with a tread pattern that suggested someone wearing outdoor boots. "He's close," Talbot said, his voice excited. "Let's keep moving."

The warmth in the air intensified as they approached the suspected location of the cabin. Miller, his breath increasing with every step, scanned the area. "Nothing visible yet," he reported, peering into the distance. "But the cabin isn't far. If he's still inside, he's not trying to stay low."

Talbot signalled the team to spread out, their movements calculated and deliberate. The sense of anticipation was unmistakable, each officer focused and prepared for what might lie ahead. "Let's surround the cabin. Remember, he'll be prepared for us. Watch your step and be ready for anything."

The cabin emerged from the darkness like a forgotten relic of the past, its weathered wooden walls and broken windows blending seamlessly with the surrounding forest. Carter and Miller approached the door, their weapons drawn, each step cautious and measured. Talbot covered their backs, his eyes scanning the perimeter for any sign of movement.

Carter nudged the door open, the hinges clanking loudly in the stillness. The room beyond was dim, illuminated only by the flickering glow of a small fire in the hearth. The shadows danced across the walls, casting an eerie light that made the room feel more like a stage set for a sinister play.

A figure stood facing the fire, momentarily illuminated by the flames. The man's silhouette was unmistakable, a stark contrast to the darkness that enveloped the room.

"Freeze!" Talbot's command sliced through the silence.

The man, clad in dark clothing and a hooded coat, turned slowly, his face obscured by his balaclava. "Don't shoot," he said, his voice trembling with nervousness.

Talbot's heart pounded in his chest. This was not the moment they had hoped for. "Come out where we can see you," he ordered, his voice taut with urgency. "It's over for you Mr Fox."

The man stepped forward into the light, his ungloved hands raised in a gesture of surrender. Talbot's heart sank as he took in the man's features. He was mixed race, a stark contrast to The Fox's known description of having pale white skin. Disappointment and frustration surged through Talbot.

"Guns down everybody, it's not him," sighed a disappointed Talbot.
"What are you doing out here by yourself?" Talbot barked, trying to keep his voice steady despite the letdown.

The man slid off his balaclava, his gaze wary. "I'm in the military, sir. I'm on leave and like camping out at night. I didn't think I was doing anything wrong, sir."

Talbot's expression softened slightly, but the nervousness remained. "Well, be careful. There's a serial criminal in the area. He doesn't care who he attacks."

The man nodded, his eyes wide with concern. "I'll head back to town. I didn't mean to cause any trouble."

As the man gathered his belongings and left the cabin, Talbot and his team exchanged irritated glances.

"Let's keep searching, just in case," barked Talbot. "Don't let this deter us."

The search continued late into the early hours of the next morning, each moment stretching longer as they navigated the wood's maze. The sense of urgency was intense, with every crackling branch and rustling leaf seeming to hold secrets, and every dark corner potentially concealing The Fox.

But The Fox was nowhere nearby. It was another false alarm, unbeknown to Talbot and his team. The hours ticked by the team moved with grim determination; their every step fraught with strain.

"Spread out and search the perimeter," Talbot instructed, his voice firm. "If The Fox is still in the area, he'll be trying to cover his tracks."

The team fanned out, their flashlights cutting through the darkness as they combed the woods for any sign of The Fox. Talbot's mind raced with possibilities, each scenario more disheartening than the last. The sense of failure gnawed at him, a relentless threat that refused to be ignored.

As Talbot moved through the woods, he couldn't shake the feeling that they were being toyed with. The Fox had always been elusive, his actions calculated and precise. The false lead, the discarded footprints - it was all part of a twisted game.

"This isn't just about evading capture," Talbot muttered to himself. "He's enjoying this. He's playing us."

Carter, looking determined, moved alongside Talbot. "Guv, we need to rethink our strategy. He's outsmarted us again."

Talbot nodded, his mind racing as he considered their options. "We need to get ahead of him. If he's moving from place to place, we need to predict his next move. He's leaving a trail, even if it's not immediately visible."

At dawn, the first light of morning began to filter through the trees, casting a pale glow over the ground. Talbot and his team gathered at the base of a large oak tree, their faces drawn and tired. The search had yielded no results, and the weight of their failure hung heavy.

"We've got to regroup," Talbot said, his voice hoarse from hours of shouting over the radio. "We need to reassess our strategy and figure out our next move."

Carter nodded, her face etched with worry. "We need to re-analyse his patterns, find out where he's likely to strike next."

Talbot gathered his team, "Go home, get some rest, and come back re-energised. Thanks for your hard work tonight, I know it's not easy chasing dead ends."

As the team collected their gear and prepared to leave the woods, Talbot's thoughts were consumed by the realisation that The Fox was always one step ahead. The hunt was far from over, and he was no closer to capturing him.

Chapter 19

The scorching weather continued to rage over the 'Triangle of Terror' like a fever, oppressive and inescapable. Heat waves shimmered off the asphalt, baking the streets, but the real fire burning in the hearts of the people was a different kind - fear, raw and unrelenting. The Fox had seen to that. His reign of terror had held a long stranglehold over the area, turning the ordinary lives of residents into a waking nightmare.

Detective Chief Superintendent Mark Talbot felt the weight of it everywhere he went. It was in the faces of the people on the street, their eyes darting suspiciously from one person to the next. It was in the hushed tones of conversations overheard at the corner shops, in the way children were pulled closer by anxious parents, their steps quickening as they passed darkened alleys.

Talbot stood outside a small, nondescript hardware store in Leighton Buzzard, watching as an elderly woman exited with a new set of locks clutched tightly to her chest. She glanced around nervously, her hands trembling, before hurrying away. Inside the shop, a line of customers waited, every single one of them there to buy some form of protection - locks, bolts, chains. Anything to keep The Fox at bay.

"Extra deadbolts, door chains, window bars," muttered Talbot under his breath, shaking his head. "People turning their homes into prisons."

Beside him, Detective Sergeant Sarah Kendrick took a long drag from her cigarette, blowing the smoke out into the hot, sticky air. "Can you blame them? They're terrified, Guv. And it's not just locks they're buying." She nodded toward a gun shop further down the street, where a small crowd had gathered. The owner, a heavyset man with a grim face, was talking to a customer, gesturing to a rack of shotguns behind him.

"Gun sales are up three hundred percent," Kendrick continued. "People who've never even held a gun before are stocking up like it's the apocalypse. And those who can't get their hands on a firearm? They're keeping kitchen knives under their pillows. Some are even making their own weapons."

Talbot rubbed his eyes, feeling the fatigue seeping into his bones. "It's a tinderbox," he muttered. "One spark and this whole place could go up in flames."

They'd already had several close calls - frightened residents firing shots at anything that moved, mistaking stray cats for intruders. One man had nearly put a bullet through his own son, coming home late after a night out. And then there were the vigilantes - groups of people, some armed, patrolling the streets after dark, ready to take the law into their own hands.

"They're scared, Guv," Kendrick said quietly. "And scared people do stupid things."

Talbot nodded, "That's what I'm afraid of."

They had tried to calm the rising panic, holding press conferences, distributing flyers, warning people to stay vigilant but not to take matters into their own hands. But the fear was too deep-rooted now, and every new victim The Fox left behind only fed the flames.

The sun was setting as the officers arrived at the local community centre, where a meeting had been called for residents. The hall was packed, a sea of anxious faces. Talbot could feel it, a live wire humming just beneath the surface. As he made his way to the front, he could hear snippets of conversation, voices raised in anger and fear.
"We can't just sit around waiting for the police to do something!"

"How do we even know if we can trust them?"

"They keep telling us to lock our doors, but what good is that when he breaks in easily?"

Talbot took a deep breath, stepping up to the makeshift podium. The chatter died down, all eyes turning toward him. He could see the distrust in their faces, the frustration. They wanted answers, and they wanted them now.

"Ladies and gentlemen," he began, his voice steady but firm, "I understand your fear. I understand your anger. We're doing everything we can to catch this man, but we need your help. Stay vigilant, yes, but don't take the law into your own hands. We're dealing with a dangerous individual here."

A man in the crowd stood up, his face flushed with fury. "And what happens when he comes for one of us, eh? Are we supposed to just sit around and wait for you lot to show up after he's already done his work?"

Murmurs of agreement rippled through the crowd. Talbot could feel the heat rising, along with his blood pressure.

"I understand your frustration, sir," Talbot said, trying to keep his voice calm. "But going out there with guns and knives, forming vigilante groups - that's not the answer. You could get yourselves hurt, or worse."

"Or we could stop him!" the man shot back. "I've got two kids at home. I'm not going to sit around and let some psycho come for them. If the police won't protect us, we'll protect ourselves."

Talbot's eyes swept over the crowd. There were others nodding, muttering in agreement. He knew he was losing them, the fear too deep to reason with. "We're doing everything we can."

"Not enough!" someone else shouted. "We're the ones living in fear every damn day!"

Kendrick stepped up beside him, her voice sharper, more commanding. "We understand that, believe me. But the best thing you can do right now is follow our advice. Lock your doors, yes, but also report anything suspicious. Don't engage. Let us handle it."

A woman's voice cut through the clamour, trembling with emotion. "Handle it? Like you handled it with Emma Harcourt? She was found bound, gagged, beaten and raped in her own bloody home!"

That one stung. Talbot felt the sting of it deep in his chest. Emma Harcourt was another victim of The Fox. And they had nothing - no solid leads, no standout suspects, just an area gripped by fear and a violent criminal who seemed to vanish into thin air after every attack.

"We're close," Talbot insisted, but the words felt hollow, even to him. "We've got leads, we're following up every line of enquiry. It just takes time."

"You're not close enough," the man spat. "And until you are, we're going to do what we have to do."

Talbot knew when he was beaten. The resentment - it was too much. He looked at Kendrick, who gave him a slight nod, her face grim. They were fighting a war on two fronts now - against The Fox, and against the fear he'd unleashed.

"Just be careful," Talbot said finally, his voice tired, almost pleading. "We don't need more blood on the streets."

Back at the station, the atmosphere was no less tense. Officers moved with a hurried purpose, phones ringing off the hook, radios crackling with constant updates. The fear wasn't just out there - it had seeped into the station itself.

Talbot slumped into his chair, rubbing his face with his hands. He hadn't properly slept in days, his mind a tangle of dead ends and false leads. Every time they thought they were close, The Fox slipped away, leaving another victim in his wake.
Kendrick dropped a file onto his desk, snapping him out of his thoughts. "You need to see this."

He opened the file, his eyes narrowing as he scanned the contents. "What am I looking at?"

"A report from one of the vigilante groups," Kendrick explained. "They've been using codewords to identify each other - so they know if it's one of their own coming to the door or someone else."

"Codewords?" Talbot raised an eyebrow. "Like some sort of secret society?"

"Exactly," she replied. "They're getting organised, Guv. They're serious. And if they get their hands on him first…"

Talbot leaned back, the weight of it all pressing down on him like an oversized stone. "We're losing control, Sarah. We're supposed to be protecting these people, and now they're taking matters into their own hands."

"And can you blame them?" Kendrick shot back. "The Fox is still out there, and every day we don't catch him is another day people are living in fear."

Talbot looked at her, his eyes tired but resolute. "We have to find him, Sarah. Before they do. Because if they catch him first, this whole area is going to explode."

The night was hot and stifling, the kind that pressed down on you, making it hard to breathe. Talbot sat in his car, parked on a quiet secluded street, the engine off. He was waiting, watching, his eyes scanning the darkened houses. He had followed one of the main suspects, Anos Kempster, from his house in Leighton Buzzard to the Stewkley area.

He wasn't alone. Kendrick sat beside him, her eyes fixed on the same row of houses. "You think he'll strike here?" she asked, her voice barely a whisper.

Talbot nodded. "Metal Mickey alerted us to Anos. He's a serial burglar and spent five years inside for aggravated assault. He matches the description of The Fox too."

"Why's he in this area late at night?" Kendrick asked.

They waited in silence, the minutes stretching into hours, the tension thickening like a rope tightening around their throats. And then they saw it - a flicker of movement. A figure, moving low and fast, darting between houses.

"There," Kendrick hissed, pointing.

Talbot's heart pounded in his chest as he reached for his radio. "All units, we've got movement on Finchley Avenue, suspect may be on-site. Move in quietly, do not engage until we have confirmation."

Talbot and Kendrick slipped out of their car, moving swiftly and quietly. The figure was moving toward a house at the end of the street, an elderly lady lived there alone, she was the perfect target.

Talbot's eyes caught the glint of metal in the figure's hand. His pulse thundered in his ears, each breath shallow and quick. "Steady," he hissed to Kendrick. "We need to catch him in the act."

A shout shattered the tense silence - a man stormed out of his front door, a baseball bat raised high. "Oi! You there!"

The figure spun around, and in that instant, Talbot's gut tightened. Everything was about to go sideways. "Stop!" Talbot roared, surging forward.

The resident charged, bat brandished, as the figure bolted around the side of the house. Talbot and Kendrick were in hot pursuit, feet pounding against the ground.

"Stop, police!" Talbot commanded, but the resident was deaf to his warning, disappearing after the figure. Talbot reached the corner, breath ragged. "Round the back, now!" he shouted, adrenaline spiking.

They rounded the house to find the resident pressing the figure against the wall, the bat wedged against their throat.

"Drop it!" Kendrick yelled, her voice slicing through the chaos.

The bat clattered to the ground. Kendrick lunged forward, shoved past the resident, and locked her grip on the figure. She twisted his arm behind his back and slapped on the cuffs.

"Spread your legs. Don't move," Kendrick ordered.

"Careful, Sarah, he's got a knife," Talbot warned, whilst trying to catch his breath.

Kendrick's fingers moved delicately, patting down the suspect before dipping into his hoodie pockets. Out came a set of keys and a cheese grater.

"What the?" Kendrick's brow furrowed. "Where's the knife?"

The suspect, barely more than a boy, stammered, "What knife?"

Kendrick's eyes widened as she pulled back the hood, revealing a teenage face, no older than sixteen.

"My nan lives here. She called my mum and said she needed a cheese grater. I was just bringing it over," he said, voice trembling.

"Christ," Kendrick breathed. "Guv, it's not him."

Talbot's gaze fell, his stomach twisting into knots. Just a kid. Not The Fox. The taste of defeat was bitter on his tongue. Excitement morphed into fury as he realised the truth: they'd failed. Again.

Meanwhile Anos Kempster, a main suspect, was on the front doorstep three houses down, meeting up with a female companion he had become familiar with. Talbot and Kendrick past them on their way back to their car.

Talbot clocked Anos acting amicably. "Oh great, another dead-end," he blurted out. "This is getting worse."

Chapter 20

The next morning, Detective Chief Sergeant Mark Talbot sat at his kitchen table, staring into the black void of his coffee. It was early, too early, and the world outside was shrouded in the dim, grey light of a dreary morning. He'd been awake since four a.m., tossing and turning, his mind running through the endless details of a case that had come to dominate his life. The Fox - the elusive, cunning serial burglar and rapist had been terrorising the local towns and villages for weeks, slipping through the fingers of law enforcement like water. Every step forward was followed by two steps back, and the pressure to catch him weighed on Talbot like a lead cloak.

It didn't help that his superiors at headquarters were breathing down his neck. The media had latched onto The Fox case with fervour, and Talbot, the man in charge, was their favourite scapegoat. Every failure was his failure, every delay his incompetence, at least in the eyes of the public and his bosses. The stress was unrelenting, and even the little things, the simple routines of life, seemed to slip out of his control.

He glanced at the clock. Six thirty a.m. He poured himself a fresh coffee. The milk should be on the doorstep by now.

Talbot got up slowly, his body stiff from sleeplessness, stress and chasing teenagers down the road. He shuffled to the front door and opened it, expecting to see the usual glass bottle of fresh milk waiting for him. Instead, he found nothing but an empty milk bottle lying on its side, rolling gently in the morning breeze. Frowning, he bent down to pick it up, and it was then that he saw it - a small slip of paper tucked inside the bottle.

Pulling out the note, Talbot squinted at the hastily scrawled message:
"YOU'VE BEEN MILKED BY THE MILK BANDITS!"

For a moment, he simply stared at the note, unable to process it. He read it again, slower this time, but the words didn't change. "Milked" by the Milk Bandits? Was this some kind of sick joke? Or was it The Fox leaving him a message? His hand tightened around the bottle, and a surge of anger swelled in his chest.

Talbot closed the door behind him with more force than he intended, the slam reverberating through the house. As he walked back into the kitchen, his mind raced. He could feel the frustration building in him, the way it had been building for weeks. This wasn't just about the milk. This was about everything - his job, the pressure, the sleepless nights, the feeling that he was losing control.

He sat back down, the note crumpled in his fist. The absurdity of it only made him angrier. Detective Chief Sergeant Mark Talbot, head of a major police investigation, reduced to dealing with a milk thief.

His coffee had gone cold. He couldn't drink it anyway.

By lunchtime, Talbot had regained some measure of composure, though the incident still simmered beneath the surface of his thoughts. He'd decided not to mention it to his colleagues at the station. The last thing he needed was for his team to see him rattled by something as trivial as stolen milk. Besides, he had bigger problems to worry about - like finding The Fox before the man struck again.

But word travelled fast in a small town.

By two p.m., Claire Milford, the local journalist who worked for the Leighton Buzzard Observer, had somehow heard about the incident. Claire was relentless when she sensed a story, and Talbot knew that if she was on the case, it would be plastered all over the front page of the local paper by morning.

Sure enough, just as Talbot was wrapping up a meeting with his team, his phone rang. It was Claire.
"DCS Talbot, I've heard some rather...curious news," she began, her voice laced with barely contained amusement. "Something about a milk theft at your house this morning?"

Talbot closed his eyes, a wave of irritation passing through him. He should have known the town's grapevine would get hold of this. He hadn't planned on giving it any attention, but with Claire sniffing around, he knew he couldn't avoid it.

"Claire," he said, his voice clipped. "This isn't a story. It's a childish prank. There are far more important things going on right now."

"Oh, I'm sure there are," she replied, "but the public loves a good laugh, and right now, the town could use something to take their minds off The Fox. Don't you agree?"

Talbot could hear the smile in her voice. She wasn't going to let this go. He rubbed his temple, feeling a headache coming on. Fine. He'd give her what she wanted - just enough to get her off his back.

"Alright," he sighed. "Yes, someone stole my milk this morning. Left a stupid note about being 'milked by the Milk Bandits.' But that's it, Claire. There's no story here."

"Well, it sounds like the local kids are getting creative," Claire said lightly. "Mind if I pop by for a quick interview? I promise I won't take up much of your time."

Talbot could hardly refuse without it looking like he had something to hide, so he reluctantly agreed. Thirty minutes later, Claire Milford was sitting in his office, her notepad ready and a sly smile playing on her lips.

"So, DCS Talbot," she began, "how did it feel to wake up this morning and find yourself the victim of the notorious 'Milk Bandits?'"

Talbot stared at her, unamused. "I don't find this funny, Claire. Someone trespassed on my property, stole from me, and left behind a note mocking me. It's not exactly the highlight of my day."
Claire raised an eyebrow. "You don't think it was just a harmless prank?"

"A prank, sure," Talbot said, his frustration barely contained. "But it's also a reminder of how little respect some people have for the law. If they think stealing and taunting is funny, they're part of the problem."

He leaned forward, fixing her with a sharp look. "Let me be clear, Claire. This kind of behaviour might seem small to you, but it represents a larger issue. If people can't respect the basics - other people's property, their privacy - then it's no wonder we have criminals like The Fox out there."

Claire scribbled in her notepad, nodding along but clearly relishing the drama of it all. "So, you're taking this seriously?"

"I'm a police officer, Claire. I take all crimes seriously," Talbot replied, his tone making it clear that the interview was over.

Claire stood, gathering her things, her smile never faltering. "Thank you for your time, DCS Talbot. I'll let you get back to the real work of catching The Fox. But you know, I think the town will get a kick out of this story."

Talbot saw her out, his mood soured even further. This wasn't what he needed - a public spectacle over a stolen bottle of milk. He had a real case to focus on. The Fox was still out there, and Talbot was no closer to finding him than he had been weeks ago.

The next few days passed in a blur of meetings, paperwork, and dead-end leads. Talbot tried to put the Milk Bandits out of his mind, but every time he stopped by the corner shop to buy something, he saw bottles of milk and was reminded of the prank. Worse, the local newspaper had run Claire Milford's story on the front page, complete with a photo of an empty milk bottle. The headline read:
'MILKED BY THE MILK BANDITS: EVEN THE POLICE AREN'T SAFE!'

It was meant to be light-hearted, but to Talbot, it felt like another jab at his authority. He was supposed to be the one protecting the town, and now he was the punchline to a joke.

A week after the incident, despite Talbot not pursuing it, the case of the Milk Bandits took an unexpected turn.

Liam Knowles, a local teenager who worked part-time at the bakery in Tesco, had been overheard bragging to a friend about the prank. He was laughing about how he and his mates Adrian Petrie, Martin Lynes, and Max Macleod - had been out drinking that night and decided it would be hilarious to take some milk on their way home and leave the note. What they didn't know at the time was that they had chosen the home of the town's top police officer.

A shopper overheard the conversation and, recognising Talbot's name, immediately reported the boys to the police.

Within hours, Liam Knowles was sitting in Dunstable police station, pale-faced and sweating as he confessed to the crime. The prank had seemed funny at the time, but now that the police were involved, it didn't seem so funny anymore. He gave up the names of the others quickly, and soon Adrian, Martin, and Max were brought in for questioning as well.

Talbot was informed of the arrests, and though he was still angry about the situation, he took little satisfaction in it. The boys were young, foolish, and had been drinking. It wasn't a calculated crime, just a stupid prank that had spiralled out of control.

In the end, all four boys were issued cautions. They had learned their lesson, and Talbot didn't see the need to drag them through the court system for something so minor. Still, he made it clear that any further incidents would result in more severe consequences.

With the Milk Bandits dealt with, Talbot turned his attention back to the real issue at hand: The Fox. The elusive criminal had struck again, this time burgling a house in Wolverton.

Talbot knew that catching the Fox would require all his focus and energy. The media circus surrounding the Milk Bandits had been an unwelcome distraction, but now it was over. He could put that nonsense behind him and get back to the work that really mattered.

As he sat at his desk that evening, reviewing the latest reports on The Fox case, Talbot felt a renewed sense of purpose. The prank had rattled him, but it had also reminded him why he did this job. There were real criminals out there - dangerous ones - and it was his job to stop them.

The milk could wait. The Fox, on the other hand, would not slip through his fingers. Not again.

Talbot leaned back in his chair, the fatigue of the past few weeks catching up to him. The road ahead was long and uncertain, but he was ready for it. He had to be. Everybody was depending on him.

Chapter 21

The warm summer rain came down in a relentless sheet, blurring the edges of the town of Dunstable under a shroud of bleak grey. The streets were slick with it, the gutters overflowing, and the distant wail of a siren cut through the damp air like a hot knife through butter. Detective Chief Superintendent Mark Talbot stood by the large windows of his office, staring out at the town he'd sworn to protect. His eyes were heavy, dark circles etched beneath them, testament to the endless hours he'd spent chasing dead ends.

The Fox continued to prowl the underbelly of the area, striking without warning, leaving a trail of destruction in his wake. A cold-blooded criminal, calculating and precise, he took great delight in playing games with the police. The entire force was on edge, frayed nerves barely holding together under the mounting pressure.

"Three hundred calls an hour, sir," muttered Detective Sergeant Sarah Kendrick, leaning against the doorway of his office, her face as pale as the fluorescent light overhead. Her voice trembled just slightly, betraying the fear that was seeping into the bones of every officer on the case. "Every damn hour. It's like the world's gone mad."

Talbot turned to face her, his face a mask of exhaustion and resolve. "And every single one of them needs to be followed up, Sarah," he said, his voice a low, gravelly rumble. "Every lead, no matter how small or absurd. We can't afford to miss anything. And it all gets fed into Metal Mickey."

The office was bursting with the smell of stale coffee and the sour tang of sweat. Files and paperwork were piled high on every surface, overflowing from their folders, each one a different thread in the tangled web they were trying to unravel. Talbot rubbed his temples, feeling the pressure coiled tight in his neck and shoulders.

"We're hunting a master of deception," Kendrick muttered, shaking her head. "The bastard's always two steps ahead of us."

"A fox is clever, but he's still an animal," Talbot replied, his eyes narrowing. "Animals make mistakes. We just need to wait for him to slip up."

He moved back to his desk, a scarred thick oak thing that had seen better days and sat down heavily.

"Observation and protection of the public," he murmured, almost to himself, repeating the mantra that had become his lifeline. "Alongside the detective work. That's our job. We can't afford to lose focus."

Kendrick nodded, her face grim. She had been with him from the start, her sharp mind and unyielding determination making her one of his best. But even she was beginning to show signs of wear.

"Speaking of observation," she said, "we've got the surveillance teams doubling up on the red zones. More eyes, more ears. If he so much as breathes out of line, we'll know."

"Good," Talbot replied, though his voice lacked the confidence he wished he could muster. "And what about the profiler's report?"

Kendrick handed him a thick dossier. "Fresh off the press. According to Dr Hardwick, he's not just in it for the assaults. He's in it for the thrill of outsmarting us. He wants us to know he's observing, ready and waiting. It's a game to him."

"A game," Talbot repeated softly, flipping through the pages. His eyes skimmed over words like 'narcissistic tendencies' and 'compulsive behaviour', but his mind was elsewhere. "Every game has an end. And when we find him..."

The phone on his desk rang. Talbot snatched it up, his voice terse. "Talbot."

"Chief, it's Harris from Dispatch," came the hurried voice on the other end. "We've got another one. Same MO - north side of the triangle, house near an old railway bridge. Patrol's on-site, but it's not looking good."

Talbot's eyes met Kendrick's, and she could see the storm brewing behind them. "Get the car ready," he said, slamming the phone down. "Let's move."

The drive to the crime scene in Bushey was tense and silent, the only sound the rhythmic thud of the windshield wipers fighting against the relentless downpour. Talbot stared straight ahead, his mind racing. Next to him, Kendrick sat rigid, her fingers tapping a nervous rhythm against her thigh.

When they arrived, the area was already crawling with officers, the blue and red lights of the patrol cars casting a surreal glow over the scene. The old railway bridge loomed overhead, a rusting giant against the darkened sky. Yellow police tape flapped in the wind, cordoning off the area.

"Jesus," Kendrick muttered as they approached. Sprawled on an ambulance stretcher, a woman, her face pale, bruised, battered and pouring with blood.

"Same as the others," muttered Detective Sergeant Jake Miller, one of the first responders, his face drawn and white. "No witnesses, no prints, nothing."

Talbot crouched beside the woman, his eyes scanning every inch, every detail. He could feel the weight of the scene pressing down on him, the cold, creeping realisation that they were once again too late. "He's not perfect," he said quietly. "He's just good at hiding."

For a moment, there was silence, broken only by the distant rumble of thunder. Kendrick stood beside him, her arms crossed tightly over her chest. "How the hell does he keep doing this? Right under our noses."

"He's good at what he does," Talbot replied, his voice hardening. "And he wants us to know he's still out there. That we can't catch him."

Miller stepped forward, his voice tinged with frustration. "We're running ourselves ragged, Chief. People are terrified. If we don't get a break soon."

"We will," Talbot cut in sharply, his eyes never leaving the woman. "We don't stop until we do."

The forensic team moved in, their white suits ghostly in the rain. Talbot, his back aching from being overworked, turned to Kendrick. "Get back to the station. I want every detail of this cross-checked with the other scenes. There must be something, we're just not seeing it yet. And get the team to follow up on our top suspects. Where were they when it happened and where are they now. Check their alibis twice if you must."

Kendrick nodded, "Ok Guv. And what about you?"

"I'm staying," Talbot said. "I want to take another look around."

As she walked away, Talbot's gaze lingered on the gloominess beneath the bridge, the dark places where the light didn't reach. He could feel The Fox was relishing in yet another easy escape.

Hours passed, and the rain began to let up, tapering off into a light drizzle. Talbot stood beneath the bridge, his clothes soaked through, but he didn't care. His eyes were fixed on the distance, scanning the deserted streets and fields for any sign of movement.

He pulled out a cigarette, lighting it with shaking hands. The first drag filled his lungs with a rough, bitter warmth, and he closed his eyes for a moment, letting the smoke curl out into the night. "Where are you, you bastard?" he muttered under his breath.

Talbot's eyelids drooped, the weight of exhaustion pulling them down like lead. The rain hissed around him, relentless, drumming a rhythm that seeped into his bones. He swayed, catching himself with a jolt as a sudden, soft rustle split through the downpour. His eyes snapped open, darting to the edge of the light cast by his torch. There, near the field, a figure shifted, half-concealed in shadow.

"Who's there?" Talbot's voice cracked, then steadied, echoing with forced authority.

The figure stood motionless. Talbot's vision blurred, and he blinked rapidly, trying to refocus. The edges of the world shimmered, morphed. His pulse thundered as the silhouette twisted, reshaping until the head of a masked man sat unnaturally atop a fox's sleek body, eyes glittering with cunning.

"Back again, are you?" Talbot's voice trembled, addressing the impossible creature as though it was an old adversary. The masked fox tilted its head, a sneer playing at its lips. Its mouth moved as though speaking, but only silence came forth. Talbot's breath quickened, panic licking at his mind.

"Why now?" he demanded, taking an unsteady step forward, gun wavering. "I told you... I told you to stay away."

The fox-thing blinked slowly, the rest of its body perfectly still, statuesque. A sense of dread seeped into Talbot's chest. He rubbed his eyes, but the image remained, mockingly solid.

A sudden, guttural laugh - his own - escaped his lips, jarring him. The absurdity struck him like ice water. Talbot staggered back, eyes wide, and in that instant, the vision dissolved into the night.

He blinked, breath ragged, and found himself staring at a patch of empty grass, rain soaking into his collar. His torchlight caught the gentle leap of a baby deer bounding away into the distance.

He sagged, lowering his gun with a shuddering sigh. "Get a grip, Talbot, you're losing the plot," he muttered, shaking his head. His fingers flexed around the cold metal of the gun before he holstered it and turned away. His mind was playing tricks on him. He shook his head and called it a night.

Chapter 22

Phoenix Close in Leighton Buzzard was as quiet as ever, bathed in the soft glow of a fading summer sunset. The houses, neatly lined with their manicured lawns and potted plants, stood in peaceful silence. The only sounds breaking the calm were the distant drone of passing cars and the occasional bark of a dog. Yet, for all its suburban serenity, there was something unsettling in the air that evening. Something that would make Phoenix Close the centre of conversation for weeks to come.

At number eleven, Pat McBride sat in her upstairs bedroom, sipping on her usual cup of chamomile tea. The day had been uneventful, much like most days since she'd retired from her post at the local school. She had developed a routine of watching the world from her bedroom window in the evenings - observing the faint movements of her neighbours' lives as they went about their nightly rituals. It wasn't voyeurism, not in her mind at least; it was just a way to stay connected in a world that was rapidly becoming more isolated since her retirement.

Her view stretched across the street and into the back gardens of the homes that lined Phoenix Close. From her window, she could see almost everything, though not with any invasive detail - just enough to feel a sense of community. Tonight, her eyes wandered absentmindedly across the usual scene of closed curtains, dim porch lights, and the occasional glow from a television set.

But something was different tonight. A shadow, swift and deliberate, darted into her view.

Pat blinked and leaned closer to the window, pressing her forehead against the cool glass. At first, she thought it might be a stray cat or perhaps a fox, common visitors to the suburban gardens. But this shadow was too large, too quick, and much too deliberate. Her heart skipped a beat.

The figure moved stealthily along the pathway that ran along the back gardens of numerous homes. For a moment, it seemed to vanish behind a lamp post that stood on the edge of her neighbour's property at number thirteen. Diane Fletcher, a divorcee in her late twenties, lived with her two young sons, aged three and five. She was known for her immaculate gardens - filled with roses, hydrangeas, and a thriving strawberry patch.

Suddenly, the figure reappeared, clearer this time. It wasn't an animal at all. It was a man.

He was tall and lean, dressed in dark clothing that blended seamlessly into the dark of the evening. He appeared to be wearing a mask which obscured his face. He crouched low, as if trying to avoid being seen, and made his way along the fence. Then, with a swift and practiced movement, he vaulted over Diane's back fence, disappearing into her garden.

Pat's heart raced, her fingers trembling as she set her mug down on the bedside table. She hadn't seen anything like this before. Phoenix Close, wasn't the sort of place where crime happened. The most excitement they'd had in recent months was a lost dog that had wandered into a neighbour's shed. But this…this was different.

For a split second, Pat hesitated. Maybe she should alert Diane first. But what if he attacked her too. Without another thought, she reached for her phone and called the police.

"Emergency services, what's your emergency please?"

Pat's voice was shaky as she spoke. "I - I think there's a man in my neighbour's garden. He just jumped the fence. It's at number thirteen, Phoenix Close in Leighton Buzzard."

The operator's voice was calm, reassuring. "Stay on the line, ma'am, while I despatch a police unit. Can you describe the man for me?"

Pat glanced out of the window again, but the man was no longer in sight. Her eyes scanned the garden, but there was no sign of movement. "He was wearing dark clothes, a mask... I couldn't see his face. He jumped over the fence into my neighbour's garden, Diane is her name. I - I don't know where he is now."

The operator asked her to stay at home until the police arrived. Pat's eyes remained glued to the window, her mind racing. Who was this man? Was it The Fox? Was Mrs Fletcher home? She rarely went out in the evenings, but Pat hadn't seen her today. Had something already happened?

The minutes stretched on, each one feeling longer than the last. Pat could hear her own heartbeat in her ears, the tension mounting with every passing second. For her own safety, she decided to lock herself in her bathroom.

Then, as the sound of police sirens could be heard in the distance, the man reappeared in Mrs Fletcher's back garden. He moved quickly, leaping back over the fence with the same ease he'd entered. He paused for a brief moment, scanning the area as if checking to see if anyone had noticed him. Then, just as swiftly as he'd arrived, he disappeared into the darkness, slipping away into the nearby fields.

Moments later, the flashing blue lights of a police car illuminated Phoenix Close. Pat emerged from her bathroom and quickly moved to her front bedroom window. She watched as two officers emerged, quickly making their way to Mrs Fletcher's front door. One officer knocked while the other circled around to the back garden, where the man had been moments earlier. Pat could do nothing but watch, her heart pounding in her chest.

Inside number thirteen, Diane Fletcher, sat huddled with her two sons in her bedroom. The curtains were drawn, but the sound of a police helicopter now circling above, combined with the sight of flashing blue lights reflecting off the walls, made the situation impossible to ignore. Her boys, clung to her, eyes wide with fear. She had tried to keep them calm, telling them it was all a precaution, that everything was fine, but the truth was, she was just as terrified.

They had all heard the stories. The Fox had been terrorising the area for months, breaking into homes, and sometimes much worse. His methods were brutal, his evasion of the authorities a source of constant dread. Tonight, that terror felt closer than ever.

The loud knock on the front door jolted her out of her thoughts. She froze, her heart throbbing in her ribs. For a moment, all she could hear was the steady hum of the helicopter and the muffled sound of her own breathing. Her sons looked up at her, their small faces pale and expectant.

"Who is it, Mum?" the youngest boy asked, his voice trembling.

"I don't know," she whispered, trying to keep her own fear at bay. She stood up slowly, walking down the stairs toward the front door. The knock came again, more insistent this time. Her hand hovered over the door handle, unsure if she should open it.

Taking a deep breath, she moved to the living room, pulled back the edge of the curtain and peeked through the window. A police officer was stood on the front porch, their face illuminated by the harsh glow of the helicopter's searchlight.

Her anxiety eased momentarily. She opened the front door. The police officer held up a small sign, and though it was difficult to read in the glare, she could just make out the words: NOD IF YOU ARE BEING HELD CAPTIVE. BLINK IF YOU ARE OKAY.

Diane's heart leapt into her throat. It was a precaution she had heard of before, used in cases of home invasions or kidnappings, a silent way to ensure everything was safe inside without tipping off a potential intruder. She quickly blinked several times, then stepped back from the door, her breath coming in short, panicked gasps. The officer didn't move for a moment, but after receiving her signal, lowered the sign.

Diane sagged against the wall, relief and fear colliding inside her. She wasn't sure how much more of this she could take. Even though the police inspected her home and assured her she was safe, the presence of The Fox lurking so close was more than unsettling - it was suffocating.

Detective Chief Sergeant Mark Talbot had arrived on scene and was stood listening as officers relayed updates over their radios as they searched the area. Phoenix Close backed onto a series of fields, one that led to a brook running alongside two nearby schools. The dense trees made it an ideal escape route, a tangle of blind spots and cover that The Fox could easily navigate, especially in the dead of night. He had used this kind of terrain before - always vanishing into the undergrowth just as the police closed in.

The police presence remained substantial throughout the night. Officers canvassed the area, knocking on doors, asking questions, combing through back gardens with flashlights. But no results. The Fox had evaded capture once again.

By the next morning, Phoenix Close was buzzing with nervous energy. The Fox was still at large, but the residents had a new layer of fear to contend with. At every front door and garden gate, neighbours gathered, exchanging hurried words about the events of the previous night. Gossip spread like wildfire.

"I heard he was hiding in somebody's shed in Hydrus Drive," one man muttered as he stood by his gate, talking to his next-door neighbour.

"They had dogs out all night," the woman responded. "Nothing. Not a single trace of him. It's like he just vanished."
"He's done it before," another neighbour chimed in. "That brook runs all the way down past the school. If he's clever enough - and he is - he could've slipped through the fields and been gone long before the helicopter showed up."

Detective Chief Sergeant Mark Talbot was sat at his desk, piecing together the information gathered during the hunt. The neighbour's sighting had been credible, but as always, The Fox had vanished before they could get close. They had tracked his trail to the edge of the playing fields, but from there, the scent had gone cold.

This was his MO - always sliding away just as they were closing in. Talbot knew the pattern well, and it was maddening. The Fox seemed to be everywhere and nowhere all at once, sneakily moving through the suburban streets and woodlands, impossible to catch.

The rumour mill churned furiously throughout the day. Some said he was long gone, having fled the area, while others believed he was still hiding nearby, waiting for another chance to strike. Parents kept their children close, refusing to let them play outside, even in broad daylight. The police continued to patrol, but a sense of unease hung over Phoenix Close.

By dusk, the adrenaline from the previous night had started to fade, but the fear remained. The Fox had slipped through their fingers again, and no one knew when - or where - he might strike next.

In the small community of Phoenix Close, one thing was certain: The Fox had come too close for comfort, and until he was caught, no one would truly feel safe again.

Part Three: Closing In

Chapter 23

The village of Eggington, nestled in the English countryside near Leighton Buzzard, was the kind of place where secrets didn't stay buried for long. With its thatched cottages and narrow, winding lanes, it was a tight-knit community where everyone knew everyone else's business.

On most evenings, the village was quiet - an idyllic picture of rural life - but tonight, the hot summer air bared down on the cottages like an invisible force.

Helen Thompson's cottage, with its ivy-covered walls and neatly trimmed garden, was one of the older homes in the village. A single woman in her thirties, Helen lived alone, but she liked it that way. She kept to herself, a private person by nature, and most of her neighbours respected that.

Two of her neighbours, Alan Briggs and his wife, Susan, were out walking their Labrador, Max. They strolled along the narrow lane, the dog trotting contentedly beside them. They were a good-humoured couple, retired and settled into a life of routines. Walking the dog was part of that routine. As they passed Helen's cottage, they heard something that stopped them in their tracks.

"Alan, did you hear that?" Susan whispered, her brow furrowing as she tugged on Max's leash.

Alan paused, tilting his head towards the sound. It was faint but unmistakable - a woman's muffled cries. He turned to Susan, his face creased with concern. "Sounds like it's coming from Helen's place," he said quietly.

They moved closer, straining to see through the semidarkness. The late evening summer haze seemed to creep closer, wrapping itself around the small stone cottage. Susan's eyes widened as she spotted something up ahead. "Look, the bedroom window...it's open," she said, pointing to the second floor.

Alan's breath hitched. The window was indeed open, the lace curtains fluttering slightly in the breeze. But that wasn't what drew their attention. In the dim glow of the bedroom light, a male silhouette could be seen moving behind the sheer fabric. A sense of dread gripped them both.

"Do you think it's him?" Susan whispered, clutching Alan's arm.

"Who?' Alan replied.

"The Fox" Susan whispered.

"I don't see a car out front," Alan replied, his voice tense. "And Helen wouldn't have a guest over without a car parked outside. I don't like this, Sue."

The muffled sounds of whimpering continued, more pronounced now - a desperate, muted sound. Susan's heart pounded in her chest. "We need to call the police, Alan. This doesn't feel right."

Alan didn't hesitate. He raced home and dialled for the police, his voice steady but urgent. "Yes, I'd like to report a possible sighting of The Fox. We can see a man in a neighbour's house, and it sounds like a woman is in distress. Please, hurry."

The operator responded quickly, and within minutes, the peacefulness of the village was shattered by the sudden approach of police sirens. Blue lights flashed across the stone walls of the cottages.

An armed response unit arrived first, skidding to a halt outside Helen's gate, their doors flying open. Officers in tactical gear spilled out, weapons drawn, they took up positions around the property.

Alan and Susan stood across the street, clutching Max's leash tightly. Their eyes were wide with the gravity of the situation they had inadvertently set into motion. They hadn't expected such a dramatic response.

"Bloody hell," Alan muttered. "I didn't think they'd send in the cavalry."

Susan swallowed, her eyes never leaving the cottage. "What if it is The Fox? You heard what's been happening. It's been all over the news."

The officers moved quickly, some taking cover behind cars while others positioned themselves at the front and back doors.

The lead officer, Detective Chief Superintendent Mark Talbot, signalled his team to move in. His face was set in a grim expression; they couldn't afford to take any chances. The sound of a woman's muffled groans, paired with a strange rustling noise, drifted from the open window above.

"Back entrance, now," Talbot ordered, his voice commanding. "We're going in quiet but be ready for anything."

Two officers, flanked by Talbot, moved to the rear of the cottage, their footsteps soft on the well-trimmed lawn. There were no signs of a forced entry, so with a swift motion, one of them used a pry bar to pop open the back door.

They entered silently, their boots making only the slightest sound on the wooden floor. The house was dark, save for the sliver of light from the partially open bedroom door upstairs.

Talbot nodded to his team. "Everyone in position. On my count." The three officers crept up the stairs, each step slow and deliberate, their breathing controlled, weapons at the ready. As they ascended, the sounds became clearer - heavy breathing, a man's low, urgent whispers, and the distinct, muffled grunts of a woman. The hairs on the back of Talbot's neck stood up. He'd been in enough high-pressure situations to recognise when things were about to go sideways.
"Three, two, one - go!" he barked.

They burst through the bedroom door, guns raised, laser sights cutting through the dim light like sharp blades. "Armed police! Hands where we can see them!" Talbot shouted.

The scene that unfolded before them was not what they expected. Not by a long shot.

A man and a woman lay tangled in the sheets, their faces flushed with surprise and…embarrassment. The man, startled and clearly naked under the covers, threw his hands up instinctively. Beside him, Helen Thompson's eyes were wide, her cheeks a deep shade of crimson. She was not tied up. She was not crying for help. She was very much there of her own free will.

"What the - what's going on?" the man blurted out, his voice half-strangled with confusion.

Helen pulled the sheets up to cover herself, her mortification plain as day. "Oh my God, I - this isn't - there's been a mistake!"

The room fell into an awkward, stunned silence as the officers slowly realised what was happening. Talbot lowered his gun, his shoulders sagging slightly as he turned to his team. "Stand down, everyone. False alarm."

The younger of the two officers couldn't help but stifle a laugh, which quickly earned him a glare from Talbot. "Quiet, Roberts."

Helen, still clutching the sheets, could barely meet anyone's gaze. "I'm…I'm so sorry," she stammered. "I didn't realise my window was open, and we must have made some noise…I can't believe this is happening."

The man beside her, who looked just as mortified, nodded. "I'm Jack. Uh…I'm sorry too. I didn't think our night would end like this."

From outside, Alan and Susan stood rooted to the spot, watching the officers file out of the cottage with sheepish expressions. When they saw Talbot approach them, they knew they were in for it.

"Are you the ones who made the call?" Talbot asked in a stern voice, though he already knew the answer.

"Yes, that was us," Alan admitted.

"It was a false alarm, it appears your neighbour has a 'friend' staying with her," replied Talbot.

Alan, his face flushed with embarrassment. "We thought…we thought she was in trouble."

"We didn't mean to cause a fuss," Susan added quickly. "It just sounded so strange, and with all the news about The Fox…"

Talbot sighed, the strain of the night finally easing from his frame. "Look, I appreciate you being vigilant, but next time, maybe knock on the door or call your neighbour first. No harm done tonight, but let's try to avoid getting the whole armed response unit involved in people's private affairs, yeah?"

Alan nodded sheepishly. "Right. Got it. Sorry about that."

A few minutes later, Helen stood on her front step, wrapped in a blanket and looking utterly mortified as her neighbours passed by, offering awkward waves and apologies. The last of the police vehicles were pulling away, the street slowly returning to its quiet, rural stillness.

Jack stood beside her, still half-dressed but trying to lighten the mood. "Well, that's definitely a first for me," he said with a chuckle.

Helen managed a small smile, though her cheeks were still burning. "I don't think I'll ever live this down."

"Hey," Jack said softly, nudging her with his elbow. "If nothing else, you've got one hell of a story for your next dinner party."
"I suppose you're right," Helen chuckled.

As the last police car disappeared down the lane, Helen took a deep breath, she'd deal with the embarrassment in the morning, but for now, she was just grateful it was over. She looked up at the stars that were starting to peek through the clouds, thinking to herself how life in a quiet village could suddenly turn chaotic in the blink of an eye.

But in Eggington, a quiet life didn't necessarily mean a boring one. And tonight, had been anything but boring.

Chapter 24

The Fox sat in his brother's small, cluttered living room in Leighton Buzzard. To the world outside, he was just another labourer, another man making his way through life with little trace. But to the police, he was an elusive criminal who had terrorised communities across Herts, Beds and Bucks for months, leaving only sporadic clues in his wake.

His brother, a quiet man named Steven, had no idea who he really was. To Steven, he was simply his brother, someone who had always been a little rough around the edges, prone to disappearing for long stretches of time, but family, nonetheless.

Steven had never been one to ask too many questions. His brother would be around some evenings, they'd have a few drinks, reminisce about old times, and other evenings he would disappear again, as he always did. The brothers were close, in a way, though there was a certain distance between them, an unspoken understanding that some things were better left unsaid.

Steven was a builder by trade, a hardworking man who lived a quiet life in his modest home on the outskirts of town. He had lived there for years, his days a steady routine of early mornings and long shifts. His home, though small and unassuming, had become something of a sanctuary for his brother in recent weeks. It was the perfect place to lay low while the police dragged their feet in the pursuit of the faceless criminal haunting their nightmares.

The newspapers were full of reports about The Fox - the clever, calculating criminal who always seemed to be one step ahead of the authorities. The Fox had always taken a certain pleasure in hearing about himself, seeing how the media and the police spun their theories, all the while completely oblivious to the fact that he was sitting quietly in the comfort of his brother's home, right under their noses.

But The Fox couldn't read. He had never learned, and the irony of it wasn't lost on him. The newspapers printed daily updates about his exploits, but he had to rely on his brother, oblivious to his true identity, to read them aloud.

Steven sat across from his brother, his reading glasses perched on the end of his nose, flipping through the pages of that day's newspaper. The headline caught his eye: 'POLICE CLOSE IN ON ELUSIVE 'FOX' - DOOR-TO-DOOR BLOOD TESTS TO BEGIN'.

"They're really coming for him now," Steven said, his voice a mixture of fascination and apprehension as he scanned the article. "They reckon they'll get him soon."

His brothers face remained impassive, though inside, his mind raced. He leaned back in the worn armchair, feigning nonchalance.

"Is that so?" he said casually, running his hand through his hair. He had learned long ago that showing emotion was dangerous - it gave people a glimpse into the chaos within.

"Yeah," Steven continued, his eyes glued to the paper. "They're gonna start going door to door, taking blood samples from every man in the area. They think he's local, you see. They reckon he's hiding somewhere, maybe even around here."

The Fox felt a chill run through him. Blood tests? This was new, and it was dangerous. It was one thing to stay a step ahead of the police, but if they were taking blood samples, it meant his days of running were numbered. His hands tensed slightly, but he kept his expression neutral.

"They really think that'll work?" he asked, keeping his tone light. "Dunno," Steven said with a shrug. "But it's a hell of an operation they've got going. Must've roped in half the bloody country to help. They're bringing in experts, too. Some newfangled science stuff. They'll match it to the crime scenes."

The Fox had heard whispers about it, but he hadn't considered it would be used against him so soon. The police were smarter than he had given them credit for, it seemed. He knew that if they came to Steven's door, they would demand his blood too - and that would be the end of him. No clever disguise or hastily forged identity could save him from the truth written in his own blood.

Steven, oblivious to his brother's inner turmoil, continued reading. He occasionally chuckled at the sheer scope of the police efforts, shaking his head at the idea of the infamous Fox living in some unsuspecting village. "I mean, can you imagine it?" Steven said with a grin. "The bloke could be right under our noses, just sitting there while everyone's looking for him."

The Fox forced a smile. If only his brother knew.

As the afternoon wore on, Steven suggested working on some odd jobs around the house. His windows were old and needed reinforcing. He was planning to nail them shut to try and prevent The Fox from gaining entry. His brother, eager to maintain appearances and appear helpful, followed him around the house.

Steven hammered away at the windows with an absent-minded determination, chatting about the case as he worked. "You know, they say he's been seen all over the place – Leighton Buzzard, Luton, even Tring. But no one ever seems to get a good look at him."

The Fox said nothing, watching the nails go in one by one, the windows sealing shut with each strike of the hammer. His brother was effectively locking him in, oblivious to the fact that he was the very criminal the world was hunting for. The irony wasn't lost on The Fox. In a strange way, it felt comforting. Safe. But he knew it wouldn't last.

When the windows were secured, the brothers settled back into their routine, sharing beers and watching TV. But the mention of the blood tests had unsettled The Fox, and he knew he couldn't stay much longer. He needed to get out of Leighton Buzzard before the police started knocking on doors.

That night, The Fox lay awake in his bedroom, staring at the ceiling. He couldn't stop thinking about the police, about their relentless pursuit, about the blood tests that would eventually lead them to him. He needed to act fast, to disappear again before they could pin him down.

Somewhere far enough away like Milton Keynes would be the logical next step. It was far enough from his brother's home to give him breathing room, but close enough that he could slip back into anonymity if necessary. And there were plenty of new opportunities there - new marks, new crimes. The temptation was already pulling at him.

But first, he needed to visit his wife and kids.

The Fox's family lived up north, in a small town in Durham that had remained largely untouched by his crimes. The drive from Leighton Buzzard was long and cumbersome, he set off early evening, once he had finished a local gardening job for a repeat customer.

Several hours passed before he reached the M18, an area he knew well, having driven through it so many times. It cut through the South Yorkshire countryside like a scar, a dark ribbon stretching toward an unknown end. The Fox drove along it with a sense of detached purpose, the summer heat swirling around, wrapping the vehicle in a stifling cloak of mystery. The night was still, the kind of oppressive calm that made every sound seem louder and every shadow more foreboding.

It was ten o'clock, and the warm air seemed to seep into the car, settling deep into The Fox's bones. A feverish heat of anticipation coursed through him, mingling with an anxious undertone - a nagging worry that tonight might be the one where his meticulous plans unravelled. Yet, the thrill of his predatory control over his victims was intoxicating, and the buzz of it drove him forward.

Brampton-en-le-Morthen, the village he had chosen for tonight's encounter, was a quaint, almost dreamlike place, its streets lined with sleepy cottages and narrow lanes that meandered through the landscape. The soft glow of streetlamps created a sense of eerie calm that perfectly suited his intentions. The Fox navigated the winding roads, his eyes scanning for the perfect spot to park his car. He eventually found a secluded wooded area, hidden from view by a dense thicket of trees.

As he parked and turned off the engine, the silence was punctuated only by the distant call of an owl. The Fox emerged from his vehicle. He looked around, scanning the area for reasons not to proceed. The coast was clear, so he reached for his bag and set off across a field.

He eventually approached his target, a secluded cottage at the end of a lane, its single porch light beaming over the neatly kept garden. The window of the downstairs toilet was slightly ajar - an oversight he intended to exploit.

With deft movements, he slipped through the gap in the window, the action smooth and soundless. Inside, the cottage was static. The Fox paused to listen, his breath slow and measured.

He located the phone in the living room and pulled out the cable ensuring the occupants would be unable to call for help. Carrying the cable with him, The Fox made his way to the bedroom, slowly and methodically. In the dim light, he could make out the silhouettes of the occupants, their recurring breathing a signal of their deep slumber.

The bedroom door creaked softly as he nudged it open. The couple lay in peaceful repose, their faces relaxed in sleep. The Fox's heart quickened, not from fear but from a twisted excitement that had become his driving force. The balaclava he wore clung tightly to his face, hiding his identity but not the intensity of his dark pleasure. He raised the shotgun, the weight of it familiar and comforting.

"Wake up," he said, his voice a cold whisper that cut through the stillness like a sharp blade.

The couple, Michael and Abigail Jones's eyes snapped open, their peaceful expressions transforming into ones of horror as they took in the sight of the masked intruder and the gleaming shotgun. The husband's eyes extended in dread, he stumbled out of bed, his voice cracking with a mix of fear and confusion.

"What do you want?" he asked, his voice barely more than a whisper.

The Fox's response was sharp and unyielding. "Quiet. Get up. Both of you."

The couple's panic was deep, their movements shaky. Abigail clung to her husband's arm, tears streaming down her face. Their eyes darting around the room, trying to grasp the gravity of their situation.

The Fox pushed them back down on the bed. He swiftly secured Michael's wrists with the phone cable. His attempts to maintain some semblances of courage were overshadowed by his visible dread. Abigail, trembling and sobbing, was ordered to bind her own feet. Her movements were frantic, her fingers fumbling with the cable The Fox had handed her.
"Face down," The Fox commanded, his voice accepting no argument. "And stay quiet."

As the couple complied, their breaths coming in short, terrified gasps, The Fox's gaze swept the room with cold detachment. He tied Abigails hands behind her back, lifted her night dress, and pulled down her underwear.
"Please, no," cried Michael.

The Fox slammed the butt of the shotgun into Michael's mouth, knocking out his two front teeth. Michael's head snapped back, blood squirted from his mouth onto the bed. The Fox slammed the shotgun into his nose, just to make sure he understood who was in control.

His actions were orderly, driven by a routine that had become disturbingly familiar.

Michael lay semi-conscious, while the Fox assaulted Abigail with swift and aggressive attacks. She was frozen to the spot. Unable to defend herself.

Once the ordeal was over, The Fox, content with his night's work, dressed himself with an evil smirk appearing through his mask. As he turned to leave, he noticed his semen on the bedsheet. A rare mistake. He retrieved a knife from his coat pocket and sliced through the sheet ensuring the evidence was removed. The portion of the sheet he targeted was a dark reminder of his recent act. This was his signature - a taunting memento of his dominance.

With the stained fabric in hand, The Fox worked quickly, stuffing it into his coat pocket along with his gloves and balaclava. The act was performed with clinical efficiency, every movement calculated and unemotional. He cast a final, disdainful glance at the restrained couple before slipping out of the cottage.

Outside, a thick fog had formed, the world around him reduced to a swirling mist. He trudged across the open field back to where his car was parked. A million thoughts were racing through his mind, the break-in, the assault, the semen spill. Oh no, the semen spill - he needed to make sure that vital clue would never be found.

He approached his car, and ever cautious but growing more careless with each passing crime, discarded key items near the spot where it was parked. The balaclava he had used to conceal his face, leather gloves, and the semen-stained piece of bedsheet, were hastily buried in a shallow grave nearby. These items, seemingly insignificant in the vastness of the landscape, held the potential to unravel his carefully constructed anonymity.

The Fox got into his car, the engine roaring to life and accidentally shifted it into reverse. The crunch of gravel and the scrape of the rear bumper against overgrown bushes filled the night air.

"Damn it," he muttered, his voice tinged with irritation. He quickly shifted the car into drive and sped away, his mind racing as he left the scene behind.

Inside the cottage, the couple lay bound and paralysed with fear as the night stretched endlessly before them. After what felt like an eternity, they mustered the courage to free each other and sat huddled on the bed, clinging to one another, sobbing. It was hours later before they finally called the police.

Chapter 25

Later that morning, Detective Chief Superintendent Mark Talbot and his team were alerted by South Yorkshire Police. Responding to a distress call from The Fox's latest victims, the local officers had swiftly connected the dots - it bore all the hallmarks of another chilling crime committed by The Fox. It all felt very familiar, despite it being a long way away from The Fox's usual crime area. A Forensics team also descended on the scene, their movements careful as they began their investigation.

In a nearby field, Farmer John Wilkins guided his tractor across the wide expanse. He had lived on this land for over four decades, and the rhythm of the seasons had become second nature to him. Due to the extended heatwave, the soil was tough to plough, but thanks to a recent downpour it was just damp enough to turn easily under the weight of his tractor. As the engine rumbled along, the large plough blades sliced through the earth, carving neat rows that stretched from one end of the field to the other.

It was a monotonous task, one that allowed his mind to wander as he worked. He'd been thinking about his livestock, which needed to be moved to a different pasture soon, when something caught his eye - a small object against the dull green of the hedgerow that bordered his field. Squinting into the near distance, the farmer noticed something unusual. There, tangled in the thorns and branches, was a glove.

He slowed the tractor to a stop, curiosity getting the better of him. Stepping down from the cab, the farmer approached the hedge, wiping his hands on his overalls. The glove was odd - out of place, it didn't belong in his field, as there was no public footpath nearby. It wasn't the sort of thing you found around here, where the only litter was usually a stray plastic bag blown in from the motorway.

Reaching out, he tugged the glove free from the hedge. It was leather, stiff from exposure, and looked like it had been there overnight. What was strange, though, was that he knew this glove hadn't been there when he'd been in the same field a day earlier. It seemed new, dropped or discarded recently. He turned it over in his hands, frowning. A chill ran up his spine, and without knowing why, the farmer felt the hairs on the back of his neck prickle with unease. This wasn't right.

His thoughts were interrupted by the sight of police cars in the distance. The farmer saw them parked at the cottage of Michael and Abigail Jones. The glove still in his hand, he climbed back into his tractor, tossed the glove into the cab, and drove toward the Jones' house. Whatever was happening over there, he figured the police might want to know about this strange discovery in his field. As he arrived, the officers outside the house took notice, and the farmer waved them over.

"Morning, officers," he said as he climbed down from the tractor. "I found something in my field that I think you'll want to see."

Detective Sergeant Jake Miller stepped forward. "What have you got?"

"This." The farmer held out the glove. "Found it caught in the hedge. Wasn't there yesterday."

Miller took the glove, examining it with interest. "Where exactly did you find this?"

"Just over that rise, down by the far side of my field."

Miller turned to the others, his face gloomy. "Let's get a team out there, now."

Inside the Jones' cottage, Talbot sat interviewing the couple, going over events from the previous night. His thoughts were interrupted by the sound of hurried footsteps in the hallway. Miller entered the room, his expression tense.

"Sir, there's been a development. A farmer found a glove in the hedge near to here. Looks like it could be connected."
Talbot straightened, his pulse quickening. "Where?"

"On the far side of the field. We've got a team heading out to search the area now."

Talbot didn't hesitate. "Let's go."

The scene by the M18 was eerily quiet. The search team had cordoned off the area near the hedgerow where the glove had been found, and forensic officers were already combing through the site with painstaking care.

Talbot stood at the edge of the field, watching as the team worked. His gut told him that this was it - the break they had been waiting for. The glove could be the key to unlocking the mystery of The Fox's movements. But they couldn't take any chances. They needed to act fast, especially if The Fox realised that he had left something behind.

"Jake," Talbot said, turning to Miller, "we need to expand the search. If he left something as obvious as a glove, there could be more. Check all of the fields and any area he may have walked to or parked in."

"Forensics, continue to sweep the area, I want every last detail he has left behind. Miller, I've got a plan. Come with me."

Within an hour, the nearby section of the M18 was awash with flashing lights of emergency vehicles. Talbot had decided to stage a seemingly routine traffic accident involving a bus, hoping to divert any suspicion. Officers, dressed as paramedics and emergency workers, moved swiftly, blending seamlessly into the scene.

"We need to search the area, now," Talbot ordered, his voice resolute. "We can't risk him coming back before we've gathered everything. If he realises we're onto him, he'll disappear."

The forensic team worked methodically, inch by inch, scanning the area for any other signs of disturbance. It was slow painstaking work.

There was nothing else of interest in and around the Jones' cottage or the field where the farmer had discovered the glove. So, the search moved to a secluded wooded area, not far from the field. And it wasn't long before one of the forensic team called out.

"Sir! Over here!"

Talbot and Miller hurried over to where the forensic officer was kneeling by tyre marks in the earth and a patch of recently disturbed earth. The forensics officer carefully brushed away some of the loose soil, revealing the edge of something metallic.

"Keep digging!" barked Talbot.

The forensic officer dug further, revealing a shotgun, buried just below the surface. The discovery sent a jolt of adrenaline through Talbot. This was no ordinary piece of evidence. The shotgun was exactly the kind of weapon they had suspected The Fox of using in most of his attacks. But finding it here, not far from the Jones' cottage, confirmed their suspicions: The Fox had been in the area.

"Get that bagged and tagged," Talbot ordered. "And keep digging. There's more here, I can feel it."

The forensic officer continued to dig. More vital pieces of evidence were revealed.

"Sir, look, a piece of cloth and a glove."

Talbot and Miller's eyes lit up. "That has to be the other glove to what the farmer just found," said Miller, excited.

"Get them bagged, tagged and sent to the lab for examination, The Fox has slipped up big time. We are finally onto him," said an almost joyous Talbot.

The forensic team, buoyed by their discoveries, continued to sweep the area.

Moments later, they uncovered the most crucial piece of evidence the investigation had seen.
"Sir, over here."

"What is it?" demanded Talbot.

"A tiny speck of paint on a broken twig. It is barely visible to the naked eye, but could this be from a vehicle?" replied the forensic officer.

"Get it bagged and tagged. It's worth investigating." A very happy Talbot responded.

The forensic officer collected it carefully, sealing it in a bag for further analysis. And then studied the bushes more closely. She focused on the height of the branch which had the speck of paint.

"Sir, it measures forty-five inches from the ground. That's the typical height of a hatchback car model."

"Excellent work officer. Get this all sent to the lab. I want to know every car make and model with this paint type and colour," replied Talbot. And with that, Talbot afforded himself a rare smile. Was this the breakthrough he had been waiting for.

"Keep searching the area, I want this place turned upside down," demanded Talbot. But no further evidence was uncovered.
It was a major breakthrough; one Talbot had been praying for.

The next day at the Crime lab in Huntingdon, Cambridgeshire, the paint sample was analysed under high-powered microscopes. Talbot stood in the observation room, watching as the technicians worked. They had sent the gloves, the shotgun, and the sheet for testing, but it was the paint that intrigued him the most. A tiny, nearly microscopic fleck of paint was often all it took to link a suspect to a crime scene. Talbot was hoping that in some way, it would help him to finally nail The Fox.

After several hours of analysis, the results were in.

"DCS Talbot?" The forensic technician called out. "We've got something."

Talbot stepped inside the lab, his heart pounding. The technician held up a report.

"We began by physically examining the paint sample, which matched the questioned sample in the first stage of our analysis. Next, we conducted a chemical analysis using Fourier-transform infrared spectroscopy, which identified the binders, pigments, solvents, and additives unique to the paint formula. Using our colour charts, we matched it to sample seven-nine-one-nine Harvest Yellow. The key detail? This specific type of paint was exclusively used on Austin Allegro models produced in the last two years."

Talbot's mind raced. The Fox drove a yellow Austin Allegro. They had already linked the car to several of the crime scenes, but they hadn't been able to track down the exact make or model. This paint sample narrowed the search considerably. They now knew the car driven by The Fox, and with the forensic evidence linking the gloves and shotgun to The Fox, they had taken a huge step forward in capturing him.

"Excellent work," screeched an almost euphoric Talbot.

In the days that followed, the investigation intensified. Talbot and his team focused on tracking down every yellow Austin Allegro that matched the paint profile. They combed through vehicle registration databases, and discovered there were fifteen-hundred owners of this type of vehicle.

The discovery of the glove had been the turning point. It had led them to the shotgun and sheet, which had, in turn, led them to the paint. Every piece of evidence was falling into place, and for the first time in months, Talbot felt that they were closing in on their elusive target.

Talbot stood tall in the operations room, his chest puffed out. "Everybody, listen up," he called out.

"We finally have a major breakthrough in our search for The Fox. We now know he drives a yellow Austin Allegro. Miller, Hughes, I want you to review each and every owner of a yellow Austin Allegro against the five-thousand names Metal Mickey has given us. Any matches, you let me know straight away," barked Talbot.

"Yes sir," Miller and Hughes responded simultaneously.

"And if there are no matches, find every person on that list of fifteen hundred car owners, visit them, rule them in or out of this investigation," demanded Talbot.

"Crikey, this is going to take us ages, Guv," retorted Hughes.

"Well, you had bloody well start now then, son," countered Talbot.

And with that, both Hughes and Miller, grabbed the list of car owners, and set about what could prove to be the most important task in the hunt for The Fox.

In the quiet village of Brampton-en-le-Morthen, the search for justice had begun in earnest. The relentless pursuit of The Fox was no longer a matter of chance but of time, as the investigation unfolded with increasing urgency. The fog of anonymity that had once shielded him was beginning to lift.

But The Fox was still out there, still watching, still waiting for his chance to strike again. Talbot knew that time was running out. They needed to find him before he disappeared for good - or worse, before he claimed another victim.

Chapter 26

The morning after his assault on the Jones', The Fox had arrived home in Durham. His wife, Sarah, was a practical woman who had learned long ago not to ask too many questions about her husband's comings and goings. Their relationship had always been one of convenience rather than passion, but it worked for them. Sarah ran the household, raising their two children with a quiet resilience, while The Fox drifted in and out of their lives, always returning just long enough to remind them he was still around.

This time, he had planned something special. His birthday was coming up, and he had promised to take the family on holiday to the Scottish Highlands - a rare treat, something to make up for his frequent absences.

When he arrived at their home, Sarah greeted him with a mixture of surprise and suspicion, as she always did. But the promise of a holiday softened her. She smiled when he mentioned the Highlands, and the children were thrilled at the idea of a road trip.

For a few days, The Fox allowed himself to slip into the role of a family man. He played with the kids, helped Sarah around the house, and even managed to push the thoughts of the police and the blood tests to the back of his mind. But the itch was still there - the pull toward the hunt, the need for control. He could feel it gnawing at him, growing stronger the longer he stayed in one place.

The Fox, an attacker cloaked in anonymity, manoeuvred his vehicle through the narrow streets of Peterlee like he'd never been away. He drove around like any other normal person going about his business. Inside his car, the temperature was cool, the vibration of the engine a soothing backdrop to the dark thoughts that churned in his mind.

He'd been successful so far, eluding capture and spreading fear wherever he went. Tonight, Peterlee would be his stage, the town's calmness shattered by the violence he had planned. He had chosen his targets carefully, selecting two homes on the outskirts of town, isolated enough to ensure that his presence would go unnoticed until it was too late.

The first house was a modest, two-story structure, its garden overgrown with weeds and unkempt hedges. It was the kind of house that blended into the background, easily forgotten in the hustle of daily life. He parked a short distance away, and he watched, and he waited, making sure the house was still and silent.

Inside, the family was unaware of the impending danger. A young couple, David and Laura McGinn, were asleep in their bed, dreaming of an untroubled life. Their bedroom was a cosy haven, filled with the warm glow of bedside lamps and the soft whizz of an old fan.

The Fox approached silently, slipping through the garden gate and down the side of the house. He moved quickly, his footsteps muffled by the thick grass that clung to the ground. He made his way to the back door, which he knew from his prior reconnaissance would be poorly secured. A quick flick of his screwdriver and the turn of the handle, and the door was open, creaking softly as he snuck inside.

The interior was eerily quiet, the only sound the soft murmur of the fan. The Fox lingered at the threshold of the bedroom, his breath sturdy and relaxed. He had done this many times before, but the thrill of the hunt never faded. He stepped inside, his movements deliberate and controlled.

David and Laura stirred slightly as he approached, but their slumber was deep. The Fox's presence was a dark cloud in their dreams, an invisible threat that they could not perceive. He moved closer, his heart pounding with a mix of anticipation and cold determination.

Laura woke first, her eyes fluttering open as she sensed something amiss. She saw the shadowy figure standing beside the bed and let out a soft gasp, her face a mask of confusion and fear. David stirred, his eyes slowly focusing on the intruder. The Fox acted swiftly, his gloved hand clamping over Laura's mouth as he brandished a knife glinting menacingly in the dim light.

"Stay quiet," he whispered, his voice a chilling growl. "No one needs to get hurt if you cooperate."

David's eyes widened in terror as he tried to grasp the horror unfolding before him. He struggled to stand, but The Fox overpowered him effortlessly. The fight, though brief, was vicious - filled with desperate gasps and muffled cries. Within moments, a sickening silence fell over the room. The Fox's attack left David with two broken ribs, a shattered nose, a detached testicle, and several missing teeth. Blood streamed from his face onto the bed as he gasped for breath.

Laura's ordeal was even worse. The Fox headbutted and elbowed her into submission, leaving her battered and bruised, her face a mess of injuries as she had no option but to comply with his violent demands. The bottom of her nightie was soaked in blood from the brutal sexual assault she endured.

The aftermath of The Fox's brutality would leave David and Laura scarred for life.

After the grim assault was complete, The Fox exited the house, leaving behind a scene of horror that would soon shake the small town to its core. He moved back to his car, the summer heat adding to the sweat already dripping from his forehead. He drove away with the same calculated calmness he had arrived with.

The following night he was back on the prowl. The second house was a similar picture of suburban normalcy, a single-story home with neatly trimmed hedges and a small garden. This time, the occupants were an elderly couple, Harold and Margo Lynch. They were nestled in their sofa in the living room, the soft glow of the television flickering across their faces.

The Fox was hiding under the sofa, having slipped into the house through a side window earlier in the day. The house was quiet, the kind of silence that spoke of an ordinary, untroubled life, albeit apart from the sound of Harold and Margo's favourite TV show blasting out. They both sat, blissfully unaware of the danger.

The Fox continued to observe them, his expression hidden behind the mask of his balaclava. He relished the moment, savouring the contrast between the peaceful domestic scene and the horror he was about to unleash. He slowly moved out from under the sofa, so he was positioned at the back, out of eyesight.

And then he pounced.

Margo was the first to spot him, her eyes widening as the shadow approached. Her scream was cut short as The Fox lunged, clamping his gloved hand over her mouth and wielding his knife with deadly precision. Harold rushed to intervene but was met with brutal force - The Fox swung the handle of the knife with chilling accuracy, smashing it repeatedly into Harold's face. Blow after blow shattered his eye sockets and nose, leaving him unconscious on the floor.

Margo sat frozen in horror. Moving quickly, The Fox bound her hands and feet with electrical cord he pulled from his jacket. Helpless, she was forced to watch as he returned to Harold, stripping off his trousers and underwear. He flipped Harold onto his stomach, pressing his face into the carpet.

"Don't move, or I'll slit his throat," he barked at Margo.

The Fox slid down his trousers and underwear and climbed onto the back of Harold. With each violent thrust, each guttural grunt, Margo flinched and let out soft, broken sobs.

The scene was a grotesque tableau of violence and terror. The peaceful family time broken by the harsh reality of The Fox's actions.

The assault lasted a few minutes. When he was done, The Fox stood up, pulled his clothes up and then smashed the handle of the knife into Margo's face repeatedly until she was unconscious. Her face was unrecognisable.

When he finally left, the house was a picture of horror, the aftermath of The Fox's brutality a stark contrast to the ordinary life that had existed moments before. Another two victims. Another two lives ruined forever.

The next morning, The Fox woke up with his family, and acted like he always did, as if nothing had happened the night before. They set off for Scotland, the car packed with suitcases and snacks, the children bouncing in the backseat. The Fox kept his eyes on the road, his mind already drifting to the possibilities that lay ahead. The Highlands were remote, sparsely populated. It would be the perfect place to lie low for a while, to escape the growing pressure from the authorities. But even as he thought about the safety of isolation, the darkness in him stirred.
The journey north was long, and by the time they reached the halfway point, The Fox's patience was wearing thin. They stopped at a service station for a break, and as Sarah took the children inside to use the restroom, The Fox found himself scanning the parking lot with the same predatory instinct he always had. His eyes locked on a young woman standing by her car, fumbling with her keys.

He knew he shouldn't. He had promised himself he wouldn't. But the urge was too strong. He opened the boot of his car, located the hidden compartment containing his balaclava and gloves, and snuck them on.

The Fox moved quickly, approaching the woman from behind. In a flash, the predator inside him took over. It was over in seconds. Quick, brutal, efficient. The woman's bloodied body slumped against the side of her car, her keys still dangling from her hand. The Fox glanced around to make sure no one had seen him. The parking lot was quiet, the sun just beginning to set over the horizon.

He hurried back to his car, his heart pounding, the thrill of the assault coursing through his veins. Sarah and the children were still inside the service station, oblivious to the horror that had just unfolded in the parking lot. The Fox forced himself to breathe, to calm the adrenaline surging through him. He needed to keep his composure.

When Sarah and the kids returned, they found him leaning against the car, smiling as if nothing had happened.

"Ready to go?" he asked, his voice steady, betraying none of the chaos swirling inside him.

They continued their journey north, unaware that The Fox had just added another victim to his tally.

The Scottish Highlands were everything The Fox had hoped they would be - vast, remote, and wild. It was the perfect place to disappear, to leave behind the growing anxiety in England. For a while, he allowed himself to enjoy the peace and solitude of the landscape, spending time with his family, hiking through the hills and exploring the rugged terrain.

But the respite was short-lived. The newspapers were still full of stories about The Fox, and even in the remote villages of the Highlands, people were talking about the case. Every pub, every small shop, seemed to have someone discussing the elusive criminal who had managed to evade capture for so long.

The Fox listened to these conversations with a mixture of pride and paranoia. He had always enjoyed the notoriety, the idea that he had outsmarted the police at every turn. But now, with the blood tests looming, he feared his time was running out.

One evening, as they sat by the fire in their rented cottage, Sarah mentioned the case, her voice laced with concern.

"They're saying they're getting closer to catching him," she said, her eyes flickering with a hint of worry. "This 'Fox' fellow. They're doing blood tests now. Going door to door."

The Fox tensed, but he forced a laugh, dismissing her fears.

"They've been saying that for weeks," he said, waving a hand. "They'll never catch him."

But even as he said the words, he could feel the walls closing in.

The holiday ended, and they returned home, the drive back to England long and quiet. The Fox could feel the pressure building, the need to move, to act, to stay ahead of the police. The darkness inside him stirred once more, and he knew it wouldn't be long before he had to strike again.

He had escaped the net for now, but the hunt was far from over. The Fox was still on the run, but the hunters were closing in, and he knew that his next move would have to be his most calculated yet.

As they pulled into the driveway of their home, The Fox glanced at his wife and children, their faces tired but content. He smiled, knowing that the façade of the family man was still intact.
For now.

The following day, on the way back to Leighton Buzzard, The Fox felt the familiar pull, that dark urge that had become his constant companion. The holiday in the Highlands had offered him a temporary escape, but it had done little to quench the growing hunger inside him. As he drove south with the memory of his last victim still fresh in his mind, he began thinking about his next move. He couldn't resist the need for another thrill. This time, he was looking for something more personal, more brutal, something that would assert his dominance in a way he hadn't done in a while.

The drive was long, and as the miles blurred past, The Fox's thoughts turned to a small house just off the motorway - Yvonne Chamberlain's house. He had seen it before, having studied its movements in the past. It was isolated, set back slightly from the others, and backed onto an alleyway that would allow him to disappear quickly if needed. He didn't know much about Yvonne personally, just that she lived alone and kept to herself, the kind of victim he preferred.

As the car approached the familiar turn-off, The Fox's heart rate quickened. He pulled off the main road and parked a few streets away from Yvonne's house. The sky had darkened, and the neighbourhood was quiet, just how he liked it.

He moved quickly, slipping through the night as he approached the house. The back door was locked, of course, but that wasn't a problem for him. He had a knack for breaking and entering, something he had honed over recent months. Within seconds, he was inside, his footsteps silent on the wooden floors. The house was dark, but he could hear the faint sound of a television playing in one of the rooms.

For a moment, The Fox stood in the hallway, letting the tension build, savouring the power he held. He could hear Yvonne in the living room, oblivious to the danger lurking just feet away. He tightened his grip on the knife he had taken from his car, a tool he now used since he discarded of the shotgun.

He entered the living room quietly. Yvonne was sitting on the couch, her back to him, completely unaware of his presence. The TV was so loud, The Fox could barely hear himself think. He slowly crept towards her, step by step. And then bang, he attacked her from behind. She didn't notice him until it was too late. But before she could scream, he was on her, his gloved hand clamping over her mouth.

But Yvonne was different. She didn't take prisoners. She fought back harder than The Fox had expected. She bit down on his gloved hand, breaking through the material, her teeth sinking into his flesh with a ferocity that surprised him. The pain was sharp, searing, but it only fuelled his rage. Snarling in anger, The Fox brought the knife handle down on her face, the sound of the impact echoing through the small room. Yvonne cried out, her nose breaking under the force of the blow. Blood sprayed across the couch, splattering against the walls as she crumpled to the floor.

But she wasn't done fighting. Even with her face bloodied and her vision blurred from the damage to her face, Yvonne lashed out, kicking at him with a strength born from sheer survival instinct. The Fox, momentarily thrown off by her resilience, hit her again, this time across the side of her head. Her body went limp, collapsing into a heap on the floor.

Breathing heavily, his hand throbbing from the bite, The Fox took off his glove to inspect his injury. His wound was bleeding badly, unknown to the Fox, his blood dropped onto the carpet. It was another mistake, which could prove costly.

He put his glove back on and stood over Yvonne, watching as she gasped for breath, her face a mess of blood and bruises. He hadn't expected her to put up such a fight, and now, with his blood mixing with hers in her mouth and on the floor, he knew he had to leave. This was messier than he had planned. The adrenaline was still pumping through him, but something in the back of his mind was screaming for him to get out before it was too late.

Without another word, he turned and bolted, leaving Yvonne lying unconscious on the floor. He ran through the alley behind the house, his injured hand throbbing as he made his way back to the car. His pulse was racing, his thoughts scrambled. This attack had been too close, too sloppy. He hadn't expected her to fight back like that, and now he had left behind evidence - his blood.

As he drove away from Yvonne's house, the full weight of what he had done began to sink in. This was no longer just a game. The police were already closing in on him, and now he had left behind more evidence than ever before. They would find Yvonne, they would take samples from the blood he had spilled, and they would use it to track him down.

The Fox gripped the steering wheel tightly, his mind racing as he sped down the darkened roads. He couldn't afford to make any more mistakes. Leighton Buzzard was no longer safe. If he stayed, they would find him. He had to keep moving, to stay ahead of the hunt, to disappear once again.

But even as the fear of capture gnawed at him, the thrill of the attack still coursed through his veins. The Fox knew he would strike again. It was only a matter of time.

Yvonne's house, now a crime scene, would soon be swarming with police. By the time Yvonne regained consciousness and called for help, the damage had been done. Her face was swollen and bruised beyond recognition, her broken nose making it difficult for her to breathe, and her left eye so damaged that she could barely see. But Yvonne was tough. Despite the immense pain, she managed to describe the attack to the paramedics and later to the police - though her details were vague, it was enough to give the authorities something to work with and to link the crime to The Fox.

Forensic teams arrived soon after, combing through the scene for anything that might give them a clue. Blood was everywhere: Yvonne's from the brutal blows to her face and The Fox's from where she had bitten his hand through a thin glove. The team carefully collected samples from both Yvonne and her house, hoping that something in the forensic analysis would help them narrow down their suspect pool.

The next day, back at the lab, the forensic team worked quickly to process the blood samples, and soon, they had something significant: The Fox's blood type. He was blood group O, a common group but still one more piece of the puzzle that they hadn't had before. While it wasn't enough to pinpoint his exact identity, it allowed the police to refine their list of suspects further.

But the clues didn't stop there. Through their meticulous analysis of past crime scenes and witness reports, the police had a profile of their elusive suspect. They knew he was approximately five feet nine inches to five feet ten inches tall. Yvonne's description, despite her injuries, confirmed that the man who had attacked her was of similar height. Her description of his hair - brown and curly - was also corroborated by past witness accounts, though many had only caught fleeting glimpses of him. Forensics were even able to determine that the man had been wearing gloves, as there were no fingerprints left behind. But his bite mark, recorded by Yvonne's desperate struggle, would help identify a man with a recent hand injury.

Each new piece of information brought the police closer to visualising their suspect, even if his identity remained hidden. They knew his height, his blood group, his hair colour and texture, his preference for gloves, and his left-handedness. This, combined with the make and model of his car gave them a better chance of identifying him.

The Fox had always relied on his ability to disappear into the cracks of society, to evade detection by blending into the background. But now, it seemed his time was running out. With each mistake, he was giving the police more to work with.

And there was another crucial factor: his modus operandi. The Fox had always used specific tools to break into homes. His methods were precise - doors picked, windows jimmied open with a flathead screwdriver, always something that allowed him to enter quietly and quickly. He was methodical, but with Yvonne, his impatience had led him to slip up. His usual care in leaving no trace was compromised by the sheer aggression of the attack.

As the details started to come together, Detective Chief Superintendent Mark Talbot stood in the operations room in Dunstable police station, surrounded by maps, photos, and piles of paperwork. He was hunched over the table, reviewing the profile they had built on The Fox. The pressure to catch this man was immense. The Fox was getting sloppy. Talbot knew that it was only a matter of time before they caught him.

"His blood group is O," Detective Sergeant Jake Miller, said, entering the room with the latest forensic report.

Talbot nodded. "Good. Another piece of the puzzle. Make sure you cross reference that with the list of names from Metal Mickey. Strike off anyone whose blood group isn't O."

Miller spread the papers across the table. "We've got his height, hair colour, hair type, blood type, he's left-handed and we know the car he drives.

Talbot looked up, narrowing his eyes as he scanned the papers. "He's left-handed. That narrows things even further, they're a rare breed."

"It does," Miller replied. "And we know the kind of tool he uses – flat head screwdrivers. He's got experience, maybe even spent time inside. We'll need to check records, see if anyone with a similar profile has been released recently."

Detective Constable Tom Hughes, chimed in. "It's just a matter of time, sir. A yellow Austin Allegro isn't exactly subtle. It's just a question of when we find him, not if."

Talbot sighed, rubbing his temples. "We can't afford to waste time. He's growing more erratic by the day. Yvonne Chamberlain's lucky to be alive, but we won't always be so lucky."

Talbot felt another glimmer of hope. The Fox had been untouchable for so long, but now they almost had him cornered.

But even as the investigation gained momentum, Talbot knew that The Fox wasn't going to stop on his own. He was like a bully backed into a corner, and that made him more dangerous than ever. They had to catch him, and soon, before he struck again.

The Fox, though unaware of the full extent of the police's progress, could feel the noose tightening. As he returned to Leighton Buzzard, he couldn't shake the feeling that time was running out. His instincts screamed at him to move again, to disappear, but a part of him - darker and more primal - wasn't ready to stop.

And so, as he lay low at his brother's house once more, the thought of running faded, replaced by the familiar itch to strike. He would move to a new area, yes, but he would not run. Not yet.

There was still unfinished business to attend to.

Chapter 27

The room was suffocating, bathed in darkness save for a single flickering bulb that swung slowly overhead, casting warped shadows across the walls. This was his sanctuary, a hidden nest deep within a decaying building on the outskirts of town. Here, amidst the peeling wallpaper and the smell of mildew, he could let the mask slip. Here, he could be himself.

He sat on a rickety chair, the kind that groaned under the slightest weight, and stared into the cracked mirror on the opposite wall. The man who stared back at him was not the man the world knew. No, this was a different face - a face that wore a twisted smile, eyes burning with a manic, predatory glint. He tilted his head slightly, examining his reflection like a scientist would study a specimen, trying to understand what lay beneath the surface. But he knew the answer. He always had.

He was The Fox, and he thrived in the spaces between fear and chaos.

His real name didn't matter anymore. He had left that behind like a snake shedding its skin. Out there, he was an urban legend, a phantom who stalked the night. People whispered his name in hushed tones, as if speaking too loudly might summon him. And he liked it that way. He relished the power it gave him, the way it made them feel small and helpless. It was intoxicating.

He stood up, his movements deliberate and measured. He took slow, even breaths, feeling the oxygen fill his lungs and feed the cold fire that burned within him. Each breath was a reminder of his existence, of his control over his own fate. Control was everything. Without it, he was just another man; with it, he was something else entirely.

He walked to the window and pulled back the tattered curtain, peering out into the night. The town lay before him like a carcass waiting to be picked clean. The streets were empty, but he knew they were watching. Watching for him. He could almost feel their eyes, hidden behind curtains, peering through the darkened glass, waiting for a glimpse of the monster they feared. And it filled him with a dark, euphoric pleasure.

What did they think he was? A lunatic? A common criminal? They had no idea. They couldn't see the intricate web he was weaving, couldn't comprehend the depth of his mind. He wasn't just breaking into homes or brandishing weapons for the thrill of it. No, each action was a calculated move in a game only he understood. A game that required skill, patience, and an understanding of fear.

Fear. That was his weapon. More potent than any gun or knife. Fear seeped into a person's bones, crawled beneath their skin, and took root in their soul. It paralysed them, made them weak, and he had learned to wield it like a craftsman with a finely honed blade. He could smell it, taste it, feel it radiating from his prey. And once he had it, once he had them in that perfect moment of terror, he could do anything.

He remembered their faces - those he had chosen to visit in the dead of night. Their eyes, wide with terror, their breath catching in their throats. The way their muscles tensed, the way their hands shook as they clutched at anything that could offer them some semblance of protection. It was like music to him, a symphony of vulnerability.

He smiled, running a hand through his hair, feeling the sweat and grime clinging to his skin. His mind drifted to that couple in Leighton Buzzard. He could still hear the sharp crack of the shotgun, see the flash of muzzle fire illuminating their pale, horrified faces. That instant when the gun went off - was it intentional? Even he wasn't sure anymore. He had felt his finger tighten around the trigger, almost as if guided by some primal instinct. The result was magnificent chaos.

The man had lunged at him, wild with a mix of fury and survival instinct, and The Fox had felt a thrill unlike any other. It was rare to see such fight in them. Usually, they cowered, pleaded, or froze. But this one…he had something different. And that's what had made it so exhilarating. The unexpected was always more delicious.

He turned away from the window, his smile fading into a thin, contemplative line. He walked over to a small table cluttered with newspapers; each one emblazoned with photo fits of his supposed look and of headlines that screamed of his exploits.

'THE FOX STRIKES AGAIN!', 'MASKED INTRUDER TERRORISES VILLAGE!', 'POLICE FRUSTRATED AS FOX ELUDES CAPTURE!'.

He ran his fingers over the photo fits, feeling the rough texture of the cheap print. The papers thought they understood him, thought they could reduce him to a caricature of madness and malice. They didn't understand a thing.

They spoke of him like he was a beast, a deranged animal with no sense or strategy. Fools. They couldn't see the layers, the strategy, the game unfolding before them. They thought they were hunting him, but they were just pawns on his board. Every move they made was a reaction to his. Every time they thought they had him cornered, he slipped through their fingers, leaving behind only the stench of fear and the echoes of his laughter.

He relished the feeling of being in control, of pulling strings that no one else could see. He knew the country was on edge, that people were locking their doors and peeking out their windows. Parents were keeping their children close, and men who once scoffed at the idea of a bogeyman now slept with weapons by their bedsides. And it was all because of him. He had transformed the mundane into a theatre of terror, turned their quiet lives into a never-ending nightmare.

But the game was not without its challenges. Detective Chief Superintendent Mark Talbot. That name kept coming up, etched into his mind like a stubborn stain. Talbot was different from the others, less predictable. A thinker. Someone who could see past the surface and into the deeper patterns of his work. The Fox had watched him from a distance, seen him pacing in his office, pouring over maps and reports. He could almost smell the desperation on the man. It excited him.

Talbot was a problem that needed solving. The detective was beginning to understand his methods, starting to connect the dots in a way that no one else had. It wouldn't be long before he got too close. The Fox knew it was time to turn the tables, to let Talbot know that the hunt could go both ways.

His lips curled into a smile at the thought of it. The thrill of the chase - he could feel it building inside him, a friction that needed release. But how? How to up the stakes without losing the upper hand? He wanted to draw Talbot deeper into the game, to pull him into his world where the rules were different, where fear was the currency and chaos the reward.

The Fox walked to a corner of the room where a small, battered chest sat on the floor. He opened it carefully, revealing a collection of items - souvenirs from his various exploits. A man's belt, photos from an album, a flashy tie. Each one told a story, each one was a reminder of a night well-spent. His fingers brushed over them, feeling the cold metal of the belt buckle, the soft fabric of the tie. They were pieces of lives he had touched, changed forever.

A thought struck him then, a sudden, dark inspiration that sent a shiver of excitement down his spine. Talbot. He would make the detective his next subject, his next project. Not in the way he had done with the others, no - this one needed to be different, special. He would get inside Talbot's head, make him see the world as he saw it. He would make him understand.

The thrill of it sent a jolt through him, and he laughed - a low, guttural sound that echoed off the walls of his lair. He had never felt so alive, so powerful. The world outside this room was his to mould, and the people within it, his to manipulate. They were all playing parts in a script he had written, actors in a drama of his own design.

The Fox's eyes burned with a feverish light. He could hear the rain starting to tap against the broken window, a soft, steady rhythm that filled the room. The night was calling to him, whispering in his ear, urging him to step out into the darkness and continue his work.

He grabbed his coat and slung it over his shoulders, pulling the hood up over his head. He took one last look at his reflection in the cracked mirror. The smile was gone, replaced by something colder, something more determined. This was his moment. The next act in his grand play was about to begin, and he was ready.

Tonight, he would rewrite the rules. Tonight, he would take the game to a new level. And when it was all over, they would know. They would all know what it meant to truly fear The Fox.

And so, with the night as his cloak and Milton Keynes as his canvas, he disappeared into the darkness, his mind alight with visions of terror yet to come. The hunt was on, and he was ready to paint the town red with it.

Inside their modest home in Oldbrook, Milton Keynes, Wesley and Haylee Adams were settling in for the night. Outside, the rain had consumed the skies, the summer sun having recently disappeared. Somewhere, not far from where they sat, The Fox was watching. He could almost hear their breaths, feel their anxiety.

The Fox was ready to go. He moved like a raider in his element, his senses sharpened by the thrill of the hunt. Milton Keynes was his new playground, its streets and alleys etched into his mind like an intimate map. He knew every corner, every hiding spot, every path that led in and out of this area. And tonight, he felt the pull of those streets, like an old addiction resurfacing. The failure of his last assault lingered, and he was eager to redeem himself.

The Fox's mouth slowly arched into a smile beneath the dark mask that covered his face. He could feel the fear that gripped this area like a vice. It was electric. And he was the spark that could ignite it.

He crouched low, moving with a cat-like grace along the side of the house. He could hear a TV show - laughter, a cheerful jingle. A sitcom, perhaps. How quaint, he thought. How ordinary. He paused by a window, peeking through the tiny crack in the curtains. Inside, Wesley and Haylee sat on a brand-new leather sofa, eyes fixed on the screen. They looked tired, weary, but there was a certain comfort in their togetherness. The Fox watched them for a moment, feeling a strange mix of amusement and contempt. They were so blissfully unaware, so wrapped up in their little bubble. It would be so easy to shatter it.

He could feel his pulse quickening, his senses sharpening. This was the moment he lived for - the anticipation, the buildup to that perfect, terrifying crescendo. He had planned it carefully, mapped out every detail in his mind. This time, there would be no mistakes.

The Fox moved closer to the backdoor, his footsteps silent on the long grass. He knew the layout, knew exactly where he needed to be. He had chosen his entry point carefully - it would take only a moment to slip inside.

With the precision of a seasoned hunter, his gloved hands gently forced open the door. The sound was barely audible, drowned out by the loud television. He crept through the opening, and he waited, listening to every sound. He could hear their voices in the living room, discussing the program they were engrossed in.

Carefully, he edged toward the doorway, his eyes adjusting to the dim light. Wesley and Haylee were blissfully oblivious of the intruder who stood so close to them. He remained out of sight, watching them, feeling the rush of power that came from being so close, from being unseen. It was intoxicating.

Wesley's eyes flicked toward the doorway, and for a moment, The Fox thought he had been seen. But Wesley turned away. The Fox smiled to himself. They were still so vulnerable. He could push them further, break them completely. But he needed to do it right.

He moved back into the darkness, deeper into the kitchen, his mind racing with possibilities. He could wait for them to go to bed, slip into their room as they slept. Or he could make a noise, draw them out, let them feel the terror of knowing he was inside, so close they could almost touch him. The thought sent a shiver of excitement down his spine.

But he decided on something simpler, he would be more direct.

He took a breath, clutched his knife tightly in his left hand, and burst into the living room. Haylee and Wesley startled; their eyes wide with fear as The Fox seized the moment. He wasted no time in letting them feel his presence. He smashed the handle of his knife into Wesley's face, breaking his nose with a sickening crunch. Wesley slumped forward, hands instinctively covering his blood-soaked face.

Before Haylee could react, The Fox turned, silencing her with a swift blow to the jaw that left her gasping in pain. Her scream barely escaped before his hand clamped over her mouth, muffling it to a whimper.

Wesley, hunched over and shaking, looked up through blood-streaked eyes. "Please, don't hurt her," he pleaded, voice cracking. The Fox's expression remained impassive as he struck again and again, until Haylee crumpled to the floor. He stepped toward Wesley, delivering a brutal kick to his jaw that sent him sprawling, unconscious.

Moving quickly, The Fox bound their hands behind their backs.

He then prowled the house, eyes flicking over every detail, his twisted mind piecing together a message for Talbot that would echo long after he left.

Minutes passed before he returned, eyes gleaming with dark intent. His search had yielded items that would etch the memory of this night into Talbot's mind - a toilet brush and a marrow from the fridge.

The Fox ripped at Wesley and Haylee's clothes like a dog ripped at a chew toy. He was sending a message loud and clear to Talbot. He was in control and there was nothing he could do about it.

What followed was vile and vicious. Relentless violence at its worst. The toilet brush snapped in half; such was the force used on Wesley. The marrow was reduced to mush. Both items were soaked in blood.

Once The Fox had finished his tirade of abuse, he calmly stood up, fixed his clothes and walked out of the house.

Wesley and Haylee remained bound, broken and unconscious. Their simple quiet lives would never be the same again.

Outside, the dark night sky swallowed The Fox as he ran for his life. His mind was racing, but there was a grin on his face. This was what he lived for - the thrill of being so close to the edge. Tonight, had been a warning to Talbot, a taste of what was to come.

He eventually slowed to a walk, his grin fading into a cold, calculating smile. His mission was complete.

Minutes later both Haylee and Wesley stirred from their unconscious states and called the police.

Detective Chief Superintendent Mark Talbot received the news with a heavy heart. It was another grim reminder that The Fox was growing increasingly erratic and vicious.

"Milton Keynes?" Talbot repeated, his voice taut with barely concealed anger. "He's back in the area then."

At the scene, the devastation was immediate and horrifying. Officers stood in stunned silence, their faces pale and drawn as they gathered inside the house now marked by the violence of The Fox.

As the team worked to comfort Wesley and Haylee and to gather evidence, Talbot's office phone buzzed with updates. Each new piece of information only deepened the sense of urgency. The Fox's latest act of aggression wasn't just an attack; it was a deliberate provocation, a challenge to the task force.

"I want all available officers to increase patrols in the Milton Keynes area. The Fox is back, and if we don't catch him now, he's going to tear the place apart," Talbot ordered, his voice steely. The pressure on Talbot's shoulders was immense.

The next day, the media frenzy was immense, and public fear was at an all-time high. The headlines screamed about the attack, each one more sensational than the last.

"THE FOX STRIKES AGAIN: POLICE FAIL TO PROTECT!" read one banner.

The police task force convened for an emergency meeting, the room buzzing with urgent voices. Talbot addressed his team with a steely determination.

"Listen up. The Fox is back. He's more dangerous than ever. Last night's attack was the worst so far. He's taking things to an unprecedented level. We have more boots on the ground in the Milton Keynes area, our focus switches there."
"He's a sick man. Who thinks to assault somebody with a toilet brush?" replied a distraught Detective Sergeant Sarah Kendrick.

"A twisted individual that's who. Hughes, Miller, where are we with the list of car owners, we must be getting close?"

"We've got through eleven hundred and fifty-nine of them, guv. Nothing but dead ends so far. Only another three hundred and forty-one to go," confirmed Detective Constable Tom Hughes.

"Keep going, I want an update every morning and every afternoon," barked Talbot.

The team discussed The Fox's return and his likely motives for moving to a new area. The meeting ended with Talbot sighing a huge sigh of frustration. The time for hesitation was over. He needed to put an end to The Fox's reign of terror once and for all.

Part Four: The Trap Is Set

Chapter 28

Since his return, The Fox had emptied his brother's bedroom of any evidence linking him to the crimes – the photographs, the ties. He was wary of a knock on the door from police asking for a blood test, so he decided against staying at his brother's place again. Unknown to all but himself, for the past few years, he also rented a secret residence, a quiet hideout in North London. He parked his car at the house to keep up appearances, and mostly used his work van for day-to-day operations.

Inside his house, he was rarely idle.

Now, he was ready to strike again, this time with a torrent of violence that would shatter the uneasy calm of Milton Keynes. Eleven houses. Eleven lives. Eleven brutal, calculated attacks.

The Fox was ready.

Milton Keynes wore the early hours like a shroud, a sprawling, soulless expanse of roundabouts and concrete cows under a blanket of darkness. The weight of a summer storm was waiting to break. The town felt tense, almost sentient, as if it knew what was coming - an onslaught of madness and horror that would leave its mark in blood and terror.

His mind was a dark place, a labyrinth of twisted thoughts and perverse desires. He fed off the fear, the chaos, the control. Every house he broke into, every terrified face he saw, was another piece of his puzzle, another stroke in his masterpiece of insanity. He had been haunting the dreams of his victims, but tonight, he would be something more. He would be their worst nightmare.

The first house in Shenley was a modest bungalow at the end of a quiet cul-de-sac, its windows dark as the occupant, Clara Compton was leaving to run an errand. The Fox, sharp and calculating, observed from a distance, waiting for his moment. When the coast was clear, he slipped into action, his gloved hands picking the back door lock with practiced precision. His heartbeat steady, almost calm. The door swung open with a soft click, and he slipped inside. The bungalow was silent except for the chirp of a canary, oblivious to the dangers The Fox presented.

After a quick scan of the surroundings, he wasted no time. He made himself at home, setting up a makeshift den with blankets as though it was his own. He brewed a cup of tea, rummaged through the kitchen, and helped himself to quiche Lorraine and a cheese and pickle sandwich. Then, he waited.

Hours later, Clara returned, unsuspecting. As soon as she stepped inside, The Fox emerged from his hiding spot, knife in hand. His eyes locked on her, cold and calculating. Without hesitation, he threatened her, waving the blade to assert control.

"Make a sound, and you die," he hissed, his voice a low, menacing growl.

The Fox felt a cold smile spread across his face beneath his mask. He reached into his pocket, pulling out a length of cord he had prepared earlier.

He moved quickly, efficiently, looping it around Clara's neck. She was about to scream. But The Fox was ready. He clamped a hand over her mouth, leaning close to whisper in her ear.

"Keep quiet, or you won't see tomorrow."

Clara froze, her eyes filled with tears, her body trembling beneath his grip. She gasped for breath, her hands clawing at the cord around her throat. The Fox tightened his grip, feeling the rush of power surge through him. This was control, pure and unfiltered. This was his art.

Fear flooded her face. Without warning, The Fox struck her with his fist, sending her crashing to the floor. And with another swift movement he kicked her in the stomach. The assault continued, blow after blow rained down on her. By the time he had finished, The Fox had inflicted serious injuries to Clara. Injuries both physical and mental. Injuries that would never heal.

As she lay on their floor, bruised, battered, covered in blood, The Fox collected his thoughts, regained his composure, and slipped out the back door. He didn't need to linger any longer. The damage was done.

The next day, The Fox was back on the prowl. The house was a semi-detached in Bradwell Common, its narrow front facing a row of identical homes. He knew this one well - a young professional, Sabrina Townsend. He approached from the back, scaling the garden fence with ease. He moved quickly, finding the rear door and creeping inside.

Sabrina slept soundly upstairs, oblivious to the intruder crawling through her home. The Fox moved with quiet accuracy, exploring the ground floor until he found an old, worn duvet in a closet. With a quick glance around the living room, he dragged some chairs together, fashioning a makeshift den. Satisfied with his hidden nook, he settled in, sipping milk he'd taken from the fridge and munching on a packet of biscuits he'd found in a cupboard.

For hours, he watched videos on the tv, the stillness of the house around him, biding his time. When the moment felt right, he rose silently, leaving behind the comfort of his temporary nest, and made his move up the stairs toward the slumbering occupant.

His footsteps were slow and deliberate as he ascended the stairs, each creak muffled beneath his weight. The house quiet, broken only by the rhythmic breathing of Sabrina sleeping soundly in her bedroom. He reached the door and pushed it open, the hinges barely whispering as he slipped inside.

The room was dimly lit by moonlight streaming through the curtains. The Fox approached the bed, looming over her for a moment before prodding Sabrina awake with the cold blade of his knife. She jolted, eyes wide with confusion, as The Fox brought a finger to her lips in a gesture for silence.

"Not a sound," The Fox hissed, his voice low and intimidating. "Do exactly as I say, or things will get ugly." The threat hung over her like a thunderstorm, as she lay frozen in the grip of terror.

Her eyes locked on him, her body trembling with fear. The Fox felt a dark satisfaction wash over him. He could see the helplessness in her eyes, could feel the power he held over her. He moved closer, his knife trained on her. He wanted her to know how close she was to death, how easily he could end it all.

He didn't though. That wasn't his style. He had other plans. He ordered her out of her bed and to drop to her knees. Without a moment's hesitation he slammed his fist into her face, sending her crashing to the ground. The onslaught that followed was beyond evil.

While she lay on the carpet, dazed, confused, bloodied, The Fox went hunting. He found a purse on a bedside table, emptied the cash into his pocket and when he had taken what he wanted, he left her there, broken and terrified, her life forever changed by his abuse.

Day after day, house after house, he moved through Milton Keynes like a dark tide, his presence felt but never truly seen. Talbot and his team were scrambling, their radios crackling with frantic orders and garbled communications. They were always two steps behind, chasing their tails. The Fox revelled in it. He could feel Talbot's desperation.

By the time he reached the seventh house, he was intoxicated with his own power. This one was different - a small, single-story dwelling on the outskirts of Stony Stratford. An elderly woman lived there, alone since her husband passed away. She had been easy to track, easy to follow. The Fox slipped in through a back window. He found her in the living room, asleep in a recliner, the television casting a dim, flickering light across the room.

He watched her for a moment, his breath shallow and steady. She was frail, vulnerable. She would break easily. He moved closer, his shadow falling over her like a death shroud. She stirred, her eyes fluttering open, and she gasped when she saw him. He moved quickly, one hand over her mouth, the other pressing the blade of his knife against her temple.

"Shh," he whispered. "No one's coming to save you."

Tears streamed down her face, her body shaking with silent sobs. The Fox felt nothing. No pity, no remorse. This was the game. This was what he lived for. He took his time with her, drawing out the fear, the helplessness. He wanted to see her spirit crumble, to watch the light fade from her eyes. When he was done sexually and physically assaulting her, he left her there, broken and alone.

The Fox continued his rampage through the area, each house a new chapter in his twisted narrative. He was writing his story in blood and fear, each scene meticulously crafted, each victim chosen with care. He was an artist, and this town was his canvas.

But even artists grow tired. By the time he reached the eleventh house, he could feel the fatigue setting in, the weight of his work pressing down on him. This one was a detached home on the edge of a wooded area in Blakelands, secluded, isolated. It was perfect.
He approached cautiously; his instincts honed to a razor's edge. He could see movement inside - a male figure passing by a window, a glimmer of light. He waited, watching, letting the tension build. He could feel the storm brewing, both inside and out. The wind was picking up, rattling the branches of the nearby trees, sending litter skittering across the ground like whispers of the dead.

He moved to the back of the house, finding a side door. It was locked, but that wasn't a problem. He pulled out his tool, the lock clicked open, and he snuck inside. He could hear him now - his voice, hushed and urgent, coming from a room down the hall. He moved towards him, his heart pounding in his chest, his senses alive with anticipation.

The door to the room was slightly ajar, and he pushed it open slowly, peering inside. A middle-aged man, Jonathan Meakin, sat on his sofa, eating crisps, watching tv, minding his own business.

The Fox moved fast. Without hesitation he stormed towards Meakin. The Fox felt a dark, cold smile spread across his face. This was it - the final act. He raised his knife, taking a step forward. Meakin finally saw him coming and foolishly lunged at him, a desperate, futile attempt to protect himself. The Fox sidestepped him easily, slamming the handle of the knife into the back of his head. Meakin crumpled to the floor.

The Fox stood over the semi-conscious Meakin, his chest heaving, adrenaline coursing through his veins.

The Fox took a step toward him, his presence looming over him like a black cloud. He watched him for a moment, savouring the sight of his terror. This was what he had come for - the pure, unadulterated fear, the raw power it gave him.

He slowly lowered the knife and reached out with his free hand, taking a handful of his hair and yanking him forward. He whimpered, his hands clawing at his gloved fingers. He pulled him close, his breath hot against his ear.

"Remember this feeling," he whispered. "Remember it every time you close your eyes. I want you to wake up every night, drenched in sweat, afraid that I'm still here, watching, waiting."

The physical assault that followed was bone breaking and relentless. Blow after blow rained down on Meakin's body until it was limp. The Fox wanted more. He stripped Meakin naked and violently assaulted him, leaving scars that would be felt for the rest of his life.

The Fox took a deep breath, surveyed the scene, and smiled to himself. He slipped out through the back door, the summer heat blasting against his skin like a furnace, humid and relentless. It was suffocating. Sweat trickled down his neck, clinging to his clothes as if the heat itself had wrapped around him.

As he made his way through the back streets, his mind was a whirlpool of dark thoughts and twisted satisfaction. The police would be converging on the scene soon, late again. He could almost hear their frantic voices, see their frustrated faces as they realised just how thoroughly they'd been outplayed.

He ducked into a narrow alley, his senses still on high alert, his eyes darting back and forth. He could feel the town around him, its heartbeat pounding in time with his own. He had become a part of it, a phantom etched into its very bones. His presence would be felt in every corner, every alleyway, every darkened room.

The Fox knew he needed to get to his car which he had stashed nearby, make his exit clean and quiet. But even in the chaos, his mind was already racing ahead, plotting the next move, the next act in his ever-escalating game.

He reached the car and slipped inside. The engine turned over with a low growl, and he pulled away from the curb, merging into the sparse late-night traffic. His face was impassive, his eyes scanning the road ahead, but inside, a fire burned. Eleven houses in Milton Keynes. Eleven lives shattered. But it wasn't enough. Not yet.

As he drove, he could feel the adrenaline beginning to fade, leaving behind a hollow emptiness that gnawed at him. The thrill, the power - he needed more of it, needed it to fill the void that seemed to grow larger with every passing day. His mind raced, thinking of the next town, the next unlucky souls who would cross his path. There was always another place, always another game to play.

The headlights of a passing car swept over his face, and for a moment, his eyes seemed to glow in the darkness. He grinned, a cold, thin smile that held no warmth, no humanity. He was The Fox, and he was far from finished.

Later that evening, Detective Chief Superintendent Mark Talbot stood still, his eyes locked on the house in front of him, the front door swinging open in the wind. Inside, he could see the paramedics moving frantically, their faces grim and gaunt in the dim light. He had seen this scene too many times before, and each time, it gnawed at him a little more.

"Eleven in this area now," he muttered. "He's relentless."

Beside him, Detective Sergeant Sarah Kendrick nodded, her face drawn with exhaustion. "He's back with a vengeance. How many more is he going to clock up."

Talbot nodded, his eyes never leaving the house. The detective felt the weight of eleven assaults pressing down on him. The Fox was still out there, somewhere, and he needed a breakthrough to help catch him.

On the night of ninth of September 1984, The Fox, a man whose criminal exploits had spread fear throughout the region, was preparing for yet another assault. His pattern of breaking into homes, building dens and assaulting the occupants, had earned him a chilling reputation. For months, he had successfully preyed on unsuspecting families, couples, and individuals, sneaking into their homes, instilling terror before slipping back into the night. His attacks were calculated, his movements precise. He had evaded the law and remained a faceless enigma. But that night, he would encounter an unexpected force: a woman who would refuse to be another victim in his long line of conquests.

It was a sweltering night. The summer heat was suffocating, and the suburban streets were empty, save for the occasional distant drone of a passing car or the chirp of crickets hidden in the grass. The Fox moved through the darkness with the same fluid, predatory grace that had served him so well. His target was a house on the edge of Wolverton, its lights long extinguished, the sole occupant asleep inside. From his observations over the past few days, he had learned that the woman who lived there was alone, no children, no partner. It was perfect, he thought. Easy, like all the others.

He approached the house with confidence. The back door was his usual entry point, and as he had done countless times before, he knelt and began to work the lock with his gloved hands. His heartbeat steady, his breathing controlled. There was a thrill in these moments - the anticipation, the power of knowing that he was in control. Within seconds, the door clicked open, and The Fox glided inside, as silent as a whisper in the night.

The house was still, the faint ticking of a clock the only sound that greeted him as he moved through the kitchen and into the hallway. He paused, listening for any sign that the woman might have stirred. Nothing. The house felt almost lifeless, as if it was holding its breath, waiting. The Fox advanced, his movements careful and deliberate. He had done this many times before. His victims rarely woke up until it was too late. He imagined it would be the same tonight. He would subdue her quickly, instil fear, maybe take a few valuables as a memento of his visit. Then, like always, he would vanish before dawn.
But as he made his way up the staircase, something shifted in the air. A faint creak of wood beneath his foot, perhaps a bit louder than intended, caused him to stop abruptly. He stood still, his muscles tensing as he listened. From the room at the end of the hall came the faintest rustle, the sound of someone stirring. The Fox continued forward, more cautious now, his steps as light as a feather.

The bedroom door was ajar, and through the sliver of space, he could see the outline of the bed, the figure beneath the sheets. The woman was still asleep, or so he thought. He pushed the door open slowly, his hand hovering near the knife tucked into his pocket - his insurance. He had learned that the fear of violence was often enough to render people compliant. But tonight, something would be different.

As The Fox stepped into the room, the woman's eyes snapped open, her body reacting instinctively to the presence of danger. She had been in a light sleep, the oppressive heat making it difficult to rest, and some sixth sense had alerted her to the intrusion. Before The Fox could fully comprehend what was happening, she sprang up, her eyes wide with shock and adrenaline.

The Fox moved to grab her, but she was faster than he had anticipated. In one fluid motion, she lunged toward him, her hands pushing against his chest with a force that caught him off guard. He stumbled back, momentarily losing his balance. She screamed, a sound that ripped through the stillness of the house, piercing the night.

The Fox, now panicked, raised his knife, but the woman was relentless. Fuelled by terror and the instinct to survive, she fought with everything she had. She clawed at his face, her nails scraping against the skin of his neck, her legs kicking with furious strength as she struggled to push him away. She was not going to be another victim, not tonight.

The Fox, used to quick and quiet control, was overwhelmed by the unexpected resistance. He had never faced someone who fought back with such intensity. The woman's screams echoed through the house, and in his mind, he knew it was only a matter of time before someone nearby heard the commotion. Panic set in, overriding the calculated precision that had defined him for so long.

He swung his arm wildly, trying to strike her, but she ducked, managing to evade his knife. Her knee came up, colliding with his midsection, and for the first time that night, The Fox felt real pain - a sharp, blinding shock that knocked the wind out of him. The woman seized the moment, shoving him back with all her strength. He crashed into a nearby bedside table, knocking over a lamp in the process.

The Fox staggered to his feet, his mind racing. This was not how it was supposed to go. He could feel his control slipping away, and in that moment, he made the decision to flee. Without another thought, he turned and bolted out of the bedroom, the woman's voice chasing him down the hall as she screamed for help. He nearly tripped down the stairs in his rush to escape, but managed to catch himself, sprinting through the house and out the back door where he had come in.

The hot night air hit him like a sledgehammer, the sweat drenched his body. He ran blindly through the darkened streets, his pulse thundering in his ears, heart pounding from a combination of exertion and disbelief. He had failed. The Fox had been humiliated.

The woman he left behind stood trembling in her bedroom, her breath coming in ragged gasps as the reality of what had just happened sank in. She had fought him off. She had survived. And though the terror still clung to her, she knew that she had done something that no one else had managed before - she had stopped The Fox.

Chapter 29

The date eleventh of September 1984 would go down in criminal history.

Detective Chief Superintendent Mark Talbot had faced many challenges in his career. He had led investigations into some of the most high-profile cases the country had ever seen, but none compared to the pursuit of the predator the media had dubbed "The Fox". For nearly six months, The Fox had terrorised the region, leaving a trail of destruction and taunting the police with flawless execution. Talbot's reputation was on the line, and he knew that if this case wasn't cracked, it would stain his otherwise exemplary career.

But today was different.

The small flick of yellow paint had been a breakthrough - though at the time, it was unknown how significant it would be. It was just a tiny shard, barely noticeable to the naked eye, scraped from a branch. Forensic teams had poured over the scene, hoping for something, anything, that would offer a clue. And there it was, a trace of yellow paint. Ordinary. Unremarkable. Yet, to the trained eye, it could mean everything. After hours of analysis, they had identified it: the paint belonged to a specific make of car, an Austin Allegro.

The discovery was a long shot, but when the forensic team had narrowed it down further - the yellow paint was used only on a particular model of the Allegro, and only fifteen hundred of those had ever been registered in the UK - it felt like the needle in a haystack had just grown a little larger. But it was still a needle. Detective Sergeant Jake Miller and Detective Constable Tom Hughes, the police officers working on the case knew the gravity of what they were dealing with. They had been chasing The Fox for months. He had slipped through their fingers at every turn, leaving a trail of terrified victims.

Now, they had something. Something tangible. A list. A frustratingly long list of fifteen hundred registered Austin Allegro's, scattered across the UK. Their first task had been to review the list against the names Metal Mickey had provided as potential suspects. It bore no fruit. None of the key suspects were registered keepers of an Austin Allegro. So, that meant, five thousand suspects could be written off, all thanks to a single piece of evidence.

The next task was to sift through the list, cross-referencing names and addresses, methodically checking each lead. It was the sort of painstaking police work that didn't make the headlines - boring, monotonous, gruelling. But it was necessary. Many of those cars had been sold, resold, scrapped, or shipped off to unknown destinations. And with every change of ownership came a new challenge - tracking down the current owners, finding addresses, and hoping one of these cars would lead them to The Fox.

The late summer days of 1984 had blended into a blur. Detective Sergeant Jake Miller and Detective Constable Tom Hughes worked sixteen-hour shifts, barely stopping to catch their breath. Dunstable police station had become a second home, the scattered files and overflowing coffee cups evidence of their dedication. Every day felt the same: reviewing names, calling former owners, tracking down scraps of information, and more often than not, hitting dead ends.

Miller had grown used to the grind. His wife, Emma, understood - mostly. She had grown tired of hearing, "Just one more case, love. It'll be done soon," knowing full well it wouldn't be. His children, two boys aged seven and nine, were starting to get used to him not being around at dinnertime. It gnawed at him, the time lost, but Miller was a man driven by duty. He had been in the police force for nearly ten years and had never encountered someone like The Fox. His elusive nature, his ability to disappear without a trace - it had turned the case into an obsession.

Hughes, on the other hand, was younger and still new enough to believe in the system, in the idea that if they just worked hard enough, long enough, justice would prevail. But even he was starting to crack under the weight of the investigation. His girlfriend had left him three months ago, tired of the late nights and missed dates. Now, he had nothing but the case, and it seemed every time they thought they were getting closer, The Fox would slip away again.

There were moments - long stretches - when both men questioned whether The Fox was even catchable. Maybe he was too clever, too careful. Maybe he was just lucky. But then, on the morning of eleventh of September, they got a hit that would change everything.

It had been a routine start to the day, the list of names still as long and daunting as ever. That morning, the two detectives found themselves sifting through more files. Miller was on the phone, tracing another dead end. Hughes was reviewing the list of owners when a new name stood out: Malcolm Fairley.

"He's listed as having moved to this address in Kentish Town a couple of years ago," Hughes said, rubbing his tired eyes.

Miller looked up from his notes. "That's not far."

Hughes nodded. "Worth checking out, don't you think?"

It was more a formality than anything. They had followed leads like this before. But it was one of the few that hadn't required hours of searching for a forwarding address, and they needed a break from the office. Within an hour, they were on the road, driving toward North London.

The atmosphere in Kentish Town was grim and oppressive. The heavy scent of impending rain filled the environment, while dark, bruised clouds loomed low over the terraced houses like a suffocating blanket. It was the calm before the storm - a storm that echoed the nervousness gripping the nation, as if the streets themselves sensed that the abuser who had haunted them for so long was nearing his end.

The address was unassuming. Sixty-Five Oseney Crescent, Kentish Town - a row of Victorian terraces with narrow gardens, all squeezed together in a crooked line. There was nothing remarkable about it, nothing that screamed of a man capable of such acts of brutality. Evil never wore a uniform; it blended in, wore the same faces, spoke the same words, lived the same lives.

Miller and Hughes pulled up to the curb outside the house. Miller glanced at the house. Nothing special. "Think this could be it?"

Hughes didn't answer right away. He stared out the window at the figure on the pavement - a man bent over with tools laid out by the side of a yellow Austin Allegro. The car looked as tired as its owner, but the scratches on its rear told a different story. His pulse quickened. "Maybe," he said finally. "Let's find out."

The two officers stepped out into the cold air. The man didn't look up as they approached, too focused on his task, his tool moving in slow, deliberate circles on the car's wheel. Up close, he looked ordinary – average height, brown curly hair and a face that could fade into any crowd.

"Morning," Miller called, his voice cutting through the stillness.

The man finally looked up. His eyes were dark, like two dirty marbles. He blinked, wiping his forehead with the back of his hand, smearing water and sweat across his skin. "Morning, what can I do for you?" he replied, in a soft Geordie accent.
Miller's senses sharpened. "We are looking for a Malcolm Fairley, is that you sir?"

"That'll be me. How can I help?" replied Fairley.

Miller gave him a smile that didn't quite reach his eyes. "Nice car you've got there. Austin Allegro, isn't it? 'Harvest yellow' they call it?"

Fairley's lips twitched in what might have been a smile. "That's right. She's a bit old, but she gets the job done."

Miller nodded, glancing at the scratches again. "Had some trouble with it, though, by the looks of it. Those scratches... any idea how they got there?"

Fairley's eyes flicked to the back of the car, a flash of something dark and sharp crossing his face before he masked it. "Oh, that? Just some kids mucking about. You know how it is."

Hughes stepped closer, his eyes narrowing. "Kids, huh?"

Fairley shrugged, his gaze sliding away, back to the car. "Yeah, well, you know how they can be."

Hughes meanwhile noticed a screwdriver which matched the description of what had been used to break into homes. And in the back seat of the car, two pairs of green overalls, one of which had a missing leg.

Miller watched Fairley closely. There was a stiffness in his movements now, a difficulty that hadn't been there a moment ago. He was hiding something. He decided to push a little harder.

"Mind if we ask you a few questions?" Miller asked, his tone casual. "Just routine."

Fairley hesitated, his hand tightening around the tool in his hand. "Sure. What about?"

"Do you know Bedfordshire at all?" Miller replied.

"Erm, yeah, my brother lives in Leighton Buzzard." Fairley looking more uneasy on his feet.

"Oh right, you must've visited him there then?" quizzed Hughes.

"Yeah, I've been a few times," replied Fairley.

Miller noticed a watch on the front seat of the car, and thinking on his feet, made a final shot at piecing all the evidence together.

"Ok, well I tell you what, let's pop inside your house and have a chat away from your neighbours. Maybe put your watch on, you don't want to leave that out here, in case those kids steal it. You know how they can be eh," Miller afforded himself a slight chuckle.

Fairley opened the passenger side door to his car, and with his left-hand picked up the wristwatch, placing it on his right wrist. And with that, Miller and Hughes looked at one another. They both felt a chill run down their spines. Victims had described The Fox as left-handed - something only someone trying to disguise their true nature would be aware of. And here was Fairley, putting on his watch on his right wrist.

Miller caught Hughes' eye, a silent understanding passing between them. They were close, so damn close. Miller kept his voice steady, calm, as if he were talking about the weather. "Shouldn't take but a minute."

Hughes opened a car door, reached in, grabbed the overhauls. He then bent over and picked up several screwdrivers and tools from the toolbox on the ground. "I think we might need to talk about these too," as he placed them into a clear plastic evidence bag.

Fairley's eyes darted from Miller and Hughes and back again. His shoulders tensed, and for a moment, Miller thought he might bolt. But then he sighed, a long, weary sound, and nodded. "Fine. Let's go."

All three men walked towards the entrance of Sixty-Five Oseney Crescent. Hughes and Miller's eyes not once leaving Fairley. As they reached the front door, Hughes noticed scratches on Fairley's neck, consistent with those reported by the last victim of The Fox. And he noticed teeth-shaped scar on his right hand. The pieces of the jigsaw were all falling into place.

Once inside, Hughes held up the evidence bag containing the overalls. The fabric was rough and faded, but there was no mistaking the fact that the leg had been cut clean off from one pair. His heart began to pound, a cold sweat breaking out on the back of his neck. "What happened to these?" he asked, keeping his voice level.

Fairley shrugged again, but there was a tremor in his voice now. "Work clothes. They get torn up sometimes."

Hughes moved in closer, holding up an evidence bag containing screwdrivers. "These look pretty worn, too. You use these a lot?"

Fairley swallowed, his Adam's apple bobbing. "Yeah. I do a bit of repair work, here and there."

But Hughes wasn't listening anymore. His mind was racing, pieces falling into place like the final moves in a deadly game of chess. The overalls, the missing leg - perfect material for a mask, crude but effective. The screwdrivers - tools that had been matched to the marks left at several break-in scenes. And the scratches on the car – the same height the forensics team said they'd be. Fairley matched the height the victims all said he was, he had brown curly hair, a Geordie accent, scratches on his neck and above all, he was left-handed.

Miller looked up, locking eyes with Fairley. "Malcolm Fairley, I think you'd better come with us, you're under arrest."

Malcolm Fairley's face went pale, his eyes wide with a sudden, naked fear. For a second, Miller thought he might fight, might try to make a run for it. But then his shoulders sagged, and he nodded, defeated. "All right," he muttered. "All right. Just…let me get my coat."

Miller stepped forward, his hand moving to his belt. "No sudden moves, Malcolm."

Malcolm Fairley nodded again, his movements slow and deliberate as he turned around and placed his hands behind his back.

Miller snapped the cuffs around Malcolm Fairley's wrists with a practiced efficiency. Hughes watched, his heart still hammering in his chest, as the reality of what they'd just accomplished began to sink in. The Fox had been caught.

As they led Malcolm Fairley out into the cold, grey morning, Miller and Hughes felt a sense of grim satisfaction settle over their bodies. The nightmare was over. But the scars - the fear and the trauma - would linger long after The Fox had been put away. And as the rain began to pour in earnest, the officers knew one thing for certain: darkness like this never truly disappeared. It only hid in the shadows, waiting for the next moment to strike.

And so, as the officers breathed a huge sigh of relief, Malcolm Fairley was detained and driven to Dunstable police station for questioning.

Chapter 30

Malcolm Fairley - The Fox - was finally in handcuffs.

The weight of the manhunt lifted, but there was no victory to savour. The dark clouds above Herts, Beds and Bucks wept tears of joy. The flickering lights of the squad car sliced through the darkness, casting long, twisted shadows that danced and wavered across the slick pavement. It was as if the day itself was reluctant to bear witness to the end of this grim chapter.

Malcolm Fairley arrived at Dunstable police station and was greeted by Detective Chief Superintendent Mark Talbot. A stern look addressed Fairley, Talbot took no pleasure in seeing the man he had chased for many months. As Fairley was led toward the building by Detective Sergeant Jake Miller and Detective Constable Tom Hughes, Talbot followed a few paces behind.

The tension was clear, a heavy, oppressive atmosphere filled with anticipation and anxiety. Talbot's chest heaved with each breath, a testament to the gruelling pursuit that had worn him down to the bone. His truncheon felt like an anchor, every step felt heavy.

Fairley's face showed a look of pure defiance. Even now, with his hands shackled behind his back and a drizzling rain soaking through his clothes, he wore a twisted smile. It was as if he found some perverse satisfaction in the spectacle of his own downfall. As the officers nudged him toward the building, his sneer seemed to mock not only them but the entire effort that had gone into capturing him.

"Keep him steady," Talbot barked to the two officers flanking Fairley. His voice was rough, edged with the strain of a long and bitter hunt. "I want him breathing when we get him inside."

Detective Sergeant Jake Miller drenched to the bone and his face as grey as the rain-drenched sky, approached Talbot. His eyes, though tired, remained sharp and focused. He was the epitome of fatigue and resolve, but even he couldn't hide the tremor of doubt in his voice. "Is that it, then? Is it really over?"

Talbot turned to Miller, his stern expression not faltering for a moment, despite the weight of the question hanging over him. Rain dripped from the brim of his hat, and for a brief second, he let out a sigh, deep and laced with uncertainty.

"Over?" Talbot echoed, his gaze fixed on Fairley, who was being ushered into the station. "Not yet. It's only over when we know why, and he's behind bars."

Miller nodded, his throat tight. It was supposed to feel like a victory - the end of an exhausting, relentless pursuit. But as the grim-faced detectives made their way into the station, the anticipated satisfaction was nowhere to be found. Malcolm Fairley, the monster they had dubbed The Fox, had been caught, but the damage he had done left a deep wound that no arrest could heal.

Inside Dunstable police station, the atmosphere was charged. Officers who had spent countless nights chasing leads and dead ends now looked at Fairley with a mixture of relief and disgust. His presence was an uncomfortable reminder of the terror he had wrought, and no one wanted to be too close to him.

Fairley was seated in a small, dimly lit interrogation room. His twisted smile had faded, replaced by a steely indifference as the cuffs were removed from his wrists and his wet jacket was peeled off. His hands, now free, twitched slightly, but there was no sign of panic or fear. He leaned back in the chair, his eyes scanning the room with the cool detachment of a man who believed he still had control.

Miller stood just outside the door, staring through the one-way glass at Fairley. Hughes joined him, shaking rain from his coat, his face a picture of exhaustion.

"He doesn't look worried," Hughes muttered.
"He's not," Miller replied. "Not yet at least. He still thinks he's got the upper hand."

Hughes' brows furrowed. "After everything? After what he did? He thinks we're the ones losing?"

Miller glanced sideways at his partner. "Men like him...they thrive on the game. It's not just the crime, Tom. It's the chase. He's been playing us for months, and now he's in here, he's still playing."

Hughes leaned against the wall, shaking his head. "I don't understand it. After all that...how can he still think there's something to win?"

Miller didn't answer immediately. He was too focused on Fairley, on the slight upturn of his mouth and the way his hands rested, unnervingly calm, on the table in front of him.

"We'll find out soon enough," Miller said. "We've got him in a box now."

Inside the interrogation room, Talbot sat across from Fairley, his face stony. A pile of case files sat to his right, documents full of evidence, testimonies, and crime scene photos that painted the picture of Malcolm Fairley's reign of terror. But it wasn't the paperwork that would break Fairley - it was the weight of truth, the relentless exposure of his cruelty that Talbot was prepared to unleash.

Fairley leaned forward slightly, his eyes locking on Talbot. "You look tired," he said with a casual smirk. "Was it hard catching me?"

Talbot didn't respond immediately. He simply stared at Fairley, his hands clasped tightly in front of him on the table.

"You've spent months terrorising innocent people," Talbot finally said, his voice cold and sharp. "Breaking into their homes. Stealing their lives, their safety. For what? For power? For fun?"

Fairley's smile widened. "It wasn't personal. Not really. They just...got in the way."

Talbot clenched his jaw, his anger barely contained. "They were families. Husbands and wives. Mothers and fathers. You left them broken."

Fairley's gaze didn't waver. "Like I said, it wasn't personal."

Miller and Hughes, still watching from behind the glass, exchanged glances. They could feel the unease mounting in the room, the delicate balance between Fairley's twisted calm and Talbot's growing fury.

"He's baiting him," Hughes whispered.

"Talbot knows what he's doing," Miller replied, though his own doubts were creeping in.

Inside, Talbot pushed the stack of files across the table toward Fairley, opening the first one. Photos of Fairley's victims stared up from the pages - blurred snapshots of faces contorted in fear, hands bound, eyes wide with terror, covered in bruises and blood. It was the raw evidence of his crimes, laid out in excruciating detail.

Fairley glanced at the photos, his expression unchanged. He leaned back in his chair, crossing his arms casually, as if he were above it all.

"You don't even care, do you?" Talbot asked, his voice low and full of disgust. "About the people whose lives you've destroyed. You don't care about anything."

Fairley's smirk returned. "Care?" he repeated. "I'm just very…good at what I do."

Talbot slammed his fist down on the table, the sound echoing through the small room. "You're nothing but a coward. A sick, pathetic coward who hides behind a mask. And now, we've got you. There's nowhere left to run."
Fairley didn't flinch. "Do you think this is a victory? You may have caught me, but you'll never understand."

"Understand what?" Talbot asked, his voice ice-cold.

"The thrill," Fairley said, leaning in, his voice dropping to a whisper. "Of being in control. Of knowing that when I walk into a room, everyone's life changes. I owned them, Talbot. I owned their fear."

Talbot stared at Fairley for a long, intense moment. But then, slowly, a hard, determined look crossed his face. "You don't own anything anymore. Not your freedom, not your control, not even your fear."

With that, Talbot stood and walked out of the room, leaving Fairley sitting there, alone, his smirk fading slightly. The door clicked shut behind him, and Talbot rejoined Miller and Hughes outside.

"Well?" Miller asked, his voice tense.

Talbot sighed, rubbing the back of his neck. "He thinks he's still in control, but that's the thing about men like him - they're only powerful when they're on the outside. In here, he's just another prisoner."

Hughes nodded slowly. "Do you think we'll ever understand why he did it? Why he hurt all those people?"

Talbot shook his head. "There's no real understanding it, Hughes. Men like Fairley - there's something broken inside them. Something we can't fix. All we can do is make sure they can't hurt anyone else."

Miller glanced through the glass at Fairley, who now sat in silence, his hands twitching slightly as he stared down at the table. "And what now?" he asked.

"Now," Talbot said, "we let him stew. He's got nowhere left to hide. Sooner or later, he'll crack. They always do."
As they stood there, the rain continued to tap against the windows, a steady, unrelenting rhythm. Outside, the storm raged on, but inside Dunstable police station, for the first time in months, there was a sense of finality.

Malcolm Fairley - the man who had haunted their every waking moment, the monster they had called The Fox - was no longer a menace to society. He was just a man, stripped of his power, trapped by his own arrogance.

The hunt was over. Now came the reckoning.

Later that day, Detective Chief Superintendent Mark Talbot stood behind the podium at the Dunstable police station, his heart pounding in his chest. Reporters jostled for position as they aimed their cameras and notepads toward him. The buzzing of conversations filled the space, a cacophony of voices blending together in an excited zing.

As he glanced down at the array of microphones positioned in front of him, Talbot felt a wave of pressure wash over him. It was a moment he had envisioned countless times during the relentless months of the manhunt for The Fox. He had imagined it would feel triumphant, a celebration of justice. Instead, a sense of sombre duty gripped him.

He cleared his throat, and the noise subsided, the room falling into a tense silence. Talbot straightened his back, adopting a stance that spoke of authority tempered with fatigue.

"Good afternoon, everyone. Thank you for being here," he began, his voice steady but firm. "I stand before you today to announce that the man responsible for a string of violent home invasions and assaults across Hertfordshire, Bedfordshire, Buckinghamshire and beyond has been apprehended. Malcolm Fairley, known to the public as The Fox, is now in police custody."

A flurry of cameras flashed, capturing the moment. Talbot felt a flash of irritation at the bright lights momentarily blinding him, but he pushed it aside. This was bigger than him; it was about the victims, the families whose lives had been shattered by Fairley's actions.

Talbot continued, "The arrest follows a meticulous investigation that has involved many dedicated officers from various departments. I want to take this moment to commend Detective Sergeant Jake Miller and Detective Constable Tom Hughes for their tireless efforts in bringing this case to a close."

He paused as the two officers, standing in the back, nodded slightly, their expressions a mix of exhaustion and relief.

"Malcolm Fairley has been charged with three counts of rape, two counts of indecent assault, three counts of aggravated burglary, five counts of burglary and also for the possession of a firearm."

"Malcolm Fairley has been a figure of fear for many in our communities. His criminal activities have left scars on countless individuals and families, and I assure you, the police force remains committed to seeking justice for every one of his victims." He held their gazes, the seriousness of his words resonating in the room.

"Fairley's capture was not without challenges. His ability to evade law enforcement for so long speaks to the tenacity with which he operated. However, through collaboration and perseverance, we were able to gather the evidence necessary to locate and apprehend him."

A reporter in the front row raised a hand, and Talbot gestured for her to speak. "Detective Chief Superintendent Talbot, can you provide any details about the circumstances of the arrest? Was it a violent confrontation?"

Talbot took a breath, noting the curiosity in her tone. "The arrest was conducted without incident. Fairley was taken into custody at his residence in Kentish Town after a thorough investigation into his whereabouts. I assure you, there was no threat to public safety at the time of his arrest."
Another hand shot up. "Can you tell us if Fairley has cooperated with police since his arrest? What do you expect will happen next?"

Talbot's brow furrowed slightly. He knew the media would want to dissect every detail, but he had to be cautious. "As of now, we are still in the early stages of our interrogation with Fairley. He has shown a certain level of cooperation, but we are prepared for a lengthy process. Our primary focus is to build a strong case against him and to ensure that the victims receive the justice they deserve."

A reporter shouted, "What can you say about the charges made against him, why aren't there more charges?"

Talbot nodded, acknowledging the urgency of the question. "Fairley faces multiple charges, including burglary, assault, and other related offenses. We will ensure that every crime he has committed is accounted for in the charges brought against him."

The questions came rapid-fire, each one probing deeper into the case and the man behind the mask of The Fox. Talbot felt a familiar weight settle on his shoulders, the responsibility of not just delivering news, but representing the countless lives affected by Fairley's actions.

"Are you concerned about Fairley's potential for a plea deal?" another reporter inquired, her voice sharp.

Talbot steeled himself. "That is something we will have to address as the case develops. I am more focused on ensuring that justice is served and that the victims' voices are heard throughout the legal process."

With each question, the atmosphere in the room shifted slightly. The reporters, initially buzzing with excitement, began to realise the complexity of the situation. The nuances of a criminal case, especially one as harrowing as this, were not lost on them.

Talbot continued, "I want to take a moment to acknowledge the victims and their families. Their courage in coming forward and sharing their stories has been instrumental in this investigation. It's important to remember that behind every statistic is a person, a life impacted by this man's actions."

A hushed silence fell over the room as Talbot's words sank in. He could see the cameras shifting, the reporters exchanging glances. The gravity of the situation was becoming intense.

"Going forward, I encourage anyone who has information or has been affected by Fairley's actions to reach out to the police. We are here to support you, and we will do everything in our power to ensure your safety and well-being."

As Talbot finished his statement, he took a moment to scan the room, his eyes resting on the faces in the crowd. Some looked sceptical, others hungry for more information, and a few appeared genuinely moved. He felt the weight of their expectations, the hopes and fears of a community that had lived under a blanket of fear for too long.

With a final nod, Talbot stepped back slightly from the podium. "Thank you for your time. I'll take a few more questions, but please understand that some details are still under investigation."

The room erupted once more into a frenzy of raised hands and shouted questions, each voice vying for his attention. He answered a few more inquiries, but his mind was already racing ahead, thinking about the next steps in the investigation and the task of helping the victims find closure.

As the press conference drew to a close, Talbot stepped away from the podium, wiping the sweat from his brow. He felt an overwhelming mix of relief and anxiety; they had caught Fairley, yes, but the battle was far from over.

Later that evening, in the quiet of his office, Talbot leaned back in his chair, staring at the framed photographs on the wall - moments from his career that now felt like a lifetime ago. The weight of the day settled heavily on him, and he rubbed his temples, trying to ease the stress that had built up over the previous few months.

The phone rang, breaking the silence. Talbot picked it up, his heart racing slightly, half-expecting it to be a reporter or a colleague needing something urgent. Instead, it was his wife, Claire.
"Mark," she said, her voice warm and familiar. "How did it go?"

"Exhausting," he admitted, sinking back into his chair. "But we caught him. The Fox is in custody."

"That's incredible news. I can't imagine how you must be feeling," she replied, a note of pride evident in her voice.

"It feels like a relief, but…it's complicated. There's still so much to do. The victims deserve to have their stories told, and I need to ensure we do right by them."

"I know you will," she said softly. "You always do. But don't forget to take care of yourself, too."

He chuckled lightly, despite the fatigue weighing him down. "I'll try, but it's hard to switch off when the job feels like it's never really done."

They talked for a few more minutes, the mundane details of their day grounding him, reminding him that life still existed outside the walls of the station. After hanging up, Talbot felt a flicker of warmth in his chest, a reminder of why he did this job - why he fought for justice every day. His Press Officer Katie McGee entered his office.

"Well, that went better than I expected. The press seemed satisfied. You handled their questions perfectly," sighed a relieved McGee.

Talbot nodded with a hint of a smile. "I've had plenty of practice. Although, it helps to have a good press officer steering the show." "Flattery noted. But seriously, this is a huge win. The Fox has been a thorn in our side for months. The media's been relentless, and now that he's in custody, they'll finally ease off…for a little while, at least."

Talbot rubbed his temples. "For a little while. I'll take any reprieve I can get, though I suspect they'll be back as soon as they catch a scent of the trial. Still, the team deserves the praise they're getting."

McGee agreed. "This case was…personal for a lot of people. It's not every day we get to tell a story with a satisfying end."

Talbot nodded thoughtfully. "True. Capturing him took everything we had and then some. If it weren't for you keeping the press at bay and managing the narrative, we'd have been hounded at every turn."

McGee smiled softly. "All part of the job. And with someone like The Fox, we had to be careful. The public pressure was intense, but I think today helped show people how hard everyone worked."

"Let's hope it reminds them we're here to protect, even when it's messy and…slow-going. And Katie - thanks for everything. It wouldn't have been this smooth without you," replied a very grateful Talbot.

McGee nodded feeling touched. "Just doing my part. Now, let's enjoy the peace while it lasts."

The following days were a whirlwind of activity. Talbot's team worked tirelessly, sorting through evidence and gathering testimonies from the victims.

Talbot spent countless hours in the interrogation room, meticulously peeling back the layers of Fairley's defences. Each session revealed snippets of his twisted mindset.

Talbot made a silent vow to the victims: he would seek the truth, no matter where it led. The stakes had never been higher, and as he prepared to delve deeper into the twisted world of Malcolm Fairley, he felt the weight of their expectations settle firmly on his shoulders once again.

This was not just about catching a criminal; it was about unearthing the darkness that had haunted his community for too long. And he would see it through.

Part Five: The Aftermath

Chapter 31

On the twelfth of February 1985, Malcolm Fairley went on trial at St Albans Crown Court.

On day one of the trial, the courtroom was packed to the rafters. Reporters jostled for space in the gallery, their cameras trained on the dock where Malcolm Fairley - The Fox - sat like a stone statue. He wore a dark suit, his hands resting casually on the table in front of him, and his expression was unreadable. The trial of the decade had begun, and the room was charged with anticipation.

Detective Chief Superintendent Mark Talbot sat behind the prosecution's table, his eyes fixed on Fairley. Even in the controlled environment of the court, Talbot could feel the man's unsettling presence. It was as if a wild animal had been trapped in a cage, dangerous and unpredictable. Talbots face was lined with exhaustion, but his eye was steady. For months, he had chased this monster through fields, woods, and darkened streets. Now, he wanted to see justice served.

Judge Mary Crawley, a formidable woman with silver hair pulled into a severe bun, banged her gavel. "Order in the court," she commanded, her voice slicing through the murmurs.

"Ladies and gentlemen of the court, today we gather in pursuit of justice - justice for a summer dominated by violence, a community haunted by acts of terror, and a truth that lies tangled in shadows. At the heart of this trial stands a figure who has captivated and divided us, a man known as The Fox. A name that evokes cunning and survival, but also secrecy and suspicion. Yet we must remind ourselves that this courtroom is not the forest, and the laws we uphold demand evidence, reason, and fairness, not instinct or conjecture.

The defendant, Mr Malcolm Fairley, is entitled to the presumption of innocence. It is the solemn duty of the prosecution to prove their case beyond reasonable doubt. Likewise, the defence is here to ensure every detail is explored, every doubt magnified, so that justice may be served.

This case will ask us to confront uncomfortable truths, to look beyond appearances, and to weigh the facts without prejudice. The eyes of the country may be upon us, but our focus remains fixed on the evidence and the law.

This trial, like all trials, is not a spectacle nor a stage for personal agendas. It is a solemn process, guided by law and respect for justice. As we proceed, I will not tolerate interruptions, theatrics, or attempts to derail the pursuit of truth.

To the jury, your role is one of utmost importance. You are the impartial finders of fact, tasked with setting aside personal biases, preconceived notions, or sensational stories that may have reached you outside these walls. You will hear evidence - some of it straightforward, some of it complex, some of it upsetting, and it is your responsibility to weigh it carefully and decide what is credible.

To the prosecution, you have the burden of proving your case. Assertions alone will not suffice; you must present evidence that leaves no reasonable doubt. To the defence, your task is equally vital: to hold the prosecution to that standard and to advocate for your client with integrity and clarity.

This case, though extraordinary in its implications, is no different from any other in its core purpose - to seek justice, not vengeance.

Remember that this is not a trial of character, but of actions, facts, and law.

With these principles clear, we shall now proceed. Prosecution, you may make your opening statement."

And with that, the lead prosecutor, Mrs Harriet Whitman, rose with a calm authority.

"Ladies and gentlemen of the jury, today we begin a trial concerning a series of heinous and calculated crimes. The defendant, Mr Malcolm Fairley, stands accused of the following charges:

Five counts of burglary.

Three counts of aggravated burglary.

Three counts of rape.

Two counts of indecent assault.

One count of possession of a firearm with intent to cause fear of violence.

These charges are not mere allegations but are supported by compelling evidence, which I will now outline.

Firstly, let us consider the unique connection to Malcolm Fairley's vehicle. A key piece of evidence is a distinctive speck of yellow paint identified as seven-nine-one-nine Harvest Yellow. This paint was used exclusively on Austin Allegro cars, of which only fifteen hundred were manufactured in this country. It is an irrefutable fact that Malcolm Fairley owned one of these vehicles.

At a wooded area in Brampton-en-le-Morthen, connected to all the crimes, a branch bore traces of this same paint at the precise height of a scratch found on the defendant's car. This is not coincidence; it is direct evidence tying him to the scene.

In addition, we found at the same crime scene, a pair of gloves, a shotgun, a semen-stained bedsheet, all which link to many crimes committed by the same person, and some of which bear Malcolm Fairley's DNA.

Witnesses to these terrible crimes have provided a clear and consistent description of the perpetrator - a man with a northern accent, who was approximately five feet nine to five feet ten inches tall. He had brown curly hair and was of slim build. During many of his attacks, the assailant wielded a shotgun, holding it in a way that suggested he was his left-handed. During other attacks, he held a knife in his left hand.

Malcolm Fairley has the same appearance and is left-handed.

During one attack, the victim bit the attacker's hand, drawing blood. Forensic analysis confirmed the blood was type O, matching Malcolm Fairley's blood group. Upon his arrest, Fairley bore a scar on his hand, consistent with a bite mark.

In another incident, the victim fought back, scratching the attacker's neck. When Fairley was apprehended, he had a scar on his neck that aligned with the victim's testimony.

Forensic analysis determined that a flathead screwdriver was used to break into the victims' homes. Upon Malcolm Fairley's arrest, officers recovered an identical tool from his car, matching the forensic evidence.

A pair of overalls with one leg missing was also found in Fairley's vehicle. One victim identified the fabric as identical to the material of the mask worn by "The Fox" during the attack.

Finally, and perhaps most damning of all, Malcolm Fairley confessed to his crimes during his initial arrest. While the defence may attempt to discredit this confession, we will demonstrate its reliability and truthfulness.

We anticipate that the defence may argue it was mistaken identity – suggesting that someone else committed these crimes and pointing to gaps in the timeline or evidence. Contamination or mishandling of evidence – questioning the integrity of forensic methods used to identify his DNA or the specks of paint. Coercion in obtaining the confession – claiming that Malcolm Fairley's confession was made under duress or was involuntary.

Ladies and gentlemen, we will demonstrate beyond a reasonable doubt that these arguments hold no weight against the overwhelming body of evidence. Malcolm Fairley is the perpetrator of these vile crimes, and justice demands a verdict of guilty.

The Crown calls its first witness, Mrs Lizzie Chambers."

A hush fell over the courtroom as Lizzie Chambers took the stand. She clutched a handkerchief as if it were a lifeline. She sat down, and the bailiff swore her in. The weight of what she was about to say settled over the room like a fog.

"Mrs Chambers," Whitman began, her voice gentle but clear, "can you tell the court what happened on the night of sixteenth of April 1984?"

Lizzie Chambers nodded, her eyes darting to Fairley for a split second before quickly looking away. "It was late," she said, her voice trembling. "My husband and I were asleep. I - I heard something downstairs. A creak on the floorboards. I thought it was just the house settling, but then...then I saw him."

"Who did you see, Mrs Chambers?"

Her eyes filled with tears. "Him," she said, her voice breaking. "The man they call The Fox."

The gallery erupted in murmurs. Judge Crawley rapped her gavel sharply. "Order!"

Lizzie Chambers continued, her voice gaining strength despite her fear. "He was wearing a mask. All in black. He...he had a knife, in his left-hand."

"And what did he do then?" Whitman asked, leaning in slightly, her eyes steady on Lizzie Chambers.

Lizzie Chambers' breath hitched. "He told us to be quiet, to not make a sound. He...he wanted us to know he could do anything, that no one would come to help us. I - I thought we were going to die."

Across the room, Fairley watched her with an eerie calm. There wasn't a flicker of emotion on his face, not even a twitch. Talbot stared at him, his blood simmering. This was the man who had stolen sleep and safety from countless families. And now, with the country watching, he didn't even have the decency to flinch.

"And can you please describe the appearance of the person who broke into your home," asked Whitman.

"Well, he looked like him, the man seated over there, Malcolm Fairley. He was the same height, same build, same curly brown hair sticking out of his mask. And his voice. It was a Geordie accent," replied Lizzie Chambers, while wiping away tears from her eyes.

Whitman guided Lizzie Chambers through the rest of her testimony, detailing the terror, the threats, and the psychological games Fairley had played. Each word tightened the grip of horror in the courtroom. Faces turned pale; eyes were wide. When Lizzie Chambers was finally excused, she left the stand as if she'd been carrying a great weight, her shoulders sagging with exhaustion.

One by one, the survivors took the stand: Markus Longman - the man who was beaten to a pulp, Clare and Nigel – the brother and sister who were forced to grope one another, Michael and Louise Stamp – the elderly couple who were sexually assaulted. Each testimony painted a clearer picture of the violence Fairley had inflicted, the lives he had shattered.

The courtroom grew colder with every word, but Fairley remained unyielding. His eyes were flat, his lips a thin line, his demeanour almost bored. When the court broke for lunch, Talbot could hardly eat. He leaned against the railing outside, the bitter wind whipping around him.

"He doesn't care," Detective Sergeant Sarah Kendrick said, coming to stand beside him. "Not a flicker of remorse. It's like he's proud of it all."

"That's because he is," Talbot replied. "To him, this is all a game. And he thinks he's still winning."

The afternoon session saw a harrowing procession of victims take the stand, their numbers overwhelming. Testimonies filled the courtroom with raw emotion, bringing tears to many in the gallery. The accounts painted a chilling picture of senseless violence, lingering nightmares, and the enduring trauma inflicted by The Fox. One by one, these courageous individuals recounted how Malcolm Fairley had broken into their homes and shattered their lives. They all confirmed that Fairley's accent and appearance perfectly matched those of The Fox.

Throughout, Fairley sat unmoving, his expression cold and devoid of emotion.

As Judge Mary Crawley adjourned for the day, the weight of the proceedings was palpable. Whitman and her team exchanged weary glances, releasing deep breaths of strain. They knew this was just the beginning - an uphill battle lay ahead to ensure Fairley would never harm another soul again.

Day two began, with the prosecution calling forensic experts to the stand.

The courtroom was tense as Dr Evelyn Carter, a seasoned forensic expert, adjusted her glasses and leaned into the microphone. The lead prosecutor, Harriet Whitman, paced deliberately.

"Dr Carter," she began, "is it your professional opinion that the yellow paint particles found embedded on a branch near the crime scene in Brampton-en-le-Morthen match the paint on Mr Malcolm Fairley's car?"

"Yes," Dr Carter replied, her voice steady. "The chemical composition and shade are consistent with the factory-standard paint used on Mr Fairley's vehicle."

Whitman nodded. "And the scratch on his car - would you say it aligns with the height and width of that very branch?"

Dr Carter hesitated for a moment, choosing her words carefully. "The dimensions are consistent, yes. The scratch appears to have been caused by a similar object, and the height aligns with the branch recovered from the scene."

The defence counsel, Ms Clara Lane, rose swiftly, her tone sharp.

"Dr Carter, would you agree that paint transfer could occur in many situations? For example, if Mr Fairley's car had been parked near a wooded area, could the branch have fallen naturally?"

Dr Carter frowned slightly. "It is possible for paint transfer to occur in other circumstances, but-"

Lane interrupted. "And regarding the height of the scratch, could it not have been caused by something else? A different branch, or even vandalism?"

Dr Carter glanced toward the jury. "While those scenarios are possible, the evidence strongly suggests-"

"Suggests, Dr Carter?" Lane pressed. "Not proves?"

The courtroom murmured as Lane sat down, leaving an air of doubt lingering over the forensic testimony.

Whitman leaned on the witness stand, a quiet confidence in her tone. "Dr Carter let's address the sequence of events. The paint transfer on the branch - does its placement suggest that it was stationary when struck by the vehicle or when it was moving?"

Dr Carter clasped her hands in her lap. "Yes, the pattern of transfer and the indentation on the bark indicate the vehicle made contact with the branch while it was reversing."

"And does this match the reported location of the branch found near the scene of the attack?" Whitman asked, her gaze fixed on the jury.

Dr Carter nodded. "Yes. The branch was positioned approximately forty-five inches above ground level, which is consistent with the height of the scratch on the rear of Mr Fairley's car."
Lane, stood abruptly, a sly smile creeping onto her face. "Dr Carter, forgive me, but isn't it true that branches of that size and shape could be found in almost any wooded area within the area in question?"

Dr Carter tilted her head slightly. "Branches of a similar size could exist, but the paint transfer and its specific location are what make this one relevant."

Lane stepped closer to the jury box, her voice dropping into a conversational tone. "Ah, but relevance isn't proof, is it? A fallen branch - perhaps carried by the wind - could have made contact with the vehicle. Or even a different car entirely might have brushed against it before."

Whitman interjected. "Your Honour, the evidence presented by Dr Carter is consistent with-"

Lane raised her hand. "Let the witness answer, please."

Dr Carter sighed, her professionalism intact. "Yes, theoretically, there could be alternative explanations, but the totality of evidence, including the specific chemical composition of the paint, strongly implicates Mr Fairley's vehicle."

Lane seized on the opening. "So, you admit there's room for doubt. And in the absence of direct evidence - like a witness who saw Mr Fairley at the scene, or his car strike the branch - this remains just an interpretation, doesn't it?"

Dr Carter hesitated, glancing at the jury. "That is for the court to decide."

A murmur rippled through the courtroom, the tension between prosecution and defence evident as Lane returned to her seat, her expression triumphant.

The room seemed to hold its breath as Whitman resumed her questioning. "Dr Carter, earlier you mentioned that the branch was found embedded with paint transfer. Were you able to determine the precise force required to cause such an imprint?"

Dr Carter adjusted her glasses, her calm demeanour unshaken. "Yes. Based on the analysis, the force was consistent with a vehicle travelling at a slow speed - approximately five to ten miles per hour."

"Interesting," Whitman said, her voice cool and deliberate. "And if this force occurred, would there not also be damage to the branch? Perhaps broken or splintered wood?"

Dr Carter straightened. "The branch was partially splintered, yes. But the paint was found only on the intact portion, which indicates direct contact without full breakage."

Lane stood up. "But you cannot definitively say the vehicle in question was Mr Fairley's, can you? After all, paint transfer could occur from other vehicles with similar colours and chemical compositions."

Whitman interrupted; her frustration barely concealed. "Objection, Your Honour. The evidence ties the defendant's vehicle to the scene."

The judge raised a hand. "Sustained. Please keep your argument focused, Ms Lane."
She smiled, unbothered. "Of course, Your Honour," she replied as she sat back down.

"Dr Carter, one last question," commenced Whitman. "Would you say the condition of the branch could have been influenced by weather, perhaps strong winds or heavy rainfall, prior to the alleged contact?"

Dr Carter's composure wavered for the first time. "Weather can alter physical evidence, yes. But in this case, it was summer, there were no strong winds or heavy rainfall that day-"

Before she could finish, Lane cut in, her voice rising. "So, we're not only dealing with uncertainties about the vehicle but also possible environmental interference! Members of the jury, is this the kind of evidence you'd bet a man's life on?"

A sudden voice broke through the tension. "I'd like to hear her finish that thought." It was Judge Crawley, her tone sharp, silencing the defence.

Dr Carter inhaled deeply. "What I was going to say is that while weather can influence evidence, the timeline and specific conditions of this case make it highly unlikely that wind or rain caused the branch to break. The alignment is simply too precise."
Whitman seized the moment, stepping forward. "Thank you, Dr Carter. Your expert analysis has clarified the facts."

But Lane wasn't done. Leaning back in her chair, she smirked. "Clarified? Or muddied? I'll leave that for the jury to decide."

The courtroom buzzed with whispered speculation as Judge Crawley banged her gavel, calling for order. "The jury will disregard the speculative tone of the counsel's remarks," she said, her voice commanding. "This court will base its judgement on evidence, not conjecture."

Dr Carter exhaled quietly and returned to her seat, her testimony complete. Whitman and Lane exchanged glances - both knowing the battle for credibility was far from over.

The courtroom was silent as Dr Rachel Morgan, a forensic scientist from the same team as Dr Evelyn Carter, stepped up to the witness stand. She adjusted her jacket, her sharp eyes scanning the room as she prepared to testify. The prosecution lead, Harriet Whitman was the first to approach.

"Dr Morgan," Whitman began, holding up two clear evidence bags for the jury to see. "Can you confirm the items in these bags?"

"Yes," Dr Morgan said, her voice steady. "The first is a leather glove found in a field near the crime scene in Brampton-en-le-Morthen. The second is a matching glove discovered buried in a wooded area nearby."

Whitman nodded, pacing slightly. "You conducted a forensic examination of these items, correct?"

"That's correct," Dr Morgan replied. "We identified traces of rabbit fur lining inside both gloves. The fibres are consistent with rabbit fur found at several crime scenes linked to The Fox."

"Could you explain how this fur matches?" Whitman pressed.

Dr Morgan leaned forward slightly. "Using microscopic analysis and DNA testing, we confirmed the rabbit fur lining in the gloves shares identical characteristics - both structurally and genetically - with fur found on the upholstery and carpets of several victims' homes. This strongly suggests the gloves were present at those locations."

Whitman smiled faintly, turning to the jury. "In other words, Dr Morgan, these gloves are not only linked to the crime scenes - but they're also linked to each other?"

"Yes," Dr Morgan replied firmly.

The defence counsel, Clara Lane, stood abruptly. "Objection, Your Honour! The prosecution is leading the witness."

The judge waved her off. "Sustained. Proceed."

"No further questions at this time, Your Honour," replied Whitman. Lane approached, her heels clicking against the floor, her expression sharp. "Dr Morgan, you mentioned DNA testing. Are you suggesting that the presence of rabbit fur definitively links these gloves to Mr Fairley?"

Dr Morgan held her ground. "I'm suggesting that the evidence strongly supports a connection."

Lane smirked. "Strongly supports? Or implies? Rabbit fur is not exactly a rare material in the countryside, is it?"

"No, but the specific genetic markers in this fur are an uncommon match," Dr Morgan countered.

Lane seized the point. "And yet, no DNA from Mr Fairley was found on either glove, correct?"

"That's correct," Dr Morgan admitted, though her voice remained steady.

Lane turned to the jury, her voice tinged with mockery. "So, we're supposed to believe these gloves - lacking a single shred of DNA evidence tying them to my client - are somehow crucial to this case? Or could it be that they're just gloves discarded by someone else entirely?"

Dr Morgan opened her mouth to respond, but Lane cut her off, whirling back to the jury. "The rabbit fur might tell a story, but it's far from proof of guilt."

Whitman, unfazed, rose to make a counter point. "Dr Morgan, isn't it true that the buried glove had soil residue consistent with the same type found embedded in boots we recovered from Mr Fairley's home?"

Dr Morgan nodded. "Yes, that is correct."

Lane's face darkened, and a ripple of tension filled the courtroom. "Can you tell us about the condition it was in when recovered?"

Dr Morgan adjusted her seat and leaned into the microphone. "The glove was buried approximately eight inches below the surface. Despite its condition, forensic analysis revealed traces of the same rabbit fur lining as the glove found in the field. Additionally, the exterior contained faint but detectable fragments of the same soil composition present on the soles of Mr Fairley's boots."

"And this soil composition," Whitman continued, "was it unique to the area where the glove was buried?"

Dr Morgan nodded. "Yes. The soil contained a specific mix of chalk and clay minerals found only in that field and a handful of nearby locations."

Whitman turned to the jury. "So, not only do we have matching gloves with the same rare rabbit fur, but one of them was buried in a location that can be tied to the defendant's footwear." She paused for effect. "In your expert opinion, Dr Morgan, is it reasonable to conclude that these gloves were handled by Mr Fairley?"

Before Dr Morgan could answer, Lane was on her feet. "Objection, Your Honour! The question calls for speculation."

The judge raised an eyebrow. "Sustained. Rephrase your question."

Whitman nodded. "Dr Morgan, does the evidence you've presented suggest a connection between Mr Fairley and the gloves?"

"Yes," Dr Morgan replied firmly. "The combination of soil, fur, and location strongly supports that conclusion."

Lane was already rising, her voice sharp. "Strongly supports? Dr Morgan, isn't it true that no fingerprints, DNA, or other direct identifiers were found on the gloves?"

"That's correct," Dr Morgan admitted. "The gloves were slightly degraded, likely due to exposure to the elements and burial."
"And yet," Lane said, pacing before the jury, "we're expected to believe these gloves are crucial evidence in this case? Gloves that could have been discarded by anyone, at any time?"

Dr Morgan's eyes narrowed slightly. "The timeline of the burial, based on soil analysis, places the second glove at that location and is consistent with the timeline of the crimes."

Lane raised a hand dramatically. "But without DNA or fingerprints, you cannot definitively tie them to my client, can you?"

"No, we cannot," Morgan admitted, her tone calm but firm.

Lane turned to the jury with a triumphant smile. "Exactly. This is all conjecture, not proof. And in a case like this, where a man's life is on the line, conjecture simply isn't good enough."

The courtroom murmured softly, the sound of uncertainty filling the air.

Whitman, unwilling to let the point drop, stepped forward again. "Dr Morgan, one final question. Can you again explain the significance of the rabbit fur found in these gloves?"

Morgan straightened. "The rabbit fur is a unique link. It was found at multiple crime scenes - places where The Fox entered homes undetected. The fact that this fur is present in both gloves suggests that they were used repeatedly by the same individual, and the soil ties one glove to the area where Mr Fairley's boots once trod the ground."

Whitman turned to the jury. "Ladies and gentlemen, while the defence may argue otherwise, the evidence doesn't lie. These gloves were tools of a predator - and every piece of evidence ties them closer to the defendant."

Lane shook her head, but the seed of doubt had been planted. Dr Morgan stepped down from the witness stand. Judge Crawley called a break for lunch.

The courtroom felt stifling as Dr Morgan returned to the witness stand. The prosecutor, Harriet Whitman, approached her with a measured stride, holding an evidence bag containing a sheet of fabric.

"Dr Morgan," Whitman began, her voice steady and authoritative, "let's address the stained sheet recovered from the burial site in Brampton-en-le-Morthen. Can you describe what your analysis revealed?"

Dr Morgan cleared her throat. "The sheet was heavily soiled, but forensic testing confirmed the presence of semen stains. Further DNA analysis determined that the semen matched the DNA profile of the defendant, Malcolm Fairley."

Whitman nodded, her gaze sweeping over the jury. "How certain is this match?"

Dr Morgan replied confidently, "The DNA match probability is greater than one in a billion. There is no reasonable doubt that the semen came from Mr Fairley."

Whitman continued, her voice gaining intensity. "And was this sheet connected to any of the crime scenes?"

"Yes," Morgan said. "The size of the sheet and the fibres were consistent with a bedsheet found at the victim's home in Brampton-en-le-Morthen, with a hole cut out of it."

The jury exchanged glances, the weight of the evidence clearly sinking in.

The defence counsel, Clara Lane, rose, her tone piercing. "Dr Morgan, let's talk about contamination. This sheet was buried in the ground, exposed to soil, moisture, and who knows what else. Isn't it possible that external factors could have compromised the DNA results?"

Dr Morgan remained composed. "Contamination is always a consideration, but the DNA profile extracted was clear and uncontaminated. The soil or other environmental factors did not affect the validity of the match."

Lane smirked. "So you say. But were there any other DNA profiles found on the sheet? Perhaps from third parties?"

Morgan hesitated briefly. "No, only Mr Fairley's DNA was present in the semen stains."

Lane seized the moment. "Only his? Curious, isn't it? A single sheet supposedly linked to a crime and the home of two people, yet we're left with just one DNA profile. Couldn't this sheet have been planted to incriminate my client?"

Dr Morgan frowned. "There is no evidence to suggest the sheet was planted."

Lane leaned closer to the jury, her voice laced with scepticism. "No evidence. That seems to be the recurring theme here, doesn't it? A buried glove, a shotgun, and now a sheet - no witnesses, no direct connection to the crimes, just circumstantial evidence tying my client to this so-called burial site."

Whitman stood abruptly. "Objection, Your Honour! The defence is editorialising."

Judge Crawley banged the gavel. "Sustained. Ms Lane, stick to questioning."

Lane shot a glance at Whitman, then turned back to Dr Morgan. "One final question. Can you definitively place this sheet at a crime scene prior to its burial?"

Dr Morgan's expression remained firm. "The fibres link it to a crime scene in Brampton-en-le-Morthen, and the DNA evidence ties it to Mr Fairley. That is the extent of the forensic findings." Lane smiled thinly. "Thank you for your carefully worded response."

The courtroom buzzed with hushed whispers as Judge Crawley banged the gavel once more. "Court will resume after a short recess," she declared, but the weight of the testimony lingered as everyone left their seats, the implications of the evidence impossible to ignore.

The atmosphere in the courtroom was electric as Johnson Lamble, a forensics firearms scientist, took the witness stand. He looked unflinching under the scrutiny of the defence counsel, Clara Lane. Seated nearby, Ashton Hartwig, the key witness whose fingers were mutilated in an attack, awaited his turn.

Lane paced before the witness, holding an evidence bag containing a shotgun. "Mr Lamble, this shotgun was recovered buried near a crime scene, correct?"

"Yes," Lamble replied. "It was found alongside the glove and the semen-stained sheet in Brampton-en-le-Morthen."

Lane nodded. "And Mr Lamble, you've examined this shotgun extensively. Are you absolutely certain it's the same weapon used in the attack on a Mr Ashton Hartwig?"

Lamble adjusted his glasses. "Yes. The markings on the spent shell recovered from Mr Hartwig's property match the firing pin and breech markings unique to this shotgun. There is no doubt."

Lane raised her eyebrows. "No doubt, you say. Yet this gun was buried, exposed to elements that could degrade evidence. Isn't it possible the markings were compromised?"

Lamble shook his head. "The markings are etched into the metal by the firing mechanism. Environmental exposure would not alter them in any significant way."

"What about fingerprints or DNA? Was there any evidence tying my client, Malcolm Fairley, to the shotgun directly?"

Lamble kept his voice steady. "No fingerprints were recovered, but DNA consistent with Mr Fairley's was found on the trigger guard. It's likely the burial process and environmental conditions degraded other potential evidence."

Lane smirked, turning to the jury. "Convenient, isn't it? A gun buried just long enough to erase crucial evidence but still somehow ties itself to my client."

Lead prosecutor Harriet Whitman stood abruptly. "Objection, Your Honour. The defence is speculating."

"Sustained," Judge Crawley said sternly.

Whitman approached the stand. "Mr Lamble, let's clarify. You're saying the unique markings on this shotgun and the shell found at the crime scene are a perfect match?"

"Yes," he affirmed. "This is the gun used in the shooting."

"Mr Lamble, did you find any forensic evidence specifically tying this weapon to the crime scene other than the spent shell?" asked Whitman.

Lamble nodded. "Traces of wood and fabric consistent with debris from Mr Hartwig's home were found in the barrel and stock of the gun."

Whitman offered half a smile. "No further questions, Your Honour." Next up in the witness stand was Ashton Hartwig.

Whitman turned toward Ashton Hartwig. "Mr Hartwig, please tell the court about the night you were attacked."

Hartwig, his voice steady but emotional, recounted the events. "It was dark. The man — The Fox - slipped into the house unnoticed. He had the shotgun. When I tried to fight him off, he aimed it at my hand and pulled the trigger." He lifted his hand, to show his mutilated fingers.

Whitman gestured toward the shotgun presented as evidence. "Mr Hartwig, is this the weapon he used?"

Hartwig's eyes narrowed as he looked at the gun. "Yes. I'll never forget it. That's the shotgun."

Lane rose, her voice cutting through the heavy silence. "Mr Hartwig, it was dark, wasn't it? And you were under extreme duress. Are you absolutely certain this is the same weapon?" Hartwig didn't waver. "I know what I saw. That's the gun."

"And Mr Hartwig, please describe the characteristics of the person who attacked you in your home," asked Whitman.

"Well, despite the limited light, I would say he was the same height as me, five foot ten. He was slim. He spoke with a Geordie accent. And he was holding the gun left-handed. That's all I can remember really," replied Hartwig. Tears streaming down his face.

Whitman, sensing the defence was on her heels, made her final statement. "Thank you, Mr Hartwig. Ladies and gentlemen of the jury, you've heard it from multiple sources. The forensic evidence, the firearms analysis, and the eyewitness testimony all confirm one thing: this shotgun is not just a weapon. It's a tool of terror, wielded by the man seated right there." She pointed directly at Malcolm Fairley, who stared blankly ahead.

The judge's gavel struck once. "Court is adjourned until tomorrow."

As the room emptied, the air was thick with the certainty of guilt, leaving only the question of how much longer the defence could hold on.

"Talbot," Whitman said as she packed up her notes, "we've got him, but it's going to be a fight to make sure it sticks."

"He won't win," Talbot replied, his voice steady and his eyes hard as steel. "Not this time."

The courtroom emptied slowly, the atmosphere still full of gloom from what had been revealed. As Fairley was escorted out in handcuffs, his eyes locked on Talbot's. That twisted grin returned. "See you tomorrow, detective," he called out, his voice taunting, echoing off the walls.

Talbot didn't flinch. "Yeah, you will," he muttered under his breath. "And you'll see me every damn day until you rot in that cell."

He turned away, the faces of the victims fresh in his mind. Justice wasn't just about the trial; it was about making sure the nightmares ended for good. Talbot and Whitman were prepared to see it through to the bitter end.

Day three commenced. It was the day everyone had been anticipating. Malcolm Fairley, the man accused of countless heinous crimes, took the witness stand.

As Judge Mary Crawley struck her gavel to open proceedings, the air in the courtroom crackled with tension.

Fairley, dressed in a stark black suit, sat motionless - his face expressionless, his eyes unblinking, betraying no hint of emotion. Leading the charge for the prosecution, Harriet Whitman rose to begin her questioning.

"Mr Fairley," Whitman began, her tone steady but pointed. "Let's revisit your whereabouts on the night of sixteenth of April 1984. You stated you were at home. Is that correct?"

"Yes, that's correct," Fairley replied, his voice measured.

"And you were alone?" Whitman pressed.

"I was in my bedroom. My brother was in his," he responded calmly.

"So, your brother can confirm you were home?" she asked.

"That's right," Fairley replied, maintaining his composure.

Whitman leaned forward slightly, her voice sharpening. "Interesting, because when your brother was interviewed by police, he stated you often went missing at night - a behaviour he considered routine since your teenage years."

Fairley shifted slightly but said nothing, and before he could respond, Whitman continued. "In fact, he told investigators that on the sixteenth of April 1984, you weren't home all day. He distinctly recalled hearing you return in the early hours of April seventeenth."

Fairley wiped a bead of sweat from his forehead, his confidence wavering. "I'm sorry, I don't recall being out that day," he muttered.

Whitman didn't miss a beat. "So, being out all day and night wasn't unusual for you?"

Fairley hesitated before answering, "No, not at all. I like to keep to myself."

Whitman thanked Fairley and returned to her seat.

The defence counsel, Clara Lane, stood with a measured calm. She adjusted her glasses and walked toward the witness stand, her demeanour soft yet purposeful.

"Mr Fairley," Lane began, her tone warm, "you've told the court you like to keep to yourself. Could you elaborate on that? What do you enjoy doing in your alone time?"

Fairley nodded, visibly relaxing. "I enjoy the quiet. I like walking, especially at night. It's peaceful - no one around, just me and the outdoors."
Lane smiled slightly. "That sounds quite tranquil. What do you do during these walks?"

Fairley leaned forward a bit, his voice gaining some animation. "Sometimes I just stroll, clear my head. Other times I stop to look at the stars. I've always been fascinated by the night sky. It's...calming."

"So, to clarify, these nighttime walks aren't unusual for you?" Lane asked.

"Not at all," Fairley replied. "I've been doing them for years. It's how I unwind."

Lane nodded. "And you mentioned earlier that your brother might not always know when you're out. Is that because these walks are a personal escape for you?"

"Exactly," Fairley said. "I don't always announce when I go out. Sometimes it's just a spur-of-the-moment thing."

Lane moved a step closer. "On the sixteenth of April 1984, you told the prosecution you don't recall being out. Could it be that you went on one of your nighttime walks and simply forgot?"

Fairley considered this, then nodded. "It's possible. I don't keep track of every walk I take. It's not something I think much about - it's just part of my routine."

"During these walks, do you often interact with people?" Lane asked.

"No," Fairley said firmly. "That's the whole point. I like the quiet. It's just me, the fresh air, and the stars."

Lane paused, letting his words settle with the jury before continuing. "Now, the prosecution has suggested that being out late is suspicious. Do you find it unusual to enjoy solitude and nighttime walks?"

"Not at all," Fairley replied confidently. "It's when I feel most at peace. Some people like the bustle of the day; I prefer the stillness of the night."

Lane smiled gently. "Thank you, Mr Fairley."

She turned back to the jury, her voice steady. "Let the record show that Mr Fairley's nighttime habits are neither unusual nor incriminating. He is simply a man who finds solace in solitude and the beauty of the night sky - a far cry from the villain the prosecution paints him to be."

She returned to her seat, her calm confidence echoing through the courtroom.

Whitman stood up, holding an evidence bag containing a screwdriver. Her tone was calm but deliberate. She leaned forward, her gaze fixed on Fairley. "Mr Fairley let's discuss a screwdriver recovered from your property. Forensic analysis confirms it matches tool marks left at multiple break-ins. Do you recognise this tool?"

Fairley glanced at the evidence bag, his expression unreadable. "Yeah, it looks like one from my toolbox."

"So, you admit this screwdriver is yours?" asked Whitman.

"I believe it is," he said carefully. "But I've lent my tools out before. It wouldn't be unusual if I have lent this one out."

Whitman's eyes narrowed. "You've lent tools out before. Do you recall lending this specific screwdriver to anyone?"

"No," Fairley replied, shifting in his seat. "Not specifically. But I've lent plenty of tools over the years. It could have been one of them."

Whitman's voice sharpened. "Are you suggesting that someone borrowed this screwdriver, used it in multiple break-ins, and then quietly returned it to your property without your knowledge?"

Fairley paused, wiping at the sweat forming on his brow. "I'm saying it's possible. I wouldn't know if someone did that."

Whitman let the silence hang for a moment, her eyes never leaving him. "Possible? Or convenient? Let's get specific, Mr Fairley. Tool marks left on the Chambers back door was an exact match to this screwdriver. Are you denying using that tool at their property?"

"I've never been to the Chambers' property," Fairley said quickly, his tone defensive. "I don't know how those marks got there."

Whitman's voice rose slightly, pressing the point. "So, you've never been there, yet your screwdriver left tool marks consistent with forced entry. How do you explain that?"

Fairley wiped his forehead again, his voice faltering. "I can't explain it. I've lent my tools to others - maybe someone else used it."

Whitman leaned closer, her tone cold and deliberate. "This isn't about one break-in, Mr Fairley. This screwdriver has been forensically linked to multiple crime scenes. At each one, the tool marks match perfectly. Are you asking this court to believe that all these crimes were committed by someone else using your tool without your knowledge, over a period of six months?"

Fairley's jaw tightened. "I don't know what else to tell you. I didn't do it. I can't control what people do with my tools."

Whitman straightened, her eyes glinting with satisfaction. "No further questions for now, Your Honour."
She returned to her seat, leaving the courtroom in a tense, uneasy silence as Fairley shifted uncomfortably under the weight of her words.

Lane, rose from her seat. "Mr Fairley," she began, "the prosecution claims this screwdriver was used in several break-ins. Who have you lent your tools to?"

"I've lent tools to neighbours, my brother, and people I've worked for." Fairley replied.
Lane nodded. "And when you lend tools, do you always get them back right away?"

"No, not always," Fairley admitted. "Sometimes I don't even realise I've lent something until someone returns it."

Lane stepped closer. "Would you recognise every tool you own if you saw it in someone else's possession?"

"Probably not," Fairley said with a shrug.

"Now, about this screwdriver," Lane continued, holding it up. "When was the last time you recall using it?"

"I honestly don't remember," Fairley replied. "It's been sitting in my toolbox for ages."

"So, it's possible someone could have borrowed it, used it, and returned it without your knowledge?" Lane asked.

"Yes, absolutely," Fairley confirmed.

Lane's voice sharpened slightly. "The prosecution suggests that you - and only you - could have left those tool marks on several victims' back doors, including the Chambers. But given that you've lent out your tools before, is it possible someone else could have used this screwdriver?"

"Yes, it's possible," Fairley replied firmly.

Lane paused briefly before asking, "Do you recall ever being at the Chambers' house?"

"No, I've never been there," Fairley said, shaking his head.

"So, to be clear, you're saying you have no connection to their property and no knowledge of how your screwdriver may have been involved?"

"That's correct," Fairley stated.

Lane turned to the jury. "Thank you, Mr Fairley. Let the record show that there is no direct evidence tying Mr Fairley to the scene - only the presence of a commonly used tool, which the defendant regularly lent to others."

Lane returned to her seat, her calm demeanour unwavering.

Whitman emerged from her seat, her sharp stare fixed on Fairley. She moved to the centre of the courtroom with the evidence table beside her.

"Mr Fairley," Whitman began, her voice careful and cautious. "Let's start with the paint fleck found in Brampton-en-le-Morthen. Forensic analysis confirms it matches the paint on your Austin Allegro. Have you driven near or through the woods in question?"

Fairley shifted slightly. "I've driven near there, yes, but I've never stopped or gone into the woods."

Whitman raised an eyebrow. "You've never stopped? Not once? Yet this particular fleck of paint - a rare colour, Harvest Yellow seven-nine-one-nine, found on only a limited number of Austin Allegros - is tied directly to your vehicle. How do you explain that?"

"I can't," Fairley replied, his voice low. "Like I said, I haven't been in the woods."

Whitman stepped closer, her tone hardening. "Let's talk about the scratch on the rear of your car. It aligns perfectly with the height of the branch where the paint fleck was found. Do you recall how your car got the scratch?"

Fairley hesitated. "Not exactly. I've had that car for years. It's been scratched before - parking, brushing against things."

Whitman nodded, her expression sceptical. "So, you expect this court to believe that the scratch - perfectly matching the height of the branch in Brampton-en-le-Morthen – both with the exact same paint - are a coincidence?"

Fairley wiped at his brow. "I don't know. Maybe."

Whitman's lips pressed into a thin line. "Let's move on. The gloves recovered near the crime scene. Do you recognise them?"

"No," Fairley replied quickly. "I've never seen them before."

Whitman picked up the evidence bag containing the gloves. "Forensic testing found rabbit fur contained within these gloves was consistent with fibres found at several crime scenes, where a screwdriver you own, was also used to break into. How do you explain that?"

"I - I don't know," Fairley stammered. "I've lent out gloves before. Maybe someone else used them."

Whitman's voice sharpened. "Lent them out? To whom?"

Fairley shifted uncomfortably. "I don't remember. It could've been anyone."

"Convenient," Whitman shot back, her voice cold. "The DNA found inside these gloves isn't incidental, Mr Fairley. Are you saying someone else borrowed these gloves, used them during the break-ins, and then left them in a location near the crime scene?"

"I'm saying it's possible," Fairley replied defensively.

"Possible," Whitman repeated, her tone cutting. "Or implausible?" She didn't wait for a response. "Let's discuss the shotgun found in Brampton-en-le-Morthen. Do you recognise this firearm?"

"No," Fairley said quickly, avoiding her gaze.

Whitman gestured to the weapon. "Forensic testing revealed your DNA on this shotgun. Have you ever handled it?"

"No," Fairley repeated firmly.

"Never?" Whitman pressed. "Then how does your DNA end up on a shotgun tied to multiple crimes?"

Fairley hesitated. "I've been hunting before, handled other shotguns. Maybe it transferred somehow."

Whitman's tone grew icy. "Transferred? From where? From whom?"

"I don't know," Fairley said quietly.

Whitman stepped closer, her eyes narrowing. "Let's address the bedsheet recovered in Brampton-en-le-Morthen - the one with your DNA on it. Can you explain that Mr Fairley?"

"No," he muttered. "I have no idea how it got there."

Whitman's voice rose, cutting through the tense courtroom. "This bedsheet didn't just happen to appear in Brampton-en-le-Morthen, Mr Fairley. Your DNA - your semen - was found on it. Are you still claiming you've never been there?"

"That's right," Fairley said quickly.

Whitman's expression was unyielding. "Then tell me, Mr Fairley, how does your DNA end up on a sheet buried in the woods, alongside evidence from other crimes? And how does soil from the same crime scene end up on your boots. Is the court supposed to believe all of this is coincidence?"

Fairley's face reddened. "I don't know how it happened. I didn't do it."

Whitman's tone turned steely. "So, the paint fleck, the gloves, the shotgun, the bedsheet, the soiled boots - all of these are accidents or misunderstandings? Mr Fairley, you claim to have no explanation for any of it, yet every piece of evidence ties you to the many crimes committed by The Fox."

Fairley sat silent, his hands gripping the edges of the witness stand.

Whitman turned to the jury, her voice resonant. "Ladies and gentlemen, the defendant's answers today were not explanations. They were evasions. The evidence is not circumstantial - it is conclusive. No further questions, Your Honour."

She returned to her seat, leaving the courtroom heavy with tension and unanswered questions.

Lane rose and approached the witness box with deliberate calm. She paused, letting the tension in the courtroom settle before addressing the defendant.

"Mr Fairley," Lane began, her voice steady and measured. "Let's discuss the paint fleck found in Brampton-en-le-Morthen, which the prosecution claims match the paint on your car. So, you have driven near Brampton-en-le-Morthen but not been in the woods nearby?"

Fairley sat up slightly, his hands resting on the stand. "Yes, that is correct."

Lane nodded, pacing a few steps before continuing. "And the scratch on your car – you do not recall how it occurred?"

Fairley shook his head. "No. I've had that car for years. It's been scratched a few times - parking in tight spots, brushing against bushes. Nothing unusual."

"So, it's entirely possible the scratch happened in a completely unrelated situation?" Lane asked, her voice calm.
"Yes," Fairley confirmed.

"And the paint - there's nothing unique about it, is there?"

"No," Fairley said. "It's just standard factory paint. Any car like mine would have it."

Lane turned to the jury. "So, the paint fleck found in the woods could have come from another car entirely, or been transferred by other means?"

Fairley nodded. "I suppose so."

Lane pivoted smoothly. "Let's move on to the gloves. So, you do not recognise these gloves, Mr Fairley?"

"No," he said, his expression neutral. "I've never seen them before."

"You mentioned earlier that you sometimes lend out tools and gloves?"

"Yeah," Fairley replied. "Sometimes."

"And you do not always get those items back?"

"Not always," he admitted.

"So, is it possible that someone else could have used gloves that you owned?"

"Yes," Fairley said firmly. "It's possible."

Lane let the answer hang for a moment before shifting. "Now, about the shotgun. So, you do not recognise the firearm presented in court?"

Fairley glanced at the evidence table, then back to Lane. "No, I don't."

"The prosecution claims your DNA was found on it. Have you ever handled firearms before?"

"Yes," Fairley said. "I've been hunting a few times."

"And where do you typically handle firearms?"

"At shooting ranges or on hunting trips," he said.

Lane's voice grew firmer. "Is it possible that your DNA transferred to a firearm through those activities?"

"Yes," Fairley admitted. "It's possible."

"To be clear, you've never seen this particular shotgun, but you acknowledge handling similar firearms in the past, which might explain the presence of your DNA?"

"That's correct," replied Fairley.

Lane moved a step closer to the stand. "Finally, let's address the bedsheet found in Brampton-en-le-Morthen. The prosecution has drawn attention to the fact that your DNA - specifically, your semen - was found on it. Can you explain how that sheet ended up in the woods?"

Fairley hesitated, his brow furrowing. "I have no idea how it got there."

"Have you ever had any relationship with the victims who were attacked nearby?"

"No," Fairley said emphatically. "Never."

"And do you know how a bedsheet with your DNA might have ended up buried in a wooded area in Brampton-en-le-Morthen?"

Fairley shook his head. "No. I can't explain it."

Lane's tone grew sharper, her words precise. "Is it possible the bedsheet - or your DNA - was stolen or planted?"

"Yes," Fairley said, his voice resolute. "That's the only thing that makes sense."

Lane faced the jury, her expression neutral but resolute. "Mr Fairley, you've been cooperative, yet all we've heard today are allegations tied to objects you cannot connect to personally. Do you believe someone might be trying to frame you?"

Fairley exhaled heavily. "I don't know why someone would, but it feels like that's what's happening."

Lane nodded. "Thank you, Mr Fairley." Turning to the judge, she added, "Let the record reflect that the defendant has consistently denied knowledge of or involvement in the crimes alleged, and that the evidence presented by the prosecution is circumstantial at best."

With that, she returned to her seat, leaving the courtroom buzzing with quiet mutters.

Whitman and Lane then probed Fairley over the scratches on his neck, the cut on his hand and the blood found at a crime scene which matched his DNA. Fairley remained consistent with his answers, claiming they were likely to be work related accidents, and he must have worked at the property where his blood was found.

By the end of the day, the courtroom was drained, the ambiance saturated with unspoken thoughts and unresolved tension.

All the evidence had been heard, the case was adjourned, the hostility in the courtroom evident as Judge Mary Crawley rose to deliver her final remarks. Her voice echoed through the chamber, firm and authoritative, as she reminded everyone present of the seriousness of the charges against Fairley. "This court will reconvene in one week to allow for closing statements from both the prosecution and defence. I urge the jury to reflect deeply on the evidence presented and the impact of the defendant's actions on his victims."

With that, the gavel struck decisively, marking the end of the day's proceedings. The room began to empty, but Talbot remained seated, taking a moment to collect his thoughts. He glanced over at the families of the victims, their expressions a mix of hope and anxiety, and felt a renewed resolve swelling within him.

Chapter 32

On the twenty-sixth of February 1985, the courtroom was a pressure cooker of anticipation. Every seat in the gallery was filled, every eye trained on the twelve men and women who now filed back into their places. Detective Chief Superintendent Mark Talbot could feel his pulse in his throat as he watched the jury foreman, an older man with a weary face, rise to deliver the verdict.

"All rise," the bailiff called out, and everyone stood, the tension thick enough to choke on. Judge Mary Crawley took her seat, her face stern and unreadable. She looked at the foreman and gave him a nod. "Have you reached a verdict?"

"Yes, Your Honour," the foreman said, his voice hoarse. He glanced at the slip of paper in his hands, then cleared his throat.

"On the three charges of aggravated burglary, we find the defendant, Malcolm Fairley, guilty.

On the five charges of burglary, we find the defendant, Malcolm Fairley, guilty.

On the three charges of rape, we find the defendant, Malcolm Fairley, guilty.

On the two charges of indecent assault, we find the defendant, Malcolm Fairley, guilty.

On the charge of possession of a firearm, we find the defendant, Malcolm Fairley, guilty."

Talbot didn't realise he'd been holding his breath until the final word was spoken. He exhaled slowly, a tight knot in his chest beginning to loosen. A murmur rippled through the room - relief, satisfaction, and a lingering unease. The heavy weight of months of working long hours and sleepless nights was finally coming to a head.

Malcolm Fairley - The Fox - stood in the dock, his expression impassive, though a faint smile played at the corner of his lips. Even now, he seemed to find some dark amusement in it all. He glanced around the room as if daring anyone to meet his gaze.

Judge Mary Crawley's voice was cold and clear as she spoke. "Malcolm Fairley, you have been found guilty on all counts. There are degrees of wickedness beyond condemnatory description. Your crimes fall within this category. You desecrated and defiled men and women in their own homes. You are a decadent advertisement for evil pornographers. The court hereby sentences you to six life imprisonments, with a minimum term of thirty years. You will be transferred to a maximum-security facility where you will remain until the end of your natural life."

There was a moment of silence, a collective breath held, and then the room erupted. Reporters jotted furiously onto their notepads, victims' families clutched each other, tears streaming down their faces. Talbot felt a wave of relief wash over him but knew it was a temporary reprieve.

"He got what he deserved," said a jubilant Detective Sergeant Sarah Kendrick, coming up beside Talbot, her voice a mix of satisfaction and weariness.

"Yeah," Talbot replied, eyes still locked on Fairley. "But it doesn't change what he did. Not for the people who'll never forget."

Fairley's eyes flicked to Talbot as he was led out by the guards. His smile widened, a mocking twist of his lips. "See you around, detective," he said, his voice low and venomous.

Talbot's face remained stoic, but inside, he felt the old anger stir. "Not if I can help it," he muttered. "Not if I can help it."
The courtroom slowly emptied.

Outside the courthouse, a crowd had gathered - victims, their families, curious onlookers, and, of course, the media. The moment the doors opened, cameras flashed, and microphones were thrust forward.

"Lizzie! Over here, Lizzie!" Claire Milford from the Leighton Buzzard Observer shouted. "Can you tell us how you feel knowing The Fox will spend the rest of his life behind bars"

Lizzie Chambers, the elderly woman who had testified with such courage, paused. Her face was drawn but determined.
"I'm glad it's over," she said, her voice trembling slightly. "But we'll never really be free of what he did to us. None of us will."

Across the steps, Selena King, a young mother who had faced Fairley and lived to talk about it, held her husband close. "He's gone," she whispered, though her own eyes remained haunted. "He can't hurt us anymore."

Yet the scars ran deep. For every family, every victim, this was a day of both justice and reckoning. Some stared into the cameras with defiance, while others looked away, unable to face the bright lights after months of darkness.

Inside, Talbot watched through the window. He knew that while Fairley might be behind bars, the true damage he'd done - the nights stolen by nightmares, the homes that no longer felt safe - would take years to heal, if ever.

"He's not a man," he muttered, almost to himself. "He's a disease. And it'll take time to clear him from their systems."

Harriet Whitman joined him. "You did good, Talbot," she said. "We all did."

"Yeah," he replied, his tone distant. "But it doesn't feel like enough. Not really."

She nodded, understanding all too well. "Justice doesn't always mean closure. You know that."
Talbot sighed, his eyes scanning the faces of the victims and their families. "Yeah, I know," he said quietly. "But it's a start."

The crowd began to disperse. Some of the victims found solace in the company of others who had lived the same nightmare. Ashton Hartwig spoke softly to Lizzie Chambers, the two of them finding a strange kinship in shared horror. Others, like Benjamin Young, stared off into the distance, still lost in a fog of disbelief.

Talbot finally stepped outside, feeling the weight of months begin to lift, if only a little. Claire Milford spotted him and hurried over. "Detective Chief Superintendent Mark Talbot!" she called. "What's next for you after this case?"

Talbot looked into the lens of her camera, feeling the eyes of the community on him. "For now, I think we all just need to breathe," he said. "It's been a long road, and there's still healing to be done."

Milford nodded, sensing there was more he wasn't saying, but she didn't press. Talbot turned away, walking down the courthouse steps, feeling the chill of the afternoon air cut through his coat.

As he reached the bottom, he paused and looked back. Fairley was gone, but his presence would linger. It would take time, and maybe it would never fully disappear. But today, they had taken a step - a small step toward something better.

Justice had been served. Now came the hard part - finding peace in the aftermath.

Chapter 33

Several weeks later, Detective Chief Superintendent Mark Talbot stood at the front of the briefing room in Dunstable police station, scanning the faces of the officers gathered before him. It was a typical spring afternoon, the sky outside bright blue, and inside, the mood was buoyant. The room hummed with a quiet sense of triumph, the kind of understated satisfaction that came after long hours of hard work had finally paid off.

At the centre of this achievement were two men - Detective Sergeant Jake Miller and Detective Constable Tom Hughes. They sat near the back of the room, trying to blend into the crowd, but today that would be impossible. Their efforts over the past few months had brought an elusive criminal to justice, and everyone in the department knew it.

Talbot straightened his posture and raised his hand for quiet. The chatter in the room died down, and all eyes turned to him.
"I won't keep you long," Talbot began, his voice calm but commanding, the mark of a man used to leading. "But I think it's important to acknowledge the work that's been done here, especially considering the circumstances."

He paused for a moment, letting his words settle in the room. "We're living in an age where technology is starting to take over much of what we do as police officers. But this case - this one - was solved without any of that."

There was a murmur of agreement from the crowd, and Talbot's eyes drifted to Miller and Hughes, who were sitting in the back row, clearly uncomfortable with the attention. He offered them a nod before continuing.

"What we had were lists - long, exhaustive lists - and two detectives who knew how to do good, old-fashioned police work."

"For most detectives, a list of fifteen hundred registered owners of yellow Austin Allegro's would have been a dead end. It was an overwhelming number of people to track down, a needle in a haystack. But for Miller and Hughes, it was just another challenge to be methodically worked through."

"It's easy to get lost in the glitz of modern policing," Talbot continued, his gaze still fixed on the two men in the back. "It's easy to think that with the new technology we have, the answers should come quicker. But technology doesn't solve cases - detectives do."

He allowed the weight of that statement to hang in the air for a moment. It was something he firmly believed. No matter how advanced their tools became, it was still the instincts, the patience, and the determination of his officers that made the difference between success and failure.

"And that's what we had here," Talbot said, pacing slowly across the front of the room. "Two detectives who refused to give up. They went through that list, person by person, knocking on doors, making calls, tracking down leads, following up on even the smallest details. It was painstaking work - days and nights spent combing through records, interviewing people, chasing down dead ends. But they stuck with it, and because of that, we caught our man."

Talbot turned to face Miller and Hughes directly, his expression softening.

"Jake, Tom," he said, his voice warm with appreciation. "You've both shown exactly what it means to be detectives. You didn't rely on shortcuts. You didn't wait for some piece of technology to hand you the answer. You went out there, you talked to people, you followed leads, and you put the pieces together. That's real police work. And for that, you have my respect and my gratitude."

There was a smattering of applause in the room. Miller and Hughes exchanged embarrassed glances. Neither man was particularly fond of the spotlight, but they both knew how much this case had meant to the department - and to Talbot, personally.

"You two proved that-" he said, nodding to Miller and Hughes. "You proved that no matter how much the job changes, some things stay the same. It's still about hard work. It's still about dedication. And it's still about knowing how to put the pieces together."

Talbot looked around the room, making eye contact with each officer. "Let that be a lesson to all of us. We should embrace the new tools we have at our disposal, but we should never forget what it means to be a detective. To follow the evidence, wherever it leads. To knock on doors, to ask the right questions, to listen to what people aren't saying as much as what they are."

There was a quiet rustle of agreement in the room. Talbot could feel the respect his team had for Miller and Hughes. It wasn't just about solving a case - it was about showing everyone that the fundamentals of policing still mattered, that the core skills of a detective were as relevant now as they had ever been.

Talbot returned to the podium, his voice becoming more formal once again. "In recognition of your hard work and dedication, I'm proud to present you both with commendations for outstanding detective work."

The room burst into applause once more as Talbot held out two certificates. Miller and Hughes reluctantly stood, making their way to the front of the room. Talbot shook their hands firmly, offering each of them a quiet word of thanks before handing them their awards. The applause continued as the two men stood side by side, clearly uncomfortable but honoured, nonetheless.

As the applause died down, Talbot stepped forward again. "This case was solved because of the determination of two detectives who refused to give up. But let's not forget that we all play a part in making this department what it is. Whether you're knocking on doors, analysing evidence, or managing the paperwork, every role is important. Every contribution matters."

He looked out at his team, his voice firm and resolute. "We're only as strong as the people who work here. And today, I'm proud of what we've accomplished."

The briefing concluded shortly after, and as the officers began to file out of the room, Talbot caught Miller and Hughes on their way out.

"Well done, both of you," he said quietly, his voice full of genuine appreciation. "You reminded all of us of what it means to be a detective."

Miller smiled sheepishly. "Just doing our job, sir."

Talbot clapped a hand on his shoulder. "Maybe so, but you did it damn well."

As they left the room, Talbot lingered for a moment, looking out the window at the blue sky beyond. He knew that the job was changing, evolving in ways that no one could have imagined even a decade ago. But today, at least, he felt a deep sense of pride in the work his team had done. No matter how much technology advanced, no matter how many new tools they were given, the essence of detective work - the persistence, the instincts, the dogged pursuit of the truth - would always remain the same. And that was something worth holding onto.

The operations room was eerily quiet, stripped of the frantic energy that had filled it for months. Desks that once overflowed with maps, notes, and coffee-stained files were now bare, ready to be reclaimed by the mundane routines of other cases. The whiteboard that had chronicled every lead, every theory, every dead end was wiped clean. It was as if The Fox had never existed, though the remnants of his crimes still clung to every corner.

Detective Chief Superintendent Mark Talbot stood alone. The task force had officially disbanded that morning - case closed, as they say. But for Talbot, it was anything but. He could still feel it - the chase, the failures, the sleepless nights replaying in his mind like a bad film reel on a loop.

Detective Sergeant Sarah Kendrick wandered in, breaking the silence. "So, this is it, huh?" she asked, her voice flat but tinged with something Talbot couldn't quite place. Relief? Resignation? "All that work, and it's like we were never here."

Talbot nodded, not tearing his gaze away from the window. "Feels strange, doesn't it? We spent months hunting him, and now - poof - everyone just goes back to their lives like nothing happened."

Kendrick snorted. "I don't know if 'back to their lives' is quite right. I mean, look at us. None of us are walking out of this the same way we walked in."

Talbot turned, studying Kendrick's face. The lines around his eyes seemed deeper, his posture more slumped. "Yeah," Talbot said quietly. "I suppose not."

A silence settled between them, both of them reflecting on what had been lost and what had been learned. Finally, Kendrick broke the quiet. "What about you, sir? You thinking about taking some time off?"

Talbot's lips curved into a humourless smile. "Time off? Christ, Kendrick, I wouldn't even know what to do with myself." He looked around the empty room, the emptiness suddenly feeling vast. "But maybe it's time I figure that out."

Kendrick nodded, understanding the weight behind those words. "You did good, Sir. You did what no one else could. Doesn't feel like much now, but…you caught him. You got the bastard."

"Yeah," Talbot replied. "But at what cost?"

He didn't wait for an answer. He wasn't sure there was one. Instead, he walked out of the room and down the hall, past the faces of his colleagues who'd been there with him through every twist and turn. He saw the exhaustion in their eyes, the haunted looks that would linger long after they filed away this case.

In his office, Talbot closed the door behind him and leaned against it. His desk was still cluttered with remnants of the investigation - photos of victims, reports, sketches of possible hideouts. A map of Fairley's attacks stared back at him from the wall, the ink of his own notes and theories now faded and redundant.

He crossed to his chair and sank into it, feeling the weight of every decision, every mistake. The manhunt had consumed him, made him question everything he believed about himself, about justice. He'd told himself he was prepared to catch a monster, but no one prepared you for the aftermath.

Talbot picked up a photo of a young woman - one of Fairley's victims Her face was smiling in the picture, but he knew she hadn't smiled like that since. He thought of an elderly woman who'd faced The Fox and survived but who'd never feel safe in her own home again. Faces like theirs haunted him, each one a reminder of what they'd lost. And what he couldn't give back.

A soft knock on the door pulled him from his thoughts. He looked up to see Harriet Whitman, the lead prosecutor, standing there. "Mind if I come in?" she asked, her voice gentle.

"Sure," Talbot said, waving her in. "But if you're here to ask me about next steps, I haven't got a bloody clue."

Whitman chuckled softly and sat down across from him. "No, I figured as much. Just wanted to check on you. See how you're holding up."

Talbot sighed, rubbing his temples. "Honestly? I feel like I'm still chasing him, even though he's locked away. Can't shake the feeling that I missed something, you know?"

"You didn't miss anything, Mark," Whitman said firmly. "You caught him. He's not blending in with the crowd anymore. You brought him into the light."

"Maybe," Talbot murmured. "But there's a part of me that wonders…if it was worth it. All those nights, all that…obsession."

Whitman leaned forward, her expression softening. "Listen, it's natural to feel that way. You were in deep, Mark. We all were. But it doesn't mean it was for nothing."

Talbot nodded slowly, but his mind drifted. He thought about his wife, and the nights he'd come home late, reeking of sweat and cigarettes, his eyes wild with exhaustion. How many dinners had he missed? How many mornings had he left before she woke up, a stranger in his own home? She'd stood by him through it all, but the strain was there. And it hadn't gone away.

"What now?" he muttered, more to himself than to her. "What does a man do when the monster's gone?"

Whitman smiled gently. "He learns to live again. He finds his way back to the things he loves, the people who matter. And maybe, just maybe, he figures out that there's more to him than the chase."

Talbot looked up, meeting her eyes. "You make it sound so easy."
"It's not," she replied. "But it's worth a shot, isn't it?"

For a moment, they sat in silence, two weary souls who'd stared into the darkness and come out the other side. Finally, Talbot stood, his eyes scanning the room one last time. He picked up his jacket, slung it over his shoulder, and looked back at Whitman. "Maybe you're right," he said. "Maybe it's time to see what's left of me after all this."

She smiled, a real one this time. "Good luck, Mark. You've earned it."

As he left the police station, the sun began to dip below the horizon, stretching golden light across the pavement. Talbot stood there for a moment, feeling the cool breeze on his face. He took a deep breath, feeling the weight of the past months start to lift, if only just a little.

The Fox was behind bars. The hunt was over. But for Talbot, a different journey was just beginning. One that would take him back to the things that mattered to the parts of himself he'd left behind in the darkness.

He took a step forward, not entirely sure where he was headed, but knowing that for the first time in a long time, he was ready to find out.

Chapter 34

Benjamin Young's house was quiet - too quiet. He stood in the bathroom, staring into the mirror, his eyes vacant and hollow. His face looked like a stranger's, pale and drawn, with bruises blossoming along his cheek and neck. He could still feel the trace of his touch on his skin, and it made his stomach turn.

The faucet was running, water pooling in the sink. He'd been washing his hands for what felt like hours, scrubbing his skin raw, trying to erase the feeling of him. His breath came in ragged gasps, his chest heaving, but he couldn't stop. The water had long turned from warm to icy cold, but he barely noticed. He was numb, his body moving on autopilot.

"Get it off. Just get it off," he whispered to himself, his voice trembling, barely audible over the sound of the rushing water.

The clock on the wall ticked relentlessly, a cruel reminder of the minutes passing. How long had it been since he left? Minutes? Hours? Time had lost all meaning. He could still hear his voice in his ears, his breath hot against his skin. The way he'd smiled when he realised, he was too weak, too terrified to fight back.

A sob caught in his throat, strangling him. He sank to the floor, his back against the cold tile wall, pulling his knees to his chest. He wanted to scream, to rage, to tear the whole world apart, but all he could manage was a soft, broken whimper. He pressed his hands to his mouth, trying to stifle the sound, as if letting it out would make everything too real, too impossible to bear.

There were bruises all over his body, deep and angry, each one a mark of his cruelty. He'd fought, he'd tried to push him off, but he was stronger, relentless. He could still feel his weight pressing down on him, the cold metal of his belt buckle biting into his skin.

He squeezed his eyes shut, trying to block out the memories, but they played out behind his eyelids like a nightmare he couldn't wake up from.

In his mind, he was back there again. The room was dark, he could smell his sweat and feel his breath hot and ragged in his ear. His gloved hand was clamped over his mouth, muffling his screams, his voice a low, guttural growl. "No one's coming for you," he'd whispered, and he knew he was right. He was alone. Utterly alone.

The cold tile floor of his bathroom seeped into his bones, but he welcomed the chill. It was something – anything - to feel other than the terror still coursing through his veins. He had never felt so small, so powerless. Every muscle in his body ached from fighting, from struggling, but none of that mattered now. He'd lost. And the world felt darker for it.

He heard a knock at the door - a soft, tentative rapping that broke through the fog of his mind. His heart seized in his chest. Was it him? Had he come back to finish what he started? He could barely breathe, his pulse thundering in his ears. He stayed where he was, frozen on the floor, unable to move.

"Benjamin? It's Sara. Are you in there?" The voice on the other side was gentle, familiar. His sister.

Benjamin's breath came out in a shaky rush, relief flooding through him. He wanted to get up, to open the door, but his legs wouldn't cooperate. He felt like he was made of lead, every movement a monumental effort.

"Benjamin, please, talk to me. I'm worried about you."

His voice was a whisper, raw and broken. "I'm here...I'm here."

There was a pause, then the sound of the doorknob turning. Sara pushed the door open, stepping inside, her eyes widening at the sight of Benjamin crumpled on the bathroom floor. She was a petite woman, but at that moment, she seemed to fill the entire room with her presence, her concern palpable.

"Oh my God, Benjamin," she breathed, rushing to his side. "What happened? Who did this to you?"

Benjamin tried to speak, but the words wouldn't come. He shook his head, tears streaming down his cheeks, his whole-body trembling. He couldn't say it. He couldn't make it real.

Sara knelt beside him, wrapping her arms around him, pulling him close. "It's okay, it's okay," she murmured, rocking him gently. "You're safe now. You're safe."

But Benjamin didn't feel safe. He felt shattered, broken in ways he couldn't even begin to understand. He buried his face in Sara's shoulder, the sobs finally breaking free, racking his body with a force that took his breath away. He cried until there were no more tears left, his throat raw and his chest hollow.

Sara held him through it all, whispering soothing words, but Benjamin barely heard them. All he could hear was The Fox's voice, whispering in his ear, telling him he was his, that he'd never escape him. He knew those words would haunt him for the rest of his life.

VICTIM SUPPORT
If you've been impacted by crime or a traumatic event, please know that you're not alone. There are many support services available to offer guidance, emotional support, and medical assistance.

Victim Support is a national charity dedicated to helping people recover from their experiences, and they are here for you too.
You can reach them at www.victimsupport.org.uk **or call 08 08 16 89 111 for compassionate help whenever you need it.**

Part Six: The Real Fox

Chapter 35

Malcolm Fairley, known as "The Fox", was born in 1952 in Silksworth, near Sunderland.

He was born to Hannah and Ambrose and was the youngest of nine children. He was often described as "shy and introverted" and had a difficult childhood. Bullied at school, he frequently played truant, unable to read and only able to sign his name. His severe stammer made him shy around strangers, and he left school at fifteen.

He often disappeared at night, taking his dog to camp in the nearby Tunstall Hills. Relatives described him as a quiet and lonely child who was close to his mother but distant from his father. He enjoyed cartoons as a child, but as he grew older, he began illegally importing violent pornographic films. His father passed away when he was still young. The only criminal record in the family was Ambrose keeping a dog without a license.

Fairley's first job was as a labourer at a dairy, but it lasted only a few months. He then worked for sixteen months at a coal washer plant before briefly trying his hand as a trainee welder. However, much of his time was spent unemployed.

But beneath that meek exterior lay something darker. As a teenager, he began his descent into crime with theft and burglary, early signs of what was to come.

Aged nineteen, Fairley met Joan Sinclair in a ballroom. Joan was impressed by his sharp appearance and dancing skills. Soon after, she became pregnant, and the two hastily married. Joan's mother had saved £100 for their wedding cake, but Fairley stole the money. After staying with Joan's parents for a while, the couple moved into their own place - though Joan later discovered that everything inside had been stolen. She even suspected that Fairley's nice shirts and ties were likely stolen as well. Fairley was violent toward Joan, and although she divorced him, he somehow managed to gain custody of their son. Despite his abusive nature, Joan's mother described him as a "dance floor Romeo" with a certain charm.

Fairley also stole cars but initially left fingerprints behind, which led him to start wearing gloves during his thefts.

Fairley later married Georgina Bell, whom he met at an ice-skating rink. They had two children and lived in County Durham, but their marriage was plagued by violence and Fairley's frequent unemployment. Georgina worked at Woolworths, but her income wasn't enough to support the family.

For the next decade, Fairley was a regular in and out of jail, unable or unwilling to break free from his pattern of crime. Fairley's roots trace back to the Fairley clan of Scotland, whose name means "beautiful woodland." Their motto, "I am prepared," was a fitting irony for Fairley, who meticulously planned his burglaries.

He often scouted hilltops to track potential victims and felt comfortable navigating through woodlands to evade capture.

In 1983, Fairley moved to Leighton Buzzard to live with his brother, hoping to find work. He took various labourer jobs in Hertfordshire, Bedfordshire, and Buckinghamshire, becoming familiar with the area.

His criminal resume grew steadily - burglary, theft, car crime - a persistent offender. But his crimes escalated in a disturbing new direction when he stumbled upon a shotgun. The chance theft of that weapon unlocked a new, twisted hunger within him - a need for power, control, and fear. And so began the reign of terror that would earn him his chilling nickname.

Nicknamed "The Fox" by the press and police alike, Fairley earned his moniker for his uncanny ability to evade capture, often slipping away into nearby woods after his attacks. More than that, he was known to build makeshift dens inside his victims' homes, like a predator setting up his lair. Throughout the sweltering summer of 1984, The Fox unleashed a campaign of terror that would shock the nation, committing over eighty crimes and sparking one of the largest manhunts in British history.

On the morning of the fourteenth of September 1984, Malcolm Fairley finally faced justice at Dunstable Magistrates' Court. The atmosphere outside the court was electric, bristling with rage and fear. A hostile crowd had gathered, their hatred unmistakable, their voices a chorus of condemnation. The police, fearing for his safety, had covered Fairley's head with a blanket, shielding him from the stones and insults hurled his way.

But that was just the beginning. On the twenty-sixth of February 1985, The Fox stood trial at St Albans Crown Court. The charges were staggering - three rapes, two indecent assaults, three aggravated burglaries, five burglaries and the possession of a firearm. In a chilling display of arrogance or perhaps a twisted attempt at repentance, Fairley asked the court to consider an additional sixty-eight cases. His crimes were not a series of unfortunate events; they were a calculated spree of violence and terror.

Standing before the court, Malcolm Fairley tried to explain himself. "I wanted to stop it," he said, his voice steady but devoid of remorse, "but I couldn't. When I got the gun, I felt I could get what I wanted." His words fell like stones in the courtroom. There was no empathy, no understanding. He was a man who had crossed the line into monstrosity. His claim that he had no experience with guns and had accidentally shot someone's hand only deepened the horror. The gun had been a catalyst, an enabler of his darkest desires.

Some of his crimes were too horrific to be made public. Many of the details remain known only to his victims, the police and the trial judge.

Mr Justice Caulfield presided over the trial with a heavy but unwavering hand. When it came time to deliver his sentence, his words were cold and final. "There are degrees of wickedness beyond condemnatory description. Your crimes fall within this category. You desecrated and defiled men and women in their own homes." With that, he handed down six life sentences. The Fox's reign of terror was over, but the scars he left on his victims and their communities would never heal.

Even in prison, Fairley remained a symbol of fear and danger. The Parole Board denied him parole in October 2023, declaring that he was still a "real risk to the public." Retired Superintendent Brian Prickett, who had led part of the investigation that finally captured Fairley, agreed. "He hasn't changed," Prickett said. "Men like Fairley don't change."

And he never did. On the twenty-eighth of May 2024, Malcolm Fairley died in his cell at HM Prison Hull. The news brought a grim sort of closure to those who had lived in fear of The Fox, the man who had hidden in their homes, watched them in their sleep, and violated the sanctity of their lives. His death marked the end of a dark chapter, but his legacy - a legacy of horror - would never be forgotten.

Meet The Author

Soren Lyman, a native of Bedfordshire, England, brings a fresh voice to the world of crime fiction with his debut novel, *Manhunt: Chasing The Fox*.

Born and raised in Leighton Buzzard, Soren developed a fascination with mystery and suspense, drawing inspiration from both real-life events and the hidden complexities of small-town life. This passion ultimately led him to pen his first novel, weaving dark, compelling narratives that explore the human psyche.

A lifelong reader of crime fiction, Soren combines this passion with a fresh, immersive style that explores themes of fear, control and the thin line between justice and vengeance.

Manhunt: Chasing The Fox marks the beginning of his journey as an author, with more suspenseful tales already on the horizon.

Printed in Dunstable, United Kingdom

I am a born romantic who loves to read romantic novels and write sizzling page turners. I met the love of my life on a pub crawl in Cyprus and for the last 33 years we have been inseparable. We have been very blessed to have a beautiful daughter, Emily, who is the light of our lives. Together with Emily's fiancé Jack, we enjoy travelling and seeing amazing places around the world. Based in the West Midlands, we have amazing families and friends. I also love British blue shorthair cats and would love a kitten, so when my gorgeous husband reads this, please, please, please, can we have one (or two!)?

I am dedicating this book to the love of my life, my partner in crime, best friend, my rock, my soul mate. Parky, I will love you to infinity and beyond.

A.R Kimberlin

ART OF LOVE

AUSTIN MACAULEY PUBLISHERS
LONDON * CAMBRIDGE * NEW YORK * SHARJAH

Copyright © A. R Kimberlin 2024

The right of A. R Kimberlin to be identified as author of this work has been asserted by the author in accordance with sections 77 and 78 of the Copyright, Designs and Patents Act 1988.

All rights reserved. No part of this publication may be reproduced, stored in a retrieval system, or transmitted in any form or by any means, electronic, mechanical, photocopying, recording, or otherwise, without the prior permission of the publishers.

This is a work of fiction. Names, characters, businesses, places, events, locales, and incidents are either the products of the author's imagination or used in a fictitious manner. Any resemblance to actual persons, living or dead, or actual events is purely coincidental.

Any person who commits any unauthorised act in relation to this publication may be liable to criminal prosecution and civil claims for damages.

A CIP catalogue record for this title is available from the British Library.

ISBN 9781035879519 (Paperback)
ISBN 9781035879526 (ePub e-book)

www.austinmacauley.com

First Published 2024
Austin Macauley Publishers Ltd®
1 Canada Square
Canary Wharf
London
E14 5AA

I would like to thank Parky, Em and Jack for being incredibly supportive and for always being there when I need a cwtch. A huge thank you to Em who, once again, was the first to read my latest novel and give me such wonderful feedback. Thank you to my big brother. Gav. You have always been my hero and the only one who knew my second book was being published. Thank you for your advice. Thanks to my besties, for all the love, laughter and tears we share, I don't know what I would do without you. A special to Mr Gregory Ho-Yen, and all the staff at Wolverhampton Eye Infirmary. Thanks to your incredible skill and dedication, you saved my sight and I will be forever grateful. Thanks to everyone at Austen Macauley, for helping me publish my second book. From the editors, art department and all of you who have developed my novel and brought it to life. Finally, thank you to all my readers, you are simply amazing.

Chapter 1

As the teenagers lined up outside the gallery entrance, there was a humdrum of excited, nervous chatter. The Worcester Institute of Fine Art was a place they had only dreamt of, up until today. It was a private educational institute, with a long waiting list of well-to-do sixteen and seventeen-year-olds clawing to get through the door. It has also been awarded several important accreditations and awards over the last ten years since opening in a lavish and prestigious ceremony. The students were waiting anxiously with little composure outside the main art building.

They were the cream of the world's society and their designer-labelled clothing screamed more money than sense to the average teenager. The site had been founded by Professor Millward, a philanthropist and multi-billionaire with a love of fine art. His huge financial contribution meant he was involved in everything, including the design of the buildings and carefully choosing each member of staff. Investing heavily in the institute, he had been rewarded tenfold financially and was now receiving massive yearly dividends in return for his initial payout. He genuinely wanted the younger generations to learn about and value the arts in general, with a particular focus on paintings.

He was a fine art junkie and had many masterpieces in his own huge collection. Ten years on, the institute had gone from strength to strength, charging extortionate prices for young adults of great wealth to learn about art. Millward had also ensured that each course intake had at least two scholarship students, who he would sponsor personally. The lucky students would meet Professor Millward and his personal fine arts team on the annual, invitation-only open day. They would discuss all forms of art and bring along pieces of their own work that they had created.

These chosen talented few would be put forward by their secondary schools from around the world and considered for a sponsorship, covering the different genres of the courses on offer. They would be asked to attend the college alone on these special days, bringing their artwork with them. This ranged from sculptures and pieces of written work to dances and acting performances. Professor Millward favoured paintings and sketches on these rare occasions, spending most of his valuable time pouring over the details of each piece of art and personally seeking out the artists he decided showed the most talent.

He would then engage in conversation with the young artists and personally assess their knowledge and passion for art itself. He had been hoodwinked a couple of times over the years when students had presented fake work. This was soon discovered at the beginning of the college year and any cheating students would be removed from the site and the scholarship given to the next deserving candidate on the list. The faculty was made up of well-educated professors from around the globe, each of whom had studied art, created art or in a number of cases actually did both.

Professor Harper and Professor Denton were two of his favourite teachers, who lived and breathed for art. Their proficiency and talent lay in painting and drawing and together they ran the 'Art' department, specialising in painted works. They both had the same enthusiasm for art, which meant they could teach with passion and keep their young muses enthralled and enraptured within the teaching sessions. Some of the more literary professors could drone on about a certain writer or actor but Harper and Denton adored all art and whilst making their lessons enjoyable, they managed to still fill their students' heads with knowledge and appreciation of the art itself. They hoped this would stay with these youngsters for the rest of their lives.

Today, they were teaching the first classes of the new intake with the assistance of their support staff. They had been sitting inside the ground floor studio, sipping coffee and checking their session planners, ensuring they had left nothing to chance. They wanted their lessons to be uplifting and inspiring, sharing their in-depth knowledge and skills so that their students could actually learn something. The 'Art' facility within the institute consisted of an expansive set of buildings, all linked together by glass corridors, some of which ran underground. The students referred to these as 'the Mole Tunnels'. These were air-conditioned tubes, that if exposed to daylight, the glass automatically shaded.

At the main entrance was a huge reception area and welcome gallery, where the students and staff displayed some of their daily artwork. A huge modern reception desk sat in the middle of the area, where Mrs Bushell was busy fussing with paperwork. Glass doors led off to the left of reception into the first tunnel which took you to a large comfortable seating area and toilets. To the right of the reception area, huge double doors opened up into 'Studio One'. To the left of these doors stood a significant wrought iron, spiral staircase which led to the first floor and the same huge double doors as below, opening up into 'Studio Two'.

Studio One was spacious, with high-tech glass walls on each side. These are also automatically shaded and can be controlled with a touch of a button. They could shade the light as much as was needed to calm the sun's rays; another click would turn them into solid walls of opaque glass, giving complete privacy to the studio. The entrance and back wall were decorated with more paintings and drawings from students; the back wall also housed a ginormous whiteboard and a projector hidden in the ceiling. A large wooden door in the left corner led to the stores where there were copious amounts of art equipment and accessories. A modern glass door on the right-hand side opened into another tunnel. This led to a large rest area and the vast 'Main Gallery'.

It had been designed and laid out to look like a French museum, displaying not only each student's end-of-year work but also priceless masterpieces that were on loan from other famous galleries around the world. Security was high around the site but the basement levels had maximum high-tech security measures in place. Several doors led off the rest area, leading to an auditorium used for art lectures, the professors' offices, another seating area, and more toilets. Studio Two had the same layout, only the right door on the back wall led to the second-floor toilet area.

"Better get this show on the road, Maggie," Philip said enthusiastically, his American accent still as clear and unchanging as the day he had arrived in England.

"Go get 'em, Pip," she responded, smiling widely. She had been working alongside this handsome man for the last four years when he had transferred over from the States. He was a favourite of Millward, the man who owned the whole shebang and was also the youngest professor on the academic team of staff. Although devastatingly handsome, Philip Denton was also single. A brooding loner, he had no time for polite conversation with the rest of the faculty and his one and only goal in life was to spread the knowledge and appreciation of incredible artwork from around the world. Quiet and offish in day-to-day life, he came alive when he taught.

He became emboldened by discussing each work of art and teaching young adults how to create their own masterpieces. Maggie had taken to him straight away when they had first been introduced. The other faculty members were either pompous brown noses or outrageous flirts who wanted nothing more than to get inside her knickers. Philip had been polite but apathetic. When she had brought him to look around the 'Gallery' buildings, he had been blown away by his surroundings. Knowing the place had an incredible reputation, standing in the Main Gallery, he felt at home. Having his own private studio in the basement was also an amazing bonus and somewhere he felt safe and happy.

He had left his comfortable job as a lecturer at Stanford after being headhunted by Professor Millward himself. Millward's eagerness and energy when he told him about the institute were infectious, however, nothing had prepared him for the unprecedented equipment, space, and wages this job would bring him. Being able to see and touch fine art from some of his favourite masters was another bonus. The art department included several basement levels where masterpieces were sent for meticulous restoration. The young professor had quickly purchased a luxury loft apartment on the banks of the River Severn, a stone's throw from campus.

He also had an apartment on campus which he rarely used. Occasionally, the river would flood and he wouldn't be able to gain access to his home, so it was a good bolt-hole to have. Maggie had been the only down-to-earth human he had met in the extensive list of staff. Once meeting him, they had all believed one of two things. Firstly, that he was smoulderingly hot stuff and they wanted to, and would try to, get him into bed. Or, secondly, he was above himself and as the rumour mill had spread the word, he was close to the owner of the institute. To some, he was an enemy to keep a watchful, jealous eye on. Being the focus of attention for most of the females and some of the males on campus (both student and staff), meant nothing to him. He was aloof with them all.

Maggie knew that within the next few minutes, most of the young female students and some of the males would be forming crushes on her dear friend, that would last through their next four years of academic life. Sighing at the fact that Pip (as she had lovingly nicknamed him) was still very much single, she turned her focus back to her studio. Casting one last look around to ensure everything was as it should be. Maggie was happy that it was ready for her new students. One or two of the teenagers who attended this college were doing so as it was 'the' place to be. They had signed up for several of the offered courses and would be studying full-time.

At sixteen and seventeen years of age, most of these individuals would have no clue of what fine painted artwork looked like, even if the canvas itself fell on their supremely coffered heads and knocked them out. There were strict protocols for those students who couldn't cut the mustard, so any thinking they were in for an easy time of it, were mistaken. The professors had no qualms about ending their student's education should they believe that they were not interested in learning or wanting to be proficient in painting. Most of the parents had enough wealth to send them to this well-established, modern institute.

Some of the teenagers were well aware that when their four-year course was over, they would probably have no use for this knowledge in their future careers. They could, however, say that they had attended the most oversubscribed fine art institute in the world. A plaudit to be added to their curriculum vitae, enabling them to name-drop at interviews, with what may be the deciding factor in getting their dream job. For many, it would be a mention in conversation, to show themselves as intellectuals and get one up on their peers. For the rest of the students, it was the most incredible opportunity to learn new skills and hone their talents.

It was a bright and warm September morning, the new students looked more like models waiting to shimmy down a runway. Outfits varied from Tom Ford chinos to Valentino blouses, most of them dressing to impress. One girl stood at the back, looking along the queue of fellow students, admiring the designer outfits. Like most of them, she was holding her phone in her hand. Never knowing when it would ping to say she was needed. She wore an oversized black hoodie, dark grey loose-fitting tracksuit bottoms, and black trainers with white rubber soles. She was hiding behind a black baseball cap with no logo and mirrored sunglasses.

Her mousy brown hair had been pulled through the catch hole at the back in a long ponytail. Unlike most of her fellow youth, she had never been under the plastic surgeon's knife or had her face and body filled with chemicals. Without a scrap of make-up on, she looked the youngest there, something she was actually pleased about. "I love your sweat top. Is it Balenciaga?" A blonde American girl asked as she reached out and without asking, felt the material of the hoodie's sleeve. "I'm so envious," she gushed. "I'm Mindy Moore…I'm sure you already recognise me from my Tik-Toks…" She paused waiting for some recognition, but as she couldn't see this girl's face behind her cool mirrored shades, she couldn't make out her expression.

"Your sunglasses…are they Cartier?" She questioned, slightly going off track and leaning in a little too closely to this pale girl's face. She hadn't moved a muscle and Mindy was used to fuss and attention. A lad walked past and joined the end of the queue, with a white rucksack slung over one shoulder. "OMG…" Mindy squealed with delight. "…Is that an AMIRI?" The blond-haired boy pulled his pods from his ears and looked at the blonde bombshell up and down. She was dressed like a cheerleader in a ridiculously short white, pleated skirt, hemmed in red. Her tight-fitting white crop top had the number one sewn onto the back.

The front was so low, her straining bosom was only just being contained. Her tanned midriff was showing, along with a large percentage of underboob. Moving quickly over to the gangly boy, she was practically drooling over his bag; he in turn was drooling over her body, most of which was on show. The pale girl in the mirrored glasses stood back and looked on, glad that the attention on her had been taken away and her mouth twitched into a small smile. She watched the lad lusting over the barely dressed simpleton, hoping that the cheerleader was in her class, enabling herself to fade into the background.

Although hidden behind the sunglasses and baseball cap, her expression was being scrutinised. He had been watching the insignificant exchange with interest. He was fascinated by real people, taking in individual expressions and memorising them, recreating them at a later date in detailed sketches. His attention had been drawn to this young girl, who, unlike the other gleeful students, looked pale and serious. She was wearing loose-fitting dark clothes and her whole demeanour was as if she was trying to be invisible. From the narrow sliver of a window at the side of the reception gallery, he had also observed the blonde, underdressed teenager hurrying over to the good-looking boy.

His eyes were immediately drawn back to the pale girl's face. Instantly, he was rewarded as her mouth twitched and a small smirk appeared on her full pink lips. The students bustled about nervously as Mrs Bushell the 'Arts' receptionist pushed the main doors button on her desk. Unlocking the colossal glass automatic doors, which gently slid open and allowed the nervous but excited teenagers to file in. There were two sets of doors with a buffer area in-between. This allowed the reception area's cooling and heating system to work more effectively.

As the students trailed in, he stood stock still, gazing out of the window. Behind him, a large canvas and easel were hiding him from view. He couldn't take his eyes off the girl, whose small smile had quickly fallen from her face, her tongue now trailing her bottom lip with nerves. For some reason, he was willing her to remove her sunglasses; he wanted to see her eyes. Instead, she moved towards the entrance of the building, slowly following the other students into the building. Watching until she was out of sight of the narrow window, he stood for a few more seconds, feeling a little bewildered.

"Good morning, you lucky humans," Maggie's loud English voice penetrated his thoughts. "I am Professor Harper and I will be teaching those of you who have been assigned to Studio One." She was as excited as her students and could not hide the thrill in her voice. "Those of you who have been assigned to Studio Two will be following Professor Denton up those stairs…" She turned to point towards the spiral staircase as some of the students made their way towards them. "Umm…Professor Denton?" She called out, realising he was not in sight. He quickly stepped out from behind the canvas, frightening a ginger-haired lad who had been admiring the painting.

"I'm right here, Professor," his serious American tone drew the attention of everyone in the reception area. Once the students took in his drop-dead good-looking features, they were even more in awe. "Studio Two, this way, people," he said walking determinedly towards the staircase. In his head, he had decided already that the shadow of a girl was probably like all the other students here. She was probably full of her own self-importance and thought she knew more than anyone else about everything there is to know. "Put your cell phones away as I will not tolerate mobile devices in my studio," he said sternly as he stood on the first step of the staircase, visually assessing the teenagers as they nervously stepped passed him.

The scared students instantly stowed their devices safely into their pockets and bags as they made their way through the doors of Studio One and alighted the stairs to Studio Two. Professor Harper followed her brood in, shouting happily to them all to find a seat. As the last student had walked past him, he made to walk up the staircase, when he noticed a figure still standing in the gallery. It was the 'shadow' girl and she was facing away from him, her attention focused on a painting on display, entitled 'Dreams'. She seemed completely taken with the painting and for a thrilling moment, he thought she was one of his classes.

"I'm missing someone," Maggie's voice broke his thoughts as he saw her walk out of her studio door and call over to the student enamoured with the painting on the wall. "Hello, dear…" she shouted over, making the young girl jump. She spun round to face the voice, her mouth opened slightly in shock.

"Sorry." The young girl spoke quietly and made her way towards the smiling Professor Harper.

"Oh, don't worry, my lovely. I'm just excited to get started. So come on in and take a seat," her teacher replied kindly. Maggie turned and caught sight of her friend on the stairs, a serious expression on his handsome face. "You okay, Pip?" She questioned worriedly, a frown appearing on her forehead.

"Yes…of course." His mouth had set into a grim line. As he made his way up the stairs, his eyes flicked back to the shadow girl walking into Studio One. She was still holding her cell phone in her hand. He had given a clear, concise instruction and was more than annoyed that she had not complied. Why did it bother him so much? He shook his head and returned his full attention to his new intake, who had already entered the studio. As he walked through the gigantic doors, he asked them all to take a seat, whilst Miss Dench, his studio assistant, fussed around them all like a mother hen.

Chapter 2

As the students chose their seats in Studio One, there was a rush to be at the front, nearest the professor. "Alright, alright, slow down," Mademoiselle Dubois called out in her thick French accent. She had proudly been Professor Harper's assistant for the last two years and absolutely adored her job. Having had her heart broken by the love of her life, she had fled Paris and stayed with an old school friend in England. Having worked at the 'Louvre' restoring old masters and with her love and knowledge of art, she had been snapped up by the institute when she had applied for an undergrad post just to make ends meet. Maggie had been like a mother to her and had taken her under her wing when she arrived.

For the last two years, they had worked well together and were now close friends as well as colleagues. She also had a great deal of respect for Professor Denton, although she still felt intimidated by his presence even after all this time. She and Miss Dench spent a lot of time together and were also firm friends. Ida had also left her home and family in Denmark but there was no heartbreak involved. She was now doing her dream job by helping to teach young people about art. Ida also worked in the restoration department, a highly sort out post. There they worked on bringing some of the greatest paintings in the world back to their original glory.

The students had all taken to their seats and Maggie had made her way to the front of the studio. "Welcome, welcome," she said warmly with her hands raised in the air. "I am Professor Harper, but whilst we are inside the Art buildings, you can call me Maggie." She was beaming, happy that her studio was full of young inquisitive minds again after the long summer break. "This lovely lady you see here…" She waved her hand in Miss Dubois's direction, "is my beautiful assistant, Miss Cadence Dubois. Again whilst in these buildings, you can call her Cadence, but outside these walls, she is to be addressed as Miss Dubois."

She finished and grabbed her large yellow mug of tea, knocking back the last dregs. "Right then, drinks are over there…" She pointed to a large desk by the store's cupboard, which neatly housed a hot water dispenser, a tray of multi-coloured mugs, a selection of beverages, and a large plate of biscuits. "Please help yourself, but remember if you use a mug, you have to wash it up yourself." The blonde cheerleader who had made it onto the front row snorted loudly. "We are not your servants. I don't care who does it for you at home, but here, if you want a drink, you have to clear up after yourself…No exceptions."

Maggie looked directly at the cheerleader, who seemed completely oblivious that this information was meant just for her. "I have ten new students here today and I am sure over the next few days, we will all become good pals. But first, I think we could all do with a drink. So, help yourselves and feel free to look around the studio." Cadence made her way over to the drinks table to show the youngsters how to use the hot water dispenser, well aware that most of them would have no idea how to make themselves a hot drink. Shadow girl had found a seat at the back right-hand side of the studio, near the main double doors.

Each student had a modern tall stool which could spin around. It had a comfortable backrest and was placed in front of a large beech desk, which was set at a slight angle. To her left, underneath the desk was a large beech cabinet. On the top of the cabinet sat a silver remote control, neatly stowed in its holder. There was also a cup holder that you could swivel out when required. Pulling open the top drawer of the cabinet revealed a tray of brand-new sketching pencils and accessories. Wow. She sat there taking in the high-spec desk and admiring the bright and airy studio. Being in the corner, she had already checked her mobile twice and no one had noticed.

She was also nearest to the main doors, so hopefully, she could sneak out as and when she was needed. Due to the students being spread out in this immense room, the nearest person to her was a fellow student to her right. In the same position as she was, at the back of the room, but on the other side, with a row of large Belfast sinks and wooden draining boards behind him. Each draining board had glass jars of various sizes already housing damp brushes that had been freshly washed that day. She turned to her right to see who her neighbour would be for the next few years. To her surprise, she found a good-looking lad smiling at her. She nodded politely and turned her attention back to her desk.

He kept watching her, his arms folded, as he leant on his amazing new desk. He had watched her anxiously check her cell a few times and was hoping she wouldn't get caught. Most of the students were hanging around the drinks table, introducing themselves to Cadence. A few of them were talking to Maggie about some of the artwork displayed on the front wall at the side of the huge whiteboard. Shadow girl checked the second drawer of her cabinet as her neighbour approached stealthily and made her jump when he said ''ello' practically in her earhole. She spun round in her chair and almost fell off.

He grabbed the tops of her arms to support her and she flinched at his touch. Quickly letting go, he sensed her discomfort. "My name eez Guy," he spoke with a French accent, as his inquisitive green eyes tried to see behind the mirrored shades. She let out a small steadying breath and slowly removed her sunglasses. Looking up at him in the brightness of the natural sunlight and spotlights that covered the studio's ceiling, he looked like a god. He smiled a sexy confident smile and held out his hand. She paused, then extended her hand out to shake his, a small crease forming on her brow.

"I'm Hallie," she spoke quietly.

"Ahh, you're English. Ashante," he said smiling broadly, taking her hand. Instead of shaking it, he pulled it to his mouth and kissed it gently, never breaking eye contact. "I am French," he said still smiling.

"You don't say," she said sarcastically, making him laugh heartily. She smiled and his heart melted. She was still wearing the baseball cap but he was close enough to be able to admire her luminescent blue eyes. They chatted briefly about how cool the studio was and how lucky they were to be here. They were messing with the remote control, which they discovered also inclined the desk and controlled the glass panel window she was sitting by. The professor asked them all to take their seats and with a grand bow, Guy returned to his desk opposite her. She smiled and shook her head at his bow. Not only was he a romantic French male, but he was also a teenage boy with raging hormones.

She made a note in her head to keep him at arm's length. Her mind was still on the handsome man she had seen on the staircase. He had made her feel uncomfortable, although she didn't know anything about him and had only seen him for a couple of seconds. "Right then, just to let you know that I love the radio on whilst I work; it soothes my soul and you will all grow to love it." She smiled quickly scanning the faces of all ten students to ensure they were engaged. She was happy to see the quiet student in the corner had taken off her sunglasses. She was obviously very shy but Maggie was expecting big things from her.

'Hallie Whitmore's' artwork had blown her away. Professor Millward had shown herself and Pip after his intake day back in March. The sketches and paintings were utterly brilliant, detailed and perfectly executed. Cadence and Ida were both convinced that Miss Whitmore would be a fraud and had a fifty-quid bet that she would be found out and expelled from the institute within the first week, but Maggie had hoped she would be that elusive undiscovered talent that everyone was waiting for. The radio chirped into action. The young adults in the room would have been disappointed if they were expecting Capital or some hip radio station.

Instead, the smooth tones of local disc jockey, Gregory Parsons (or GP as Maggie loved to call him), rhythmically announced the next tune to be played. A gentle seventies tune filled the room and the youngsters either smiled or grimaced at the music.

"So, we have music, you have seen where you will be sitting throughout the course. Can I ask that you keep to the same desks, as it helps me remember your names? You will find a well-stocked cabinet of art equipment to your left and we have a large store if there is anything else you require. You will also see a small remote control; this enables you to alter the angle of your desk to suit yourself and it also shades the windows if the natural light becomes too bright. Your seats are specially designed to adjust to any size or shape that sits in them, so they should be nice and comfortable." Maggie again looked around and a few students nodded their heads.

"When do we start to paint?" A German accent from the front row called out.

Maggie turned to see a gangly fair-haired boy. "And you are?" She waited for him to reply.

"Fynn Schulz," he said without humour. Mindy Moore had nabbed the adjacent desk and sighed longingly when he spoke. He was so cute and he had great taste in clothes and accessories, her type of boy.

"Well, Fynn, we will be sketching after lunch as this morning I'm going to show you around if that's alright with you?" She smiled, used to tenacious, overbearing youngsters. Master Schulz nodded his head, his face staying serious. "That's settled then." Still smiling she continued, "So if you would all like to follow me, I will give you a tour of the gallery's buildings." Along with her now full, yellow mug of tea, she made her way to the door on her left which led to a tunnel. With more excited chatter, the students followed. Mindy stayed at Flynn's side and smiled inanely, whilst pointing out that she loved his sweater and that Gucci was her favourite designer.

As the youngsters of all nationalities entered the glass corridor, two had hung back. Cadence, the assistant, was fussing around the drinks table, tidying it up.

She had OCD and liked everything in its place. She was oblivious to the two students who hadn't moved from their desks. Guy was watching Hallie with interest. She had observed the others as they were filing into the corridor, waiting until last, wanting to be invisible and not draw any attention to herself. She turned to look at him and again seemed surprised that he was watching her. With a tilt of his head in the direction of the corridor, she bit her bottom lip with nerves.

She stood and started walking towards the door to the mole tunnel, which had closed behind the last student. At the door, she stopped and turned to see Guy right behind her. He stopped at her side and opened the door, holding it open for her to walk through, "Thank you," she said softly.

"You are welcome," he said, playing the gentleman. A few steps downwards led to the conveyor belts like you find at any airport. As they stepped onto the left-hand conveyor belt, it moved them gently through the cool glass tube. This was a semi-submerged tunnel that was surrounded by elegant gardens on either side.

"So, this is what a hamster feels like," she said attempting a little humour to counter her nerves. The corridor made her feel claustrophobic and she longed to be outside.

"I agree." Guy laughed and took in the wonderful flowers in line with his view that he would simply love to sketch. At the end of the tunnel, they stepped off the moving floor and walked through an automatic glass door. An expansive seating area with several doors on either side greeted them.

"We will start with the Main Gallery. This room contains the final paintings of our year four students. We also use it to exhibit paintings we are offered on loan and therefore this is a high-tech security system that covers this area. No students are permitted in here on their own. The 'Gallery' buildings have their own security team, so please don't get any ideas of trying to sneak out an expensive work of art." She laughed at this and put her palm against the scanner at the gallery entrance doors. There was a click and the large doors gently opened. As they walked into the vast hall, there were oohs and ahhhs as the new intake realised this was a seriously amazing space.

There was different-sized artwork framed and hung professionally on the walls, under which exhibit plaques gave information about the artist and an explanation of the painting. Long padded benches sat neatly down the middle of the hall, allowing the viewers time to sit and inspect each painting. Hallie was completely in awe and immediately went to the right-hand side of the colossal hall which was empty. The other students had followed their professor and were admiring the artwork on the left-hand side. Voices echoed around the vast space but Hallie was oblivious. She loved art and this place felt like heaven.

"I am a landscape painter," Guy spoke quietly at her side and she realised she was not alone. After staring up at him for a few seconds, she glanced over to where the others were having a lively debate about their favourite types of paints.

"Wouldn't you prefer to be with them?" She looked back at him, his moss green eyes not blinking.

"I prefer to be with you," he purred, with the nuances of his French accent giving the words a seductive twist.

"Look, Guy…" She raised both hands in the air as if he was pointing a gun at her. "I'm really not interested. I am so lucky to be on this course and I want to concentrate and work hard…" She paused trying to find the right words. "I'm sure you're lovely, but I do not want a boyfriend." Her serious expression showed she meant business.

He smiled with his head nodding, making his brown short curls bounce slightly. "I understand, Cherie." A slight grimace on his handsome face showed his disappointment. "Would you mind a friend who 'eez a boy?" His eyes widened as he waited for a response.

Hallie sighed and shrugged her shoulders as her hands fell to her sides. "I would like a friend," she said sincerely. A radiant smile was his response and they both relaxed a little and discussed the incredible portrait in front of them. A magnificent Katrina Hart painting of an Asian lady in a beautiful orange sari. She held her hands together and was praying. You could see every wrinkle on her wizened face, the work was exquisite. An hour later, Maggie ushered them out of the Main Gallery and back into the seating area with all the doors leading off it.

"Toilets are at the far end over there." She helpfully pointed to where they were situated. "Can I ask that you make use of them now as we are heading into the auditorium for a joint session with Studio Two? Once we are in there, we won't be leaving until the twelve pm bell." She finished and checked her watch; ten-fifty, right on track. In fact, she might visit the ladies' room whilst she had a few minutes to spare. Some of the students were also making their way to the toilets. A few had sat on the comfortable settees and chairs, flicking through the pages of the various art magazines that had been scattered about. Hallie and Guy had been the last to leave the gallery.

Maggie then scanned her hand, thus securing the artwork. Hallie felt the side pocket of her trousers vibrate. "I have to go," she whispered to Guy, although the other students were nowhere near them. "I need to answer a call," she said as his face contorted with confusion. "I will go into the auditorium." She nodded over to the door, which was clearly labelled with an artistic plaque. She made it through the auditorium door with no one noticing, relieved that most of her classmates were so full of themselves, that they had no care what others were doing. She pressed redial and as she took in the large room, she was again overawed. Her old school had been nothing like this place.

As the phone started ringing, she put it to her ear, at the same time making her way to the back seats of the auditorium which had a viewing gallery and exit doors behind them. At least, she could sneak out unnoticed if it came to it. "Hi, it's me," she spoke hurriedly. "I'm in my lessons and I can't really talk now." She broke off. She listened to the impassioned words being spoken on the phone. "I understand, but I did explain..." Again she was interrupted and with a nervous glance at the main door, she gave in. "Okay, put him on, but I have to be quick."

Guy stood by the auditorium doors keeping a watchful eye on things. Luckily, Maggie had been distracted by some magnificent artwork in one of the magazines that had been waved in front of her by a keen Japanese student and she was in deep conversation with the group. Suddenly, the tunnel door swished open and the dominant figure of Professor Denton appeared, strolling briskly towards the auditorium. He was followed by his own group of students who were chattering eagerly about their morning so far. Guy froze, trying to think of a reason to delay his new friend being discovered using her phone.

He glanced nervously around the room to see where the nearest fire alarm was but rethought this immediately as it may set off sprinklers that would ruin all the artwork on display. Denton had seen this dubious-looking student and picked up on his mischievous look. Spinning around, he addressed his group, who had made it through their first mole tunnel with much delight and animation. "The restrooms are at the far end to the right; I suggest you go now as we have a combined session with Studio One in less than five minutes time." They all nodded enthusiastically and as he approached Guy, every single one of his students made their way to the toilets.

He noticed Maggie deep in conversation and as he came face-to-face with her curly-haired student, he eyed him suspiciously. "You're keen?"

Guy wasn't sure if this was a question or a statement, but in order to delay, he replied, "Yes, Sir, I am." His polite reply did not seem to endear him to this professor, so he decided on another tact. He burst into song, surprising himself as much as the bewildered man in front of him. "I can see clearly now the rain 'as gone…" His loud singing penetrated through to the auditorium and 'shadow girl' paused.

"I have to go now; I will be with you later," she said clearly and concisely. "Goodbye." She finished and waited for the other end of the call to go dead.

"…I can see all obstacles in my way!" Guy's French accent didn't really help the song but he persevered.

"Enough!" Denton stopped him with that one sharp word. Moving his foot discreetly from the door, which he had been holding slightly ajar, Guy stepped back. Professor Denton shook his head looking past the French singer towards Maggie, who was staring open-mouthed with the rest of the students. "I'm going in to set up, give me a few minutes," his American drawl both chilly and to the point.

"Of course," she replied smiling, used to his tone. As Denton pushed the door open, Guy was about to protest but simply could not think of a reason to prevent him. He could have just hit him but Guy was happy to be on this course and did not want to be expelled on his first day. So, he begrudgingly stood aside and watched as the serious-looking professor disappeared into the other room.

Chapter 3

As he purposely strode into the auditorium, the door closed silently behind him. He stood and looked from the huge screen on the front wall, to the plinth, desk and seat on the stage and across the rows of seats and desktops, sloping up the viewing gallery. His eyes stopped on a small figure sitting on the last seat of the back row. He instantly recognised the 'shadow girl'. She was still wearing the black baseball cap but he couldn't see her face. Her head was resting on her folded arms, leaning on the desktop which ran the length of the row. Several thoughts rushed through his mind. He wanted to go to her and put his arm around her slim frame to comfort her but that was not appropriate.

Maybe he should call over and check if she was alright, but he didn't want to frighten her. The memory of her jumping when Maggie had called out to her in the reception gallery appeared vividly in his mind. Was she crying? The thought disturbed him. Deciding he should not approach her, he called out, "Can I help in any way?" His tone was softer than before, his American accent apparent in every syllable. The girl's head shot up and though she was some distance away, he was relieved to see she had removed her sunglasses, the peak of her cap still giving her face some protection from whatever she was trying to hide from.

Her eyes were wide and bewildered but from the gap between them, he could not make out their colour and for some reason, this annoyed him. He could make out her expression, even under the protection of her baseball cap. She looked as if she had the weight of the world on her shoulders. She hadn't replied to his question, so he tried again. "Is everything alright?" He was genuinely concerned. In all of his teaching years, he had never had a student look so intensely sombre, especially on their first day.

She had seen him earlier on the staircase but he now stood on the other side of the room and his suit jacket had been removed. He was wearing dark grey trousers with a thin black belt. His pale pink shirt was fitted and a pale grey tie was knotted neatly at his throat. He was tall and his body toned; he obviously kept fit and she wondered briefly what he would look like without the smart, expensive clothes. As she was thinking this, he had spoken; with no idea what he said, she took in his face. He was devastatingly handsome, with full lips and chiselled cheekbones and jawline. She was sure that he must model for the sculpture department, as he literally looked like a Greek god.

With light brown cropped hair and a clean-cut jawline, he looked as if he had just stepped out of a barber's shop. She was just wondering what he would look like with stubble, sending her insides squirming, when he spoke again. She watched his mouth move and she knew he was addressing her, but her mind was elsewhere and she again just stared at this gorgeous man. His expression was serious, his brow furrowing in concern for this vulnerable young girl who didn't seem to understand him. For a few more seconds, they just stared at each other, him not knowing what to say or do next and she was simply dumbstruck.

Suddenly, she jerked raising her right hand, placing it firmly on her right hip. She looked down at her hand and back at the handsome professor with a look of panic on her pretty face. He did not know how to react to her, his mind overthinking it and telling him to stay put, his heart screaming at him to go to her. He took his first step forward just as the door burst open at the side of the auditorium and Maggie bustled in. She was closely followed by Guy and the rest of the noisy students. Philip Denton froze mid-stride and watched as the French student, who had sung to him, traipsed past, heading in the direction of the 'shadow girl'.

He watched as she saw the lad approach the girl. She looked back to her right hip and again his heart tightened at the thought she was in pain. "Everything okay, Pip?" Maggie whispered as she linked her arm with his, looking in the direction of his glare. "Hmm, I will talk to you about her later," she spoke quietly her voice full of concern. "Alright, you lot, everyone takes a seat." She called out, back to her bright and bubbly teacher mode. She linked Pip's arm with hers and pulled his attention away from the back row of the auditorium. They made their way onto the stage. Maggie flicked a switch on a small remote control that had been resting on the plinth that stood elegantly in the middle of the stage.

Behind her, a huge screen powered to life and the institute's crest appeared. Sensing that Pip was out of sorts, she decided to take control and start the lecture. Today, it was more of a welcome introduction and as Maggie's teaching style was informal and relaxed, it wasn't much different to her usual lectures. Pip sat on the chair behind the desk that was also on the stage. He focused on the folders and paperwork that had been methodically placed in order on the desktop. Cadence had been busy. Maggie was passionately informing the apprehensive students exactly what was expected from them. After seeing the quality of work on display in the Main Gallery, the teenagers were slightly overwhelmed by the task ahead.

After ten minutes of trying to read the same document and not taking a word in, Pip decided to look up at the back row of the auditorium. He found the curly-haired songster sitting alone. Scanning the rows of scattered students, he was searching for the 'shadow girl' and her black baseball cap but she was not there. Fuck, was she ill? How had she managed to leave the auditorium without anyone noticing? Why was he so bothered? Breathing slowly, he returned his attention to where she had been sitting on the back row. Her fellow student had the decency to look sheepish as they caught each other's eye.

Guy quickly turned his attention back to Maggie who was describing the seven arts that made up the fine arts institute. He tried to listen intently but was unnerved by the severe look he was getting from the Studio Two professor. As he had taken his seat, Hallie retrieved her mobile phone from her right trouser pocket and with a grimace, whispered, "I have to take this." She quickly escaped the room by the exit door that was practically next to her, leaving Guy with his mouth agape in silent shock. He was hoping that no one would notice her disappearance and was glad that the German student, Fynn, was shooting questions at Maggie, gaining the whole room's full attention.

He tried to focus on the lecture but his mind wandered off to his new friend and he looked to his side where she had been sat a few minutes before. As he raised his head to look at the stage, he had caught Professor Denton's pensive glare. He broke eye contact and looked back at Maggie. The man behind the desk looked bloody furious.

In an attempt to subdue his thoughts, Pip returned his focus to the document he had reread several times since taking his seat. Half listening to the mostly inane questions being fired at Maggie, he tried to take in the information on the page in front of him. After a few more minutes, he closed the document, unable to recall any of its information. He glanced up at the back row and there she was. In her black baseball cap and dark baggy clothes. He caught his breath and quickly looked down at the papers on his desk. So, she thinks she can sneak in and out on her first day's lessons? She needed to learn some respect, as Maggie was trying to impart information about the sessions they would be having.

As the lecture was drawing to an end, Maggie called on her learned colleague to add anything she may have missed in her welcome lecture. "Professor Denton?" She called over to him but his mind was elsewhere. He stood and walked to the plinth nodding politely at Maggie, who made her way over to sit in his seat.

"Ladies and gentlemen…" He began in his strong American accent, his tone serious. "I would like to remind you all that there is a two-year waiting list of potential students who would literally do anything to be sat in your seats today. I will not tolerate any student who does not show one hundred per cent commitment to their placement here." He glanced up at the back row and saw the peak of the black baseball cap dip. He couldn't see her face but he knew she was getting the message. The group of teenagers fidgeted uncomfortably in their seats. Although intimidated, the female students could not look away as he domineered the stage. His handsome features were taut and grave as he continued.

"You are the lucky ones, the talented ones. You have all earned your place here in this spectacular institute, however, you must all strive to deserve it." He finished and glanced over at Maggie who was sat wide-eyed, her mouth forming a small 'O', slightly perplexed by Pip's speech. She stood and shook out her full skirt as she walked over to him, restoring her usual happy smile. She stood beside him behind the plinth, grabbing his hand and squeezing it in reassurance. Their hands were hidden behind the podium, so no one could see, a small gesture of comfort. He looked down at her and smiled, his breathing slowing and becoming even.

The tension in the room instantly lifted when the teenagers observed this daunting man actually smile. An electronic bell rang out and everyone in the room seemed to let out a relieved breath. "Okay, folks, see you all in an hour after lunch. You will find us in our relevant studios; be ready to create some actual art." She beamed at the thought of seeing what this new group were capable of. Pip was just about to add that a certain student should stay behind when he glanced up to see that the 'shadow girl' had disappeared again. Fuck, how did she manage to do that? He had leant over the plinth to ask her to remain but she had already somehow escaped.

"Enjoy your lunch break…and I need to speak to you…on the backrow." All eyes turned to the curly-haired songster; the other students were relieved that he wasn't ordering them to stay behind. "So do not disappear." His tone was serious and his face looked like it had turned to stone. He returned to the desk to retrieve some documents he had wanted to read during lunch. Guy gulped and his face paled. Maybe singing wasn't the best idea for distraction; the professor looked 'en colere'. As the students streamed out of the auditorium, Guy bravely remained in his seat. He was used to being shouted out by his domineering father, who thought his son was wasting his life away with this 'La peinture merde', as he called it.

Maggie walked over to Pip. "What's going on?" She asked quietly.

Looking up at her kind face, he smiled, leaning back on the chair. "I will fill you in. Give me five, meet me in my office." He finished looking up at the nervous boy still sitting in the back row. He beckoned to him with his hand. "Why don't you come down and join me?" He said standing himself. Maggie paused for a moment as she looked up at the good-looking French lad, who had also stood and was making his way across the row, heading for the middle aisle. Sighing in resignation and winking at Pip, she left them to it.

He smiled again at the wink, a little habit Maggie had when she didn't know quite what to say and they were not alone. Pip stepped off the stage and walked over to the front row, where he perched on the desktop. With his arms folded, he looked formidable as Guy approached him with apprehension. "I am zorree for ze zinging," Guy began apologetically.

Pip shook his head. "I don't want to discuss your singing, this is the 'art' department," he said not hiding the sarcasm in his voice. "What is your name?" Pip asked, trying to remain calm.

"Guy Rousseau," the intimidated student replied quickly.

"And the disappearing student who was sat beside you?" He waited for Guy to understand and continued, "What is her name and do you know why she thought it appropriate to leave the lecture several times this morning?" His voice was now even and cool, defying the young man to even try and lie about it.

"Err name 'eez allie Whitmore," he spoke quietly, his French accent thick with emotion that Pip couldn't quite place. "She 'ad no choice to leave, she 'ad an emergenzee to deal with." The lad finished, hoping he had said enough to get this professor off his back but not enough to get Hallie in trouble. He knew

Denton had spotted Hallie leave from the 'le mal' looks he had been giving them both during the lecture.

"Emergency?" Pip queried, his brow furrowed.

"Zat's all I know," Guy said honestly, shrugging his shoulders.

Pursing his full lips together, one eyebrow raised as he assessed this nervous teenager, now looking at the floor in front of him. "You may go," he said sternly. The lad looked up for a moment as if deciding whether or not to speak. Wisely, he chose not to say another word and turning on his heels, he walked silently out of the room. Pip rubbed his hands over his face and after retrieving the necessary documents from the desk, made his way to his office, taking a last look at the seat on the back row just in case she had returned. It was empty.

Chapter 4

As he pushed open the door to his spacious office, Maggie greeted him with his favourite coffee made on his treasured Tassimo machine. A large plateful of ham and salad sandwiches, mini scotch eggs, and a bowlful of plain crisps were also laid out on the coffee table. They took it in turns to get lunch and Maggie had gone traditional for the first day back. "Looks amazing," he said gratefully as his stomach rumbled. Breakfast was hours ago and he was famished. He placed the documents he wanted to read on his desk and made his way over to the coffee table full of food. Pip sat himself down unceremoniously on the large comfy sofa, next to his work partner and friend.

"Sooo…" Maggie said through a mouthful of the sandwich. He took a serviette and placed a sandwich on top. He sighed; his handsome face creased in a frown. "Hallie Whitmore," he said not really knowing where to begin.

"Ahh yes, I have all my hopes set on her being a master of fine art." She smiled knowingly. "There is something about her that draws the eye…" She said as she looked up from her sandwich and saw he was watching her intently.

"Go on," he encouraged.

"This morning, I had to force myself not to stare at her…" She said honestly, pausing as she crunched on some crisps. "And those eyes, wow." She finished looking up again at Pip. He was looking at her as if mesmerised.

"What colour are they?" He tried to sound nonchalant but failed miserably.

Maggie stopped eating, putting her pile of crisps back on the table and looked at him bemused. "They are the most heavenly deep blue I have ever seen, but don't tell Clara," she said, knowing her wife would be very jealous if she heard her talking about another female's blue eyes and good looks.

"Heavenly deep blue…" He repeated, closing his eyes and trying to picture them.

"What's going on?" Maggie said sipping her hot tea from her favourite huge yellow mug, which Pip had brought her a few years before. "Why all the interest?" She questioned. The two professors knew each other inside out and back to front. When they had met four years ago, they had decided to break the ice by having a late night in the staffroom. They had ordered pizza and drank a ridiculous amount of wine between them. For the first time ever, Philip Denton let down his guard and was open and honest. Maggie had been warm and welcoming and for some odd reason he still hadn't fathomed, he trusted her immediately.

They regaled each other with stories of their childhoods, education and love lives. Both were fascinated and shocked by some of the details that came out. It was the beginning of not only a firm friendship but a close relationship between them both, so much so, that they thought of each other like family. He had told her that night that he was a little jealous of her. Maggie's love and adoration for her partner, Clara, was all consuming and powerful. He had never felt that overwhelming passion for anyone. His parents were still together after many years of marriage and although he knew they loved each other; he had never seen any real passion between them.

At twenty-eight years old, he had slept with many women, his looks never failing to attract. Before leaving the States, he had been seeing a much older woman. She had picked him up one night in a bar, using her feminine wiles to lure him back to her penthouse suite. He was cocky and full of himself at the time, thinking he was worldly-wise and an Adonis in the bedroom. He had been wrong. She had opened his mind and body to incredible sex and taught him tricks he hadn't known. He had been left deliriously elated and sated in her experienced hands. They had been sexual partners for over three months and she had taught him many skills, in regards to the knowledge and skill of sex.

Occasionally, she would talk down to him, pointing out his young age, as if it was detrimental to her pleasure whilst having sex. She pressed all of his buttons on purpose, knowing he would get angry and respond by domineering her during sex. The strange relationship had ended as quickly as it began when he announced he was leaving for the United Kingdom. There was never any closeness or love but he really thought he meant something to her. Expecting her to be heartbroken and that she would try and convince him to stay, she had laughed, her coldness now exposed. Telling him he was nothing to her, just bad sex.

She had also thrown in a comment that she was married, a fact he had been blissfully unaware of. After a blazing row, he had left her penthouse suite never to return. Copious amounts of alcohol and feeling a little lost, he had recounted this tale to Maggie. She had listened and helped him analyse this part of his life many times, over drinks, when they were alone. He had told her that on the evening he had argued with the older woman, he was so angry and upset, he was scared of what he might do. He had never hit a woman in his life but he had been so hurt and angry, he had come close. He hated the anger and knew it was no way to deal with a breakup.

He had managed to keep his cool and ended up having a fight outside a local bar, where he had badly beaten a loud-mouthed yob who had dared to spill some of his drink over Pip's shoes. Luckily, he had stopped before he killed the lad, but the anger he felt and the violence he had carried out had frightened him. Maggie had put his violent behaviour that night down to him being heartbroken and in the four years they had known each other, she had never seen him angry or lose his temper. She knew he attended an exclusive, private club named 'The Oyster Club', where he saw the same mistress each time.

He neither trusted nor had time for a real relationship. He had not had any girlfriends or one-night stands apart from this woman since he had arrived in England, and he had not had sex with her. He liked her company. No complications, just someone he could spend time with and talk to. Although bright and confident when teaching, Maggie knew Pip was lonely and wanted nothing more than for him to fall in love and live happily ever after. Clara loved Pip as much as Maggie. They were both outgoing and loud and looked fondly at Pip as their younger brother.

Maggie and Clara had a lot in common, including their cheery dispositions. They enjoyed having fun and doing new adventurous things. This year, during the summer holidays, they had gone skydiving. Pip had gone to watch them, initially being concerned for their safety as they threw themselves out of the plane hatch. He was soon in stitches when they reappeared on the ground after the exhilarating experience. Maggie had been gushing about 'flying like a bird' and the immense feeling of freedom. Clara had described how she had nearly knocked herself out with her ample bosom and if they ever attempted to do this again, she needed a much better bra.

He adored them both and although they were in their early fifties, he looked affectionately on them as spritely older sisters. Having four sisters and a brother back in the States, he was used to sibling rivalry, but Maggie and Clara were his dearest friends and the closest thing he had to family in the UK. He would occasionally fly over to Los Angeles to visit his parents and large family. He also had aunties, Uncles, and cousins whom he cared for, but somehow over the years, he had distanced himself from them all.

"I ask again, why all the interest?" Maggie repeated patiently, taking a huge slurp of her tea.

"I'm not really sure," he replied honestly. "I saw her earlier from the window in the welcome gallery, there was something about her…" he answered honestly. "A vulnerability?" He shook his head and took a bite out of his delicious sandwich. "Watching her, it seemed like she was trying to hide. I have no idea why, but like you said, I felt drawn to her and couldn't stop watching her." He raised an eyebrow and she threw a scotch egg at him. "Hey." He laughed.

Maggie looked serious for a moment. "You're not attracted to her sexually?" She questioned, watching his response closely. Nothing ever shocked Maggie and she always said exactly what she was thinking. The look of earnestness on her pretty face meant that for the first time since they had met, he could not be honest and open with her.

"Of course, not," he replied quickly, although he didn't really believe his own answer.

"Thank god for that." She scoffed puffing out air exaggeratingly. "'Cos she's only a child you know," she said seriously, her eyes knitted together in a frown.

"I know, of course, I know…Now let's change the subject. What are your new students drawing this afternoon?" The mood significantly lifted as she told him all about the large box of seashells she had found in the art store. Studio One students would be attempting to draw them and she was hoping to assess their art skills from the work that they would hopefully be completing this afternoon. "What about yours?" She asked, stuffing another crisp in her mouth. He smiled and shook his head at her un-lady-like and un-professor-like behaviour.

"Studio Two will be drawing boots and shoes," he replied, still smiling at his friend. At twelve-fifty, they both made their way to their own studios in readiness for the afternoon sessions. As he stepped through the double doors from Studio One to make his way up the staircase, he saw Hallie Whitmore once again standing in front of the 'Dreams' painting. With her head tilted, her long ponytail was resting on her left shoulder. Instead of taking the staircase to his right, he walked towards her. As if she sensed his presence, she flinched, spinning around to face him.

Head tilted up, he could now see her truly exceptional blue eyes, framed with long dark lashes. She had a button nose and full rosebud pink lips. A faint blush appeared on her pale cheeks. There was not a sign of make-up or cosmetic procedure on her porcelain skin. "Miss Whitmore." He nodded a hello and held out his hand in greeting. As he did so, her head moved back a fraction as if in response to his proximity. She stared at him, mouth closed, with no intention of shaking his hand or speaking. His austere look was enough to turn flesh into stone.

His stance changed from polite to imperious as he quickly became angry with this young girl. Who the fuck did she think she was? Not speaking, not shaking his proffered hand. Suddenly, she flinched, her right hand moving to her right hip pocket. Her eyes widened in alarm as she nodded her retreat and turned to walk away, retrieving her phone from her pocket. He was so furious that he strode after her and grabbed her arm tightly, pulling her around to face him. He was about to let rip and tell her how disrespectful she was being to a professor when he saw her face. Her mouth open in shock, her incredible blue eyes dilated, wide in alarm. Her whole body had recoiled and he realised she was frightened.

He let go immediately, opening his mouth to apologise, but she had already turned and practically ran through reception and out of the double doors. He stood for a few moments, bewildered by what had just happened. He had scared her, something he had never dreamt of doing. "Everything all right, dear?" Mrs Bushell called from behind the elegant reception desk having witnessed the interaction.

Pip turned and addressed her, "Mrs Bushell." He nodded and tried to summon up a convincing smile. He liked this charming old lady a lot and just her cheeky wink made him feel a little better.

"You ok, my love?" She asked again, her Black Country accent still present in every syllable. She smiled warmly at this handsome man.

"Yes, thank you, Mrs Bushell, all is well. How are you doing on our first day back?" He asked kindly as he walked towards the massive desk, which she was sitting behind.

"All good here, my dear," she answered, delighted to be back at the heart of the gallery's building. Pip took in her genuine smile and surveyed this crazy old broad in front of him. She had altered her chair so it was as high as it could go, giving her a good view of the reception area and unknown to Pip, her feet were dangling, like a child. She had white long hair piled into a messy bun, with a bright green scrunchie, securing it. She always wore make-up and had the same pink lipstick on that she had the day they had first met. An outrageous flirt, she was always kind and funny. Today, she was wearing a dark green silk blouse, which had a large bow at the neck.

Mrs Bushell adored chunky jewellery and her ears were sagging under the weight of the large diamante, clip-on bows that were hanging on for dear life. A matching chunky bracelet with the same diamante bow was secured around her bony wrist. She looked like a Christmas present waiting under the tree. She was still smiling when there was a low rumble and odd noise emitting from her direction. Her smile fell and her eyes widened in alarm. "Are you alright, Mrs Bushell?" Pip asked, his face showing his concern. She nodded slowly as her nose wrinkled and her eyes tightened.

Suddenly, the most horrendous smell hit Pip's nostrils and he stepped back, making his apologies. "Sorry, but I have to get back to the studio. Catch up with you later, Mrs Bushell." He smiled and politely stepped away from the smell which seemed to have been omitted from Mrs Bushell's bottom. As he walked away, she looked up at the ceiling, shaking her head in mortification. Pip's thoughts had reverted back to the incident with the young student and with a great sense of remorse, he turned and made his way up the staircase to Studio Two. Luckily, the welcome gallery had been deserted, so no one else had witnessed the interaction.

As he sat at his desk, he slammed the documents down hard, the look on the young girl's face replaying clearly in his mind. He opened the papers and saw a photo of the same girl he had just grabbed and scared. He felt sick to his stomach. No female had ever reacted to him like that. Fuck. He scanned through the documents containing Hallie Whitmore's application form, photographs of her artwork, fee papers, and an emergency contact sheet. He glared at her date of birth; she was only sixteen years old. This information alone put him in a fouler mood than he was before. Skimming through the photographs of her work, he could see that she must be a fraud.

They were stunning pieces. A landscape, a portrait, and several paintings and drawings of individual objects. They were all executed to a high, professional standard and there was no way a young girl could have possibly achieved this level of skill. Her emergency contact details showed mobile numbers for both of her parents and a local address. The afternoon bell trilled out, breaking his thoughts, as he slammed the document shut and threw it in the top drawer of his desk. Something about Miss Whitmore bothered him, her frightened face replaying in his mind and tormenting him for the rest of the afternoon.

As the students re-entered Studio One, they were presented with a large shell on each of their workstations. Hallie had a beautiful conch shell, with a shiny coral pink centre. She loved shells and the sight of it lifted her dark mood. The male professor had caught her in the welcome gallery and she guessed by his reaction that students were not allowed into the building over the lunch period. After trying to shake her hand, her phone had silently vibrated in her pocket and she knew she had to answer it quickly. He had followed her and grabbed her arm. She pulled her left sleeve up to see a dark mark on her pale white skin.

She bruised easily and she knew that she would be left with a purple-black contusion from her first day here. The thought was depressing. The fact he had caught her using her phone and that he obviously hated mobiles was even more daunting. What if she was going to lose her sponsorship and get kicked out? "You are lucky, look what I waz given." Guy's French inflexion was close to her ear as he moved beside her. She jumped looking up to see him holding a large sea urchin in his hands. "I'm not good at objects," he said despondently.

Seeing that he looked as dejected as her, she tried to help. "Draw what you're good at then," she said with a small smile, trying to be positive. His dark brows raised as he pulled a face, having no clue what she was talking about. He was now holding the urchin away from himself as if it were about to explode. Hallie couldn't help but laugh and he smiled in response. "Draw a landscape and add the shell into it," she said simply and he realised that she had had a good idea. He beamed at her, grateful for her input. With a final wink, he made his way over to his desk. Before he had even taken his seat, Hallie had begun sketching her shell on the large crisp white paper that had been laid out before her.

The radio was on in the background; another seventies tune echoing around the studio. Maggie was pouring another mug of tea and a couple of the students had formed a line for the drink's tables. The others were all chatting animatedly, having survived their first morning's session and enjoyed their first campus lunch. Mindy was leaning provocatively over Master Schulz's desk and he was paying no attention to her face. His eyes were focused on her overstretched breasts which were barely contained by her cheerleader top. She had chosen to have her hair in pigtails hoping to emanate a Britney Spears vibe. This had the opposite effect of making her look younger as it was combined with a large amount of dramatic make-up.

Along with the chemical fillers and enhanced breasts, she looked older than her seventeen years. After half an hour of general chatter and wasting time, Maggie called for everyone's attention. Armed with her large yellow mug of tea, she instructed the students to take their seats and study the shell they had been given. They were to sketch it and use only HB pencils to shade and shape it. She also informed the students that she and Cadence enjoyed listening to 'Heartbreak Half Hour' on the radio where the presenter would recount a romantic story, some ending happily, some ending sadly.

"You will all grow to love this slot on the radio," Maggie called out loudly. "So enjoy it and take your time with this, your very first piece of artwork on your course." She clapped her hands together in excitement, gleefully happy to have her new intake of students. As the chatter died down, the students began to intently observe their seashells in preparation for drawing. Maggie scanned across the studio to ensure the teenagers were all engrossed in their work, to find the back right desk empty. Hallie Whitmore was not sitting in her chair. With a furrowed brow, she walked over to the back of the room. She picked up the piece of paper left on the worktop.

Her mouth agape, she blinked her eyes several times in case she was imagining it. She then stared at the shell, neatly sat on the desk and a row of different numbered HB pencils. She looked back at the paper where a perfectly executed image of the shell had been skilfully recreated. It was incredible work and Maggie checked her watch. The other students had only started their drawings a few moments ago but it seemed that Hallie had already completed the lesson. "She az gone to ze ladiez room," Guy called over from the safety of his workstation. Maggie carefully replaced the conch drawing and approached Guy. She opened her mouth to speak and stopped as she saw his sketch.

His desk was at a forty-five-degree position and he had lightly pencilled a beach. Its sandy shore aligned with palm trees and shrubs, with waves gently melting into the soft shore. After taking in the scene, Maggie smiled. "You were supposed to draw the shell," she questioned, delighted with another skilful drawing, although this one was just being started.

"I 'ave, Madame," he answered, his French accent and good looks having no effect on his new professor. He pointed to his drawing and there in complete proportion to the beach scene was, in fact, a dried sea urchin. "Eet 'as washed up on ze beach with ze tide." He smiled at Maggie and she beamed back. Amused yet delighted with his interpretation, she was always happy when students thought for themselves. Thinking outside the box meant that they usually had excellent imaginations and this, in turn, would lead to better artwork. Remembering he had mentioned Miss Whitmore visiting the ladies, she turned back to Hallie's desk to see her sitting in her seat and sketching her shell from another angle.

Maggie decided to speak to her at the end of the day as she didn't want to upset her and affect her exceptional work. She could not, however, let students leave the studio and not inform her where they were going. An hour later, the radio blared out an eighties one-hit wonder after an emotional 'Heartbreak Half Hour', which had brought most of Studio One to tears. A sad story was told of two lovers who had to face many obstacles in their disastrous courtship. In the end, they had just made it to their first kiss when the boyfriend had dropped down dead.

Some of the class had finished their drawings, others had a long way to go when the bell rang out at three-thirty to announce the end of the academic day. "Right then, ladies and gents…" Maggie called out. "Please leave your desks tidy and wash up your cups before you leave. Also, can you make sure you have written our names on your work so I know whose is whose?" Cadence was bustling around the studio, collecting completed artwork, carefully holding them as if they were precious priceless drawings. The chatter grew as the students discussed what they would be doing for their first proper evening at the institute. The campus contained coffee bars, restaurants, and a nightclub.

Most of the students were going for food and then drinks as the next art class was on Wednesday morning. Other students were attending different courses, so Tuesday would be Sculpture and Dance sessions in the other buildings. Hallie was about to slip out of the back door when Maggie called over to her. "Hallie, can I have a word before you go, please?" She said smiling and waving to students who were now leaving for the day. Hallie checked her watch and nervously paced back to her desk as the last student left the studio. Cadence went into the store room, returning the unused paper neatly in its place. Maggie watched Hallie for a while, noticing she was continuing to check her watch.

When they were finally on their own, Maggie put down her mug and walked over to her student, who had now donned her mirrored sunglasses. "Have you enjoyed your first day, Hallie?" Maggie started brightly.

"Yes, thank you," Hallie replied quietly. Maggie wished she could see her beautiful face properly as it was now covered by the shades and the peak of her baseball cap.

"I noticed there were a few times this afternoon where you were not at your desk," Maggie questioned. Hallie's face did not respond with any movement, so the professor continued. "If you could just let me know if you need the toilet because if there is ever a fire, I will know where I have to look for you." She finished and was a little perturbed that this young girl had not responded. She must be terribly shy. "Do you understand, Hallie?" She tried again.

"Yes, Miss. Sorry, Miss," Hallie whispered. She again checked her watch and bit her bottom lip.

"It's Maggie and it's okay, you obviously have someplace to be. Don't tell me you're off to the coffee shop for a hot date?" Maggie laughed, trying to be friendly and break the ice. Hallie simply nodded her head and turned to walk towards the exit door to the studio. As she went to reach out and pull the door, it was pushed open from the other side. Professor Denton walked through causing Hallie to freeze, hand still raised and mouth popped open as she took a breath in. Maggie looked on as Pip took in this teenager's statue-like appearance.

"Miss Whitmore…" Pip spoke his tone and demeanour serious. Hallie turned to look at the other exit door, which led to the Main Gallery and other rooms. This was the only door to the main entrance and he was blocking it. "About earlier…umm…" he said in his usually concise American drawl, not really knowing what to say.

"I'm late," Hallie said quietly as she again checked her watch.

"Oh…alright," he stuttered, then standing to the side and holding the door open. Hallie turned to face Maggie, who was looking completely befuddled. "Have a good evening, love," Maggie tried to say brightly. Hallie looked at Professor Denton, her lips pursed and her face pale, and then walked out of the studio. When she got to the reception area, she waved at Mrs Bushell and literally ran out of the door. She kept running until she reached her destination, the bike shelter. Cadence had reappeared from the stock room and had started noisily rearranging the cups on the drinks table. Maggie grabbed Pip's hand and walked towards the backdoor of the studio.

They didn't speak until she reached her office where she safely closed the door. Her office walls were full of paintings and sketches that previous students had drawn and signed for her. She was still positive that one day one of them would become famous in the art world. One particular favourite of hers was a portrait by Katrina Hart. She was a student at the art institute and had gone on to be a world-famous artist. She went over to her fridge and retrieved a bottle of prosecco. Pip sat on the corner of the settee that was a soft, plush purple. She found two mismatched mugs and put them on the coffee table in front of him.

She flumped down just as the cork whooshed off. "Pop goes the weasel," she sang, pouring the fizzing liquid into the waiting mugs. She took a large gulp and burped loudly, making Pip smile and shake his head gently. "No wonder we don't hang out in the main staff room," he said teasingly.

"Ok, mister, what happened with Miss Whitmore?" She tilted her head as if it would help her understand better.

"I saw her looking at the 'Dreams' painting before the afternoon session. I wanted to ask her why she had skipped out of the auditorium during the lecture." A frown was creasing his handsome face. "Before I could ask her, her phone must have vibrated, as she took it out of her pocket and went to leave…" He rubbed his forehead with his hand before he continued. "I was so annoyed; I grabbed her arm." He stopped as he took in Maggie's bewildered expression. Not a lot surprised her but she had never known her beloved Pip get angry. The fact he grabbed a student's arm was news to her and she didn't know what to say, so she took another huge gulp of prosecco. "She looked so scared, Mags," he said sadly.

She stood unexpectedly and walked over to her large messy desk. Grabbing papers in one hand, and holding her prosecco in the other, she sat back down by her friend. "Look at these," she said, spreading the papers out over the coffee table. She had asked Cadence to secure these in her office before the bell had rung. There were three pictures of a conch shell, all drawn from different angles. The conch itself was superbly drawn but the shading, considering it was all in pencil, was exquisite.

"Wow," he said completely blown away.

"Hallie drew them this afternoon." She smiled. "Amazing huh?"

He nodded in disbelief. "All three done today?" He questioned, taken aback. He honestly thought she was a fraud, but seeing these three sketches, she had proved she was the real deal. Three pieces of artwork were completed in an afternoon session and to this standard was incredible. "Maybe she is a new master," he said whilst scrutinising the drawings, his mind whirling at the day's strange events.

Chapter 5

Weeks had passed and the students had all settled into the art sessions in Studio One and Two. Although failing miserably in her artwork, Mindy Moore was still the centre of attention across the two floors of new students and had now slept with most of the male students on her course. She had her eye on the good-looking French dude who sat at the back of the room, but he seemed oblivious to her charms. Thinking he must be gay to not be interested in her, she had decided not to write him off completely and was keeping a sly eye on him. He seemed captivated by the nondescript girl, who looked like she needed some new clothes and a makeover.

He was, in fact, completely smitten with Hallie Whitmore. When he wasn't concentrating on his artwork, he would watch her intently. She always wore a baseball cap, her hair swinging in a ponytail and pulled through the catch hole of her cap. Baggy dark clothes covered her body and Guy spent many a night lying in bed imagining what beauty lay beneath. Hallie's shy, private nature had meant she had made no friends and she continued to receive silent messages on her mobile phone, which meant she was in and out of the studio. Since being caught on the first day, she always managed to catch Maggie's eye. With a small polite nod, she would slip out of the back door.

Maggie had realised quickly that Hallie was not some moody teenager, obsessed with her mobile phone. She thought Hallie's whole demeanour was of someone who was dealing with something much bigger than teenage hormones. Maybe there was a family upset or something private going on. Miss Whitmore was unlike any of the other students. The other nine students on Hallie's course in Studio One were all lively and outgoing. Most came from great wealth and notoriety and were all self-assured and confident. Hallie was subdued and quiet in comparison.

The art she had produced over the first term had been outstanding and she was by far the best artist not only in the studio but in Maggie's mind, possibly the world. She and Pip would sit and go through each day's artwork at the end of their sessions. Hallie's work was so detailed and perfectly executed, that they both had their doubts about what they could teach her. Both astounded by the quality of her work, with seemingly so little effort or fuss, they had photographed and logged each piece of her signed work and sent copies to Professor Millward.

Pip still had vivid memories of that first day when Miss Whitmore had made him so mad and he had grabbed her arm. Her face repeatedly occupied his dreams and he felt a strange pull towards this girl. At sixteen years old, she was still classed as a child. Pip knew that as a professor, his role was to teach and protect his students, but there was something about her. Maggie had told him that Hallie would leave the studio several times a day in response to what she believed to be a vibration from her mobile phone. A few weeks In, Maggie had again kept Hallie back after the afternoon session.

She could not fault the quality or quantity of her work, however, she made it clear that Hallie's behaviour was not normal and that no student should be leaving the studio that much to answer their phone. Hallie had apologised and without making eye contact, simply said that there was a family issue and that she had to make herself available whenever she received a call. Unfortunately, the silent calls were coming through several times a day. Maggie had dealt with teenage angst and meltdowns ever since she had become a teacher, many moons ago.

She had been headhunted by Millward to join the institute's faculty team and although delighted, had been met with the biggest student egos she had ever encountered. With celebrity parents or famous in their own right, Maggie had guided her students through parents' affairs and divorces, eating disorders, and a huge range of mental health issues and drug use. All of these dramas she had put down to the price of fame. Hallie Whitmore was not famous and neither were her parents. Having been awarded the scholarship for her outstanding artwork, Hallie was never brash or full of her own self-importance like the other students were.

Maggie had concerns and tried calling Hallie's parents, leaving voicemails for them both. She had received a text message response, late the same evening, apologising for not returning her call. Explaining they were both busy professionals, Mrs Whitmore had assured Maggie in a long message that Hallie was fine. Her elderly grandad was unwell and Hallie's close bond with him meant that whenever he wanted to speak to her, she would answer him. Talking to her would calm him down and make him feel better. She again apologised if this was affecting Hallie's work and ended the text message. Maggie was a little appeased. Soon the matter would surely right itself. If the girl's grandad recovered good health or if he sadly died from his illness, then that would be the end of it.

However, it had been three months since this message and there had been no change in circumstances regarding Hallie's odd behaviour. As soon as the afternoon bell rang, she would fly out of the door and literally sprint to the bicycle shelter to the right of the art buildings. She would then unpadlock her pale blue bike, pushing the chain lock into the wicker basket that sat neatly at the front of the handlebars. This was witnessed every Monday, Wednesday, and Friday from the large glass walls of Studio Two. The upstairs studio students were released at least five minutes before the end of the day bell tolled.

The happy students would pile out of the room and down the staircase, leaving Professor Denton to take his place at the vast glass wall in order to watch the figure that haunted his dreams. Each time she would begin to peddle quickly, picking up speed. He would watch her with clenched fists and grinding teeth. The fact she did not wear a helmet infuriated him. Why would she endanger herself like that? Each time he witnessed it, he became angrier. Surely her parents should force her to wear a helmet? He could not understand why this young girl's welfare bothered him so much.

He had ten of his own students to look after and Maggie was quite capable of caring for her own kids, but there was something about this girl. He was mortified that he was becoming slightly obsessive about her, having to watch her leave the buildings, wondering where she raced off to each afternoon. For once, this was one part of his life he was not sharing with his best friend, Maggie. She knew something was bothering him and had wondered if it had something to do with the natural beauty that was Miss Whitmore. However, he never mentioned her, only to critique her day's work when Maggie asked for an opinion. This routine had gone on for weeks and the British weather had now changed to dreary and autumnal.

Apart from donning a flimsy pakamac to keep out the torrential showers, Hallie Whitmore had not changed. Even Mindy Moore was coming in wearing tight woollen jumpers and fitted leggings to try and combat the bleak climate. Hallie wore the same loose-fitting tracksuit bottoms and long-sleeved tops. She never wore a thick jumper or a coat, which was just another irritating fact Denton had to cope with.

One Friday, it had actually been a dry, sunny afternoon, after torrential downpours all morning. The grass and foliage surrounding the studio buildings had dried out a little from the earlier storm and the sunshine seemed to lift everyone's spirits. They had an hour's combined lecture in the auditorium and then a handful of students were taken to the vault for the first time. The vault was a huge basement area nestled safely underneath the Main Gallery and art buildings. It had a state-of-the-art cooling system which kept the stored artwork at the proper temperature. This reduced moisture and any possible damage to the neatly stored paintings, drawings and sketches.

There were large shelved areas and glass rooms that housed the more expensive donations and priceless paintings on loan. As they stepped off the lift into the basement reception, they were greeted with a Liverpudlian hello and a huge genuine smile from Kiwi, one of the security team. In his late sixties, he had worked at the institute since its opening and although due to retire in a few weeks' time, he loved his job. "Ello, gorgeous people. Don't forget, if you need a handsome fella to paint, I'm always available," he said with a cheeky wink, making everyone smile.

"Alright, you lovely lot, we are splitting you up and each group will be doing some work down here in the vaults until the afternoon bell," Maggie said brightly, the powerful lighting illuminating the fine lines over her mature skin. She reeled off a list of a few names and a work area for each little group. Thankfully Hallie was put with Guy, whose relaxed and happy nature made her feel better about life in general. They had been paired with two students from Studio Two. Alexandru Balan, son of a famous Romanian Football player, and Akemi Fujioka, whose mother was a renowned Japanese clothes designer.

Alexandru was tall, dark and brooding. His forehead stayed in a constant frown and as yet, had never smiled in the art sessions. He was also avoiding Mindy Moore who had a nasty habit of rubbing her plastic, fake body up against him. As he entered the massive glass vestibule, both he and Guy were secretly relieved that Miss Moore was not part of their group. Akemi, on the other hand, was as loud and bright as her red flowered print, oversized suit. Her black shiny hair was immaculately pinned up and a trail of a small orange flower blossom, jiggled from the black comb, holding her doo in place. She was petite and apart from her bright red lipstick, she wore very little make-up.

Akemi also smelt divine, wearing one of her mother's range of perfumes. Hallie, Guy, and Alexandru, all took in the gentle blossom and vanilla scent that filled the room as Akemi entered. Maggie bustled into the strange glass-walled room after the four students, again full of enthusiasm for the next job in hand. "So, you have been specially chosen for this job. We have some of the oldest, most valuable paintings that the institute owns kept in the vaults. We sometimes lend them out to galleries and museums but we are not letting a bunch of first years loose on those." She laughed loudly and even Alexandru's mouth twitched.

"You will be looking at some new pieces though, so you are very lucky to have this opportunity." She was waving her arm around the room which had large shelving units and drawers full of artwork. There was a large beech desk which had several tubes on. Six tall beech stools were sat neatly around the desk and the students each took a seat. Maggie picked up a plastic box off the desk, pulling two white cotton gloves out, and pulling them over her hands. She then chose one of three tubes and deftly opened the lid, slowly and carefully producing a sizeable scroll. She gently smoothed out the paper to reveal a stunning landscape, sketched in pencil.

Guy was already obsessively assessing each delicate stroke that made up this skilled drawing. Hallie smiled as she took in his face, he was totally oblivious to everyone else in the room. Maggie was explaining the recording and labelling system. Pressing a button on the side of the huge desk, part of it lifted to reveal a state-of-the-art iMac laptop and a black wand-like object. Maggie explained how they would scan new pieces of artwork when they arrived at the institute. Grabbing the black wand-like stick, she waved it slowly over the drawing that was now laid out flat on the desk. Moving over to the laptop, she pressed a few buttons on the device.

Instantly, a comprehensive 3D image appeared above the desk, making all the students blink in shock. It was the drawing but enlarged several times. The fine, delicate pencil strokes could be clearly defined. It was mind-blowing and everyone in the room was awestruck. Even Maggie, who was used to this high-tech equipment, was always delighted to see her student's response when she first showed it to them. "We have had three new pieces of artwork and they need scanning and recording; you lucky lot have been specially chosen to carry out this important task." She beamed at the chosen four, each picked for their skills.

They were simply the most talented of this year's intake. As the students studied the 3D image, Maggie went on to explain the logging system on the laptop and how they would be documenting and scanning each piece of artwork. After giving the technical information and the safety equipment, including the cotton gloves they would all have to wear, she left them to it. Guy was the first to break the ice by feigning claustrophobia, clutching his throat and dramatically falling to the floor. Alexandru actually laughed and offered his hand to help this French clown back to his feet, whilst Akemi checked out Guy's handsome features.

She already fancied Alexandru, although he never really smiled until now. Hallie was also smiling at Guy's antics and for the rest of the afternoon, they scanned, recorded, and discussed all three drawings. In a light and jovial mood, the four students bonded; Akemi was completely blown away whenever Alexandru smiled, which for some reason, he was doing for most of the afternoon. Each piece of artwork was stunning. Guy's favourite was the landscape which completely captivated him. There had also been a portrait of a portly Tudor vicar and, finally to Hallie's absolute joy, was a small Klimt-like canvas. It was obviously not the real thing but was a joy to study.

She was a huge fan of Gustav Klimt and it looked like his style. It featured a pale woman's face with gold swirls and triangles. The colours were incredible and Hallie was completely taken with both the original and 3D image that was suspended in the cool air above the desk. They were all giving their opinions on the type of medium used to create such a beautiful piece when Maggie bustled in. "How are you all getting on then?" She asked brightly, taking in the beaming smiles of her students.

"It's been amazing," Akemi said simply, shrugging her shoulders. Alexandru nodded in agreement; his smile had slipped from his handsome face and the brooding expression was fixed firmly back in place.

Maggie took in the 3D painting and grinned. "Gorgeous, just gorgeous," she whispered. Then realising the four students were staring at her, she laughed. "I'm a sucker for art, what can I say," she said winking at them. "Studio Two students, can I pinch you for another task?" It wasn't a question and Akemi and Alexandru walked away from the huge desk and made their way to the exit. "You two will be ok on your own?" She asked kindly.

"Of course." Guy's French accent oozed sex appeal and combined with his smouldering look, he had somehow reduced his professor to mush. A blushing Maggie turned and left the room, disappearing from sight with Akemi and

Alexandru. Guy and Hallie exchanged looks and then laughed. "You women cannot resist my charms," he said seductively, wiggling his eyebrows.

"This one can," Hallie replied, still laughing. Guy pulled a sad face, making her laugh even more. She was really enjoying this afternoon's session. "I need to…" Guy paused. "To pee," he finished. During the first week, he had been chatting with Hallie and told her he needed to piss. Her face had screwed up and she had made it clear that the expression was distasteful. So, he had been trying to not say the word 'piss' around her since. Hallie smiled at his thoughtfulness and waved as he left the room and, for the first time, she heard the classical music playing softly in the background. She hadn't noticed it before, what with all the chatter about the artwork, but it was soothing to her soul.

She continued to record the painting and was just wondering where Guy had got to when she heard the gentle swoosh of the electric door. "I thought you had fallen down the toilet." She smiled without looking away from the image hovering above the desk.

"Is that right?" A strong American accent consumed the room. Hallie spun around on her stool, her eyes wide in shock. "Miss Whitmore." His face was now serious, sensing her alarm.

"Professor," she spoke quietly and returned her focus back to the painting. The room suddenly felt cooler and a lot smaller; Hallie shivered.

"You're cold." This was a statement and not a question. He wanted to stride over to her and wrap his jacket around her shoulders. Hallie was still shivering when she abruptly grabbed her right-hand side pocket, a frown appearing on her beautiful face. This professor didn't like students using their mobile phones and she didn't want to lose her place at the institute. She was biting her bottom lip, nervously wanting to check her phone screen but not daring to do it in front of the daunting figure of Professor Denton. Swallowing any emotion in his voice, he spoke deliberately and concisely.

"Miss Whitmore, you are perfectly allowed to check your cell outside of session times," he said seriously, watching every movement of her stunning features that lay beneath that bloody cap. Hallie made no move to retrieve her phone but her face remained screwed up in misunderstanding. "The bell went twenty minutes ago, so feel free to check your cell," he said his tone still serious.

"Twenty minutes ago," Hallie replied aghast. She quickly scrambled off the stool and grabbed her phone out of her pocket. Her eyes widened even more when she noted the time. It was twenty past three and there were already three missed calls. "Fuck," she said, not thinking and then regretting her bad language immediately as she glanced up at the imposing American man blocking the exit. "I'm late, I have to go," Hallie whispered, mortified. Six missed text messages appeared on her phone screen. Shit.

Hallie closed down the computer, the beautiful 3D image disappearing at the flick of the switch. Professor Denton observed her silently as she hurriedly tidied the desk. The laptop and wand were both stowed away safely and she went to leave the room, forgetting for a second that the intimidating professor was in this large glass cube with her. Making her way around the desk towards the exit, she stopped abruptly as she realised he still stood in the way of the exit door. She lifted her head up to see his face from under the peak of her cap. He had a serious yet somewhat bewildered expression on his handsome face.

"Will you please take that goddam hat off?" His voice was icy and stern and his words made her flinch. He had been looking into her incredible cerulean eyes as he spoke, desperate to see her full face. Noticing her eyes tighten and her mouth form a grim line, he realised that he had frightened her yet again. Completely mortified and not knowing what to say next, he simply stood to one side. The automatic glass door swished open and without saying a word, Hallie Whitmore dropped her head and walked quickly through the exit. She had made it out of the room and found herself running towards the door to the basement reception.

"You alright, kid?" Kiwi's Liverpudlian drawl made her jump as she ran into reception and pressed the button calling the lift to the ground level. She nodded in response and silently begged the lift to hurry as it seemed to take forever. When it finally arrived, she stepped in quickly, grateful when the doors pinged closed. She was relieved that the professor was not in there with her as she found him intimidating and the thought of them being stuck in an even smaller space together was disconcerting. She made it to ground level and ran past the offices and seating area, through the mole tunnel and straight through into the reception area.

She whizzed past Mrs Bushell, who shouted 'Goodbye, dear' after her. Hallie did not hear her and continued running until she reached her beloved bicycle.

Chapter 6

Hallie had felt sick as she ran. In the confinement of the air-conditioned glass cube, she had felt overwhelmed and ice cold. Now in the cool November air, she felt clammy and overheated. What was the professor's problem? Why did he stare at her like that? Her stomach flipped over and she realised she had not eaten since breakfast and that her body was objecting to her sudden burst of energy. As she sprinted towards the bicycle park, she saw Guy, leaning on the rail, next to her pale blue bike.

"Hey, I waz wondering where you 'ad got to?" His French accent was thick with pretend indignation. His face dropped as he took in her pallid complexion and harsh breathing. "What 'appened?" He said genuinely concerned.

"I'm late, I have to go," was all she could manage as she quickly undid her chain lock and threw it into her basket, whilst mounting her bike at the same time.

"'allie?" Guy said seriously, grabbing the handlebars to prevent her from riding off.

"Please, Guy, I have to go…I'm late," she pleaded. Letting out a frustrated sigh, he stood back, letting go of the handlebars and stepping out of her way.

"'allie!" He called after her, raising both hands in the air trying to get her back. She didn't hear him as she was busy picking up speed whilst jetting down the large sloped path. It led to a little used side gate leading off the institute grounds which was surrounded by high metal fencing and a patrolling security team. Her head reeled from the close encounter with Professor Denton, who for some reason had also been invading her dreams at night. She was also completely annoyed at herself for being late, something she found abhorrent. How could she have not realised the time? Why hadn't she checked her phone?

As she made it onto the side road that ran along the institute's border, she was so busy chastising herself for her tardiness that she didn't notice the posh sports car that was now following her.

As he followed her racing through the side streets, he grew more and more angry that she was not wearing a cycling helmet, let alone a coat. She was endangering herself and it riled him. It was Friday afternoon and luckily, the traffic was light as she raced along, oblivious of her stalker. His car was top of the range and he pursued her with ease. After taking a few turns, she entered a back alley. He held back at the end of the street and observed her jumping off her bicycle and running alongside it. She stopped abruptly at an open metal door. A tall dark-haired man, wearing an apron, appeared, clapping his hands.

A loud Italian voice carried through the air but from the comfort and warmth of his car, he couldn't make out what was actually being said. Hallie obviously knew the Italian and as he took her bike off her, he patted her shoulder and she disappeared into the building. Knowing the alley ran alongside 'The Shambles' area of the city, he quickly retrieved his phone and googled the location to see which building Hallie had entered. 'The Shambles' was a popular pedestrianised row of eateries and pubs that ran adjacent to the large main high street. Although there were a few antique shops to mooch through, it was full of craft ale bars, pubs, and restaurants providing cuisine from around the world.

Studying the street map, he figured out that the back entrance belonged to 'Amores', a fine Italian restaurant. He had actually dined there several times with Mags and Clara and they had enjoyed both the authentic, tasty food and the welcoming surroundings. Why would his student be going to the back entrance? Surely, she did not work there. He knew she was a scholarship student, so surely, she didn't have to scrape around for money. The thought of her being hard up for money saddened him as he drummed his fingers on the steering wheel and contemplated what to do next. Stay in the car and wait, or go into the restaurant and order food?

He was very tempted by the latter as the food there was really good, however, he didn't want to risk missing her exiting the building unseen. Turning off the engine, he decided to wait for her. After an hour, his patience was rewarded when he saw the Italian man pushing her pale blue bicycle out of the building and into the dark back alley, with Hallie Whitmore following. She was still wearing that baseball cap and long sleeve sweatshirt, but no coat. Although it was still dry, the pre-evening chill was bitter. He clenched his fists at the thought of her being cold. The Italian man was cheerily saying 'Ciao' and as she mounted her bike, he put his hand on her shoulder again.

She froze for a second and the man didn't seem to notice as he continued gabbling on. The bright street lights shone down on Miss Whitmore's boy-like frame, the baggy clothes hiding any feminine features. The jolly chef had gone back into the building and reappeared with two large brown paper bags, which he placed neatly into the wicker basket at the front of Hallie's bike. With a wave of a hand, she began to peddle off down the back alley, the Italian man shouting 'Ciao Bella' after her. He had already started his car, the quiet engine not giving away his stealth position. Within seconds, he was trailing behind her; as she weaved through the traffic, he kept up with ease.

The folder full of Miss Whitmore's personal information sat on the front passenger seat; he had already memorised her home address. He followed her back towards the institute and past the cathedral and its gardens. The traffic was heavier now but he knew the direction she would be heading to, if going home, so he continued that way. Passing his own apartment building, he drove a little further until she turned off to a quiet suburban, cul-de-sac, to the left of the river. As she slowed her bike down, she jumped off and walked quickly, turning onto a large, block-paved driveway belonging to a huge detached house. A black Mini sat neatly on the drive and he assumed that one of her parents was home.

Equally spaced modern, lantern effect lights helped light the building, giving it a warm and welcoming feel. Three large-sized terracotta pots, displaying three different types of palm trees, adorned the left corner of the huge driveway. Brightly coloured winter pansies ringed each palm and even in this light, he could see the house was well-kept. The house was massive and he suddenly questioned the fact that his student should require any support in attending the art institute. This was an affluent area, literally minutes away from the city centre and a stone's throw from the River Severn.

His brow furrowed at the thought of her being a fraud. Hallie had walked alongside her bike towards the right-hand side of the house. Disappearing through a tall iron gate, which opened into a wide dark alleyway at the side of the double garage, presumably leading straight to the back garden. The neighbouring street lights were lit up, illuminating the house frontage. It was clean and well-kept, so the Whitmores obviously had a handyman and gardener. They must have money. He had pulled over to the kerb and was about to turn off his engine when Hallie appeared at the front door.

Still wearing the same baggy clothes and baseball cap, she pulled the front door closed and wrapped her arms around herself. She must be feeling cold. He grimaced at the thought of it. With her head down, she made her way down the street and sprinted down the quiet road, past his car. He ducked down but she was oblivious to anything and anyone. Without the trademark sunglasses, she still wore that bloody baseball cap and baggy tracksuit. He turned the car and drove slowly now, keeping his distance. She turned right and then another right before another secluded cul-de-sac which led to a number of joined buildings and a small car park.

He watched as she entered the 'Waterside Village' building. When she disappeared through the automatic doors, he immediately googled the building's name, which he read off the large, well-lit board, displayed outside the neat foyer. It seemed it was a supported living facility for elderly people with a large range of health issues. Maggie had filled him in on the reason Hallie Whitmore constantly left the studio after being texted on her mobile phone. It must be where her ailing grandad was being looked after. Again, he drummed his fingers against his steering wheel and made a decision that would change his life forever.

He turned the car around and made his way back to Hallie's house. Pulling up right outside it, he slipped Miss Whitmore's file under his seat and undid his seatbelt. For some reason, he felt nervous. Stepping out from the warmth of his DB10, he shuddered from the cold air that hit his skin. In smart chinos and a teal Ralph Lauren polo shirt, he hadn't had a chance to grab his coat. The British weather was something he still hadn't got used to after all these years. The thought of Hallie Whitmore facing the elements without a coat passed through his mind again and he slammed the door a little too forcefully than he had meant to.

Determinedly marching up the driveway, he hammered the door knocker, still annoyed at a young girl going out on a cold, dark evening and not being appropriately dressed against the elements. The door swung open and a tall, skinny lad greeted him with a huge endearing smile. "'ello." He smiled again this time not showing his teeth, his cheeks lifting, revealing dimples Michael Douglas would have been proud of.

"Good evening," he started but was quickly interrupted.

"You're American?" The lad looked like he had just completed *The Times* crossword.

"Yes, I am American," he replied, smiling back.

"What can I do for you then?" The boy smiled and now showed all of his large white teeth.

"My name is Phillip Denton and I work at the art institute where Hallie studies…" Pip trailed off as the boy's face fell, a worried look now replacing the welcoming smile.

"Oh my god, is she ok?" The lad stepped out into the cool air and looked up and down the street. "What has happened to her?" The bravado from when he had opened the door had gone and he looked a lot younger than before.

"No, no, she's perfectly well, nothing has happened to her," he finished and placed a calming hand on the youth's shoulder. The young lad let out a long breath and rubbed the back of his neck, relieved at the news.

"She's my sister," he said looking up at Phillip. He could see the boy had the same large blue eyes as Hallie, but instead of her long black lashes, his were blonde.

"I'm sorry, I didn't mean to frighten you. I just have something that belongs to her," Pip finished. He wasn't handling himself well, he needed to sort himself out.

"Oh, then you'd better come in." The lad's jovial manner was completely endearing and as it was chilly standing on the doorstep, Philip accepted with a grateful nod. He felt the warmth and comfort of this immaculate home as soon as he crossed the threshold. An expansive hallway, with a huge wooden staircase to the right and a number of doors leading into the right-hand side of the house. On the left of the staircase was a large hallway, with a long light oak side table holding an elegant table lamp whose base was shaped like Ducks feet, emanating a soft glowing light to the hall. A house phone sat neatly next to it, along with a black wire basket which looked like it contained some unopened post.

The walls were all white and set off the beautiful dark wood, Parquet floor. There were two doors on the left and hanging on the wall in-between them were three large photographs. They were lit by elegant picture lights, illuminating each print. Pip turned to admire the first photograph. It was a PlayStation gaming remote, a very modern photo to have in a hallway and Pip was immediately intrigued. "Oh, that's mine," the lad offered in explanation. "We all choose our favourite item to go on the wall," he said cheerily.

"Very modern and excellent photography," Phillip stated, impressed with its uniqueness.

The lad laughed. "It's not a photo, my sister drew it," he replied shaking his head at the stranger's mistake.

"Your sister drew this?" Phillip pointed at the large picture and took a step closer to study it properly. It was so clear and defined that it literally took his breath away. The skill and artistry that had gone into it was nothing more than amazing and the thought of her being so talented elated him. "Hallie really is a master at art," he said to himself, forgetting he was in company.

"Hallie?" The lad questioned, still smiling pleasantly.

Phillip turned to address him. "Yes, Hallie. She did draw this?" He pointed to the gaming remote.

"Oh…" He hesitated. "Oh yeah, Hallie drew that and these." He walked further down the hall and the same size print adorned the wall. This one was a football. A simple object but drawn to perfection. It was in such high definition, it looked as if you could lift it off the wall and start kicking it about. They had walked past the long table and two more doorways on the right. There on the left was the last large picture. This one was of a pencil and an artist's paintbrush. The detailed image again looked real, the work that had gone into each picture was immense and he was simply blown away.

Viewing Hallie's work at the institute was a pleasure, but here in her own home, it felt even more special. Feeling a movement by his right ankle, he flinched. Looking down, he saw a large, grey cat, rubbing against his leg. "Oh, that's just Ernie," the lad said, bending over and grabbing the purring bag of fur.

Pip loved animals and on seeing the relaxed temperament of the cat, he just laughed. "Ahh, so I've made a new friend," he said as he stroked the cat's head, being rewarded with a louder purr.

"No, he just likes a fuss," the lad said smiling lovingly at Ernie. "This way…" and with that, he turned and walked towards the bright light emanating from the room at the end of the hallway. As Phillip followed him through the open French doors, he found himself in a gorgeous open-plan kitchen. Closed French double doors on the left and then a vast open space on the right, with large glass walls giving an unobstructed view of an enormous garden, only not fully visible due to the darkness of the autumnal evening. As he turned to the right, there was a large beech kitchen table with six chairs, three lined up on either side.

A huge comfortable-looking corner settee was beyond that, with a low beech coffee table. A pile of magazines was neatly stacked on top. Beyond that a breakfast bar with modern black bar stools, behind which was a splendid sleek cream gloss, kitchen. Pip was about to comment on the great space when he realised what was behind the table and chairs to his right. The whole wall had been covered in Monet's Lily Pond print. He paused and took in the beautiful print. "She's good, isn't she?" The lad spoke from behind the breakfast bar. He had put Ernie down and was retrieving two cans of lemonade from the stainless-steel American fridge freezer.

Pip couldn't reply for a few minutes as he walked forward to feel the wall. It wasn't flat and smooth, like paper. To his utter joy, he realised this was a real painting and like the everyday objects depicted in the hallway, this was an enlarged image of Monet's masterpiece. It was truly spectacular. His concentration was broken when he felt a nudge on his left arm. It was the lad offering a can of soda. "Thanks, kid." He smiled.

"Sorry, I can't remember your name," the lad said, a little embarrassed he had forgotten it.

"Phillip Denton, but my friends call me Pip," he said, unsure why he had added the part about his nickname. Only his family and very close friends called him that.

The lad's face lit up and changing his can to his left hand, he held out his right hand. "Hello, Pip, my name is Jay," he said beaming. "Well, actually it's James, but they only call me that when I'm in trouble," he recounted thoughtfully. Pip laughed as he shook his hand, genuinely liking this lad's persona.

He was just about to ask Jay more about the huge wall painting when they both heard the door slam. "Hi, honey, I'm home," a female voice shouted from the front door. "And guess what…" And with that, the female started singing, "We are the champions!" She sang very loudly and out of tune. Jay was rolling his eyes and shaking his head. A girl appeared in the large doorway of the kitchen and on seeing Pip, she stopped singing abruptly and stared at him. She stood there for a moment, open-mouthed.

She was shorter than Hallie but had the same mousey-coloured hair, which was tied up in loose pigtails, perhaps making her look younger than her years. Bright pink cheeks, due to the cold evening air, and the wide-eyed stare were simply down to the shock of finding an unexpected visitor in her home. She was wearing a navy vest top and shorts, piped in red edging, with a large number seven embroidered in red on the front. A pair of neon green, muddied football boots were hanging around her neck. She dropped her sports bag, rucksack and coat, heavily on the floor at her feet and her eyes flicked to Jay, waiting for an explanation.

"This is Pip," he said smiling at the fact he had made a new friend. "Pip, this is my sister…"

"Liv!" She shouted out, interrupting him.

Jay looked crestfallen for a moment and then thought he would cheer things up by saying, "Pip likes the paintings, he works at the art institute, teaching our sister."

Liv didn't seem happy with this and looked sourly at her brother. Taking a few steps into the kitchen, she looked at Pip directly. "She is really brilliant at it. She did us our favourite paintings on our bedroom walls. I've got Flaming June by Frederic Leighton," she finished, her mood lifting slightly on discussing her favourite painting.

"I didn't want a famous painting, so I asked for a picture of my favourite place in the world, the Dominican Republic," Jay added brightly.

"I would like to see those," Pip said, genuinely interested to see more of Hallie's artwork. They were disrupted by the front door closing again.

"Hello," Hallie called from the hallway. "Well, he's not too good today." There was a sadness in her voice and Pip wanted to stride into the hallway and embrace her tightly. "Didn't know who I was…" Suddenly, she stopped talking as she came to a halt in the doorway. Professor Denton was stood in her kitchen, as bold as brass.

Chapter 7

Her mouth hung open in shock and she realised that her siblings were also both standing in the kitchen with him. Oh, my fucking god!

"Pip likes your paintings." Jay tried to break the ice; his older sister didn't look too impressed that they had a guest.

"Pip?" She questioned, completely bewildered.

"He means me," her professor spoke up. "My apologies for intruding on your Friday evening but I had to return something," he said, watching her face carefully for any reaction. She still had that bloody baseball cap on and he wished she would take it off. Her eyes flitted between her brother and sister as she tried to think what she should say.

"Return something?" She asked quietly.

"Yes, you left your phone in the archives," he said producing a mobile phone from his back pocket.

She drew in a breath, her hand immediately reaching for her side pocket. "Shit," she said quietly chastising herself and walking towards him. She took her phone from his extended hand. Their fingers touched briefly and she felt a bolt of electricity run from her fingertips straight to her core. Her eyes widened and he couldn't help but stare. He had felt the same electrifying pulse and stood, stock still, looking at her intently.

"Stay for tea." Jay burst into their private moment.

"What? No…" She was mortified. Jay's face dropped and her younger sister just stared at this handsome stud muffin who was standing in her kitchen. Pip turned to Jay.

"I don't want to intrude," he said politely. Jay was crestfallen and looked at his big sister with his huge, blue, puppy dog eyes. He was enjoying having male company and didn't want Pip to leave.

"I'm sure the professor has plans, Jay, it is Friday evening." She tried to placate him but he had got the idea in his head now.

"He wants to see more of your artwork." Jay tried a different tack, "I was going to show him my bedroom before you rocked up," he said innocently. Now she looked horrified, her eyes tightening slightly.

"So, you were going to go into a teenage boy's bedroom, who you have only just met?" She addressed Pip directly, her face serious.

"Well, when you put it like that, it doesn't sound good…" Pip trailed off, a little disappointed that she could think of him so badly. "Obviously, I would have waited for your parents to get home. I take it they are not here now?"

The siblings exchanged a strange look and the younger sister spoke up. "No, they are not here," she said carefully.

"Well, I am sure they wouldn't want an uninvited guest at their evening meal." Pip smiled, genuinely not wanting to intrude.

"They're not coming back," Jay said solemnly, leaning on the breakfast bar.

"They are away for the weekend," the younger sister jumped in again.

"They wouldn't mind your teacher staying for tea." Jay again looked pleadingly at Hallie and she was a little taken back at how determined he was to have her professor stay for a meal.

"There's not enough for four," she said glaring at Jay, silently begging him not to argue about this. He obviously didn't get the message as he then pointed out that Angelo always sent far too much food for the three of them.

"Angelo?" Pip questioned.

"Yes, he owns Amores, the Italian restaurant in the Shambles. His food is amazing." Jay gushed; he loved his food.

"Ahh yes, I have had the pleasure of eating there on several occasions and the food has always been awesome," Pip replied and smiled, making Hal catch her breath. His handsome features really were breathtaking and when he smiled, his whole face lit up.

"He does always send loads…" Liv trailed off as she looked at Hal with the same Whitmore, puppy dog eyes that Jay had just used to great effect. Hallie looked at her open-mouthed. Oh my god, her too?

"Pleeeeaaasseee," Jay said putting his palms together as if to pray.

"Mum and dad won't mind," Liv added.

Sighing a big sigh and wishing the ground would open up and swallow her whole, she raised both hands in submission. "Ok, ok," she said, shaking her head gently.

Jay punched the air, shouting, "Yeah, cool," and Liv smiled broadly, glad this good-looking stranger would be with them for a little longer.

"I'm just going to shower and change," Hallie said, feeling very uncomfortable.

"I will lay the table ready." Jay beamed as he sprang into action and started sorting out the cutlery needed for the meal. Hallie was just about to turn and leave them to it when she noticed the writing on the back of her sister's sports top. Her eyes widened in alarm, but luckily, Pip's attention was on Jay, who was now happily trying to hang a spoon on his nose. Putting an arm around her younger sister's shoulders, she pulled her sidewards until they were both in the doorway of the huge kitchen. Pip now turned and looked at them both. Liv looked confused and Hallie still looked alarmed as they edged backwards down the hall.

Smirking at their strange behaviour, Pip offered his assistance to Jay in laying the table. The girls scrambled up the stairs and ran into the family bathroom, where they had an emergency conflab on what to say to their new house guest over dinner. Meanwhile, in the kitchen, a cheerful Jay was informing Pip on his gaming acquis and inviting him to have a go on Call of Duty after they had eaten. Pip chatted easily with this happy, confident young lad. "So how old are you?" Pip was interested as the lad was eloquent and at ease in his company. Some of his sixteen-year-old students felt intimidated and got tongue-tied around him.

"I'm thirteen," Jay replied proudly. Pip was surprised as Jay's whole persona seemed older. He was polite but not afraid to ask questions.

"How old are you then?" Jay asked, proving Pip's point.

"I'm twenty-eight." He laughed as he spoke and Jay whistled.

"That's pretty old, mate," he said cheekily, making Pip laugh even harder. They had laid the kitchen table with cutlery, a set of white plates, and to Pip's surprise, four wine glasses. Liv appeared first, wearing a fluffy pink dressing gown over a set of white velour pyjamas. Her hair was wet and tied in a loose bun on top of her head. She eyed Pip suspiciously as she took her seat. "Please sit." Jay pulled out a chair for his new friend and Pip gratefully accepted.

"So, you teach at the art institute?" Liv questioned sceptically.

"Yes, that's correct…although I don't actually teach Hallie unless we are in the auditorium." Liv looked serious for a moment as if she were going to say something, but instead, she bit her bottom lip and chose not to comment.

"We can show you the rest of the artwork after we've eaten..." Jay called from behind the breakfast bar. "Hurry up, I'm starving!" He yelled out. As if on cue, Hallie walked in and Pip instantly stood, ever the gentleman. She was wearing a navy V-necked lounge suit with cuffed bottoms. The hated baseball cap had finally been removed. Her hair was wet and scraped back into a bun on the nape of her neck. She had obviously showered. Pip tried to blank out the idea of her naked body under the shower head, water running over every inch of her porcelain skin. Christ, she was only sixteen and his thoughts alone would be enough for him to get arrested.

But at last, the baseball cap had gone and he could see her beautiful face in full. Incredible, large blue eyes framed with long black lashes. Perfectly arched eyebrows sat on her smooth forehead. Her cheeks were a little flushed from the hot water of the shower and her full pink lips looked desirably kissable. She looked amazing. Small lines formed on her forehead as she looked at Pip with a serious expression. "What?" She asked icily. He realised he had been staring at her and sat back down. He turned his attention to the table, where he needlessly rearranged his knife and fork.

He glanced up at Liv who was opposite, eyeing him carefully, trying to work out what he was thinking. Hallie padded past them, barefooted on the large white floor tiles. Pip's fist clenched at the idea of her having cold feet. A few minutes later, his thoughts were interrupted by Jay bringing the first lot of Angelo's reheated food in large, black and white, patterned serving dishes. It smelt delicious and Pip realised how hungry he was. Jay plopped down in the seat next to him and started naming the scrumptious dishes before them. Hallie continued to reheat four more large dishes of Bolognese, multiple kinds of pasta, and sauces, which she then brought to the table.

Returning to the kitchen area, she came back with a bottle of red wine. Pip looked at the bottle and then at Hallie. He didn't know any other sixteen-year-old who would drink red wine with their evening meal. She poured the crimson liquor into the elegant wine glasses and paused over his glass. Making full eye contact, they just stared at each other, electricity pulsing between them. "Of course, he wants some, sis," Jay scoffed, with a mouthful of creamy Carbonaro. Breaking eye contact, she realised she had been taking in all of his handsome features and with a blush on her cheeks, she poured Pip a glass of wine.

At first, the meal was a little awkward, each of them sat eating the delicious food without a word. Pip noticed Hallie had not eaten much and again this made him angry. Liv started telling them all about her game and the fact her team had won, thrashing the other unskilled lot. "What game was this?" Pip questioned, "...netball?" All three siblings burst out laughing and Liv filled him in on her love of football. It took a few seconds for him to concentrate on what she was saying as his attention had been drawn to Hallie's beautiful face. It was the first time he had seen and heard her laugh and it was enchanting.

Forcing himself to concentrate on Liv, he realised it made sense. Hallie had drawn the three siblings a picture of their favourite things and the football sketch that hung proudly on the hall belonged to Liv. They all found it hilarious when their American guest referred to football as soccer. Jay joined in the lively conversation telling Pip that rugby was better than football/soccer, and as a Worcester Warriors and England supporter, he reeled off a never-ending list of his favourite rugby players. Hallie had taken the opportunity to discreetly check her phone, which she had done several times throughout the meal.

She then sat back enjoying her sibling's bubbly, cordial banter, joining in now and again where appropriate. Once they were all stuffed with the main meal, Liv helpfully cleared the plates and re-laid the table with dishes and spoons in readiness for when they all felt like pudding. "I can't believe you all drinking red wine," Pip said bemused.

"Our dad used to drink red wine and for Friday night dinner from Angelo's, we all stick to the tradition," Liv said smiling at the memory.

"Used too?" Pip asked, picking up on the past tense. Liv was just sitting back down and turned to Hallie, her mouth open and her face paled. Hallie looked at Pip and opened her mouth to respond but Jay cut in.

"He doesn't drink alcohol anymore, not good for a surgeon," he said, demonstrating by holding up his spoon and shaking it wildly. Pip smiled but the look on Hallie and Liv's faces meant there was obviously more to it. Liv soon excused herself, not wanting any pudding. She had homework she wanted to get out of the way, so she could enjoy the weekend. Jay had retrieved a huge tub of cookie dough ice cream from the large American-style fridge freezer, which he spooned generously out into two dishes. Pip frowned as Jay placed one in front of him. He sat down and dug into the second. "You're not having any?" He questioned Hallie with a frown.

She shook her head as Jay started talking ten to the dozen about the latest gaming systems and asking Pip if he thought Xbox or PlayStation were the best. Suddenly realising the time, he jumped up, licking the last of the ice cream off his spoon and informed them that he had arranged to play Call of Duty online with his friend, Tom, at seven-thirty. "Jay…" Hallie spoke quietly compared to her excitable brother and sister.

"Yes, I know…one-hour limit on a weekday," he said dolefully giving his best puppy dog look at his older sister begging for extra time. She smirked and nodded. "You have until nine o'clock, no longer," she said firmly, clearly used to his tricks.

"Yes!" He shouted. Punching the air with delight, before literally dancing out of the room and disappearing into the hallway.

"And then there were two," Pip said smiling, glad of the opportunity to have an actual conversation with this young siren.

"Why did you really come here?" She said directly, before taking a sip of her wine.

"I wanted to return your phone." He looked at the intrigue on her face and decided to be honest. "You seem to be inseparable from it and I thought you would panic when you realised it was missing."

She rested her glass down on the coaster before she spoke. "I can't believe I hadn't checked it. I've had a lot on my mind recently, I must be losing my marbles," she said shaking her head.

"Like what?" He was frowning, the thought of her being unhappy in any way disturbed him for some reason.

"Well, my placement at the institute for a start," she said looking thoughtful.

"Hallie, you are the most skilled artist I have ever had the privilege to meet." His face darkened and his tone was serious. She looked up from scrutinising her glass to stare into his gorgeous eyes. "Look behind you, Monet couldn't have painted it better. You have no idea how talented you are and I assure you the institute is lucky to have you as their student. In fact, Millward is in raptures over the work you have done during your first term. I think he might even come over and see you before we break up for the Christmas period," he said earnestly.

Hallie had sat watching him, taking in every word. "Thank you," she sighed. "That does help, I'm never really sure what Mag…Professor Harper really thinks of me. She's so lovely to everyone and I sometimes wonder if she ever says anything bad." A small smile appeared on her full lips as she thought about her wonderful teacher. If she was completely honest, she hadn't learnt much that was new to her at the art sessions, however, having the time and opportunity to draw, sketch, paint, and look at works of art was an incredible freedom, which she was very grateful for.

"Hallie, I need to ask you something." He looked a little uncomfortable and the smile dropped from her face.

"Go on," she replied.

"This house is huge and in one of the best areas in the city and your parents…I mean, your dad's a surgeon. I presume your mum works?"

Hallie fiddled with the stem of her glass as she spoke. "She was a surgeon too," she said gravely.

"Was?" He queried, again the past tense had been used.

Hallie sighed and drank the last drop of wine. "We need more wine for this," she said looking at him. For some strange reason, she felt she could trust him, making the decision there and then to be honest.

"I only mention it because you have been given a free placement that a lot of people were desperate for and it looks like you're from an affluent family…" he trailed off.

"Let me just sort this lot out and we can talk. There are some things you need to know." She stood and started gathering the used dishes from the table.

"Please let me help." He stood and grabbed the furthest dish from her and she smiled in gratitude. He was completely intrigued and beguiled by her. He wanted to sketch her in her lounge suit, wanting to capture the soft glow on her skin from the effects of the wine. He followed her past the breakfast bar and took in the damp skin on the nape of her neck where her hair was still wet. It took all of his self-control to not wrap his arms around her and kiss her exposed neck. She had already loaded her dishes into the dishwasher and had turned with hands outstretched for the next lot, which he was carrying.

"I'm happy that you're not wearing that baseball cap." It was all he could think to say, as words escaped him. She was so beautiful; he was in such great danger of swooping her into his arms and kissing her.

"So am I." She smiled a shy, timid smile that made his groin strain. Surely, she was used to compliments, just look at her. As she loaded the glasses and flicked a switch on the high-tech dishwasher, he found himself wondering about the clothes that she wore to the institute. Why would she hide her body in a baggy dark tracksuit? Even now, she had a layer of loose material covering her up and he found it frustrating. Gathering two fresh wine glasses and a second bottle of red wine, she made her way out of the kitchen; glancing over her shoulder, she asked him to follow her.

Making her way down the softly lit hallway, she opened the last door on the right. After pressing a switch on the wall, several lamps flicked into action around the room. It was a large spacious living room, with two comfortable-looking sofas and an oak coffee table, where Hallie placed the wine and glasses. She moved to the huge front-facing window and closed the wooden blinds. "There are no paintings in here?" Pip questioned as he looked around the large room.

"Umm no, I wanted an art-free room. We don't use this room much actually," she said thoughtfully. Pip was still standing and she took a seat on the settee, then she gestured with her hand for him to join her. Deftly opening the wine, she poured some into the glasses on the table and offered him one.

"So, what is it you need to tell me?" He asked taking a sip of the delicious wine.

She had reached to get her glass but sat back on the soft cream cushions looking at him thoughtfully. "I'm trusting that this is between us and that it will go no further," she said seriously.

"Okay." He was unsure what she was about to disclose but the thought of them having a secret between them was actually endearing.

"My parents were both surgeons and obviously the pay was good…" She looked around the room and then back at Pip. "They paid for this house and we are very lucky that we have no mortgage." He was listening intently, waiting for her to disclose that her parents were committing tax fraud, or that the house was brought out of illegal gains. "They were both killed in a gliding accident over six years ago," she spoke softly and finished by biting the bottom of her lip.

Pip was stunned into silence as she watched the information sink in. "They were killed?" He questioned, completely shocked by what she had just told him.

"My dad loved adventure and was learning to fly. He took my mum up in a glider as a romantic treat for her birthday, but there was a fault on the glider and they crashed. Neither survived." She spoke so clearly and concisely, that he was completely taken aback.

"So, who looked after you all?" His tone expressed the horror he felt at the thought of three children losing their parents so young.

"Pong, our grandad. He lived close by and looked out for us the best he could."

"Looked out for you? Did the best he could? You mean he didn't move in?" He fired the questions at her, furious at the knowledge that the children must have been scared and alone.

"Please, it's alright," she said calmly, trying to soothe him.

"Alright!" He shouted, making her flinch. He immediately regretted it. "I'm sorry, it's just…you were children and needed support, so why did you say he did the best he could?" He questioned trying to quell the outrage he felt.

"Pong had early onset dementia at the time, he was very forgetful, but he did his best in his more lucid moments." Pip's mouth was gaping open in horror but she went on. "We managed to fool the social workers and on their rare visits, we made out he had gone to the shops, etc. We were very convincing and the council were overstretched and under-resourced. We were all attending school and I made sure we had clean uniforms, full lunch boxes, etc. My parents left trust funds for us all that we would get when we reach twenty-one. In the meantime, we had a payout from the glider company which also went into a trust for us."

"Pong did his best to help cover our household bills, clothes, food and so on, although we do get money to help run the house that was left in the will. My parents didn't realise the cost of living would go up and obviously uniforms, clothes, and Everything, all adds up." She paused and looked directly into his eyes.

His heart was simply melting and all he wanted to do was hold her tightly, but he stayed still, gripping his wine glass. "Please go on," he said gently. She nodded and took a sip of wine, needing its medicinal qualities for what she was about to tell him next.

"At sixteen, I started working at Amores restaurant to help out with the bills. Pong wasn't doing so well, so we couldn't depend on him. Angelo and Stacey, that's his wife, started sending food home with me. They knew our parents had died and wanted to help somehow. Now we are older, we only have it on a Friday night but they used to send food for us daily. Pong deteriorated and is now in a home a couple of streets away." She sighed and Pip knew exactly where the home was as he had followed her there earlier that evening. "I umm…" She paused trying to find the right words and he leant over and put his large hand on hers. She felt the electricity run straight to her core and took in a huge breath.

"I finished school and had to miss art college as there simply wasn't time. I looked after my sister, brother, and grandad and worked full-time, plus took extra shifts at the restaurant. Pong's health is so bad now, we don't think we will have him much longer…" She closed her eyes summoning strength to carry on. He squeezed her hand for support and she opened her beautiful blue eyes and gazed at him. He wanted to question why her grandad was called Pong but this was not the time.

"Go on," he said gently.

"I'm not actually sixteen now." Biting her bottom lip again, she looked up at him. She was trying to gauge his reaction as she waited with bated breath, praying he would not report them all. "I'll be twenty-one on Christmas Eve." As she said it, she didn't break eye contact. There was a dramatic pause and she was surprised to see the corners of his mouth turn up slightly.

"Thank fuck for that," he said, now breaking into a full smile, making her mouth pop open into an 'O'. "Honestly, Hallie, the thoughts I've been having about you have been, well…let's just say, if the institute could read my mind, I would have been sacked by now, or even arrested." His smile faltered as he realised she looked horrified.

"That's the other thing…" She looked anxious and pale in the soft lighting. Taking a deep breath, she went on. "Hallie applied to the institute for me and lied about my age…" She said looking embarrassed. Pip was confused now, his brow creased as he tried to figure out what she had just said. As a way of an explanation, she said simply, "I'm Liv."

Chapter 8

Now it was his turn to look shocked. "Liv?" He whispered.

"Olivia Whitmore," she said quietly. "I'm so sorry. Hallie was just trying to do something nice for me. I had no idea she had applied to the institute on my behalf. When she showed me the invitation, I was in shock. The art institute is the best in the world and I swear I just wanted to look round…" She had leant closer to him now, imploring him to see her side of things. "I wasn't planning on taking the placement but when I got there, I was blown away," she said trying to explain.

"I felt the same way when I saw it," he said in agreement. This poor girl had been through hell and back and had finally found her haven by attending the institute.

"Maggie, I mean Professor Harper, was so kind and so…" She couldn't find the words.

"So, what?" He asked his serious expression, not helping her to speak.

"So motherly." She paused and gulped back the emotion in her voice. "I felt at home." She ended, placing her glass back on the coffee table. There was a silence as he processed the information she had given him. Who the fuck was he to ruin her happiness and the fact she wasn't a sixteen-year-old girl was incredible? At almost twenty-one, she was a woman and his mind and body were alive with possibilities.

"Liv." He tested her name on his lips. The look she gave him was so innocent and vulnerable, that he simply had no choice. Still holding her left hand in his, he pulled her towards him into a fierce embrace. Although shocked, the feeling of this gorgeous-looking man pressing his firm torso against her was blissful. They wrapped their arms around each other and held the embrace for a long time. She was kneeling on the cushion beside him, her knees touching his toned thigh. He stroked her hair softly, taking in her ravishing scent.

Slowly, he loosened his hold; regretfully she parted from the warmth and solace of his body. Just as she thought the sweet, intimate moment was over, his hands palmed her cheeks. His intense gaze made her shiver in anticipation as he stroked her flushed cheekbones with his thumbs. "Liv." His voice was low with want.

"Pip." She returned his intense gaze and he could bear it no longer. Pulling her face towards him, his lips crashed on hers and they started to kiss. The passion with which she kissed him back torched a flame deep inside him. He roughly lifted her by her waist onto his lap, without breaking the kiss. Her arms were wound tightly around his neck, her fingers running through his short hair. His hands were free to explore as he snaked them under her top and around her equally toned body. He skimmed the lace strap of her bra, his hand finding the damp nape of her neck. She moaned into his mouth, spurring him on and sending him crazy with lust.

He broke the kiss and nuzzled her chin, making his way down her long neck. "I really want to fuck you," he growled, as his other hand gripped her hip.

She held his face and rested her forehead on his as she tried to steady her breath. "Just one more thing," she said drawing back, looking a little abashed. His fingers tightened on her hip and he reluctantly slid his other hand out from beneath her top, gripping her other hip, so she couldn't move. She gasped as she realised his hard erection was literally between her legs. "I umm…I haven't…" She swallowed and closed her eyes.

Fuck, she was beautiful. "Tell me," he growled sexily as he took in the pink blush of her porcelain cheeks.

"I've never been with anyone," she whispered. Her eyes squeezed tightly shut as she covered her face with her hands.

Pip stilled at the news. "You're a virgin?" He asked quietly, looking horrified. Without saying a word, her face still covered, she nodded slowly. "For fuck's sake, Hal…I mean Liv!" Her name change would take some getting used to. He was angry now, pushing her off his lap and standing abruptly in a furious rage. Liv was mortified. She thought he liked her, that he wanted her and after she had poured her heart out to him, he was treating her like this. Her hands had dropped to her sides, her eyes wide in alarm. "I have to go," he snapped. She stood not wanting him to leave.

"Please don't…" He didn't witness the Whitmore puppy dog eyes as without another word, he had already turned and stalked out of the room. The slam of the front door signalled his exit from the house. She watched from behind the blinds, lifting a slat, to see the man of her dreams screech off in a silver sportscar.

Chapter 9

Liv sighed deeply. She had replayed the evening's events in her mind and still had no idea what to do next. Jay had been gutted when he realised Pip had left without saying goodbye. He had been looking forward to showing his new friend the games room and whooping his arse at COD. Explaining to her siblings that Pip had received a call and was needed at the institute urgently had not gone down well. Liv made her brother his favourite drink of hot chocolate, complete with mini marshmallows and a plate of double chocolate chip cookies and amazingly, as ever, his mood improved quickly.

Hallie had been a little harder to persuade. "Why would he be called in on a Friday night?" She was appalled on his behalf. "It's not fair, he was with us here. They shouldn't have made him leave," she said most indignantly. Hallie was bubbly and outgoing, and like her brother, wasn't afraid to say exactly what she thought. She had been taken aback to see the handsome professor standing in her kitchen. The last male adult guest in their home was her grandad, Pong, and that had been years ago.

Over their evening meal, both Jay and Hallie had thoroughly enjoyed Pip's company and for some unknown reason, their spirits had lifted, even though they had not felt low. Pip's easy going and friendly nature had endeared him to Liv's younger siblings and she had also been struck by the fact that the evening was a great success. That was until she had told him that she was a virgin and he had flipped. That was hours ago and a reflective Liv had been holed up in her bedroom ever since, going over and over the conversation in her head. She had moved into the loft conversion a few years before giving Hallie and Jay some much-needed space.

The loft in the massive house had been split into two over ten years ago and although one side was still used for storage and extra bedroom space, the other had been turned into a suite of rooms by their father as a gift for their mother. It consisted of a large bedroom, a small library with a sitting area, a spacious dressing room, and a modern en-suite bathroom with a large bath and a huge walk-in shower. Liv had to be not only a big sister but also mum and dad to her siblings and although they all loved each other and were incredibly close, they also had times where they wanted to be alone. So, Liv had moved from the first floor into her parent's bedroom suite.

It was odd at first and she felt even lonelier than she had before, but she knew it was the best thing to do for her Hallie and Jay at the time. She had redecorated the whole house during the endless sleepless nights when grief would not let her rest. The bedroom area was now full of cream and gold. On the wall behind her super king-sized bed was a hand-painted copy of Gustav Klimt's *The Kiss*. It depicted a couple in a lingering embrace and to Liv, who was secretly a big romantic, it was the only painting she wanted in her new bedroom. The gold, silver, and platinum colours illuminated this passionate picture, which would catch the sun's rays or the soft light of the bedside lamps.

It always left Liv enraptured and she would easily describe it as her favourite painting of all time. She was now sitting underneath her beautiful artwork, pillows plumped up, and crisp cream sheets pulled up to her waist, the duvet neatly folded over. On her lap, Burt was stretched out on his back, purring loudly as she stroked his soft, furry tummy. Out of their two cats, Burt was the lazy lump who enjoyed cuddling, sleeping and eating. Ernie was slimmer and a lot more active, but he still loved the cuddling up and all the affection the Whitmores gave him. He was sprawled out at the end of the bed, snoring gently.

Liv couldn't sleep. She continued to replay every word she had said to her handsome professor and then that embrace. Followed by that kiss. Holy shit, he was hot. She shook her head as she tried to understand what he must have been thinking. She had expected him to go mad at the fact that she had basically committed fraud in attending the institute, but he had remained calm. When she had told him she was older than she had made out, he seemed pleased. Telling him her name was not Hallie but actually Liv, he had remained serious but then held her closely to him. Then kissing her with such force and intensity, she was still breathless at the thought of it.

Suddenly, Liv's phone beeped into action from where it sat on her bedside table. She reached out, trying not to disturb Burt, and grabbed it. Reading the front screen, she sat with open-mouthed eyes as wide as saucers. The screen was illuminated with the words 'PIP' calling. The ringtone sounded oddly familiar but she couldn't place it. She held the phone until the music stopped and just as she was letting out a long sigh, it sprang back into action, the screen lighting up with the same message as before. *How on earth did he put his details in my phone*, she wondered. *Christ, maybe he was a stalker.*

The phone went dead again and Burt mewed to get her attention, his huge soft paw tapped her hand which was holding the phone. "Sorry, Burt," she said diverting her attention back to him and stroking his tummy with her free hand. He started purring again and was quite happy that his human was multitasking, tickling his tummy with one hand and holding her ringing phone in the other. After the third round of ringing, her phone finally silenced and she let out another sigh of relief. A loud beep signalled receipt of a text message. After summoning up the courage to retrieve it, she opened the inbox with a slide of her thumb. Pip's words were short and to the point, 'Answer your phone!'.

Wow, he sounded really pissed off. She was just debating if she should reply when a second message came through. 'Answer your goddamn phone!' Another demanding request. Liv wanted to scream. He's the one who stormed out, he's the one who left her heartbroken. The phone pinged again and both Burt and Ernie sat up alarmed at the disturbance. 'If you're not going to answer your phone, just let me in!' was the next message. Fuck, he was outside. She could have sworn that her heart had stopped beating as she realised he was in such close proximity. Straining her ears, she tried to listen out for any noises from the front drive but could hear nothing.

He seemed to be angry with her and at this ungodly hour of the morning, she was not willing to have a rollicking. It was already after one am and she needed to get some sleep. *Just ignore him*, her head was telling her. Her heart was telling her the opposite. The thought of him downstairs, standing at her front door, in the chill of the winter's night made her shiver; however, she wasn't sure if it was out of fright or excitement. She flicked open the screen of her phone and typed quickly, sending the text before she could think twice. 'I'm in bed, it's late and I am not opening the door'.

It took a few minutes for his response to ping through. 'I need to talk to you'. Maybe he had calmed down.

'We can talk tomorrow', she replied swiftly.

'Liv…' was his simple response. With a trembling hand, she pressed the dial number and without it even ringing, he picked up. "Liv?" His voice was serious and it sent another shiver down her spine.

"Hello," was all she could think to say.

"Hi," his American accent thick with angst.

"It's very late." Liv began.

"I'm sorry and I'm sorry about earlier…" There was a pause. "But I need to know why you keep checking your cell," he said sternly.

Liv frowned. "Cell?" She asked confused.

"Your mobile phone, Liv. Why do you check it constantly?" His tone was still edgy and she wasn't sure what to say. "Are you sleeping with Angelo?" His solemn voice penetrated her mind.

"What?" She shrieked, losing her temper. Ernie jumped up onto all fours and disappeared under the duvet cover. Burt being too lazy to move, flumped back down and rolled up on Liv's lap, making himself even more comfortable, slightly put out by the noisy interruption to his evening. After all, Liv had told him, he thought she was sleeping with a married man. The thought repulsed her.

"Do you have any idea how often you check your cell? It's all the time. What am I supposed to think?" He tried to reason.

"Just forget everything I told you tonight. Do not contact me again," she said firmly, whilst fighting the urge to scream. Sliding her finger across the screen she ended the call, not giving him the chance to respond. Springing up out of bed, leaving a grumpy Burt discombobulated, she ran into the library which was in complete darkness. Navigating the settee, she made her way to the circular window. Lifting one of the wooden slats of the blind, she peered out at the driveway and street below. His silver sports car was parked directly to the right of the house on the road.

She watched whilst she saw the headlights flash on as a dark figure stalked its way from her drive and onto the road to the awaiting vehicle. The dark figure was tall and slim, wearing what looked like a leather jacket and baseball cap. When he reached the driver's side door, he paused and looked up at the house. She knew that the room she was standing in was dark and that he would not be able to see her, but it made her feel uncomfortable. It wasn't until he jumped into the car and it roared off, out of the cul-de-sac and into the gloomy night, that she realised she had been holding her breath. She flinched as she felt a furry body rub up against her leg.

Burt was missing her company and had come to find her. She sighed as she lifted the purring lump of love into her arms, holding him like a baby in her arms. "At least you don't ask me stupid questions," she said, kissing him on his handsome head. Returning to her bedroom, she placed him back on the cream and gold duvet, then she sat on the edge of the bed. How could he think that? She thought he was mad that she was a virgin, but that was a complete curve ball and she was still in shock.

She tossed and turned for another half hour before giving up on sleep entirely. She padded down to the kitchen, closely followed by Burt who sensed a snack might be on the cards. Ernie stayed curled up under her duvet, too cosy to move. She sprinkled a couple of cat biscuits into Burt's bowl and retrieved a can of pop and a kinder Bueno bar for herself. She didn't eat a lot of chocolate but tonight she needed it. She made her way back into the hall, opening the first door on her left. Following the long corridor to the last door on the right, she opened it up and flicked on the bright, clear spotlights of her favourite room in the whole house, the studio.

She loved this room. Her dad enjoyed painting as a relaxing hobby, and although not as talented as Liv, her mum had encouraged him and decorated the light airy room just for him. They were both surgeons and their demanding jobs meant they had very little downtime. When baby Olivia arrived, they were so delighted. She turned their world upside down and they suddenly realised that as much as they loved each other, they needed to make time for each other and their beautiful baby girl. Loving being parents, they had gone on to have Hallie and then Jay.

They felt their family was complete and still giving one hundred per cent to their work lives, they both ensured they had time for each other and their beautiful children. The studio was another room that Liv had inherited, although her work was incredibly accomplished and polished, unlike her dad's. His paintings and pictures were hung around the room, along with Liv's artwork, and she always felt a sense of her father's comforting presence when working there. Her mind was racing with Pip's words and she tried to blank them out by sketching. Hours later, she stretched her aching shoulders and spread out the drawings on her art table.

It was similar to the posh institute table and tilted as much as required, only Liv's worked via a wooden cog which you had to turn to adjust the angle. She let out an exasperated breath as she looked down at her latest work. Each depicting Pip's handsome features. Some were of his whole face, then close-up detailed drawings of his lips, his strong nose and, of course, his eyes. Instead of forgetting about him, she had drawn every picture by memory, his drop-dead gorgeous face fresh in her mind. Checking her Fitbit watch, she realised it was almost five am.

She felt too restless to sleep, even though her head was hurting from all of the concentration. She decided she needed some fresh air and quickly ran up to her bedroom and changed into her running gear. She usually wore tight-fitted running leggings, a bra-like crop top and a long-sleeved running top, however, as her black, loose college joggers and sweatshirt were thrown over the chair in the dressing room, she decided to wear them instead. With the addition of a poly base t-shirt, she again borrowed one of Jay's black baseball caps. She threw the hood of her jumper up over her head for extra warmth.

After checking the laces of her running shoes were neatly tied, she headed out of the door and into the cold darkness. Securing the front door key in the side of her sports sock, she set out in the bitterness of the frosty November morning. She loved this time of day when there was no one else around. She might bump into the odd drunk coming out of the city's many nightclubs, or maybe the milkman in his electric van. Apart from that, it was animals that she liked to see, including urban foxes skulking around the dustbins and house cats mewling at doors to be let in by their sleeping owners.

Taking the river route, she made her way onto the path that ran alongside the River Seven. At certain times of the year, this path was impassable due to flooding, but today, the river levels were quite low and Liv decided to follow the footpath up into the city. Sleeping swans and geese were her only companions and as the river was a huge tourist attraction, it was always well-lit and pretty much litter-free. This meant an easy-running route without people interrupting her thoughts. As she ran along the frosted banks of the river, her body started to adjust to the icy bitterness surrounding her.

Her long, lithe legs fell into rhythm and she felt her tense shoulders relaxing a little as she made her way along the path towards the city. As she passed the fancy, luxury apartments, they were all in darkness except for the top apartment, which reminded Liv of a lighthouse beacon. She ran on past, her body feeling warmer from the motion. She smiled as she passed the façade of the spectacular cathedral, looking stunning with the vast number of spotlights helping to illuminate its grandness, even in the darkness. She started wondering about the institute and if Pip would report her to the board to be kicked out.

Making a determined effort, she forced the thoughts from her mind, concentrating on the approaching stone bridge that brought thousands of cars a day in and out of her beautiful city. She left the path and ran up the car park, making her way over the bridge. There was already the odd vehicle crossing over it, heralding the start of a busy Saturday morning in Worcester. Still keeping an even pace, she ran on past the empty river boats, looking sad and lonely in the gloom of the dawn.

To the right of the river and moored boats, the lights of the city began. The bright LED street lights and well-signed roads, with shop facades that could be seen in the distance. She ran on past the arches and reached the start of the Pitchcroft racecourse and the beginning of Seven Terrace. This row of narrow terraced houses was where she stopped, catching her breath with her hands on her hips. The first house on the left was an elegant bistro restaurant, but Liv remembered when it was an ice cream shop. She looked longingly at the house next door.

Its simple exterior belying the large, comfortable rooms that go way back from the road. It was her first home and she had happy memories there, but today, it didn't give her the warm, happy feeling it usually did. Today, it made long for her beautiful parents. Today, it made her feel lonelier than she had ever felt before. It was still early and the dark and frosty morning had meant that she had not seen another person during her run. Taking a huge breath, she suddenly bolted, wanting nothing more than to be as far away from her old family home as possible.

Liv was a keen runner and was used to pushing herself to the limit. It was the one place she could be herself; it was the only place she felt free. Sprinting past the empty tourist boats and back over the bridge, she felt she could run forever. Her pace grew faster as she sprinted on. Suddenly, she felt completely overwhelmed and she knew it was all because of Pip and that kiss. She pushed herself even more and her legs felt like they were on fire. Her chest was burning as she took the glacial morning air into her lungs. Her arms and legs moved in unison, propelling her on at great speed. As she raced past the cathedral and approached the luxury apartment buildings, the back of a lone figure was jogging in her path.

As she flew past him, she felt her whole body scream in pain, as she pushed it to the absolute limit. Her face and fingers started tingling as the blood pumped too quickly around her body. Having veered around the jogger, her body lost direction and she swerved onto a grass verge, which was still covered in the early morning frost. She meant to slow down but the slippery grass meant she lost her footing. Falling hard, literally, head over heels into the embankment, she ended up face down and winded on the cold, damp ground. Within seconds, she felt an odd sensation in her right arm.

She heard a male voice but it was muffled and distant and she could not understand what he was saying. Face still down in the grass, she tested her legs, finding she could move them. Adjusting her body into a kneeling position, she brought her left hand to touch her face. Again, she felt the odd sensation in her right arm and turned to look at it, fearing it was broken. A large hand was wrapped around it, causing the pressure she was feeling, and as the fog lifted slightly from her brain, she recognised the voice that was echoing through her mind. "Hey, buddy, you okay?" Fuck. She dropped her head on the back of her left hand and the man obviously thought she had fainted.

"Christ…" She heard him huff. "I'm calling for help," he said gruffly, as she felt the pressure leave her arm and she knew he had let go.

She finally found her voice. "I don't need any help from you," she spoke quietly and didn't move. There was a pause, she felt pressure on both shoulders as he lifted her into the upright kneeling position. Her face was covered in mud and blood, and the hood of her baggy sweatshirt fell onto the tip of her nose. As she blew out a steadying breath and squeezed her eyes shut, she felt the hood being pulled back. There was an audible gasp and then his hands moved swiftly from her shoulders onto either side of her face.

"Liv." His voice was as icy as the embankment she was kneeling on. She kept her eyes closed. "For fuck's sake…Liv." This time, his voice was more tender and she opened one eye. There he was, the magnificently drop-dead gorgeous stud muffin, who had stormed out of her life last night.

"Hello," was all she could manage as her head swirled like a whirling dervish and she passed out.

Chapter 10

After what seemed like a few seconds, Liv stretched her aching body and blinked her eyes open. Completely disorientated, she sat up quickly, making her head spin as she tried to take in her surroundings. She was no longer lying on the cold muddy river bank. She was now on a warm, soft, navy settee with plump, mustard yellow cushions and a mustard woollen throw wrapped around her shivering body. "Lie down." This was not a request but a demand as Pip strode determinedly into the room. He was wearing a black Adidas fitted tracksuit and he looked delicious.

Liv smiled at the thought of what his body might look like underneath, making her insides squirm with longing. "Liv…" His voice was softer now, "Please, lie down," he said as he knelt down beside the settee, resting a bowl of steaming hot water on the plush carpet. She obliged, flushing slightly at her erratic thoughts. "What were you just thinking?" He questioned gently as he rang out the hot water from the black flannel. Liv closed her eyes tightly, totally embarrassed. "Olivia?" He said anxiously and she opened her eyes wide.

"Stop closing your eyes like that, I can still see you." His mouth twitched as he was slightly amused by her sweet habit. "Plus, I keep thinking that you've passed out again," he said, back to the stony glacial expression.

"Sorry," she said quietly, looking up at the ceiling and admiring the ultra-modern chandelier. "I like your lights," she said absentmindedly, making him laugh. She turned immediately, causing pain in her neck and head.

"For fuck's sake, lie still," he admonished as he watched her wince.

"I just wanted to see you laughing," she said pouting and he laughed again.

He wiped her face in a slow rhythmic motion that left her fighting to keep her eyes open. "Do not go to sleep," he demanded sternly. "You may have a concussion," he said as he continued to wipe the blood, mud and grass off her right cheek, revealing the freshly grazed porcelain-like skin underneath. Her pale skin was flushed from the running and change of temperature.

"Where am I?" Liv asked, staring absentmindedly at the chandelier. It was made up of long tubes of stone-like glass, each exploding with small rays of light; it was simply stunning.

"Hey…" He said gaining her attention. "You want to tell me what just happened?" His hand paused over her forehead where she also had cuts from the fall. She looked at him, her face ashen, and he could make out the dark skin under her eyes. "You have slept?" He was angry now. She just looked at him, taking in his impressive features and knowing she couldn't have possibly done him justice in her late-night art session. Not getting a response, he placed the flannel into the bowl of hot water by his knee. "Liv, you have slept since I left you last night?" He asked again; this time, he sounded gentle and sincere.

She dared not speak, he was so up and down, that his mood swings were giving her whiplash. Slowly, she shook her head, the pounding pain grew in her sore temples. "Fuck, Liv, what were you thinking?" He said running his hand through his mousey tresses, making him look like a hot movie star. She let out a breath, trying to urge her head and her body not to lust after this man, but failing miserably. "What am I going to do with you, Miss Whitmore?" He said seriously. Hearing her name spoken in that way did two things to her.

Firstly, she wanted to smack him hard across his gorgeous face. She wasn't a child and didn't deserve to be spoken to like that. Secondly, there was a reaction she didn't fully understand or expect. Her insides felt as though they had turned into molten liquid and she wanted to rip off his clothes and kiss every inch of his body. This thought shocked her as she had never thought that way about anyone, ever. "Liv?" His hand was on her grazed cheek, trying to hold her attention. His eyes were dark and severe as they took in her injuries and his temper took over once again.

"You need to sleep. That's exactly where you should be right now, except you may have a concussion and it's too dangerous for you to sleep right now…and what on earth were you thinking of running along the river banks at this time of day? There could have been punks about, drunken men who could have…" He shook his head unable to go on. "It's still dark out there, you could have ended up in the river for fuck's sake." His temper was rising with each frightening thought. "You're wearing the same goddamn clothes as in college. You should have proper running gear on, that would keep you insulated in this weather. What possessed you? Do you realise what could have happened to you?"

He closed his eyes at the mere thought of her being hurt; the grazes and cuts on her beautiful face made him angrier than he was showing her. He felt a movement and opened his eyes to see Liv had sat bolt upright, her face in pain but a serious expression fixed as she spoke.

"Thank you for your assistance, however, it was not needed. I run every morning. What time I run, where I run and for how long I run, is absolutely none of your business. What I wear is also none of your business and if I choose to throw myself in the river, that will also be none of your bloody business too." It was her turn to get angry now. "How dare you get annoyed at me for not sleeping? Again, it is none of your business. Maybe if you hadn't stormed out of my home like a spoilt child last night, I would have bloody slept. Maybe if you hadn't called me in the early hours and accused me of sleeping with a married man, I would have bloody gone to sleep and still be wrapped up in bed now."

Her fists were clenched with unspent anger as she decided to give him what for. He was kneeling before her, open-mouthed at her rant. "How dare you interfere in my life? I'm sorry I'm such a let-down to you and I'm sorry that I actually didn't fall in the river, then you would never have to tell me off about my behaviour again." He winced at her words and she wasn't sure where her inner bitch was coming from, but she was glad it was here as she needed to stand up for herself. She pushed both hands down on the soft settee and helped herself up into a standing position.

He sprang to his feet and gently placed his huge hands on both of her shoulders, willing her to sit and calm down. Before he could beg her to stay, she went on, "I told you everything. I was completely honest with you and you twisted it." She looked heartbreakingly sad and he wanted to take her in his arms and kiss her sorrow away. "You honestly thought I was having sex with a married man?" She said with disgust, "You don't know me at all. Please don't follow me, delete my number, forget yesterday ever happened," she finished bravely. He studied her youthful, beautiful face. She leant forward and kissed his cheek gently.

"Goodbye, Pip," she said the hopelessness prevalent in her voice as she shrugged her shoulders free and stepped away from his intoxicating proximately. Why did she kiss him when he was being a complete knob? He stood speechless for a moment as he contemplated her words. Liv exited from the main door and followed the hallway to the main front door. On finding the front door, she opened it and found herself in a small foyer with a lift. A table sat at the side, adorned with a glass vase full of gorgeous flowers. She pressed the lift button and waited, praying it hurried up and she wouldn't have to face him again.

A gentle chime signalled the lift's arrival and as the stainless-steel doors slid quietly open, she gratefully stepped into the large mirrored cube. She turned and just as the doors were closing, she saw Pip run towards her and heard him bang the door in frustration as they had closed him out; he was too late. Her mind whirled in a frenzy as she went over the words she had just said to him. She felt sick but that was probably due to the fall she had; she still felt winded. Pleasant orchestral music played softly in the background and another gentle chime signalled the arrival at the ground floor.

She stumbled out into an immaculate marble-floored lobby. Palm trees in huge terracotta pots lined the glass walls to her left and to her right, there was a modern reception desk, behind which sat a gentleman in his late fifties wearing a crisp, dark grey suit. He stood on seeing her exit the lift and although worldly-wise, looked a little confused at her presence. "Good morning, Madam," he spoke eloquently and sounded like he could have been a BBC news reader from the forties.

"Morning," Liv replied politely. She was just walking over to his desk to enquire about their location when two side doors flew open to the right of the lift behind her and Pip burst through. She didn't know if he was going to yell at her or hit her as his face was like thunder and for the first time in his company, she felt scared. As he approached, he knew he had to keep check of his temper but this girl kept putting herself in danger and it riled him. He was so angry when he realised it was her who had fallen in front of him on his morning run; he was torn between shouting at her or kissing her. His groin reacted to this thought and again he checked himself as he stood right in front of her, looking down at her huge blue eyes.

Mud and blood still covered much of her forehead and face as he hadn't had a chance to clean it off. "Liv," he said, sharper than he had intended. She had already noticed the back wall of glass, which showed the uninterrupted view of the river. They must be near to where she fell and therefore, she was near to home.

"I have to go," she said quietly, looking at the logo on his running top, rather than at his face.

"Please stay," he said softly as he brushed a muddy tendril of hair behind her ear. The baseball cap was still on his settee in his penthouse apartment. She debated for a brief moment as his handsome face was pleading with her to stay. Maybe this was fate and she was meant to be here with him. "Please," he pleaded.

"I have to go to work," she said honestly as reality kicked in and she remembered that she was due at Amores at eight-thirty.

His eyes suddenly changed from their bright blue to a smoky grey and his fists clenched tightly as he spoke. "Angelo?" He spat out and she realised he still thought she was having an affair with a married man. Gritting her teeth, she used all her force and pushed him hard on the chest. The action achieved nothing but he stepped back. He wanted to lift her over his shoulder, kicking and screaming back to his apartment, and run her a bath, where he could wash every bit of her mud-stained body. The thought made his dick strain in his tight boxers. She had not made eye contact again and had walked over to the vast glass revolving door, only it wasn't revolving.

She turned and glared at the concierge, who in turn glanced at Pip. He nodded his head and the elderly gent pressed a button on the high-tech keyboard in front of him, releasing the glass compartments as the door began to spin slowly. She stepped in nervously and walked slowly around to the opening. Liv stepped out into the crisp early morning with a sense of relief. Maybe she should be more careful when she went running. What if she had passed out alone on the riverbank? Hallie and Jay wouldn't have a clue where she was. The feeling of them being scared for her, made her feel even more nauseous.

She realised she had been in the luxury riverside apartments and tried to get her head around the fact that Pip lived so close by. Slowly walking the short distance back to the safety and warmth of her home, she was relieved when she closed the front door gently. She was greeted by Burt and Ernie, who were eagerly awaiting breakfast. She fed them and made a strong cup of milky coffee, which she took up the two long flights of stairs. Her legs were aching from the effort after what she had just put them through with her manic run. She had an extraordinary few hours and the winter sun was only just rising. What would today bring?

She stood letting the shower pound on her exhausted body, washing away the remaining mud and blood from her face and hair. Her stomach flipped over as she replayed the events from the last twelve hours. She had let a man into her home. Sharing the safety of her own private space and letting Hallie and Jay get attached to a stranger who she hardly knew. She had told him the truth about how she had gained her space at the institute and when they had kissed with such ferocity, she had been even more honest with him, explaining that she had not had any experience with men. Her insides flipped over again at the embarrassment of it all.

He was a gorgeous man and she knew most of her class had massive crushes on the professor and she wondered briefly if he kissed any of them. She abandoned the idea quickly as it was a completely depressing thought. As she dried her hair, the heat made her grazed head and cheek twinge in pain. She could cover up the bruising skin with foundation, however, the red grooves in her damaged forehead and left cheek would be harder to disguise. She decided to wear one of Jay's baseball caps and realised she must have left his black NY cap in Pip's apartment. Hopefully, Jay wouldn't notice it was missing and she would have to buy him another one.

Liv had gotten used to wearing a baseball cap as she wore one to her lectures at the institute. The idea behind it was to blend in and fade into the background, something she had successfully managed to do. She wore plain baggy clothes to evade being noticed and it had worked so far. Well, no one had paid her any attention, except for Guy and now Professor Denton, that is. She considered Guy to be a friend, although he didn't know the truth about who she really was. Her brow creased at that thought, causing her graze to sting. She sighed as she knew at some point, she would have to tell Guy the truth and how she had managed to get into the prestigious art institute.

He was such a lovely, kind young man and the last thing Liv wanted to do was to hurt his feelings. She reflected on Pip's response to the truth and the way he had held her and kissed her. The fact he had gone on to accuse her of having an affair with a married man was mortifying and she quickly pushed those memories aside and dressed for her day's work at Amores. Black leggings, a grey baggy t-shirt, and black Converse and she was ready. She always had a bag with a spare uniform in her car boot, but today, she wasn't on the restaurant floor.

Despite the fact that her aching body would probably object to the idea of gambolling around the floor, should the need arise, she made her way downstairs and fussed the cats, whilst making more fresh coffee and two pieces of toast spread thinly with marmalade jelly. They all disliked the marmalade with the rind in and the same went for jam, they always had bits free. Both Burt and Ernie were given a bit of her toast crust, one of their favourite breakfast treats. Ernie then meowed to go out into the bitterly cold morning, whilst Burt curled up on the kitchen settee to snooze off his breakfast.

A quick time check showed it was seven-thirty and grabbing the car keys out of the kitchen drawer, she pulled a hoodie on and left the house quietly. Hallie had a football match at eleven o'clock, but her friend's mum was picking her up at ten-thirty. She was then sleeping over at her best friend, Mazz's (Marianne), and wouldn't be home until after tea tomorrow. Mazz had been Hallie's best friend since nursery school and they knew each other inside out and back to front.

Esme and John had been blessed with two beautiful daughters, Marianne and Madeleine. Esme's French mother had inspired their names and she grimaced every time they were called by their shortened nicknames of Mazz and Maddie. John adored his girls and they had grown into pretty teenagers and good people. As there were three hormonal women at home, he had found solace and joy in his man cave, a large wooden shed at the bottom of the garden. It had been fitted with a battered leather reclining chair, sky TV, and beer pumps. What more could a man want?

Esme loved being in the company of her daughters and included Hallie as family. Both sisters loved Hallie and there was never a crossword between them. Instead, they gossiped and enjoyed their girlie time, talking about boys and how they would never understand them. Maddie, being two years older than Mazz and Hal, was in her first proper relationship and they discussed and analysed every small detail. The girls would giggle and whisper and thoroughly enjoy their time together.

Jay was going to meet Tom for lunch at McDonalds, then a gaming afternoon at Tom's house, followed by a sleepover. Tom's dad, Richard, was taking them both to the rugby game tomorrow and she would be lucky if she saw him before late evening. Richard and his wife, Clara, had moved to Worcester a few years ago and Jay and Tom had become instant buddies at middle school. Now they had started secondary school and were both tall and gangly, but best buddies. Their love of gaming and rugby had cemented what would no doubt be a lifelong friendship. Jay's happy-go-lucky nature endeared him to Richard and Clara on their first meeting and, as Tom was an only child, they also doted on Jay, treating him like a second son.

Jay loved having male company and going to the rugby games with Tom and Richard was always the highlight of his week. Tom also loved staying at the Whitmores. Although Liv was the mother figure, they had a lot more freedom there and he always felt respected and at home there. Above it all, Liv knew that Hallie and Jay were safe and loved by their extended families. The only blood relation was Pong, so to have her siblings content and happy when staying at their best friends' homes was a constant source of relief to her.

As she drove her Mini through the narrow streets, weaving between the growing traffic of a busy Saturday morning in the city, she contemplated the evening ahead. With Hallie and Jay both staying as friends, she would be on her own. Something she was usually not bothered about, but today, she felt sad at the thought of it. Maybe Pip embracing her tightly and kissing her passionately had opened her eyes to the concept of having someone to love. She loved her siblings and Pong of course, but to fall in love with someone, to feel you belong to someone and they feel the same way about you, must be a wonderful feeling.

She stifled a yawn as she turned into the back alley of the Shambles. Already busy with vans unloading and loading, she weaved between the vehicles and made a sharp turn to her right. A narrow road led her to a metal gate. Opening her electric window and feeling the icy blast of air hit her skin, she waved her ID card across the scanner. The massive gates rumbled into action and opened slowly, leading the way into the Amores' private car park. It was for staff and occasionally VIP customers to use. It was fully secure with cameras which were linked to a security company. The restaurant was open for prep from the early hours of the morning and would be open until late.

When she was working in the restaurant itself, she would be one of the first to turn up on a Saturday morning, arriving at four am, and she would assist with the preparation of meals for the day. Returning home around twelve and then going back again at four to work the evening shift, which depending on their clientele, could mean a two am finish. Weekdays were not usually as long, but at sixteen, it was an exhausting routine, especially when trying to keep on top of things at home. Once she had parked, she locked her little black Mini. She walked to the side gate, which opened automatically, and smiled and waved at the camera as she always did, feeling sorry for the poor chump who had to sit and stare at the computer screens all day, waiting for a human to appear.

She crossed the narrow street and was comforted by the singing she could hear coming from the back kitchens of Amore. The back gate was open as always and as she made her way through the staff entrance, she was greeted with a cheer from Angelo and the kitchen staff. This was a tradition and one she always found welcoming, although at first embarrassing. The Italian singing started up again and as she made her way up the side staircase into the private apartments, she was once again grateful for these wonderful people that she included as her family.

Chapter 11

By three-thirty that afternoon, a mentally and physically exhausted Liv made her way out of the yard and through the back gate that led onto the alleyway, Liv carefully carried a large brown bag full of goodies that Stacey had forced her to take having found out Liv was going to be alone tonight. Shivering from the chilly afternoon air, her head had started aching and all of her limbs were sore. Part of her was glad that her sister and brother were away for the night as she could have a bath and crawl into bed. There was a niggling feeling in the back of her mind that she just couldn't shake.

It was Pip. She hadn't heard a word from him all day and after checking her phone even more times than usual, she had only had two calls from Pong, which she had answered and texts from her siblings, updating her that they were both safe and well and enjoying their day. As she scanned her ID card for the private car park, she turned and glanced up the narrow street. It was early afternoon and the delivery vans had all gone. There were a few cars abandoned by lazy shoppers, all destined for tickets, as the ever-present traffic warden was on patrol. She turned back as the slim gate opened, waving at the security camera but forgetting her usual smile.

Feeling a little on edge and unsettled, she put it down to the nasty fall earlier that morning. As she drove through the now busy streets, she made her way towards home. Driving past her turn for her cul-de-sac, she continued on to Pong's home. Neatly parking, she groaned as she alighted the car, her muscles complaining about the action. Reaching into the top of the large brown paper bag, she grabbed the box of toffees she had brought as a little gift. Walking into the supported living facility was always a little depressing. Her grandad had always been active and outgoing, but now due to dementia, he could hardly remember his name, let alone who she was.

The staff, however, were incredibly kind and worked hard to make sure Pong was as safe, happy, and active, as this horrific disease allowed. Tina was Liv's favourite carer. She always greeted Liv with a huge hug and a warm smile. A buxom wench, she loved nothing more than a few pints of lager at her local when her long shifts had finished. Her children were all grown up and had children of their own. She was a devoted single mum to her three children and a fantastic nan to her ten grandchildren. She always joked with Liv that she was going to start her own football team with her many grandchildren.

Liv knew that Tina spent a lot more time with Pong, even more than she was paid for. She would often finish her shift and sit and have a cup of tea with him. Today was no different as Tina's friendly face greeted Liv as she walked into Pong's apartment. His little space was homely and comfortable and Liv's paintings adorned the walls of the living room, where Pong was sat sipping his mug of tea. "Hello," said Tina cheerfully, getting up and hugging Liv warmly. This small gesture always meant the world to Liv as she knew that Tina hugged her grandad when she was not there, so he was still getting affection and love. "What have you been up to?"

Tina's face dropped as she took in Liv's bruised and scratched face. She also had a dark bruise coming out on her cheek and she could feel it pull when she smiled. "I fell over on a run this morning, I'm fine," Liv said as she turned to her grandad. "Hello, Pong," she said smiling.

The old gentleman studied her face and recognised what he thought was his only daughter. "Elizabeth? I've been looking for you," he said grumpily. Liv was used to this and produced Thornton's toffees and his face lit up. They were his favourite and although he was angry at Elizabeth for going missing, he was happy now she was here and with his favourite sweets too. Tina made her excuses and left, giving both Liv and Pong a huge goodbye hug. The confusion set back in like a switch had been flicked. "My name is Gerald," he said eying her suspiciously. "Who are you?"

"I'm Liv," she replied a tight smile on her face as she realised, she should have given this a miss today. She could see the cogs of his brain trying to match her name and face to a memory, but sadly there was no recognition and he grabbed his walking stick from the side of his chair, waving it angrily at her.

"I don't know you," he shouted. "Get out of here!" He looked around bewildered, not recognising his own living room. Liv stood and nodded politely, used to her grandad's angry behaviour. He was getting worse and she knew there would come a point where he would be forced to go into a residential home for his own and other's safety. It was only thanks to Tina's extra care that he had lasted here for so long. Most of the other residents were of sound mind, so his progressively threatening behaviour would mean at some point, he would need twenty-four-hour secure care.

He was still ranting as she closed his front door quietly, making her way down the meticulously clean corridors and the large fish tank that sat in the beginning of the reception area. Walking through the lobby, she smiled and waved at the old ladies who were busy nattering over tea served in China teacups and saucers. She passed through the two sets of automatic doors and out into the darkness of the late afternoon. Shivering, she wrapped her arms around herself, stopping at her car and turning back to face the welcoming lights of the home's reception. It was so sad that her beloved grandad had lost most of his memories and after extensively researching the term vascular dementia, which was the type he had been afflicted with, she knew he had been given a death sentence.

Liv was not an emotional being. This was mostly down to when her parents were tragically killed and she had decided that she should be the strong one, the dependable one. Her siblings needed her to be brave and not break down. Not a single tear had fallen from her beautiful blue eyes since the knowledge of her parent's deaths. She had stayed strong for all of these years and now in the great sadness of knowing her grandad was not going to be with them much longer, she knew she could not break her resolve. With a look of new determination on her bruised face, she took a deep breath, turned back, and unlocked her car.

As she opened her front door, Liv was greeted by Burt and Ernie, both meowing loudly and rubbing around her legs, welcoming their human home. The house had been empty for a few hours and they had missed their fuss and company. Placing the brown bag carefully on the breakfast bar, she emptied the contents. A bottle of fine red wine and five large plastic containers holding a range of the delicious Amores menu. Stacey and Angelo always sent them far too much food and as this was only for one person, there was loads. She stacked them on the worktop.

Although grateful, the last thing she wanted was food. She fed the mewling cats and as they scoffed their tea, she made her way around the downstairs windows, closing the blinds and shutting out the world. Updates from Hallie and Jay put her mind at rest as they were both safe and ensconced in their second families' homes. Too tired to do anymore, she flicked off the kitchen lights, leaving only the soft glow of the hallway lamp. They always left this on overnight as they could make their way to the kitchen without burning their retinas in the middle of the night. Her heavy legs felt each and every step up to the first floor and as she passed her siblings' bedrooms, she felt an overwhelming sense of loneliness.

Finally, after climbing the second staircase, she reached her bathroom. Washing her face with her Clinique liquid soap made her graze sting. After drying her skin gently, she used clarifying lotion on a soft cotton pad to clean her skin properly; this stung even more. She moisturised and gazed at her bruised face in the mirror. Her mum had always encouraged her to look after her skin and she followed her mum's skincare routine religiously. Her porcelain skin was the result, although this morning's injuries didn't help her look her best. She shook her head despondently and decided to forget about the bath idea.

She was so tired, she just wanted to get her pjs on and get into bed. She walked into her dressing room, kicking off her Converse at the side of the tub chair and pulling off her socks, throwing them into the wooden laundry basket in the corner. Peeling off the baggy hooded jumper was a relief as the house was warm and she was starting to feel a little overheated. That too was thrown into the laundry box. She was just about to take off her loose grey t-shirt when she was disturbed by the ring of the front doorbell. The electronic doorbell had plug-in attachments on each floor so that everyone could hear if someone was at the door.

The bell was now chiming the tune of 'We wish you a merry Christmas', and Liv smiled to herself, knowing Jay must have changed all the sounds on every plug to play the same thing. The bell had been pressed again. Someone was obviously impatient and didn't realise Liv had to get her tired, aching body down two flights of stairs. She unlocked the front door and as always, the security chain stayed in place. Opening the door slightly, she caught her breath. Pip stood there peering through the gap, his expression dark and serious.

Chapter 12

"We need to talk." His tone was resolute and determined. Liv was so tired, that she couldn't be bothered to argue, so closing the door gently, and slipping the security chain off its bracket, she reopened the door fully to let him in. He looked devastatingly handsome in stonewashed jeans, a fitted, white V-neck t-shirt and an open black leather jacket, exposing his toned physic beneath the white crisp cotton. She closed and locked the door, trying to unsee the image of his fit body that was now burnt into her brain. He stood looking at her artwork on the wall, the image of the gaming remote holding his attention.

She walked past him and made her way into the kitchen without saying a word. Pressing a button on the lighting remote, the under-counter lights flickered into life and a corner lamp above the comfortable settee spread its soft glow onto the seating area and coffee table. She made her way into the kitchen space and retrieved two wine glasses from a wall cupboard and the bottle of red wine she had left on the breakfast bar. Lowering herself onto the comfy cushions of the settee, she pulled her aching legs beneath her and poured two glasses of wine into the large crystal glasses.

She knew he was watching her every move, but for some reason, she just didn't care. Maybe the last twenty-four hours had made her grow up even more, or it could just be the fact that her mind and body were so exhausted after a night with no sleep and the nasty fall she had that morning. Either way, she didn't want to argue. Ernie jumped up onto her lap, purring loudly at her presence. Burt had already made himself cosy on her bed and wasn't moving for anyone or anything. Liv absentmindedly scratched his ears as he plonked himself down on her lap.

Pip made his way to the settee in silence. Slipping off his heavy jacket, he threw it over the arm of the seat before he sat down. He wasn't sure what he had expected but this wasn't it. He studied the marks on her beautiful face, his fists clenching as he remembered the danger she had put herself in that morning. Her forehead and cheek were grazed and the red scratches looked sore. The skin around it had darkened and a tinge of blue meant that a bruise was imminent. She also had a discoloured cheek, the bluey purple skin showing another injury. How could she have done this to herself? Why did she insist on putting herself at risk?

His thoughts were broken when she reached out for her glass of wine from the low coffee table. The tight muscles in her arm and shoulder pulled painfully, making her blanch. His mouth formed a grim line as he saw her face react to the small movement. "For fuck's sake, Liv," he said angrily, taking a few calming breaths before he went on. She sipped her wine and replaced the glass on the table, with the same sharp twinge in her muscles as her body disapproved. She returned her attention to Ernie, who had sat up in response to Pip's forceful voice, his ears and eyes now on alert for any danger.

Pip grabbed his glass and took a large slug of liquid in an attempt to quell his growing anger. The warming, delicious wine did help and he replaced his glass back on the table in a slightly better mood. "I haven't stopped thinking about you all day," he said softly, making her finally look up at him. Seeing the marks clearly visible on her beautiful face made him so mad, but he knew he had to control it. If he lost his temper now, he would lose her and that was the last thing he wanted. "I just want the truth, Liv," he said gently and her mouth popped open slightly as he said her name.

Her head tilted and small creases appeared on her bruised forehead as she frowned. "I told you the truth last night and you didn't believe me," she said quietly, holding his intense gaze. "I told you I had lied to get into the institute, that I'm older than you thought, and what my real name was...and you believed me. Then I tell you something so private and so personal, and you think I'm lying?" Her voice relayed the betrayal she felt and she squeezed her eyes shut, trying to block out the world. He opened his mouth to argue but closed it again as he couldn't seem to find the right words.

He tried a different tack. "I followed you," he said simply.

Her eyes flicked open. "What?" She questioned in shock.

"I followed you home this morning; I was worried you were going to pass out again," he said honestly.

"Go on," she said, not really sure if she wanted to hear anymore.

"I waited and then followed you to Amores," he said. "I waited for you there, not knowing how long you would be." He didn't take his eyes off hers as he watched for a reaction. "I even went in..."

"You did what?" She interrupted him in a horrified whisper. Although she hadn't raised her voice, the atmosphere had plummeted, and Ernie jumped off the settee, deciding he would take his chances upstairs on the big bed, next to a snoring Burt.

"I asked where you were and the young lad looked stupefied, and said he didn't know anyone called Liv." He was questioning her again, obviously not believing her. The young lad he was talking about was the new waiter, Jason, a seventeen-year-old student, who had started his first shift at Amores that morning. Liv sighed and retrieved her mobile out of her back pocket. "There is someone I need to tell you about." She looked calm as Pip's whole universe started to collapse. "Someone I love very much," she spoke quietly, her face giving away nothing.

Pip sat stock still, his brain working overtime and his fists clenched in fury. Liv flicked her phone on, running her deft fingers in different directions, landing on the photos section. Scrolling through them, she chose an image and handed the phone to him. He looked horrified, expecting to see some good-looking twenty-something who had stolen Liv's heart. He felt sick. Taking her cell suspiciously, he studied the photograph. It showed a cute little boy sitting holding a teddy bear, his eyes looking down at the cuddly toy and not at the camera lens. Pip quickly put two and two together and came up with three. "He's yours?" Pip asked mortified.

"Oh my god, what do I have to do or say for you to believe me?" She replied getting annoyed. "This is Luca, he is three years old and he is Angelo and Stacey's son. I help look after him. There is also another man in my life." She took the phone back and swiped quickly, then passed the phone back to him. This was a photo of an elderly gent, in a three-piece suit, his short white hair neatly combed. He was smiling broadly and looked slightly familiar. "That's Pong, my grandad. The constant phone checking at the institute is because he can flip out at the drop of a hat. Not all the time, but sometimes hearing my voice can help calm him down."

"He has dementia and is deteriorating quickly. I visit them both as much as I can, but on a Saturday, I work at Amores, upstairs in Angelo and Stacey's home, looking after Luca. I used to waitress and help out in the kitchens, but for the last year, I have been helping them with Luca. Stacey is pregnant with her second child and Luca can be a handful. I have spent the day reading, playing, and making him happy." She eyed him as the information sank in. "And for the very last time, I have never had sex with anyone, ever. It's embarrassingly mortifying to tell you this for a second time, but as you didn't believe me the first time around…"

She closed her mouth, biting both lips hard between her teeth. She didn't need this hassle, she had more than enough going on in her life without the complication of a moody, sexy, stud muffin. She risked a look at his torso, trying to avoid his face. The white cotton material of his t-shirt strained at the underlying six-pack beneath. She let out a long breath and again reached out for another sip of the delicious wine. Replacing it on the table, she remembered how tired she felt and that all she wanted to do was sleep. She yawned at the thought of her comfy, warm bed, covering her mouth with both hands to stifle the sound.

She rubbed both palms over her eyes and looked up at Pip who had remained statuesque and silent. "It's not even five o'clock and you'd locked up the house?" He questioned a serious expression on his face. Liv was confused, expecting questions about Luca and her grandad.

"So?" She said defiantly.

"You were upstairs when I rang the bell?" He asked thoughtfully.

"Yes," she said simply.

"Where are Hallie and Jay?" He asked just realising how quiet the house was.

"They are both at sleepovers with their friends," she answered, wondering what business it was of his.

"Liv, were you going to bed before I arrived?" The look on his face was of bewilderment; it was only late afternoon and she had locked up the house and was going to bed. He must be thinking that she was acting more like a ninety-year-old than a twenty-year-old, but at this point, she didn't care what he thought. She leant towards him, wanting to make sure she was heard.

"This is my home and if I want to go to bed at five o'clock on a Saturday afternoon, I can." He went to answer but she carried on. "In fact, if it hadn't been for you, I would have slept last night and not felt like a complete zombie today," she finished, glaring at him. He leant forward too, so that their faces were incredibly close.

He fixed her with a steely stare before saying, "Have you eaten?" Rolling her eyes in response, she decided not to answer. Instead, she stood, grabbing her wine glass and bottle as she did so. Walking over to the breakfast bar, she put down the booze and picked up the food containers taking them around into the kitchen, placing them neatly in the fridge. She pressed a button on the light controller and the kitchen under lights and lamp flickered off, leaving the kitchen in darkness apart from the soft light emanating from the hall. Picking up the bottle and glass, she walked out of the kitchen.

"See yourself out," she said not turning back. Completely perplexed by her behaviour, Pip stood, clinging on to his own glass, and followed her. She was walking up the stairs and as he made his way up, he realised she was wearing tight-fitting black trousers. How had he not noticed this before? Her loose tee meant that her butt and upper body were covered, but this was the first time he had seen the shape of her legs. His dick hardened as he took in her long, toned limbs. Why would she hide them? They were amazing and probably all down to her daily run. He blanched at the thought of her racing past him earlier that day and ending up on the icy, muddy embankment.

She had now turned right and they were on a large landing, again a slim side table, holding a large Tiffany effect lamp, softly lit the area. Making her way onto a second staircase, he stood for what seemed like an age, giving her lots of space, her bare feet making no sound on the plush carpet. He stood stock still deliberating his next move. He looked up the flight of stairs and she had long gone. After at least ten minutes of indecisiveness, he followed in her footsteps. Again, there was a side table with a large cream, urchin effect lamp, gently lighting the stairs and landing.

He found himself on a second landing with a number of doors to his left and one set of double doors to his right. A soft light was flooding through a partly open door to his right and he decided to go in. He found himself in a spacious dressing area, with beautifully crafted frosted-glass wardrobes, all with inside lighting. The ceiling spotlights were off but the inner wardrobe's soft lights were bright enough to see clearly. He turned to see another door ajar ahead of him, a gentler hue illuminating the way. A small corridor opened out into a vast bedroom. Again, the lighting was beautiful as the soft glow of several lamps gently lit the area.

He could see an enormous bed, draped in cream and gold covers, and two grey furry mounds resting on top, where the cats lay fast asleep. Two bedside tables with matching cream shades sat neatly on either side of the bed and above the cream headboard, the glint of gold as he caught sight of Liv's favourite painting in the whole house. He stood awestruck. A long-time admirer of Klimt's work, he even had one or two of Klimt's pieces in his own private collection.

Even in this subdued light, he could see the detailed work that had gone into it. After what seemed like another age, he realised that Liv was missing.

Scanning the room, he saw a seating area to his right with one huge, cosy-looking cream sofa. Glowing embers lit the modern fireplace which was fitted inside the wall and the light of the glowing red embers lit up the features of Liv's angelic sleeping face. He walked over to her, quietly placing his wine glass down on the small side table, alongside Liv's glass and the bottle of remaining wine. He gently sat down beside her and watched her as she slept. Her breathing was soft and rhythmic and he was hypnotised by her beauty. She had wrapped herself up in a huge cream fluffy throw and looked as snug as a bug in a rug (one of Maggie's expressions).

The minutes ticked by and he could think of no other place he would rather be, than here, watching her. She was safe and warm here. He could protect her here. He had been taken aback by her response to him; most females found it difficult to talk to him. That's why he loved Maggie and Clara. They saw him as a human being and not as a well-off fuck machine. His looks had never really bothered him. The all-American playboy genes were inherited and apart from keeping fit and active, he didn't do a lot to maintain his image. He wore what he felt good in and not what was deemed fashionable and expensive.

He had actually started to use a men's moisturiser at night, a gift from Maggie last Christmas, as she said he needed to start looking after himself. He was brought back to the present by Liv's eyes snapping open. She stared at him for a moment, realising that this gorgeous man was sitting right next to her in her bedroom. Holy fuck! He couldn't help but smile at her as she gazed into his eyes, the Whitmore puppy dog look in its element. The glow of the orange embers gently lit her face and her skin looked translucent in the subtle light. He reached out and stroked a loose tendril of her hair behind her ear. The small action made both of their breaths hitch.

Liv's stomach was flipping over as the touch of his fingers on her cheek set her insides on fire. Feeling flushed and overheated, she pushed off the warm blanket that she was cocooned in. It was no good, his very presence made her feel hot, sweaty, and extremely turned on. In an attempt to control her racing heart, Liv closed her eyes tightly to shut him out, trying to focus instead on breathing in and out. She felt lightheaded and dizzy, but her eyes remained closed as she battled her body's reaction to his proximity. Suddenly, warm full lips crushed against hers, kissing her fervently.

Chapter 13

Liv's eyes flew open as she felt her temperature shoot up one hundred degrees. This sexy, hot man was in her bedroom, kneeling in front of her, kissing her. Pip had his eyes closed, enjoying the fullness of her lips against his. Kneeling up so they were face-to-face, he couldn't resist her any longer. His hands moved to her face as the kiss deepened. Her arms automatically wrapped around his shoulders as she returned the passion of his kiss. His tongue started to gently probe her mouth and she felt her body responding to this intimate action. Her insides had turned to molten liquid and a strange feeling of excitement and terror was making her whole body tingle.

Pip moved from her lips to her neck and gently kissed and nipped his way down her skin until he reached the top of her loose t-shirt. He leant back onto his heels, her hands falling to her sides, whilst his hands cupped her face. "I want to make love to you." His voice was husky and heavy with want. She thought her insides were going to spontaneously combust and simply nodded in response, missing his lips on her neck. In one swift move, he stood, scooping her into his strong arms. Standing, he lifted her easily and walked over to the end of the enormous bed. She thought he was going to put her down, but instead, he sat on the edge of the bed, still holding her in his arms.

Both Burt and Ernie had woken and started purring, hoping for some attention now that their humans had arrived. Liv laughed and shooed them off the bed with her hand. Most put out that their comfortable pitch had been disturbed, they both skulked out of the room to find somewhere quiet to curl up and sleep. He had watched her laugh, taking in her eyes lighting up with humour and it made him want her even more. The smile dropped from her face when she saw he was studying her. Shifting her whole body, she moved so she was sat astride him in a kneeling position.

She was facing him, marvelling at the hard bulge that was pushing against her core and making her wet. Serious now, she leant forward and kissed him with all she was worth. Their desire for one another ignited a flame of hot passion. This time, the kiss was wild and fiery. Tongues lashed against each other as the heat built. He moved his mouth back onto her throat and she practically purred as she clung to him. Stopping again at the neck of her grey, baggy t-shirt, he looked at her, his expression dark and seductive. She nodded slowly, ready for the next step, feeling safe with this man and knowing she wanted to take things further.

The corners of his mouth turned up and he reminded her of the Cheshire cat. He was definitely about to get the cream. Letting go of her beautiful face, he grabbed the bottom of her loose t-shirt. She obligingly raised both arms, her eyes never leaving his, trusting him explicitly. Her muscles still ached from the fall, but she didn't care. He lifted off her grey tee and she heard him suck in his breath harshly. *Oh fuck...he doesn't like what he sees*, she thought immediately. As the shirt went over her head and her vision was temporarily blocked, her nerves kicked in. When her view was clear, she quickly took in his expression. He was staring at her body and she felt completely inadequate and totally embarrassed.

When he had lifted the shirt off her body, he couldn't help but stare. Pale porcelain skin covered a toned firm stomach and a sexy black laced bra held her ample full breasts. Where the fuck had she been hiding those? His expression was serious as he was lost in his own thoughts, admiring the beautiful woman in front of him. He scowled when he took in her left-hand side, which had now had purply blue bruises from the fall earlier that day. After a few seconds, his eyes moved higher, only to see Liv's beautiful face screwed up and her eyes squeezed shut. Both of her lips between her teeth, mortified at the situation she was now in. She was as still as a statue. "Liv?" He spoke gently.

"I'm so sorry, I knew this would happen," she blurted out quickly, raising both hands to cover her face, the action pushing both of her supple breasts firmly together. The site of this almost made him come and he had to take a deep soothing breath. He raised his hands and gently pulled her hands away from her face. Still biting her lips together, she opened one eye. He laughed gently as he touched his finger to her lips, making them unfurl open.

"Liv," he almost growled with want. Liv opened both eyes wide in shock.

"What's wrong with me?" She whispered. She was more than embarrassed that she was sitting on a man's lap, half-dressed. This had never happened before and her inexperience with men was now completely obvious. Pip had probably slept with hundreds of women and her twenty-year-old body must be a huge disappointment.

He realised she was actually feeling insufficient and his whole demeanour changed. He leant in close to her face, his hands back on her cheeks holding her still. "Olivia Whitmore, you are without doubt the most incredibly beautiful woman I have ever and will ever lay eyes on," he said firmly. Her huge blue eyes opened even wider as she fought to believe his words. No one had ever said anything like that to her before. A faint blush of pink appeared on her cheeks and she closed her eyes again, embarrassed at her own inexperience. "Liv…" he rested his forehead on hers and she opened her eyes in response.

"We don't have to go on…as much as I really want to. This is all new for you and I am just happy to be here with you," he said seriously. He wanted nothing more than to make love to her but he wanted her to enjoy it and want it too. She sighed and was just about to apologise for being an unskilled virgin when his eyes darkened. "Don't apologise," he said warningly.

She knew she wanted to go on. She was totally in love with him and at almost twenty-one, she really wanted to have sex. Who would be more suitable than this handsome American hottie who wanted her as much as she wanted him? A timid smile appeared on her face, once more melting his heart. She gently cupped his face in her delicate hands and kissed him. Again, the kiss became more passionate, Pip only breaking it to whip off his t-shirt, revealing a tanned muscular body that took Liv's breath away. Lifting her gently onto the bed, he stood, kicking off his sneakers and undoing the button fly on his jeans. He retrieved a small foil square from his back pocket before stepping out of the denim and ripping off his socks.

Liv sat admiring his amazing physique, although her attention lingered on the foil packet he had thrown on the bed. Returning her gaze to him, she was face-to-face with a pair of fitted grey boxer trunks that Daniel Craig would have been proud of. His privates were straining to be released and her eyes went from the firm bulge of his pants, following his toned abdomen, up higher until she made contact with his intense gaze. He held both hands out inviting her to stand and she took them, shakily standing up in front of this sex god. Cupping her face, a gave her a chaste kiss on her lips. His hands slid onto her shoulders and he gently kissed her neck, this time carrying on and making his way down the centre of her cleavage, past the delicate lace, kissing his way down her toned stomach.

His hands had moved to her hips as he knelt down in front of her, looking up at her before he went on. She knew he was waiting for permission and although still embarrassed that the top half of her body was barely covered, a small nod confirmed she was ready to go on. He slowly peeled down her black leggings, revealing matching black lace knicker shorts. When her leggings were at her ankles, he gently lifted each foot to rid them of this excess material. Again, he noticed the bruises on her left leg and ignored the anger he felt at her being hurt. His hands gently rubbed her feet, all the way up the sides of her quivering body, to her chest.

His expression was serious and dark, entirely focused on her glorious frame. She tried not to feel inadequate, however, being a novice, she couldn't help but feel lost. Moving his hands across to cover her breasts, he squeezed gently and she felt her whole body respond by pushing against them. Her head went back and she closed her eyes, this time not to hide but to revel in this intense feeling of desire. Her whole being was on fire and she knew she was ready for what was to come next. She wanted him, she wanted to feel like a real woman. He started kissing her breasts through the fine lace material of her bra, making her blood pulse around her aching body.

He kissed and nuzzled his way to the base of her neck, stepping closer to her so her breasts were pressed against his firm chest. His closeness caused her to wrap her arms around him, so her legs didn't give way. He responded by enveloping her nearly naked form in his strong arms. Her legs felt like jelly and as he nibbled her earlobe, she turned her head and his lips found hers. Standing only in their underwear, they kissed each other fiercely. Their hands explore the other's hot, clammy skin. Pip was the one to break the kiss and again scooped her into his arms and, after making his way to the side of the bed, he laid her gently on the cream and gold covers.

She looked like a goddess. He went back to retrieve the foil packet and returned to where she lay, breathless and wanton. Her breasts felt heavy and restricted in her bra and she could feel her knickers were wet. Mortified, she crossed her legs slightly. Her attention suddenly focused on Pip who was peeling off his underwear, revealing his huge, hard penis. She had helped change Jay's nappies when he was a baby and helped bathe him and her sister, she had also studied biology at school and had sex education classes. She knew exactly what a penis should look like but had never seen an adult penis in real life, especially not so close up and with a rock-hard erection.

Her eyes widened when it struck her just where his penis was supposed to go and she squeezed her thighs together even more as the thought of it seemed quite painful. She watched as he expertly ripped open the packet and produced a condom. He rolled the protective sheath over his solid length with great ease, obviously used to the procedure. Liv found this thought depressing. He wanted to smile when he looked down and saw the look of horror on her face, but he knew she would be nervous. This was her first time and it was going to be with him, he wanted her to feel safe.

Lying down beside her, she looked into his eyes and for some unexplainable reason, she knew she trusted him explicitly. She turned on her side and he copied, his hands stroking back the loose tendrils of hair that had escaped from her plait. "Hey," he said smiling. "How are you feeling?" He continued to stroke her hair.

"Bit nervous," she replied honestly. His smile dropped and he edged his face closer, so their noses were almost touching.

"I think you're a little overdressed for the occasion," he said the corner of his mouth twitching as he kissed her. She felt his hands reach around her body and after a few seconds, she felt her bra unclip. Her whole body froze and her eyes widened in response. "Liv…" Her name on his lips eased her back to reality and she suddenly felt braver. Pushing him back, she slid on top of him, his hard dick pressing against her stomach, sending her insides on fire. She kissed him passionately as he removed her bra. "Sit up," he growled, the words echoing down to her core. She complied and he followed.

Liv was now topless and her pert, full breasts were free of the lace. She was stunning and his dick twitched and strained at the thought of soon being inside her. He kissed her hard, one hand wrapped around her body keeping her close and one hand skilfully fingering her nipples, squeezing and tweaking them, making her moan into his mouth, spurring him on. He rolled her underneath him and kissed her chin, then down her neck and onto her breasts, kissing and sucking them, the feeling utterly torturous but delicious. "I want to make love to you," he growled and her only response was 'Yes'. Edging down the bed, he pulled both sides of her knickers down and whipped them off, leaving her whole body exposed.

She closed her eyes for a moment, having another brief encounter with reality. She was lying on her bed completely naked with an equally naked sexy man lying with her. It was such a surreal feeling that Liv thought for a moment it could all be a dream. She was biting her lip when she felt his fingers move across her cheek gently, moving on to stroke her hair. "Hey," he said again. He was leaning over her, his face etched with concern. "Liv, you can talk to me…If you want to stop…" his voice trailed away.

"I don't want to stop," she said bravely, her eyes remained squeezed shut. "I'm just…" She searched for the right words. "…scared," she spoke quietly. "Scared and very wet." There was no sound or movement and she flicked her eyes open to see if he was still there and not gone running down the street. Her mind suddenly filled with the image of his naked body literally running down the street. She shook her head to rid it of the distraction. He was still there, leaning over her, his eyes wide, his face unreadable.

"Scared and…wet?" He questioned. Shit, maybe she shouldn't have said that, maybe that's not supposed to happen and she had a broken fouf! She closed her eyes again and covered her face with her hands, something she did when she was terribly embarrassed. An endearing gesture that again melted his heart. She felt his kiss on the backs of her hands and she moved them. He gently kissed both eyelids and she opened her eyes to see him. This gorgeous stud of a man, kissing her, Liv Whitmore, whilst naked! She blew out a calming breath and his hand slowly snaked its way down her face, neck, shoulder and breasts.

They felt heavy and fuller than usual, aching to be kissed and nuzzled again, but he skimmed past and as his fingers approached her cleanly shaven fouf. She didn't close her eyes; she watched as he gazed at her earnestly, his hand exploring. Using his fingers, he gently touched her where no one had ever touched her before. As he felt the wetness on his own fingers, he closed his eyes, fervently enjoying the feel of her. "Christ, Liv, you're so ready for me," he said as he deftly probed and explored her most intimately. She could feel an inner tension building and knew that she wanted this, that she needed this. "Liv…" His face was over hers.

"I want to be inside you when I make you come for the first time." His expression was serious and she found her body was responding to his fingers, pushing her hips against his hand. "Liv?" He kissed her mouth and she looked up at him.

"I'm ready," she whispered. He rolled her underneath him and with his legs astride her body, he slowly laid on top of her. The feeling was incredible and she desperately wanted him inside her. Resting most of his weight on his elbows, he kissed her fiercely and she raised her knees up in response. He gently started to ease his dick inside her, the wetness of her arousal helping to slide him in slowly.

It was a strange sensation and just as she thought he was fully inside her; he broke the kiss to speak.

"You ok?" He asked with concern. She nodded, not wanting him to stop moving, grabbing the back of his head and kissing him passionately. Suddenly, he thrust into her body and she yelped out as an excruciating pain shot through her. He stilled as she winced and adjusted her hips slightly, the feeling of her most intimate area being stretched to capacity and his throbbing hard dick being so far into her body took a little getting used to. It felt odd but wickedly good. Slowly and rhythmically, he started to move, in and out, filling her insides and making her body strain to contain him.

They began kissing again and she could feel a tension building; with each growing thrust, her body craved for more. The pain had gone and all she could feel now was a building pleasure. His movements became stronger, pushing into her body harder and harder. The feeling was exquisite and she didn't want it to stop. "Look at me," his words pierced her mind as she hadn't realised she had closed her eyes. She was now meeting each of his thrusts, grinding her body as close to him as she could get. "Liv."

Her name from his lips was her undoing as an explosion of feelings ignited at her core. Everything else faded away as the sublime pulsing of their orgasms took over their bodies. Waves of intense pleasure hit their bodies, seeming to go on forever. The delicious fullness of his dick slowly released its load into her very core, racking them both of every ounce of energy. The mind-blowing frenzy of her first sexual encounter and his most explosive and satisfying orgasm ever, both concluded as they lay in each other's arms, sated and happy, their bodies giving way to exhausted slumber.

Chapter 14

Liv felt incredibly hot. Her body was so overheated and her skin clammy. Half asleep and in an attempt to cool down, she tried to move her legs to kick the covers off but her legs wouldn't budge. They were weighed down by an invisible weight. She tried to adjust her arms and they too were pinned down, so she couldn't move at all. Liv started to feel panicky not being able to lift her arms or legs. Being swelteringly hot wasn't helping either. Her whole body jolted awake and it took her a few seconds to realise that under the duvet cover, strong muscular arms were entwined around her naked body.

A muscular leg was wrapped around hers and she realised this was why she couldn't move and felt so bloody warm. Pip Denton was holding her in a tight embrace. The soft glow of the bedside lamps meant the room was dimly lit, her alarm clock showing it was just after two in the morning. She wondered how on earth she could get out of his strong grip without waking him. Slowly, thoughts of the evening returned as she remembered that she was no longer a virgin. She had actually had sex last night. Fuck! Quite literally. Not just any old sex but sex with Professor Philip Denton, sex god extraordinaire.

Suddenly, he let go of her and his body twisted away. Her fidgeting must have disturbed him. Although, feeling boiling hot, her body immediately felt the loss of his close touch. Deciding she really needed a shower, she slipped out of the covers and padded gently over to the door of the bathroom. There was a dull ache in the pit of her stomach, a slight discomfort that she put down to her first sexual encounter. Deciding she needed a wee, she was mortified when she discovered a patch of dried blood between her thighs. She felt sick and lightheaded at the thought that she had been bleeding and scared that something inside her was damaged. What if her fouf really was broken?

With her mind reeling, she quickly entered the vast walk-in shower, feeling her muscles ease as the hot jets of water pounded her skin. Grabbing her tropical-scented body wash and a soft cotton wash pad, she squirted the orangey liquid liberally over the pad, firstly, cleaning the dried blood away and then washing the rest of her body. Removing the bobble from her hair, she undid what remained of her plait before washing her long mousey locks. Once she had shampooed and conditioned, she shoved her hair up into a loose bun, securing it with the bobble, wet tendrils falling loosely down her neck.

Without warning, she felt completely overwhelmed. Ignoring the tiled bench that ran along the length of the shower, she sat down beneath the stream of water, pulling her knees up to her chest and rested her head on her arms. Water rained over her scrunched-up body as she relived every second of last night's exploits or rather sexploits. Every touch and feeling went through her head and the mind-blowing orgasm that had left her body exhausted and replete. She had not only shown her body to another human, she had trusted him explicitly and for the first time in her life, she had sex.

No actually, she had made love. Something so huge and life-changing, although she didn't feel like she thought she would. Thinking it would make her more grown up, a real woman. Instead, she felt vulnerable and insecure. Sitting here under the hot shower, she felt even lonelier than ever. Her fouf had been bleeding and this really scared her. At fourteen, she started taking the mini pill to regulate her erratic periods. At eighteen, she changed to the Depo jab, something she only had to have once every twelve weeks and since the age of eighteen, she hadn't bled once.

She had lied to the nurse, saying she was in a sexual relationship, but really, she couldn't be doing with periods on top of the everyday worries she had about her siblings, her grandad, running a house and working. As her mind rallied, she began panicking about being pregnant. The Depo jab should protect against pregnancy and Pip had worn a condom, so surely, she wasn't at risk of that. As her head spun with the horrible consequences of what she had done, she hadn't noticed the waterfall of streaming hot water had stopped. All of a sudden, she felt the comfort of a warm, fluffy towel fall over her shoulders as strong arms scooped her up.

She screwed her eyes shut, totally embarrassed at the fact that once again she was naked and completely out of her depth. Snuggling into his chest, she didn't want to move or speak. She felt him sit and with one arm wrapped securely around her, the other had somehow procured another towel and he was swathing her hair in it, gently pressing the soft, fluffy cotton against her head. She didn't move or speak, keeping her eyes closed tightly against the world. Although her emotions were spiralling out of control, she felt snug and safe in his arms. Once he had finished patting her hair as dry as he could, he just held her tightly, his fingers rhythmically stroking her neck. Her body started to relax and she moved her arm, resting her hand on his neck.

He too was contemplating the events of the last few hours. Having woken to find her missing, he had seen the blood stain on the cream sheets. Pulling on his boxers, he made his way to the bathroom, finding Liv curled up under the hot shower, her naked body shaking. His heart sunk at the sight of her like this and he wanted to hold her, protect her. She must be feeling so overwhelmed, she had just given her virginity to him. This angelic young woman had trusted him with her incredible body, letting him touch her and make love to her. He too was overcome with the magnitude of it all.

Grabbing some towels, he turned off the powerful jets and scooped her up, holding her closely and wanting her to know he was there for her. Making himself comfortable on the settee, he had dried her hair the best he could and sat watching the glowing embers of the fire. He didn't want to force her to speak, knowing how shy and private she was, last night's events must be completely blowing her mind. When her hand gently rested on his neck, he could smell the scent of the topical body wash and without warning, his dick hardened. Trying to calm his body, he took deep soothing breaths, Liv's head nuzzling into his chest.

He looked down at her beautiful face, her pale skin being lit gently by the orangey, red glow of the fire. The graze on her cheek was healing, the bruises looking worse than before as a darker purple had pigmented her skin. An involuntary growl left his throat at the thought of her being hurt and Liv's eyes opened wide in alarm. She sat up, using both hands to secure the huge bath sheet that was wrapped around her. The smaller towel was twisted around her head and she looked like an angel. "Hey," he spoke softly, not wanting to frighten her. "I think we need to talk," he continued and she closed her eyes again. "Please don't," he said both hands cupping her face.

Her eyes opened again and she turned on his lap so she could face him. Instantly regretting the move as she felt the hardness of his dick beneath her fouf, with only the thin material of his pants between them. "I'm so sorry," she said quietly. "I thought I would feel different after…after…" She bit her lip, not being able to say the word sex in front of him.

He kissed her gently on her soft, full lips. "You have no idea how beautiful you look," he said, his lips twitching up into a smile. She looked unbelievingly into his sparkling hazel eyes as his long black lashes flicked against his strong cheeks. He was devastatingly handsome. There had to be a more experienced partner for him out there. His face darkened as he watched a frown form on her doubting face. "Talk to me," he said.

She took a deep breath. "Last night was just so…" She struggled to find the words again "So amazing and you were so bloody hot," she said earnestly. "…And I can't believe my luck that someone like you would…would…You know…" She blushed and a pink hue touched her cheekbones; he felt his dick twitch again in reaction. "You were amazing and I was so tired, I can't believe I fell asleep. Then when I woke up, I was too hot. You were cuddled up to me and when you turned over, I felt cold and lonely…" She trailed off, closing her eyes, feeling stupid.

His hands tightened on her face. "Please, go on," he implored. Her eyes were still screwed shut but she bravely went on.

"I needed a wee and realised that I'd been bleeding," she whispered, absolutely mortified. She was so embarrassed at revealing this to him but she wanted to be honest.

"Liv." His voice was deep and domineering and she blinked her eyes open, thinking he was cross with her and closed them again when she saw the serious look on his face. As he gazed at her, he shook his head gently. "Liv, you do know that bleeding is normal after you have sex for the first time." This was not a question and his American accent seemed more pronounced with each word. Opening one eye in query, she took in his appalled expression. Closing her eye again quickly, she couldn't bear for him to think she was an inexperienced idiot. "For fuck's sake, Liv, look at me."

His voice was so firm and controlling, that she opened her eyes at once, her one hand now resting on his shoulder; his hands were still holding her blushing cheeks. "We made love and it was the most awesome sex I have ever had. And you…you were breathtakingly magnificent, and your body was, and is, the most beautiful body I have ever had the pleasure to see and touch." She was staring at him, her face relaying her disbelief in her abilities. "I wanted your first time to be special and I am truly over awed that you chose me. Liv, you have no idea how much I…" He broke off.

"Pip…" She interrupted. "I bled." This was still bothering her and she looked mortified. He couldn't help but give an affectionate smile as he moved his face close to hers.

"That is completely normal, Liv, it was your first time," he said softly.

She gazed at him, slightly hypnotised by his sexy hazel eyes, and became even more aware of the firm bulge pressing against her bottom. "I haven't had a period for years and it just…it just frightened me," she replied honestly.

He grimaced at the thought of this beautiful creature being frightened. "I am right here for you, Liv. You trusted me with your body and now you have to trust me with your feelings." His voice was smooth and low.

Her stomach was unfurling and her skin tingling in reaction to his proximity. She reached up and stroked his cheek; such a delicate, sweet action. He felt as if his skin was on fire where her fingers lingered. "I'm okay, it was just all a bit much. My belly was aching too," she said as she used her free hand to pull the white fluffy towel closer to her chest.

Pip looked troubled. "Can I get you some painkillers?" He said with concern.

"It's alright now, it has worn off," she said still stroking his cheek with her long fingers. "Can I ask you something?" She looked apprehensive.

"Of course, anything," he replied, happy that she was talking to him and her beautiful were open.

"Do all couples have orgasms like that?" Her cheeks coloured again and his mouth dropped open in shock. "Oh god…I'm sorry, I shouldn't have asked that," she said, grimacing, once again mortified that she was so unskilled in this area.

"No, no, I'm glad you asked me that," he said quickly, sitting up a little straighter, his straining dick putting delightful pressure on her fouf. She was now, her legs on either side of his firm thighs and she felt her pulse quicken. "Most couples will orgasm, although I don't think as spectacularly as we did," he said genuinely not having thought about it before.

"It's just…well, I was thinking…" Her fingers had stopped their stroking of his cheek and were now resting on his broad shoulder again, the other hand still clasped tightly on the towel that was keeping her modesty. "If an orgasm feels like that, then…" She deliberated continuing, biting her lip with nerves.

"Liv?" He wanted her to go on.

"Well, if couples have orgasms like that every time they have sex, why does anyone ever leave their house?" The question was so innocent and sweet, he couldn't help but laugh out loud. She pulled her head back from him, embarrassed that he was laughing at her, her face still serious.

Catching her expression, he stopped abruptly, leaning forward so that their noses were actually touching. "That is actually a very good question," he said seriously.

"So why laugh?" She pouted and he ran his thumb over her full, pink lips.

"I'm sorry, I shouldn't have laughed," he said his eyes taking in every detail of her beautiful face. "It was a good question and one I have never thought of until now. Maybe we could find out the answer together?" His tone was low and she could feel her body responding to the gravelly pitch of his voice. Her head tilted to the side slightly as she considered his words. A small smile formed on her beautiful lips as he crushed against them. Letting go of the towel and letting it fall to her waist, she instantly wrapped her arms around his neck, enjoying the sensation of his skin against hers.

He pulled her forward towards him and their kiss became more intense, raising his hips slightly, causing a firm pressure on her exposed fouf. Her body responded to his groin movement by grinding her hips slowly over his restricted erection, causing intimate friction that made them both groan with desire. Flipping her over onto the settee, the towel falling to the floor, he stood and whipped off his boxer shorts, his impressive dick springing free. She sat up quickly and was now kneeling again. Although still shy at her own body being naked, she wasn't scared of his being exposed and smiled as she took in his sexy, muscular frame. "Liking what you see, Miss Whitmore?" He smirked.

"Just admiring you, Sir," she said smiling broadly. His face darkened at her response and he leant over her so she was looking up straight into his handsome face.

"I need to get a condom from my pants pocket. If I didn't have to move…" He blew out a breath, trying to calm his desire to be inside her.

"You don't need to," she said looking up innocently at him. Placing his hands on the back of her head, he kissed her hard. She was almost panting when he broke away, just moving his face a few centimetres from hers.

"I don't want children, Liv," he said seriously.

"Neither do I," she answered in shock.

"Then we need to use protection," he said his mouth curving up at the ends, thinking about entering her body unsheathed, just the thought of it making him even harder.

She squeezed her eyes shut and bit her lip, before whispering, "I have the contraceptive injection, so I won't get pregnant." All was silent for a long minute and she had to open her eyes to check he hadn't left the room, although she realised his hands were holding her head still. He blinked as he took in this information, his mind quickly coming to the wrong conclusion.

"So, you have had sex before?" His voice was harsh and angry. This time, it was Liv's turn to let out a calming breath. Her whole body wanted him inside her, she wanted to feel him touching her and make her come again. She closed her eyes, not used to talking about intimate things with anyone, let alone a man.

He was just about to lose his temper when she whispered, "I have not had sex with anyone until you…last night. I was on the mini pill for years to regulate my periods and I switched to the jab, so I don't get periods at all. That's why I was so scared when I found the blood earlier." She covered her eyes with both hands, absolutely mortified at having to explain herself; he must think she was such a child. Instead, he was thinking the opposite.

He was thinking what a bastard he had just been judging her wrongly, once again. He needed to trust her. Christ, the evidence of her losing her virginity to him was on the bed sheets they had slept in. He let go of her head, rubbing his hands over her bare shoulders, and skimming down her body to her waist. Kneeling down in front of her, on the soft thick pile of the cream rug, he brought his hands forward onto the tops of her thighs and gently rubbed her skin with his fingers. "Liv," he said quietly. She kept her eyes covered, so he knelt up and delicately kissed the backs of her hands. "Please, Liv," he begged as he took her hands in his and pulled them from her eyes.

Alongside the purple bruise on her cheek, a pink tinge had also coloured the pale, white skin. She kept her eyes closed and at that exact moment, he knew he had really fallen for her. She was so innocent and shy. It must be hard for her to talk about sex and periods with him, but she did it. She was brave and strong in everything she did, and this endeared her to him even more. With his hands still on the tops of her legs, he gently kissed her full lips. The knowledge that he didn't need to wear a condom this time, made his hunger for her body grow. She slowly started kissing him back, keeping her eyes closed.

His eagerness grew with the strength of his kiss and when he felt her arms snake around his neck, pulling him closer to her naked body, he could take it no more. Putting his arms around her bare bottom, he pulled her off the settee and onto his lap, her legs falling on either side of his waist. Without breaking the kiss, they went on. Their body's both naked and pressed up against each other, making them both hot and wanton for things to go further. She could feel the wetness between her legs and panicked in case it was blood. She looked down in horror but could not see any red liquid.

Realising that she was wet and scared, he kissed her forcefully in an attempt to take her mind off the fact that she had bled earlier. As the passion took over, they were both consumed with being as close to each other as their bodies allowed. He adjusted himself so his dick was directly below her and she knelt up slightly, completely lost in his kiss. With his hands still around her waist, she eased her body down slowly onto his rock-hard erection. Easing his length in gently, letting her get used to the tight but incredible feeling she was now experiencing.

As she gently moved her hips, she took his whole dick inside her and it felt even deeper and more solid than before. She felt her inner core expanding, incredibly letting him fill her. Kissing passionately, he started to move slowly, making her gasp. Their bodies were glued together. This was a whole other world Liv had never known and the feeling of him inside her was delicious. Moving in rhythm, Liv met each growing thrust, like for like, sending him wild with desire. She felt incredible. He was as enraptured with her as he moved inside her gorgeous body. Their tongues lashed against each other and the force of their movements caused a building tension in their bodies. Liv could feel the tension growing and although inexperienced, she knew that she was going to orgasm.

Pip broke their kiss, still thrusting hard. "Come with me, Liv." His ragged voice was all it took and she felt his dick twitch as he came inside her, sending her on an epic release as the powerful orgasm pulsed through her body. On and on, she moved her hips, grinding against his dick until they were both spent. They sat in the same position, with him buried deep inside her, whilst they gained control over their breathing and their heartbeats slowed back to a normal pace, their arms still wrapped around each other, their bodies together as one. They revelled in the glorious aftermath of another magnificent orgasm. Finally, Pip spoke. "I think we need to sleep," he said kissing her temple gently.

"Hmmm," she replied drowsily. He managed to stand, still holding her tightly in position, not wanting to break their intimate embrace. As he reached the bed and laid her down, she felt him pull out and moaned at the withdrawal, "Ohhh…" She pouted as she turned over falling fast asleep. Pip laughed and took one last longing look at her stunning naked body before climbing into bed beside her, pulling her close to him, and covering them both with the soft duvet before he too gave into a deep satisfying sleep.

Chapter 15

As she slowly opened her tired eyes, Liv pulled a face. Her alarm clock display told her it was only just before five am. She stretched her aching legs and moved her hips slightly, testing to see if there was any pain. To be fair, she was just achy all over. What with her nasty fall and the fact that she had probably used muscles that she had never used before? The bedside lamps were offering their soft glow as it was still dark outside. She could feel the warmth of Pip's skin on her back and she bit her lip to stop herself giggling. A gorgeous, incredibly sexy man was asleep in her bed. How did that happen?

The experiences of the last few hours made her lower belly ache with want, but she didn't think it was proper to wake him up and jump his bones, although that was exactly what her body wanted her to do. She sighed. Bloody five o'clock on a Sunday morning and she was awake. Her one day off from everything and as tired as she was, she knew she wouldn't be going back to the land of nod. Her mind was overwhelmed with the fact that she had actually, finally, had sex…twice! Sighing quietly, she decided she could do with another shower and she didn't want to fidget and wake Pip up, he too must be exhausted.

Silently, she slipped out of the cover and grabbing her mobile phone, she flicked off the lamps, plunging the bedroom into darkness. She quietly padded her way across the wooden floor and into her bathroom, which had a dim night light, gently illuminating the area. Remembering that Pip had woken when she showered earlier, she grabbed her tangle teaser, toothbrush, and Clinique set and still entirely naked, made her way through to the dressing room. She found her clean pjs on the chair. A vest top and shorts, in a pale blue silk, with pink blossoms; it was one of her favourites, plus her embroidered kimono.

Grabbing them, she quietly tiptoed down the stairs to the first floor, where she used Hallie's en-suite shower. She had considered using the main bathroom, but as that was mainly used by Jay, she knew Hallie's would be cleaner and tidier. Using the lower jets only, she washed her aching body with Hal's lime and grapefruit shower gel. The smell was uplifting and awakened her senses. When she stepped out of the cubical, Burt and Ernie greeted her with loud purrs, rubbing their furry bodies around her legs. She dried herself off and applied some deodorant.

Brushing her dry hair, she pulled it up into a tight bun high on her head. Jay called it her ballerina bun whenever she wore it like that. Putting on her pretty pyjamas and kimono, she washed, cleaned, and moisturised her face and brushed her teeth. Looking at Hal's shelf of posh perfumes, she decided on Alien, squirting some onto her neck and wrists. She picked up her phone and Burt, who was literally sitting on her feet, and went down to the kitchen, where Ernie was now waiting for her. After giving both of them lots of fuss, she fed them and changed their water bowls. The under-counter kitchen lights were on and the corner lamp was giving a reassuring soft glow to the seating area.

She poured some orange juice and made a piece of toast, realising she felt a little dehydrated. She took one bite of the toast but couldn't eat any more as her stomach twisted and turned. She gave the rest to Burt in little bits. He had stuck around for another snack and was very happy with his full tummy. Ernie had gone outside into the freezing dawn, hoping to stalk some birds. Liv's tummy rumbled as she struggled to keep the small bit of toast down. Maybe the nerves of her first sexual encounter were really kicking in. They had made love twice, so she couldn't have been that bad. Pip had told her how beautiful and wonderful she was, but with her low self-esteem, she found it hard to believe.

Her adult life had been about looking after her loved ones and her personal life had been pushed aside. Liv had never had a boyfriend, although lots of lads had tried their luck at school. She hadn't been interested as a young teenager, and at sixteen when she had lost her parents, there seemed to be more important things to worry about. She switched on the coffee machine and the smell of fresh coffee began to fill the room. She flicked on the flat-screen TV, which was hung on the side wall, turning the sound right down so she didn't disturb her sleeping sex god, even though he wouldn't hear it on the top floor.

Sipping her coffee, she walked over to the settee and made herself comfy, pulling the grey, teddy bear throw around her and flicking the channels on the TV. She liked to watch the BBC news channel at least once a day to keep up with world events, apart from that she didn't watch much television. Burt jumped up and lay with his bottom on her lap and his body stretched up over her chest. He loved the fluffy throws but he loved Liv's company more. Purring loudly, he settled quickly and went off to sleep.

It was just after six when Pip appeared, walking into the kitchen in nothing but his tight-fitting trunk pants. With a serious expression, he took in Liv cuddled up in the throw, with a snoring cat sprawled on top of her. He strode over and sat down beside her, waking Burt up. He meowed, stretched, and made his way over to the new human. Pip stroked his thick grey fur and scratched behind his ears. Purring again, Burt sniffed around. Not finding any food or offers of a snack, he jumped off Pip's lap and disappeared out of the kitchen to find a quiet spot for more snoozing. Pip pulled some of the throw over his legs and looked enquiringly at Liv.

Her eyes were wide, her pale skin showing the dark purply blue of the bruises which had come out even more on her forehead and cheek. The shadows under her eyes were noticeable and he knew she hadn't slept properly. Creases appeared on his forehead and his fists clenched. Liv noticed the small movement. "You do that a lot…" she spoke quietly. "Do I make you that angry?" She said sadly.

Without warning, he twisted his body and moved it so he knelt over Liv, in an imposing stance, with his face close to hers. "I get angry when I think about you being hurt or frightened," he said, not being able to hide the emotion in his voice. She was right, he was disappointed in her and she looked down at her hands in embarrassment. "Liv." His voice was a plea and she felt his hands on either side of her face. Tilting it up towards him. She looked up at him through long dark lashes, making him instantly hard. "Fuck, Liv, all I want to do is make love to you," he growled.

She felt her stomach flip over and a warmth spread between her legs, as she knew she felt the same way about him. "Yes please," she whispered bravely. The intensely dark look lifted and he laughed at her response, breaking the tension that was building. "Believe me, I would like nothing more, but I need sustenance first." He kissed the end of her nose and stood up. "Do you mind if I help myself to coffee?" He said, the smell of which filled his nostrils.

"I'll get it," she offered standing and throwing the fluffy blanket onto the settee.

Pip took a step back and whistled. "You look amazing," he said, admiring her silky outfit. Her kimono was open and the short set showed off all her body and beautiful curves. She smiled timidly, feeling completely unworthy, although she really wanted him to ravage her. He saw her doubting expression and grabbed her waist. She placed both hands on his bare muscular chest and felt his fingers rubbing the sides of her silk-clad hips. "Talk to me," he said seriously, watching her expression carefully, trying to read her face.

"Last night was wonderful…" She paused. "But I completely understand if you want to leave and move on," she said awkwardly, biting her bottom lip. His expression changed again, back to dark and intense.

Searching her eyes, all he could see was a vulnerable, beautiful, young woman. "I am not going anywhere; I am here and I am staying." A tight smile appeared on her pretty face as she realised he wasn't running off into the cold, dark morning. She leant forward and kissed him softly on his lavish lips. His grip tightened on hips and he kissed her back with the same ardour and intensity. Liv moved her hands up his neck and up into his hair. The kiss grew more passionate and he pulled back. "Liv, as much as I want to explore your body…" He took a deep breath. "I need coffee," he said simply.

She shivered at the thought of him exploring her body and a full smile rewarded him for his words. "Coffee," she replied as she let go of him and pulled away, noticing his straining pants. Wow. Pouring his coffee, she offered sugar and milk; he declined both. He was leaning on the breakfast bar, watching her move around the kitchen. Her stunning body looked magnificent in the sexy silk number she was wearing. He admired the stunning embroidered butterfly that filled the back of her kimono. The main background was brown and the inside was lined in a light teal. The huge butterfly was an array of embroidered colours, it was stunning like its owner.

"Can I get you something to eat?" and She said innocently as she handed him his mug of steaming fresh coffee.

"Fuck, Liv." He squeezed his eyes shut, shaking his head and blowing out a long breath.

"I can still see you," she said teasingly as she leant over the other side of the breakfast bar.

His eyes flew open and he laughed, the sound resounding down deep in her stomach. "Have you eaten yet?" He said still smiling. Her face changed and she looked as if she was going to say something but wasn't sure if she should. He walked around the bar and into the kitchen area where she was leaning. Just a glimpse of her leaning over the breakfast bar in her skimpy, silky outfit, made his dick rock-hard. She stood and stared at him as he approached. He placed his hands on her shoulders, and asked again in a softer tone. "Have you eaten?"

She bit her lips and shook her head. Wanting to close her eyes, she bravely kept them open as she gazed into his luminous pools of dark hazel brown. "I tried a piece of toast but only managed a bite…I felt sick," she said honestly. Fighting to contain his anger, Pip's serious expression held hers for the longest moment.

"Okay then, I am going to feed you," he said his eyebrows lifting and his expression lifting.

"Feed me?" She said unsure of his actual intention. He moved past her to the huge American fridge freezer, opening up the door to see what goodies it held. His fists clenched again as he took in the untouched Amores containers from yesterday afternoon. "When did you last eat?" He asked trying to keep his tone even. When she didn't reply, he pulled his face out of the fridge and turned to see her sat, with her legs dangling, on the worktop counter. "Liv?" He questioned and again she bit both her lips between her teeth. He closed the fridge door and strode over to her, parting her legs and standing between them. He placed his hands on either side of her body.

Her beautiful face was looking down avoiding his severe glare. Standing intimidatingly close to her, she couldn't help but notice his convex pants. Her legs were spread wide and she felt the tension building between them. Fearlessly, she decided to look up at his handsome face. Gently, she kissed the creases on his forehead, visibly affecting his breathing. He didn't stop her, his now resting on the counter, either side of her bottom, his eyes focused entirely on hers. She continued by kissing each temple and his eyes closed at her touch. He felt her gently kiss his nose and then his cheeks. His eyes were still closed and he was expecting her to kiss his lips but feeling her lips on his neck made him groan.

"Liv…" He wanted her to eat but his body wanted to make love to her again. She had stopped at the sound of her name, looking at him with her puppy dog eyes. "You win, but then we eat," he said seriously, his lips twitching up at the sides, making her smile. Kissing the sides of his mouth, she felt herself getting wet and debated asking him about this new experience, deciding to put it off until later. Her whole body wanted him inside her and she kissed him hard on his lips. He returned her kiss with as much force and passion, his hands snaking around her neck and into her hair, which was in a tight, neat bun on the top of her head.

Her hands were holding his 116houldders and just as she was getting lost in the kiss, his hands moved to her bottom, where with a squeeze of her cheeks, he slipped her off the bar and into his arms. She wrapped her long legs around his firm body. Not breaking the kiss, he strode around to the settee and laid her onto the soft grey throw. She looked incredibly beautiful. Lying down on top of her, he kissed her hard and fast as their bodies responded to each other once again.

Liv lay in his strong arms, completely overawed by the mind-blowing orgasm she had just experienced. Her fingers trailed a pattern down his smooth, tanned chest. The grey throw was over them both and the early morning sun was rising, lighting up the huge garden. A light frost covered the grass and plants and a spectacular spider's web had frosted and was now glistening like a diamond necklace on the bird table. Ernie was crouched down low beside it, glaring at a little robin who was enjoying the bird seed. "You don't have any window coverings in here?" Pip broke the silence as he admired the vast English garden, slowly appearing in the light.

"We have shades for when it is really sunny, but at night, we don't usually bother closing them."

"Your neighbours have just had a good show then," Pip laughed jokingly.

"We're not overlooked here," she informed him with a smile on her own face. "There's a park behind us and our neighbours on both sides can't see in here," she finished. She turned onto her stomach and revelled in the feeling of this firm, muscular sex god underneath her body. Easing herself up onto her elbows, she looked down at his handsome face. They were both beaming.

"I have a plan," he said as he moved his hand from behind his head and wrapped it around her smooth, warm skin.

"Okay," she said light-heartedly. "Shower, then breakfast…followed by a tour of your home," he finished.

"Shower?" She said, her eyes widening at the thought of him naked and in her shower.

"Miss Whitmore, you are insatiable," he teased. "I have created a sex monster," he laughed and she blushed and bit her lip. "No, no, no," he said pushing himself up and lifting her with him. "We are showering alone, otherwise we will do nothing all day but make love." His tone was light but they both knew this was exactly what they both wanted to do. He smirked. "Come on, you wanton sex goddess," he laughed, slapping her bottom and making her giggle. He carried her up the two flights of stairs like she was a rag doll. Fuck, he was fit. Putting her down on the floor of her bathroom, he excused himself quickly, leaving her feeling a little putout.

She had her third shower that day, this time washing her hair again. She dressed in loose cotton, red and black palm tree patterned trousers and a fitted sleeveless black top, with a loose belt around her waist. Plaiting her wet hair on both sides, she joined them in a bun at the nape of her neck. She looked stylish and older than her twenty years. With a spray of her favourite Olympia perfume, she walked back into the bedroom. Her attention was drawn to the bed where the bottom sheet and mattress protector had been stripped and was nowhere in sight. She heard the shower running again and walked towards the bathroom to ask him where the sheet was but she paused at the closed door. Maybe she should give him some privacy, although she was very tempted to take a peek.

Instead, she walked over to the sofa, switched off the fire, and busied herself by neatly folding the throw and placing it onto the back of the seat. Opening the wooden blinds, she let the morning winter sun dazzle through, bringing her painting above the bed to life. The golds and platinums glinted and shone in the bright rays of sunshine and Liv stood admiring it for a while. It had always been her favourite painting, but now it seemed much more. The couple embracing, holding each other so closely, their bodies merging and glorious when together. It displayed the way she felt when Pip held her.

She heard the bathroom door open and Pip walked through it. His skin was glowing and his short hair still glistened from the shower. He was dressed in his white t-shirt and tight jeans and he looked sublime. Her stomach flipped over as her lower regions ached for him. She smiled as he approached but his face remained serious. "I will need to go to my apartment at some point." His voice was low and her fouf reacted to his tone.

Get a grip, Olivia, she said to herself. He flattened down the front of his t-shirt, which was still an immaculate white. His words sunk in. Oh my god, he wants to leave. He's had his wicked way and now he's abandoning her. She turned back to her painting. Frowning at the fact she had thought it more beautiful this morning as she imagined it was her and Pip in that romantic embrace. Although still glinting in the light, it looked duller and somewhat flatter than before. "Hey." Pip had stepped forward and was now standing between her and the painting. "What's wrong?" He asked, a look of concern on his handsome face. He enveloped her in his arms and she looked up into his hazel eyes and felt a wave of sadness wash over her.

"If you want to go, just go," she spoke softly, not wanting a scene. If he was fed up with being with her already, then there was no hope of…of what? Living happily ever after? Liv knew enough about life to know this was not possible.

"Liv!" His voice was loud and strong and broke her thoughts. She hadn't realised her eyes had closed, something she knew she did when she didn't want to face what was happening. Her name was spoken so harshly, that it actually made her jump and her eyes flew open. His arms were gripping her tightly and there was literally no escape.

Well, if she had to face him, she might as well say what she wants. "You obviously want to leave, so please, just leave." She didn't actually believe her own words.

"For fuck's sake, Liv…" He took a deep breath. "I meant I need to go back to my apartment to change my clothes. I like fresh ones after showering and I would like to be in something more casual." He paused and took in Liv's confused expression. "I was intending for you to come with me…" He trailed off and her mouth gaped open. She felt like slapping her hand across her forehead. What an idiot. Watching her realise what he had actually said, his heart melted yet again. This beautiful, wonderful young woman was head of her family. She had worked hard to keep her siblings safe and well, and caring for her grandad too. She had always put everyone else before herself and now it was her time.

He was determined to make her happy and content, however, they both had a lot to learn about each other first. Smiling, he gently kissed her nose and then moved down to her mouth which was still gaping open. Kissing him back, all words were forgotten and her body began to react to his presence, wanting to be nearer, wanting him to touch her. As the kiss deepened, he stepped back. "Oh no, you don't," he said with a dazzling smile on his face.

"What?" She asked innocently.

"You and your incredible body are not going to make me miss breakfast. I love my food and even if I have to feed you myself, you need to eat." He finished with a chaste kiss on her lips. Grabbing her hand, he pulled her gently and like a dumbstruck zombie, she followed him. She had completely misinterpreted his words about leaving and then he had kissed her instead of losing his temper. Wow. Meekly, she followed him down the two flights of stairs, along the hallway and into the huge kitchen. As they walked past the breakfast bar, he suddenly spun around and lifted her with ease onto the worktop.

Another quick kiss and he made his way back into the fridge, picking out items he thought would make a tasty breakfast. He expertly prepared bacon, scrambled egg, and toast, with Liv's assistance from the countertop. She told him where to find the bowl and whisk and which frying pan to use. He was just buttering the toast when she jumped off the work surface and laid the kitchen table. Pouring a small glass jug of orange juice, she added it to the table. Her tummy rumbled at the smell of the delicious food but she wasn't sure if she would be able to eat any of it.

She sat at the table and smiled broadly as he set down the plates. It really did look amazing. "Thank you," she said shyly, secretly enjoying the fact that this had been prepared for her and she hadn't had to lift a finger.

"You didn't know I can cook?" He grinned as he picked up his knife and fork. "Please eat," he said, noticing she hadn't started. Biting her lips together, she reluctantly picked up her fork. She looked up at him and he was watching her, his eyes narrowed and his head tilted. "Talk to me," he said seriously, discarding his own fork on his plate. She swallowed and looked him directly in the eyes.

"I am hungry but I'm not..." She started and resting her fork down on the plate, she took a calming breath. "When I was sixteen, food became unimportant to me." Wanting her to go on, he didn't speak but maintained eye contact. "I knew we had to have it and that Hal and Jay needed it, but for me, it was just..." She sighed. "I'm not explaining this very well." She looked down at her plate and instead of contemplating eating it, she wanted to throw it in the bin and get rid of it. It had smelt so good and she was going to have some but when her emotions kicked in, there was no chance of her eating.

"Please go on, I want to understand." Pip's voice was gentle and she felt a lump in her throat.

"When Hal was thirteen, I had a phone call to say she had been hurt during a PE session and was on her way to the hospital. They told me that she was unconscious and I can't tell you what went through my mind..." Visibly paling, she shook her head. "When I arrived at the hospital, I was told she had lost consciousness but was now awake. She had collided with another player in a game of football and they had banged heads. She had a fractured wrist but was full of beans when I got to see her." She was maintaining eye contact but finding this extremely difficult. She had never discussed this with anyone.

"I felt so sick and devastated that she had been hurt. What would my parents think of me?" She sighed and looked down at her hands which were on her lap. "And when Jay was ten, he went on a school trip, a week away at an outdoor pursuits place. It was the first time we had been apart since…" She swallowed and bravely carried on. "I waved him off on the coach and his bottom lip was wobbling, I knew he was upset. Hal was crying and I had seven days of hardly any sleep and a lot of worry." She looked up at Pip's handsome face, his expression was fixed and serious.

"Of course, he had a fantastic time and was full of it when he got home, and then, just before Christmas last year, Pong was really ill. He had become so forgetful and a danger to himself. I knew he had to go into care but it was a hard time. Hal and Jay were all excited for Christmas and I had to deal with finding somewhere for him to live safely, moving him out, and then sorting and emptying his house." She paused, her attention returning to her fingers, which she was fidgeting with.

"The thing is, during these times, I felt overwhelmed and couldn't really eat for a few days. I think my body just has enough to cope with and isn't bothered about food," she finished. She couldn't believe she had just told someone her inner thoughts; it was an odd feeling to discuss your private life and something she wasn't used to.

"Liv, you have been through a terrible time and you are so young to have coped with it all. Do you realise you have just compared our time together with the shittiest times of your life?" He said enquiringly.

"What?" Her head jerked up and she stared at him in horror. "No, that's not what I meant, I was trying to explain how I…why I…For fuck's sake, those were all important times in my life when I felt overwhelmed. I have never done this before, Pip. I have never shared what I'm thinking, or how I'm feeling. I certainly didn't mean to offend you, but you being here and us, you know…" She paused and closed her eyes tight. "It is a really big thing for me." Opening her eyes, she pushed her plate away from her and stood up, turning quickly to escape this mortifying conversation.

He stood abruptly and his hand grabbed her arm pulling her to a stop, his strength halting her tired body. His other arm wrapped around her and he just held her tightly. She wanted to run away, embarrassed that she had overshared and sad that he thought he was a shitty experience, that is so not what she meant. Slowly, her body relaxed and she leant into him. Putting her arms around his strong frame, they clung to each other and she felt him kiss her hair. This was like her painting above her bed; this was the closeness and safety in each other's arms that made her feel like her picture had shown her in reality.

After what seemed like an age, he broke the embrace, looking down tenderly into her huge blue eyes. "I'm sorry, I shouldn't have said that. I'm not too good with sharing either. Thank you for being honest. If this is going to work, we have to be honest with each other. I hate the thought of you being upset, frightened, hurt, lonely or hungry. The list could go on," he grimaced. "It makes me so angry, Liv. I've never been in a normal relationship either, so I'm learning too." She was a beautiful woman, with a beautiful soul, and he knew he was lucky to have her In his arms. "Forget the food, show me your home," he said his tone lifting and a smile forming on his sexy lips.

Chapter 16

Calling a truce on the emotional speeches, Liv showed him around her home. Firstly, the dining room to the left of the kitchen. It was elegantly decorated with modern furniture, but the painting taking up the rear wall took all of Pip's attention. It was a copy of a Manet, *A Bar at the Folies-Bergère*. It depicted a nightclub in Paris where a woman was standing at the bar, arguably in front of a mirror. There was the hustle and bustle of the club going on in the background but your eyes are drawn to the woman's withdrawn face. Seeing this masterpiece on a wall took his breath away and once again, he was reminded of Liv's incredible talent.

Turning to admire her as much as he had the painting, she stood back, arms folded and head tilted to the side. She had been studying him, studying her work. They both smiled as he walked over to her and without speaking, he kissed her passionately. She responded with the same conviction and once again, he broke the kiss, taking a deep breath to try and halt his growing fervour. "I would like to see more of the house and not get distracted by you," he said earnestly.

She smiled as she felt his dick rock-hard against her body. "Okay, no kissing until we have finished the tour," she said stepping back, instantly regretting the distance between them. "That's the conservatory," she pointed absentmindedly through the closed double French doors that led out into a huge conservatory. He thought she was going to show him around it but she walked out of the dining room and he followed. Making their way down the hall towards the front door, she pointed to the right. "That's the living room, which you saw on Friday night." She stopped and her expression changed. She went to speak but changed her mind.

He too had replayed his actions of that night when he had lost his temper and stormed out. He kissed her forehead gently and she moved out of his reach, wagging her finger at him. "No kissing, Professor." She smiled again and he laughed. She passed the bottom of the stairs and opened the door in front of her.

"This is our chill room," she said walking through into a light airy room with yet more comfortable-looking settees. There were soft, furry throws over each. A colossal flat-screen TV hung on the wall and photos in frames covered most of the oak Kallax shelving.

Again, the main back wall had been painted, this time an exquisite copy of Claude Monet's *Sunrise*. The beautiful pastels of the sun's orange orb, shed its light across the hazy blue sky and waters below. It was a stunning piece of work and suited the calm and comfort of the room. He looked back at Liv, who was waiting by the door, smiling at her in complete awe of her talent. "I will show you the studio last but now you might need a peg for your nose." She smiled at her own joke.

"Which room next then?" He asked intrigued.

"Jay's..." she said pulling a face. "And teenage boy's smell." She laughed along with him as he held her hand and they climbed the first flight of stairs. Bearing left, they took the first door on the left. This opened up the coolest teenager's room Pip had ever seen.

"This is amazing," he said squeezing her hand and taking in the special holiday vibe surrounding him. On the main wall was a life-size illustration of a beach. The clear blue sea was gently lapping against the smooth, fine sand. Palm trees lined the shore which arched in a crescent into the distance. It looked as if you could literally step into the scene. The rest of the room was covered in posters, photographs, and paraphilia that Jay had collected over the last thirteen years. Above his bed was the Dominican Republic flag. The bed wasn't made, but for a teenager's room, it wasn't too bad.

Liv automatically scooped up some dirty boxers and t-shirts that had been thrown on the floor. Taking aim, she threw them across the room and straight into Jay's open laundry basket. "Good shot," Pip said, impressed.

"I have had plenty of practice," she replied smiling fondly. My god, she really was incredible. He walked towards her and she raised her hand, palm facing him, shaking her head. "No kissing until the tour is over," she said smiling. She turned quickly and made her way out of Jay's room. "That's the family bathroom," she pointed at the door but walked straight past. "Then this room is Jay's favourite room in the whole house," she said opening the next door.

It was another large room with a huge light blue corner settee that could fit at least ten people on it. On the right-hand wall was another epic flat-screen TV and a large beech unit underneath it, housing different gaming platforms. The side walls were home to beech shelving which displayed a huge collection of games. This was quite obviously the gaming room, but Pip's face showed his confusion as he stood gazing at the masterpiece that adorned most of the left wall. An Alma-Tadema painting. It looked a little out of place in this modern game room. He turned back to look at Liv but she had moved to his side.

"Jay's favourite painting of all time," she said quietly, staring at the painting. It depicted three beautiful women, on a balcony in Naples, during Roman times.

"It is stunning, he has good taste," Pip commented, holding her hand. She looked up at him, his face taking in every detail of her work. She felt oddly proud that he appreciated it. Hal and Jay were used to her talent and they were the ones who decided which paintings would go into which room. Except for Liv's room and the studio, those were all Liv's choices. "The women look so beautiful, Liv; you have really captured their elegance and refinement." He was completely blown away again.

"We went to Naples as children and dad always said that mum looked like one of the beautiful women in this portrait. Jay remembered that and wanted this painting so much…" She broke off whilst her mind went back to a younger Jay running up the stairs, completely overjoyed that Liv had finished his special painting. She looked up at Pip who was staring at her intently. She sighed. "Come on." Pulling his hand, she dragged him from the room. "That's the study," she said vaguely, walking past another door but opening the next on the landing. "This is Hal's room." Again, there was a contrast as this light airy, modern bedroom was full of football posters, and trophies, and yet on the side wall was a stunning copy of *The Birth of Venus*, a famous Botticelli.

An almost naked Venus stood in a huge scallop shell as she arrived at the shore. On the left-hand side of the painting, Zephyr, the wind god, blows at her. He is said to be holding Aura, the personification of a lighter breeze. On the right is said to be the Greek goddess Horae, holding out a rich cloak to cover Venus with. The detail, as with all of Liv's paintings, was breathtaking. "Did Hallie think that Venus was like your mum?" Pip enquired, genuinely interested in why these teenagers had decided on old masters being painted onto their walls.

Liv smiled. "Sadly, no. Hal has always been a romantic and as Venus is the god of love, well…" She trailed off. "That's Hal's en-suite," she pointed to a door on the right before walking out of the tidy bedroom, no dirty pants on the floor in here. Pip followed her out of the room. "That's a guest room and then the storage cupboard," she said nodding in the direction of two more closed doors and starting to alight the second staircase.

"I've seen your room," he said wolfishly, making her stop in her tracks.

"There's another room I would like to show you," she said timidly and he immediately regretted his bravado.

This was her world she was showing him, her place of safety and solace and she was letting him in. Silently chastising himself, he took the steps two at a time until he was at her side, his actions making her smile. His dick twitched again and he tried not to focus on her face or body. "So which way are we going?" He pointed to the left of the staircase and she shook her head.

"That's the loft or attic space. It's full of stuff we don't want to part with; it also sleeps four people, so it's a big space," Liv explained. "I wanted to show you this room," she said walking to the right, to the very first door at the front of the house. Pip walked in and was taken aback to find a library. One of the walls had a built-in plasma fire, similar to the one in Liv's bedroom but smaller. Above the fire was a painting in an antique gold frame. A pale beauty with dark hair stared out into the library, her gold silken robe glistening around her waist, her white off-shoulder blouse layered and loose around her arms, her hand holding her sword.

Pip walked towards it and reached out his hand to touch the ornate frame. It was completely flat, an optical illusion that he had completely fallen for. There was no frame, it was all a painting on the wall. He let out an excited breath, the depth of skill in this copy excelled the others he had seen. Turning to Liv for an explanation, she simply said, "My dad's favourite painting," with a melancholy smile. He looked back at this masterpiece, Emile Lacomte-Vernet's art recreated on a library wall. Floor-to-ceiling oak shelving units gave the room the look of a vintage library, two cosy chairs and a large, vintage chaise long sat in the middle of the room, along with a small reading table and a Tiffany reading lamp sat neatly in the middle.

"This is my quiet space," Liv whispered as she looked around the room.

"It's beautiful." He strode over and took her in his arms. "Just like you." He smiled totally in awe of this talented wonder he was holding. He kissed her hard and this time, she deepened it, running her hands around his waist and pressing her body firmly against him. "Fuck, Liv, I want you." The words left his lips as she was still kissing him, his tone alone making her wet, wanting him inside her. He growled as he lifted her black fitted top revealing a red lace bra. Kissing her neck and shoulder, his hands squeezed her bottom cheeks, firmly pulling her against his erection.

Suddenly, he lifted her bottom up, allowing her legs to wrap around him, all the while fervidly kissing. He walked through the side door and into the bedroom, over to the end of the massive bed. "Stand," he ordered huskily, his voice sending a shiver down her spine, which reacted with her core. He peeled off her trousers, revealing matching red knickers. "Fuck, Liv." He wanted her more than anyone or anything in his life. Never had he experienced this need, this attraction to another.

She felt clammy and discombobulated as he knelt and started kissing her flat stomach. Her hands rested on his shoulders and she looked up at the ceiling, knowing that her knickers were getting wet from his kisses on her bare flesh. She squeezed her thighs together. He noticed the movement and moved his hands down over her sexy arse and onto her thighs, constantly kissing and nipping her waist, making her hot with desire. The kisses were getting lower and as he reached the top of her knickers, she could barely breathe. Slowly pulling them down, he continued to kiss her, making her stomach swirl and contract.

Without warning, his lips pressed against her most sensitive skin, making her gasp out loud, her grip tightening on his shoulders. He stopped and looked up at her. "Trust me." His voice was hoarse with lust and closing her eyes, she simply nodded her response, completely lost in the moment and wanting more.

Chapter 17

As she walked down her hallway, Liv could smell the food that they had left uneaten on the kitchen table. Her stomach flipped over and she knew she had to get rid of it before he saw it. "The studio's through there," she pointed at the second door to the right under the staircase.

He grabbed her hand and pulled her backwards so she bumped into his firm body. "You're not coming in with me?" His handsome face was creased with concern.

"I won't be long, you can look around in peace." She smiled and kissed his lips, the frown slipping from his forehead. She turned and made her way into the kitchen. Maybe she was embarrassed to show him her work, although from what he had seen, she did not need to worry about him not loving it.

The door led him into a dark corridor and he made his way to the next door, which opened out into a large, bright space. There were sketches and paintings hanging on the white walls and he found he didn't know where to look first. A drawing table and stool were in the middle of the room and yet another huge, comfy-looking corner sofa sat to the right with a low coffee table in front of it. To the left of the room stood a huge light oak chest of drawers, with a large expanse of pigeon holes nestled on top. Each hole had jars with pencils, paintbrushes, and different art paraphernalia neatly stored on it. Pip approached the drawing table and found a perfectly detailed pencil sketch of an eye.

All though only drawn in lead pencil, it was incredibly detailed and impeccably carried out. Smiling, he shook his head gently at Liv's talent, she really didn't know how good she was. Lifting the stunning picture of the eye, he found himself staring at his own face. Again, drawn with nothing but a lead pencil and the use of clever shading, his face seemed to jump off the page as if three-dimensional. It was a surreal few minutes where he found himself intently studying each stroke of her stunning work. He lifted a few of the papers that were hidden underneath and they were all of him—his face, his eyes, shadows of his features. The detail in her drawings was exceptional.

Placing her current work back on the desk, his eyes were drawn to the left wall beside the storage unit. There, in a frame, was his painting. Hundreds of lanterns floated above a dark lake, a small sailing boat in the shadows of the waters. If he didn't know any better, he would have thought Liv had stolen it from the gallery's reception area; however, he had seen her copies of masterpieces all over the house and he knew she had painted it. An exact copy and a favourite piece of his own work, entitled 'Dreams'. His chest grew as he felt the pride of an artist whose work had been reproduced. They say that copying is the biggest form of flattery and in all his years teaching, he had never felt this proud.

Not only of himself but of Liv's immense capabilities and expertise. As he browsed the studio walls, a broad grin spread across his face. There had been something about this young woman from the moment he had first set eyes on her; he had been completely obsessed. The fact that he had thought she was a sixteen-year-old student had made things complicated. He had observed her, trying to blend into the background, not making a song and dance about her artwork. He had made excuses to watch her, letting his own students leave a few minutes before the bell so he could see her running to her bicycle and escape the institute.

He now knew she was almost twenty-one years old and that she rushed out of the art department to help care for her friend's little boy. She also visited her grandad daily and took care of her two younger siblings, who both seemed happy and well-adjusted. Liv really was the most incredible woman he had ever met. Even Maggie and Clara seemed to pale into insignificance and he had put them both on a pedestal. Suddenly, the door opened and Liv walked in with a tray of coffee and warm croissants covered in butter and filled with raspberry jelly. His stomach rumbled loudly as the smell of the brunch hit his senses. She set the tray down on the coffee table and sat down on the settee, tucking her legs underneath her. She took a mug of coffee in her right hand and a warm croissant in her left.

He made his way over to her and sat down beside her, his face beaming as he took one of the pastries and devoured it with relish. She ate hers slowly and he made no comment, relieved that at least she was eating something. "So…" she said when she had finished and was gently sipping her hot coffee. "What do you think of my studio?" She was looking at him so earnestly, he had to resist the urge to kiss her. As he looked around the room, he tried to think of the right words to say, but all seemed insignificant.

"Awesome," was all he could think of.

She smiled shyly and followed his gaze. "I love it in here," she said quietly.

"It's my newest favourite place," he said as he turned to look at her beautiful face. "Except for your bedroom…and your kitchen…" He trailed off, his face beaming. Liv's mouth hung open in shock and a pale pink blushed across her cheeks. Neither spoke for a few minutes and they just looked into each other's eyes. Finally, he let out a sigh and took another croissant off the tray. "These are delicious by the way." He took a huge bite, making her laugh and breaking the sexual tension that had begun to build. They both turned as they heard a loud meow and Burt sauntered into the room, jumping up onto Liv's lap.

"He knows when there's food about." Liv smiled and stroked his thick, soft, grey fur. Taking another croissant, she broke some off and fed it to a purring Burt. Breaking off more little sections, she shared them between her and her affectionate cat. Having finished the croissant, Burt having eaten over half of it, flumped down on her lap for a snooze.

"What breed are Burt and Ernie?" He asked interested in her fluffy companions.

"They are British Blues," she answered smiling.

"They are awesome too." He stood; his attention turned back to the studio. Again, he made his way around the walls, asking questions about different pieces of art. They discussed colour palettes and inspirations, Pip explaining he enjoyed landscape painting and that that was his forte. Liv, however, excelled at landscapes, portraits, and objects, her capabilities were endless. He told her that her art was breathtaking and that he was so privileged to be surrounded by her work. For the next hour, they chatted happily about their favourite artists and artwork, genuinely sharing the same passion. Pip had another two croissants and they had finished their coffee when Ernie made his way into the room.

Jumping up onto the settee, he enjoyed the attention from both Liv and Pip. "Did you have any pets growing up?" Liv asked.

Pip laughed. "My family kept horses, so I guess they were my pets," he said smiling.

"Wow, horses?" Liv asked surprised.

"Actually, my parents are breeders; they have the best studs in America," he said honestly.

"They certainly do," Liv spoke without thinking and it took Pip a few seconds to understand what she meant. They were both laughing and enjoying each other's company when they heard Jay's voice call out.

"I'm home and Tom's with me. Whose is the neat sports car?" Liv's eyes widened and she bit her lip. Ernie jumped down and ran out to greet his other human; Burt stretched and sat up lazily.

"It will be ok," Pip said gently stroking her cheek. Taking a deep breath, she stood lifting Burt at the same time.

Taking Pip's hand, she bravely led him to the kitchen where Jay and Tom were already raiding the fridge. "You're back early?" Liv said checking the kitchen clock, it was only just after midday. She placed Burt down on the floor, where he sat down by her feet in protest. Jay pulled his head out of the fridge, chomping on a piece of ham. Opening his full mouth to answer, he stopped when he saw Pip holding Liv's hand. A huge hammy smile formed on his cheeky face just as Tom turned holding an armful of food and placed it on the counter.

"My dad got called into work and as it's the 'B team' playing today, we thought we would give it a miss and have a FIFA afternoon," Tom said happily. The Whitmores was his second home and he loved it here. Liv and Hal were more like his sisters and he didn't get nagged at like he did at his house. An only child, his parents doted on him, but he loved being with his best mate and his family.

"Chew," Liv said smiling at her brother's positive response to Pip being present. Jay began to chew what was stuffed into his mouth. "Tom, this is Pip," she said introducing Jay's best friend to her new friend.

"Is that your car outside?" Tom said in awe.

"Yes, it's an Aston Martin DB10." Pip smiled; he loved his car and it had many admirers.

"Wow!" Jay's mouth was open again, showing a mass of part-chewed ham.

"Jay, close your mouth." Liv shook her head and smiled, used to his boyish behaviour.

"Can you take us for a ride in it?" Tom asked excitedly. Jay nearly choked, his eyes wide and his head nodding in agreement.

"Sure, but not right now. Liv and I have plans for this afternoon, but I promise I owe you both a ride," he said easily, making the two teenagers grin like Cheshire cats. Liv looked a little confused but chose not to speak.

"We're just making a snack, cos we're starving," Jay said, his mouth now empty. He rubbed his stomach and did the full Whitmore puppy dog eyes for them.

"Knock yourselves out." Liv smiled as she let go of Pip's hand and walked around the kitchen area, retrieving two glasses and a bottle of red wine, and without saying another word, she left the lads engrossed in their snack-making. Pip took the glasses from her, so she had a hand free to hold his. As they ascended the stairs, she whispered, "He took that well," and smiled.

"What can I say, I'm very likeable," Pip replied and she stopped on the step, kissing him softly on the cheek. She continued on up the stairs, leaving him grinning like an idiot. As they made themselves comfortable on the settee in her bedroom, she poured them both a glass of wine. Cuddling up to one another, she spent the next few hours finding out everything about him. He was born and raised in LA, with two sisters and three brothers, all older than him. They had all followed in his parent's footsteps and worked with horses in some way, either breeding or riding them. His parents also owned the largest ranch in Denver and lived between their country home and their townhouse in LA.

Apparently, they were shocked when Pip decided to take art seriously at college and university, but nonetheless, they were proud of him becoming an art professor in England. He said they made it over at least once a year when there was a break in their hectic schedule, however, he made it home several times a year due to the many university term breaks. They had run out of the wine but were both cosy on the settee. "I will go and get another bottle and check on the boys," Liv said reluctantly.

"I will come with you," Pip replied, not wanting to be apart from her for a second. Hand in hand, they descended the stairs the first-floor games room, where they heard whoops and hollers coming from behind the closed door. Liv smiled shaking her head, loving the fact her baby brother was so happy.

"Hi, guys," she said as they walked in. The lads were on the edge of the settee, the coffee table covered in crisp packets and two empty plates. Jay paused the football game and used his puppy dog eye to look at Liv.

"Is it food time?" He asked hopefully, Tom had the same impassioned look.

"What would you like?" Liv asked smiling, obviously used to their pleas for food.

"Cookies, chocolate milkshake, and are there any brownies left?" Jay asked, crossing his fingers on both hands. "Liv makes the best chocolate brownies," he said assuredly to Pip.

"My mum had the recipe but they never taste as good as Liv's," Tom chirped in looking thoughtful. Liv smiled and turned to walk out.

"Liv?" Jay had the puppy dog eye look again. She stopped and looked at her brother's pleading grimace. "Can we please have a takeaway tonight?" He asked politely. "We had a roast for tea yesterday and Tom is staying," he added to help his case.

"It's two o'clock now, so game as much as you want until five and then this all goes off." Jay went to argue and Liv raised her eyebrows and tilted her head. He closed his mouth and let her continue. "You can both shower and get your pjs on, and then, we will have a takeaway." Both boys fist-pumped and cheered. "And then sort out your school bags. You will need your sports kit tomorrow don't forget."

"My mum is dropping off my uniform and kit later," Tom said grinning from ear to ear.

Liv smiled fondly at them both. "Once you've done that, you can watch a film. Lights out at ten-thirty," she said firmly.

"Thanks, Liv," both Jay and Tom answered at the same time. As she walked out of the room, followed by a completely smitten Pip, they heard the game being un-paused and the cheering and banter continued. Whilst Liv was making the chocolate milk, with both Burt and Ernie rubbing around her legs, Pip took his opportunity to talk.

"You're really good with them," he said admiringly.

She looked up at him, a wistful look on his handsome face. "It was hard at first. I'm not his mum, I'm his sister, but I also need to be a parent. Jay's a good lad, his happy-go-lucky character means that not a lot bothers him." She focused on whisking the chocolate milk.

"What about Hallie?" He asked, genuinely interested.

Liv sighed. "Again, it wasn't easy at first. Hal is a completely different kettle of fish," she said thinking back on her sibling's reactions when she had to tell them that her parents were gone. Pip watched the lines form on her beautiful face and didn't speak. "Hal found it harder to cope with at first. There were a lot of tears and then her hormones kicked in and the usual teenage angst. To be fair, I got off lightly. We talked a lot, just the three of us. I told them I would never leave them and that I would look after them…" Her voice trailed off and her hand had stilled with the whisk.

Pip moved behind her and wrapped his arms around her flat stomach. She tilted her neck as he kissed it gently. Letting out a long breath, she regained composure and began pouring the milkshake into two big plastic cups. Pip begrudgingly let her go as she whizzed around the kitchen, procuring a tray, two plates full of cookies, delicious-looking brownies and another bottle of red wine. Placing them all on a tray and somehow managing to avoid tripping over the mewling cats, she nodded when she had finished and he followed her up the stairs, enjoying the view of her rear end.

After leaving the tray with the delighted lads, she took the bottle and second plate of brownies and cookies, and made her way up to her bedroom, with Pip at her side. "I don't know what's making me more excited, the fact that I'm with you, or that you've made brownies," he said eyeing up the incredible-looking, chocolate brownies.

"Well, they do say the way to a man's heart is through his stomach." She laughed as she saw him grab a brownie and take a huge bite.

"Mmm…delicious," he said as he ate the sweet treat.

Pouring more wine, Liv opted for a white chocolate cookie and pulled her phone out of her pocket. She had checked it a few times during the morning and he had decided not to comment. "Just texting Hal to tell her Jay and Tom are here as she will probably want to come back early." As she tapped the keypad, she took small bites of her cookie. Within seconds, her phone pinged and she smiled in response. "Hal and Mazz are going to come back earlier and Mazz is sleeping over," Liv said smiling.

Hallie had also met her best friend at nursery school and they had been completely inseparable ever since. Both sporty and athletic, they played on the same school teams, so Liv and Mazz's parents took it in turn to taxi them about. Now the girls were older, they liked the independence of getting the bus to tournaments and weekend games, but when the weather was bad, they were both grateful for lifts to and from their favourite sports venues. Marianne, or Mazz as they called her, was the youngest of two siblings and she also loved to stay at her best friend's house as often as she could.

At the Whitmores, she was treated with respect, like the young woman she was and not a child. Her French mother was a high-flying businesswoman, and although she adored her daughters, she rarely had a minute free to sit and talk.

Whereas Liv always made time for Hal and Mazz. They would talk over any problems or worries, whether they be about, school, boys, or life in general. Mazz always thought of Liv as a beautiful older sister; after all, they had known each other since Hal and Mazz were four years old.

Liv also checked her phone for Pong's calls, or messages from Tina, his main carer. Luckily, there were none. She had tried not to make it too obvious but had managed to take sneaky looks when Pip was not looking. Settling back down on the settee, it was another hour of getting to know each other. Discussing the institute and all of its facilities, Pip told Liv about its benefactor, Professor James Millward.

Pip had first met him when he was studying at Harvard, where seeing his potential, James had taken him under his wing. Liv had seen Pip's artwork in the reception to the studios and also hung in the impressive Main Gallery. His glorious landscapes are painted in amazing arrays of colours with an eclectic flair. James had gone out of his way to support Pip, introducing him to many incredible artists and art journalists over the years. Taking a special interest in his education, James was the very first person to buy a piece of Pip's artwork, a stunning landscape where a thunderstorm was rolling in on dark clouds, shadowing the lush green valleys below.

James was a prolific art collector and as a multi-billionaire, had the finances to purchase and privately display some of the most prized masters of their time. He proudly displayed Pip's work along with the great masters he had collected. Milward's art institute had been planned for years and as his favourite city in the United Kingdom was Worcester, this was where he was going to create a place of learning like no other. He had slowly acquired grounds and ten years ago, his much dreamt-of art institute was opened in great pomp and ceremony. James Millward sounded like an amazing man and Liv was a little nervous that this lover of art was visiting Worcester in a few weeks' time.

The Christmas Ball was a huge event held in the Great Gallery in the main art building. As a professor, Pip was expected to attend. The tickets were not cheap and the evening would be for the who's who in the world of art. Famous fashion designers, sculptors, artists, actors, and writers would all be in attendance. So many tickets were available for students, however, the art block had first priority. They had got on to the subject of the ball and Pip was delighted to discover that Liv, Hallie, Jay, and their best friends, Tom and Mazz, would all be there. He usually enjoyed being with Maggie and Clara but found some of the people in attendance precocious and pompous.

"I am so glad you will be going," he said beaming.

"Yes, but we won't be able to sit together," she said looking serious. "You're a professor and I'm supposed to be a sixteen-year-old student," she said frowning.

"At least I will see you," he said leaning over and kissing her deeply. He pulled her onto his lap and she weaved her hands through his hair, the kiss becoming fierce and their bodies and souls wanting more. "Hi ya," Hal's voice called into the room and they broke off the kiss, both panting and breathless. Hallie and Mazz burst in, still wearing their school sports kits. "We won!" They both cheered and waved their hands in the air, dancing.

Liv laughed as she jumped up off Pip's lap and hugged the girls tightly. "That's brilliant news, well done," she said enthusiastically. Pip also stood and walked over to them. Mazz's eyes were popping out of her head, her face agog. There was a drop-dead gorgeous man and he was in Liv's bedroom. Both girls turned to look at Liv, eyes wide and excited. "Pip's stopping for tea if that's okay?" Liv asked.

"Sure, that's great," Hal said, almost bursting with unanswered questions, she bit her lips between her teeth, trying not to explode. "Umm, we need to shower and change, then can we eat?" Hal said, seeing her pal was dumbstruck. Liv smiled and nodded.

Mazz regained her senses. "Great, I'm starving," she managed to say.

"Just speak to the lads and decide what we are going to have for a takeaway," Liv called after the girls who were already leaving arm in arm, whispering and giggling.

"Okay," Hal called without turning back. Liv turned back to Pip and he kissed her passionately.

"Where were we?" He said smirking.

After yet another shower, Liv put on her pyjamas and sat on the bed waiting for Pip. He had declined to have a shower together as he knew they would end up making love and her younger siblings would be waiting for their meal. She flumped down on her bed, making a snoring Burt jump. The biggest grin on her pretty face as she thought of the mind-blowing orgasm she had just had. She then reflected on all of the orgasms she had, again wondering why on earth couples ever left the house. She heard a phone ping on the bedside table. Crawling up the bed and stroking Burt on the way, she picked up Pip's phone.

The text read: 'Dearest Philip, we missed you yesterday evening. We hope you are well. Would you like to keep the session we have booked for next Saturday, 1 December, at nine pm? Please let us know at your earliest convenience. Sasha x Care of the Oyster Club.'

The shower was still running as Liv sat and pondered the text. Who the hell was Sasha? She had heard about the Oyster Club from the chefs at Antonio's. They were always saying they wished they could afford the exclusive men-only club to get away from their nagging wives and girlfriends. Why give him a time? It was a drinking club, probably with scantily dressed women; surely you could turn up when you wanted, especially when you paid the extortionate fees that were charged there. Without thinking, her trembling fingers pressed reply. Checking the bathroom door was still closed, she quickly typed:

'Yes, I wish to attend on the 1st December, Thank you, Philip.'

Pressing send, she then deleted both messages and returned the phone to the bedside table. She sat there absentmindedly stroking Burt, her mind working overtime with thoughts of a half-naked woman called Sasha serving drinks to her Pip.

Chapter 18

It was the best start to a Monday morning that Pip and Liv had ever had. Foregoing their early morning runs, the five am alarm gave them the opportunity of another world-stopping orgasm. Liv showered, leaving Pip to snooze after a dynamic session of passion. Making her way down the stairs, she fed the cats, made five lunches, and was just sipping her coffee when Pip strode in looking like a film star. He was wearing dark grey pinstripe trousers, which hung low off his hips. A thin black leather belt secured them to his toned body; his torso was covered in a crisp white cotton shirt with the collar undone. His mousey locks looked darker as they were still damp from the shower.

He hadn't made it back to his apartment yesterday, however, he always carried a clean suit, shirt, accessories, and toiletry bag in his car. You never know when it could be needed. This morning, he was carrying a pair of black, polished shoes and had a silver tie and dark grey suit jacket draped over his arm. Placing them on the kitchen chair, he walked around the breakfast bar and into the kitchen area, his arms enveloping Liv in a tight embrace. He smelt amazing and she made a mental note to discover the aftershave he used as it was divine. Or maybe it was just him? Her insides flipped over at the thought of him naked.

Burt rubbed up their legs, meowing for attention, making them both laugh. Letting go of Liv, he bent down and scooped up the fat, purring lump of love into his muscular arms. "You will be covered in hair," Liv reproached, but he just cuddled Burt up even closer. She smiled, loving the fact that he loved her cats as much as she did. Kissing Pip softly on his cheek, then kissing Burt on his head, she busied herself with making breakfast. The television was on quietly displaying the latest news and Pip sat down on the settee, with Burt on his lap, watching the headlines. He loved the BBC news, everyone was so prim and proper, nothing like the loud, brash American newsreaders.

Liv placed a mug of coffee on the low table in front of him, smiling at Burt who had now curled up on his lap. "I've made a new friend," he said beaming.

"He knows you will be eating soon and wants to share your breakfast," Liv replied. Burt was actually very clever. Ernie had gone out into the early morning darkness and would miss out on any extra snacks. Liv began to make scrambled eggs and bacon, returning to the kitchen table after another ten minutes of preparation and cooking. Pip carefully moved Burt onto the cushion next to him before making his way to the table. The breakfast smelt and looked delicious—bacon, scrambled egg, toast and pastries along with fresh coffee and juice.

"Looks amazing, thank you," he said squirting brown sauce on his bacon. "I love this stuff; we don't have it in LA," he said admiring the brown sauce bottle, delighted with the food on offer. Liv sat down opposite him, smiling at his enthusiasm. She was sipping another cup of coffee and had no food in front of her. Pip had just taken a hearty mouthful of bacon and eggs but stopped chewing when he realised that she wasn't eating. Looking at the coffee and then at her face, he decided not to comment. He really had to do something about her not eating with nerves; there wasn't much to her now and she couldn't afford to lose any more weight.

Liv saw him take in her coffee and was glad he didn't comment. She loved that he had a good appetite and maybe she would too once the butterflies disappeared from her sensitive stomach. This had all been such a whirlwind. Starting at the world-famous art institute, then falling in love with the art professor. Liv almost spat out her coffee, covering her mouth as she coughed at the thought of being in 'love'. She was only just getting to know this man and yet she was calling it love? Her stomach flipped over again and she told herself to calm down and just enjoy the time with him.

He was watching her with fascination. "Talk to me," he said seriously.

She responded with a heart-wrenching smile. "That's all you ever say to me," she said lightly. He relaxed and returned her smile.

"We're starving," Jay's voice bellowed around the kitchen as he and Tom walked into the room.

"Breakfast is in the oven," she said happily. "Leave some for the girls please." She smiled at them as they practically ran to the oven. "They are always hungry," she laughed.

"I know how they feel," he said looking intently into her eyes. Luckily, the boys were engrossed in dishing out their breakfasts and didn't hear the innuendo. She shook her head and sipped her coffee. By eight o'clock, the busy house was in full swing. Music pumped out from the first floor as Hallie and Mazz were putting their final touches to their make-up and neat uniforms, ready for sixth form. Jay and Tom were dressed and lounging in the TV room, watching a police chase programme. Pip had donned his tie and jacket and looked smoulderingly hot as he loaded his car boot with his overnight bag and suit cover.

Coming back to the front door, where Liv was shivering in the cold of the morning, she suddenly turned and ran towards the kitchen, shouting, "Wait a minute," before disappearing around the corner. A few seconds later, she ran back to the doorway where he was standing. She handed him a large brown paper bag and his forehead furrowed in confusion. "Lunch," she explained and was rewarded with his megawatt smile.

"Let me take you," he said putting his free hand around her waist.

"You already have," she said slightly embarrassed by her own words.

He laughed heartily and kissed her goodbye. Reluctantly, he broke away as he felt his dick straining against his pants. "I have to go," he said his voice full of regret.

"I will see you in an hour's time," Liv said reassuringly, causing him to sigh.

"Ok, it's a date." He winked and stole a chaste kiss from her lips before turning and getting in his posh car. Liv wasn't bothered about cars as long as they started. She didn't know or care about makes or models but his car suited him. It was smooth, sleek and smoking hot, just like Pip. Standing in the chill of the early morning, her fingers were beginning to tingle from the cold as she waved him off. He reversed down the drive, out onto the quiet cul-de-sac, and with a final wave, he blew a kiss in her direction and zoomed off at speed up the road. As she closed the door, she leant against it, daydreaming for a few seconds.

He was so hot and sexy and he had made love to her, several times. How could this be happening to her? Suddenly, the text from the Oyster Club filled her head. Forcing it out of her mind last night and what with the amazing wakeup call and normal Monday morning chores, she had only just remembered it.

"You ok, sis?" Jay and Tom had retrieved their lunches and were making their way to the front door.

"Yes, of course." She smiled but it didn't quite reach her eyes. "Have you got your sports kits?" She asked and they both turned to show their bulging bags full of PE kit slung over their shoulders. "Have a good day, love you," she said as she opened the door and let them through.

"Love ya," they both said simultaneously and then quickly reverted the conversation back to the best rugby player of the season as they sauntered down the drive. Realising there was something she wanted to do before her art session started, she quickly sent a text and tidied the kitchen, stopping briefly to wave off the girls to college. Putting Burt into the utility room, she made sure the back door was locked. The cat flap would allow the cats in and out, and the utility was warm and cosy as it housed the boiler for the house. Two comfy cat beds were in the corner and Burt curled up in his toasty bed. Kissing his soft head and checking he had fresh water, she locked the kitchen door.

Pulling a black sweatshirt over her head and donning a black baseball cap, she stuffed her phone in her pocket. After grabbing her bike from the alley and locking up the side gate, she was off. Free of the responsibilities of the house and siblings, her mind wandered to the Oyster Club text. Why would he attend somewhere like that? What exactly went on there? Liv decided she would try and catch Lilly at Amores this afternoon and ask her more about it. Lily had mentioned she worked the odd shift there serving drinks. Although polite, Lilly seemed quiet and a little shy, so may not want to talk to her. Maybe she could say she was interested in working there. Lilly might fill her in on its goings-on.

Liv secretly hoped that it was a casino or networking club for businessmen who drank whiskey and smoked cigars. She had heard Angelo and the male kitchen staff commenting how they would love to be members and there was a lot of jeering and wolf whistles. The thought of scantily clad waitresses dishing out the whiskey was a depressing thought, but she really had no idea what went on there. An angry driver honked his car horn as she realised she had pulled out of a side road without looking to see if it was safe. *Come on, Liv, concentrate*, she thought to herself, briefly trying to put the text out of her mind, as she tried to focus on just getting to the institute alive.

Pip had arrived at the art department with a spring in his step. Clutching the lunch bag and his leather briefcase, he strode happily into the reception area, whistling. Mrs Bushell was sat in front of her computer at the desk, half-moon glasses perched on the end of her nose. "Ooo…someone's happy this morning." She grinned. He walked up to the desk, leant over, and kissed her on the top of her latest up doo. It resembled a seventies beehive style, only bigger. She crinkled her nose. "Get away with you, Professor Denton, I don't know where those lips have been," she said tittering.

With that, his smile grew broader as he remembered exactly where they had been. He carried on with his whistling and pushed open one of the huge doors to Studio One, hoping to find Maggie. Instead, he found Cadence helping herself to coffee from the drinks table. "Good morning, Mademoiselle Dubois. Have you seen Professor Harper?" He smiled his sexy smile and she was putty in his hands.

"Oh, 'ello Professor Denton. Professor 'arper is een a meeting, I'm zorry." Her thick French accent was full of lust. Ignoring her look of desire for him, he checked his watch; it was only half past eight and Maggie was not an early bird; in fact, she would usually only just be arriving. He had already stopped at a coffee shop to get an espresso; the exertions of the weekend and very little sleep were catching up on him. The caffeine hit had woken him up and he sat in the car reliving his amazing weekend. He had ordered another shot of espresso and made his way to work.

After parking in the private art studio car park, he was practically bouncing with energy. "Meeting?" He queried, finding it odd he hadn't been informed.

"Oui, and you 'ave a visitor waiting in your office also," she said her eyes tightening slightly, showing some distaste.

"Really, I wasn't expecting anyone..." He trailed off. It had been over fifty minutes since he had left the delightful Liv, so maybe she had made it in early to fit in one more kiss, or maybe even more before the sessions started. Gulping, he quickly made his way to the tunnel. "Thank you, Mademoiselle," he called over his shoulder.

'Ee iz far too good for zat woman, she thought bitterly, as she stirred her coffee, jealous that it wasn't her draped across his desk, awaiting his arrival.

Walking through the open lounge, he noted a sign on Maggie's office door, stating she was in a meeting and no one was to disturb her. Very unusual. As he approached his office, he saw a large man in a dark suit and a buzz-cut pacing. Even more unusual. Maybe a new member of the security team? "Can I help you?" Pip asked politely. The guy shifted uncomfortably and shook his head. Pip nodded and continued to his office door. As he opened the door, his senses were attacked by an overwhelming scent of a sickly, oversprayed, floral perfume. He stepped in to find a tall, leggy female perched on the end of his desk. She was rudely skimming through some of his notes that he had left out.

The skinny, peroxide blonde looked up at him through her fake eyelashes and drag act-make-up. "I've been waiting for you, Philip," she said in a haughty tone, wagging her bony finger. "You shouldn't keep me hanging around you know." Her English/American accent sounded odd.

"Alexia," he said surprised, not able to hide his disappointment as he was hoping to find Liv. She stood and Pip took in her ludicrously high, bright yellow heels, teamed with a tight-fitting fuchsia pink dress. It looked like she was going to a nightclub and he found himself biting the inside of his mouth to stop himself laughing at her. She mistook his expression for attraction, after all, everybody wanted her.

"Daddy and I arrived last night, but he is still asleep and I wanted to see you." She leered at him.

"You wanted to see me?" He asked confused. She made her way over to where he stood and trailed her long, fake, neon orange nails across his cheekbone.

"Philip, you are the only reason I came here," she said, licking her overfilled lips in what she considered to be an alluring gesture. He grimaced and moved to her left, trying to avoid her touch. Placing his briefcase and lunch bag on his desk, he walked over to his beloved Tassimo, placing an espresso pod in, and pressing the button to start the machine off. His coffee buzz from earlier had evaporated as he had entered his office and he needed more. Taking off his suit jacket, he hung it on a hanger on the coat stand in the corner. He turned and sat at his desk, flicking on his laptop. "Excuse me."

Even her voice annoyed him. He looked up with a stern expression on his face. "What do you want, Alexia?" He demanded as she tottered over to his desk. Putting her hands on the edge, she leant over as far as she could. A provocative stance, giving the professor an extensive view of her protruding watermelon breasts, straining to be contained by the pink lycra.

"I want you, Philip," she said in her most seductive tone.

He raised his eyebrows in response. "That will never happen. Now if you will excuse me, I have work to do."

His abruptness made her stand up as she snatched her hands from his desk as if she had been burnt. "Need I remind you who my father is?" The words spewed out like poison.

"I know who he is and I look forward to seeing him, but until then…" He trailed off, spinning his chair around to collect his steaming espresso, which had just finished pouring. He turned back a little slower as he was aware he was holding a cup of hot liquid. She was still standing there. Her lips were pursed together and he thought of an expression Maggie often used, 'She looks like a bulldog's arse chewing a wasp'. The thought entered his head and he couldn't help but smile. The words summing up this dreadful woman in front of him. "Goodbye, Alexia," he said focusing his attention on his computer screen and ignoring her completely.

Stamping her foot in anger, she spun on her perilously high heels and stormed out of his office, slamming the door as she left. *How dare he speak to her like that, no one ever dismissed her out of hand. She was Alexia Millward, every woman wanted to be her and every man wanted to screw her, well nearly all.* She had always wanted to fuck Professor Denton since the first time she had seen him, but he had never been forthcoming. He was polite in general company, but on the few occasions she had managed to get him on his own, he had always excused himself and walked away from her as fast as he could.

She could take her pick of men, although it never crossed her mind that they would only sleep with her for notoriety or to get at her money. The fact was, that she didn't have any money of her own, it was all her father's. He was extremely generous but she was not an independent woman and relied on his handouts and charitable nature. Her mother had died in childbirth and her father had been utterly devastated. He bestowed all his love and money onto his only child and she had quickly grown up to be a spoilt, nasty piece of work. As she stalked through the Main Gallery's seating area and down the tunnel, she was already trying to think of ways to hurt him.

No one treated her like that and got away with it. There was no way she could get him fired, although he deserved to lose his career, her father adored him. This made her even more jealous and the fact that she had flown all this way just to see him; she was furious. She had absolutely no interest in the institute or its work, and when her father had suggested she accompany him, she had one thought on her mind—to seduce and bed Philip Denton. She stormed through Studio One, closely followed by her bodyguard and threw an evil look at the assistant, who was standing in the corner gawping at her, along with Ida who had joined her for a cuppa.

The little French bitch was obstructive when she arrived and demanded to see Philip earlier. Trying to put her off and tell her that she, Alexia Millward, would have to make an appointment. *Who the fuck did she think she was?* She pushed the studio door open and stomped through the reception gallery. Alexia completely ignored Mrs Bushell, who politely called after her as she tottered through the reception area. It's a good job she didn't hear the old woman, who shouted, "Don't let the doors hit you on the way out." Then with a huge grin, raised her mug of steaming hot tea at the fact her favourite professor had obviously kicked the nefarious princess out of the building.

Pip stood and looked out of his window, whilst thoughtfully sipping his coffee. The disappointment of his guest being Alexia and not Liv really hit him. His head was full of Olivia Whitmore. Her face and incredible body filled his thoughts. The way she looked after her family and her amazing talent, that's what you call a real woman. Not like the completely fake, pretentiousness just displayed by Alexia. The difference between the two women was immense. Liv worked hard to provide for her family and Miss Millward had never lifted a perfectly manicured finger to earn a dime. The thought annoyed him.

A multi-billionaire heiress who had everything she wanted and a young woman running herself ragged to support her family. He was used to women wanting him and Alexia had tried to seduce him several times before. She was well known for sleeping around and he had always steered clear. His choices were much more select. Having finished his coffee, he checked his watch, eight fifty-five. He wondered if Liv had arrived yet and decided to make his way to Studio One. Upon leaving his office, he noticed that Maggie's door still bore the 'Do not disturb' sign.

He hoped everything was alright as it was most unlike Maggie to take part in an early morning meeting. An unsettling feeling washed over him and as he entered Studio One, the sight of Ida waving a pack of dark chocolate digestives at him (his favourite) did nothing to improve his mood. Pip had hung around the reception gallery as the students filed in. As usual, most of the young girls flocked around him, wanting to gain the attention of their gorgeous professor. Mindy was of course first at his side, touching his arm as she tried to discuss her latest artwork with him. He had seen her work, along with every other student from Studio One and Two.

There were a handful of potential artists, Mindy was not one of them, and Liv outshone them all. Mindy looked as if she had copied her look from Alexia, wearing a tightly fitted top. Her rock-hard breasts were trying to escape out of her bra and sticking out of the scallop-necked jumper. Along with a mini skirt, opaque tights and black patent leather boots, she looked like a hooker. He smiled politely and scanned the filling gallery for the only woman he wanted to see, but there was no sign of her. She was never late and when the bell rang for the beginning of the session, his mood fell further.

With a furrowed brow, he made his way up the staircase and into his studio, closely followed by Ida and her pack of chocolate biscuits. Still frustrated that he hadn't seen Liv, Pip made his way into the store's cupboard to retrieve materials that he didn't really need. He just wanted a few minutes to gather his thoughts. The subject of his dreams was now a reality. Olivia Whitmore was now his. So where was she?

Chapter 19

At eleven-fifty, Professor Denton dismissed his class, telling them they could all have an extra half-hour lunch break and that he didn't want to see any of them back in the studio until one-thirty. The response to his announcement prompted a loud cheer and his students immediately discussed the ways they would while away this extra time. Most decided to go to the nearest local for a boozy pub lunch as most of them had fake IDs. The others decided to tackle the busy high street and get ahead on their Christmas shopping. Ida was busy cleaning brushes over at the Belfast sinks. Despite her professor being a little out of sorts earlier, he was now back to his happy, passionate self and she smiled absentmindedly as she went about her chores.

Hoping that Liv had now made it into her class in Studio One, he practically skipped down the spiral staircase. Bursting through the doors, he found a bustling room of energy. The students were checking out each other's work and standing in little clicks, discussing their latest project. The Main Gallery was being prepared for the Christmas Ball in a few weeks' time. Each student would have their best work displayed around its vast walls and so decisions were being made as to which of their art would be chosen for such an auspicious occasion. Maggie was engrossed with two students to the right of the room explaining how to give more contrast to a picture by the use of shadows as they admired a portrait painting.

He glanced to his left and found a male student leaning on Liv's drawing desk, where he seemed to spend most of his time. That thought made him angry and his fists clenched tightly. The young man was deep in conversation and Liv was sat leaning in close, her face partially hidden by the baseball cap she insisted on wearing. He strained to try and hear what was being said but Guy's quiet tone could not be heard over the music playing on the radio, Maggie's loud voice, and the general chatter of the studio. Suddenly, a hand was placed on his chest and he turned to see Mindy Moore, practically drooling over him.

"Hello again, Professor," she said looking up at him through her fake lashes. He took a step back and quickly glanced at Liv, who was now staring at him, her face unreadable. Mindy took advantage of the pause and stepped forward, filling the gap. "Do you wanna see what I can do?" Mindy's American drawl snapped his brain back into gear and he looked at her, completely appalled. As he hadn't responded, Mindy giggled and continued. "I mean, do you wanna see my latest work?" Her face was twisted into what she hoped would be a sweet, shy expression, but made her look completely ludicrous and freakish.

"Ahem, Miss Moore…" Maggie's voice made them both spin around. "Have you got nothing you should be doing?" Maggie's stern look was focused completely on her wayward student. Mindy looked at Maggie as if she had just spat in her coffee. "Well?" Maggie insisted. Mindy sighed and begrudgingly removed her hand from Pip's chest. With a last withering look at Maggie, she turned on her heeled boots and strutted back to her workstation, where two good-looking male students were waiting patiently to praise her terrible attempt at a landscape. Frowning at the sixteen-year-old's slutty behaviour, his attention returned to Liv but the annoying boy was now blocking her completely from view. "Pip?" Maggie was still standing at his side.

"Maggie," he replied, not even turning to look at her.

She wrinkled her nose and bit her lip, trying to hold in what she really wanted to say. "Your class has finished early today. Do you have time for a coffee?" She was smiling sweetly when he eventually turned to face her.

"Yeah, that would be good. Thanks, Mags," he said, grateful for the opportunity to stay in Studio One and stalk his secret girlfriend. Maggie linked her arm through his and pulled him over towards the drinks table. Neither spoke as she prepared him a fresh coffee. She passed him the mug full of steaming caffeine, just as the end-of-session bell trilled across the room. He spun around quickly, sloshing the hot liquid onto the Parkay floor. Students had started pulling on heavy coats and collecting their belongings, ready to brave the cold winter weather on the way to the institute's restaurant or nearest pub. Liv was nowhere to be seen. Her workstation was empty.

He scanned the room and glowered at the male student who had been talking to Liv when he had entered the room. Guy picked up on the bad vibes and looked up from his rucksack that he was neatly packing. For a few seconds, their eyes met and Guy suddenly blinked and turned pale. *He actually looks frightened*, Pip thought to himself smugly. Guy quickly donned the hood of his winter jacket and slung his bag over his shoulder, before slipping out of the exit door. Pip watched intently until he was completely out of sight.

Some of Maggie's students had hung back, desperate for the opportunity to bump gums with the dishy American professor. Maggie shooed them all away and as the last student begrudgingly left the room, she looked at her dear friend and laughed. "Just like flies around shit!" His mood lifted immediately as he made a mental note of another great saying from his beloved Maggie.

Having had a few missed calls from a stressed Tina, Liv had discreetly left the studio and rang to speak to Pong, who just needed to hear her voice, assuming that it was his beautiful daughter. Once she had reassured him she would be with him after her afternoon art class, she found herself walking the short distance to the bustling high street. Her stomach rumbled and she realised that the whole Pip situation had ruined her appetite and for the first time in days, she was really hungry. She made her way to her favourite café, Whoopsie-Daisies, which was just off the main street. It was a small, comfortable place with shabby chic furniture.

They displayed and sold local crafts and artwork (including some of Liv's work) and also prepared and sold the best sarnies, baguettes, cakes, and pastries in the city. Even from the outside, the café looked welcoming; strings of fairy lights hung in the old-fashioned lead windows and Liv could see people enjoying the warmth and delicious food. On entering, Rita called out from behind the counter. "Hello, stranger." She beamed at Liv and waved. Liv smiled back. She had been coming here for as long as she could remember and its unimposing, happy ambience always made her feel good.

She peeled off her baseball cap and walked over to the counter, "How are you, sweetie? Anything exciting happening?" Rita asked, genuinely delighted to see her.

"Yes, good, thank you," Liv replied, thinking it best not to mention she was no longer a virgin and was sleeping with her teacher.

"I have something for you," she said retrieving an envelope from the back of the counter. "I haven't seen you for a few weeks, so it has mounted up," Rita said cheerily handing over an envelope full of cash. "I could do with some more paintings if you have the time, selling like hotcakes they are," she said delightedly.

Liv peered warily into the envelope to see wads of notes, all neatly banded together. "Wow, Rita, how many have you sold?" Liv asked in shock.

Rita's eyebrows raised as she grinned. "All of them," she said clapping her hands together in delight. "Well, all of them except my favourite one," she said nodding to the far corner of the room where above the inglenook fireplace, complete with real glowing fire, there was a large painting of the Whoopsie-Daisies shopfront. The painting depicted the charming leaded windows and pale blue front door, covered in white and yellow daisies; it showed a bright sunny day and a family were admiring the cakes on display in the window.

Liv laughed and shook her head. "This is so great; thank you, Rita." She was already deciding what extra treats she could buy Hal and Jay for Christmas.

"Well, what will it be, sweetie?" Rita smiled as she waited for Liv's order.

"Hot chocolate and a sausage bap, please," Liv replied, safely zipping the envelope into her left jogging bottom pocket and pulling her small coin purse out of her right pocket.

"You must be joking, sweetie, put your money away, this is on me," Rita said shaking her head firmly "Craft and art sales are going through the roof, so this is my treat." She raised her hands to refuse any proffered money and the customers all hushed their conversations to eavesdrop.

"Thank you, Rita, that's very kind but…" Before she could finish her sentence, Rita had turned to make a steaming mug of chocolate, quickly turning back with the finished product and squirting an undignified amount of squirty cream onto the top of it. Rita pushed her own masterpiece towards her and Liv gave in, realising she would never win against her. Liv nodded gratefully as she carefully picked up her drink and scanned the busy room for a seat. Luckily, there was a small table with one chair, in the far corner, in front of the main leaded window.

Liv sat and gazed at the passers-by, hurriedly going about their day, wrapped up against the chill of a crisp, dull winter's day. Absentmindedly sipping her lush hot chocolate, she people-watched. It was one of her favourite pastimes and helped her to try to block out the look Pip had just given her at the studio. She had noticed his fists were clenched and had come to the decision that it must have been his anger at finding Guy talking to her. Although the way that hussy Mindy Moore was behaving, it should have been Liv who should be angry. She then tried not to think about the Oyster Club text, and as her mind raced with images of scantily dressed prostitutes in darkly lit rooms, a hand touched her shoulder, making her jump.

Her head spun around to find Rita as she placed a delicious-looking sausage bap on the small table, along with a knife, serviette, and two sachets of red sauce. "Enjoy." Rita smiled and patted Liv's shoulder, winking at her before clearing away the plates and dishes on the table opposite. Old-fashioned Christmas carols were playing in the background and she enjoyed people-watching as she demolished her lunch. After she finished her hot chocolate, Liv felt replete. Wishing she could stay here all afternoon, she checked her watch.

Begrudgingly, she donned her sweatshirt and cap, knowing she had to make her way back to the institute. As she left, Rita was busy serving customers, so she shoved a ten-pound note into the tip jar on the counter and as she opened the door, the bell tinkled and she called goodbye and thanked the lovely Rita. As she pulled her hood over her baseball cap, she walked quickly past the shop fronts and the busy shoppers. Christmas music emanated from each open shop door, even though it was only late November. Liv smiled as she knew how much Hallie and Jay enjoyed the Christmas festivities.

Suddenly, her legs stopped moving and she found herself gawping into the window of the 'Vintage Vogue' boutique. Hal helped out here when she had time for extra pocket money. Liv and Hal had visited the shop together a few weeks ago to buy Hal a dress for the winter ball. Mrs Bingley-Smyth had owned the shop for over fifty years and Liv remembered her mother taking her there as a child, where she tried on the stunning dresses on offer and Liv would sit and watch enraptured. Mrs Bingley-Smyth regaled Liv and Hal with incredibly romantic stories of her dresses like she had when they were children.

The stories involved a handsome foreign prince and some poor English girl, who was given a dress and wore it to a ball (yes, very Cinderella-like) and as soon as the prince set eyes on the beautiful dress, he fell in love with the girl. They had also enjoyed these stories as children and if they needed a dress for a special occasion, there was no other place they would dream of going. Hal had chosen a full gown for her prom from this boutique and as the institute's Christmas Ball was very prestigious, she had asked Liv to go with her to pick a new dress.

Hallie and Jay both had pocket money (from Liv's hard work and income) but Hal also babysat odd weekends and helped out at the boutique, very rarely spending her savings. She had enough money to pay for the new gown, but of course, Liv had offered to pay for it. Mrs Bingley-Smyth adored the Whitmore family and also gave them a very generous discount. The dress Hallie had chosen was a bright, red silk, with a fitted strapless bodice, which Hal loved because it pushed up her non-existent boobs, giving her cleavage. With an elegant fishtail skirt, it showed off her stunning figure and gorgeous long legs.

Whilst Hallie had been trying on dresses, Liv sat on the burgundy velvet chaise long, the same one she had sat on as a child. Mrs Bingley-Smyth had allowed Liv to address her by her first name, Edie (short for Edith), and had given her a glass of prosecco (as a child it would have been squash with a cocktail umbrella). Whilst she busied herself opening a new delivery, she told Liv a story about one of her green gowns that had magical powers. It made men fall in love with whoever was wearing it. The wizened old lady was wonderful and had such an extraordinary character, you couldn't help but like her. She was eccentric and Liv loved that.

That day, she was wearing a purple taffeta cocktail dress, with a huge ruffle on the shoulder, combined with navy tights and shiny navy court shoes. Edie looked like she was off to a cocktail bar, but it had only been eleven o'clock in the morning. Liv had never seen her without make-up and that day had been no exception. Bright pink lips, lined in a mauve lip liner, purple eyeshadow and black eyeliner with an expert flick at the corner of her sparkling blue eyes. She also had purple feathers sticking out of her pink permed hair. As she pulled out the latest addition to her gown collection, Liv's attention had left the dressing room curtain awaiting Hal's emergence as she stared in awe at the striking dress now being assessed by the delightful Edie.

The old lady realised that Liv was admiring the new frock and stood up to show it off in all its glory. It was the most amazing topaz blue and green and Liv reached out to feel the soft silk material, which seemed to glisten in the glare of the spotlights. It was so sleek and elegant, with a simple slightly cowled neck, falling into a full long skirt. "Ahh, but you haven't seen the best bit." Edie's eyes twinkled and she smiled, turning the dress around. The slim straps fell into a low plunge back.

Liv puffed out air from her mouth as she envisioned just where the plunge would end on her body. The thought of showing the crack of her bum was most alarming. The skirt part of the dress splayed out into a dramatic peacock feather effect, with glistening sequins embroidered into the delicate silk, creating stunning feathers. It was exquisite. Edie cackled at Liv's reaction. "Oh, my dear girl, this would look good on you." She eyed Liv from head to toe.

"Umm…no I don't think so." Liv sipped her prosecco nervously.

"What size are you, dear?" She was on a mission but Liv didn't want a new dress; she really couldn't justify the extra expense.

"I'm a twelve, Edie." She grimaced as she knew that most of these dresses were for skinny women and, although slim and toned, she was not petite.

Edie tutted and her eyes closed slightly as if doing calculations in her head. "Shame," she said sucking her bright pink lips between her teeth. "This is an eight to ten," she said regretfully.

"Ah well," Liv said, thinking she would feel relieved but actually feeling a bit depressed at the fact there was no way it would fit.

"I'm going to put it in the window. It's a fabulous dress and it deserves to be put on show." She nodded and gently hung the stunning dress on a padded silk hanger. Hallie burst through the thick, burgundy velvet curtain in the red fishtail gown and the incredible topaz creation was forgotten.

Now, two weeks on, Liv's feet had stopped of their own volition at the sight of 'Vintage Vouge's' Christmas display. The window was edged in thick red tinsel and the centrepiece was a lurid gold, taffeta, full ball gown. For some reason, Liv felt a tinge of sadness that the stunning topaz dress must have been sold. Frowning and with a pout on her beautiful lips, she willed her feet to start moving and in a rather sullen mood, she walked quickly back to the institute.

She was expecting to see Pip on her return, after finding out that Studio Two students were given a longer lunch break than usual, but he was nowhere to be seen. The afternoon whizzed by, with both Liv and Guy making the final decision on which piece of art to display at the Christmas Ball. They had discussed their options with each other and Liv had really valued Guy's opinions. Other students were noisily debating their own choices, some near to tears about making such an important decision. Guy had pulled his stool over to Liv's workstation where they were enjoying a latte coffee and a chat. They were both leaning on the desk, watching the commotion around the room.

Mindy Moore was practically hysterical about not having a special piece of artwork ready and for once, Maggie was not her calm and patient self; in fact, she looked like she was going to slap her. Well, someone should. Liv had been observing intently until she felt like she herself was being watched. She turned to see Guy's serious and slightly melancholy expression. "What's up?" She asked, her attention on her friend and not on the now screaming banshee that was Miss Moore.

"'allie, I need to talk to you," he said quietly, his French accent thick with sadness.

"What's wrong?" Liv put a hand over his, the guilt of him not even knowing her real name was getting too much for her.

"I know it ezz impossible but I cannot keep it secret any longer." His beautiful face was pale as he stared at her.

"Guy?" *Oh god, please don't tell me you're sick*, she thought to herself as her mind raced with unpleasant possibilities.

"I really like you, 'allie…" He paused and looked down at her hand touching his arm.

"And I like you, Guy, you're a good friend," she said reassuringly.

He let out a long sigh and turned to look at her again. "I mean I really like you." He raised his eyebrows at the word 'really'.

Liv frowned as she thought about his words, her eyes widened in shock as she realised what he actually meant. "Guy, I'm so sorry…I…" She stuttered.

"ees okay, 'al, I know you don't love me," he said sadly. "I know you love someone but it ezz not me," he finished sadly.

Liv's mouth gaped open and she wasn't sure what to say to him. "I need to talk to you but not here. Come to my house later for tea?" She pleaded with him.

"Of course," he said smiling graciously, although the melancholy never left his eyes. She scribbled down her address on a piece of paper and he took it from her. They both fell silent and turned their attention to the commotion going on with Mindy and her fan club.

Liv had ducked out just before the bell as she really wanted to catch Lilly at Amores, the Oyster Club text still playing on her mind. On sprinting out of the art building, she called goodbye to Mrs Bushell, who was busy sipping tea from her bone china cup. "Goodbye, dear," she replied, placing her delicate cup back on its matching saucer. "Now, that is who you need to spend time with, Bunny." She watched Liv run out through the double doors and turn right towards the bike shelters. "Amazing, young woman, I have been watching her with great interest," she said knowingly.

"Why would I want to spend time with a young whippet like that when I could be with you?" Bunny's smooth American accent made her heart melt slightly, but Joyce Bushell was no man's possession. After a miserable marriage to a controlling curmudgeon, she was finally released at the age of fifty-one when Mr Bushell died unexpectedly. Whilst attending a local cricket match, the ball had been belted out wide, heading in an odd direction. It had landed with some force on Mr Bushell's head. He died instantly. Whilst all around her were sad at his demise, Joyce was in fact relieved. He had made her life miserable and now at fifty-one, she was a widow, with no family or friends to speak of.

He had never wanted children, even though she had been desperate to be a mother. Her family had all passed away and as she was an only child, there were no siblings to support her. She sold their large, cold house on the outskirts of Worcester and moved into a modern apartment in the city centre. She lived there happily with the only male she ever trusted and adored. She was free to go where she wanted when she wanted. After corresponding with Bunny, her oldest and dearest friend, he helped her by giving her a job as a receptionist at the art institute. They were both passionate about art, it was their mutual love.

Art had actually brought them together as teenagers, many years before she had met Mr Bushell. Now here she was, loving life and sat drinking tea with her Bunny. Wasn't life strange?

Liv had run to her bicycle and hopping on it, she began peddling fast down the hill to the gated exit. She felt her lungs ache as the chill of the afternoon air hit her chest. She was trying to regulate her breathing, something she was used to with running, but it had grown colder through the day and she knew that winter was definitely here. They had a mild autumn but there was now speculation of snow on Christmas day, something that hadn't happened in years. On entering Amores, she had her usual greeting in way of a cheer from all of the chefs and kitchen staff.

She smiled at her warm welcome, as she always did, but instead of taking the back stairs up to the apartment, she made her way through to the main restaurant. For a Monday afternoon, the restaurant had quite a few customers, its reputation for good food in a relaxing, friendly environment meant it was seldom empty. She spotted Lilly serving an elderly couple their main and side orders and waited patiently for her to finish with her customers before approaching. Lilly was tall with jet-black long hair tied back into a neat ponytail. She was wearing the Amores waiting staff uniform of black tailored trousers, a white short-sleeved shirt, a thin black tie, and a black apron with dark red edging.

Liv was always impressed by how smart the staff looked and actually enjoyed it when she donned her own uniform to help out when the place was extremely busy. There were a few large groups having their early Christmas parties, laughing and chatting loudly. Although tall and pretty, Lilly wore no make-up and although polite, seemed shy and slightly awkward. "Hi, Lilly," Liv said cheerfully.

"Hello, Liv, it's good to see you," Lilly replied as they hugged. She was genuinely happy to see Liv as they usually missed each other when on shift.

"Have you got a minute? I just wanted a quick word," Liv asked, trying to keep her tone bright. Lilly looked around at her tables, all happy and content with the delicious food they were enjoying.

"Sure," she said and made her way over to an empty booth. Liv followed and took a seat opposite Lilly, who sat meekly waiting for Liv to begin.

"So, I umm…" Liv stuttered and started fiddling with her fingers, the nerves kicking in. "I was just wondering if you could tell me…Umm…" She was really struggling and now Lilly's face was full of concern.

"Liv, what is it?" She asked worriedly.

Taking a deep breath, she opened her mouth again. "What actually happens at the Oyster Club?" The words tumbled out of her mouth before she could stop them and she looked up at Lilly, Who was completely taken back. "I'm sorry to have to ask you but you're the only one here who actually knows."

Lilly took in Liv's anxious expression and spoke gently. "I'm sorry, Liv, anyone employed at the club has to sign an NDA when they start."

Liv was confused. "NDA?" She questioned.

"Sort of like a gagging order, Liv," she finished as though that was the end of the matter.

Liv pondered quickly about how to go forward and decided as always that it was best to tell the truth. "I've met someone. He's amazing and good-looking. I have no idea what he sees in me…" She whispered the last bit. Lilly sat silently, making no movement. "Anyway…" She took another deep breath. "He had a text from the Oyster Club asking if he would be attending this Saturday at nine." Liv's eyes were wide and she was watching Lilly's every move in case she gave something away.

"Liv, I really can't tell you; I cannot afford to lose my job," she said honestly. "I only pick up a few shifts here to stop my family and friends questioning me about how I afford a mortgage and bills. I can't risk my job at the club by giving you information. I'm so sorry," she finished, obviously not feeling comfortable in continuing any conversation about the Oyster Club.

Liv's face fell. Of course, she wouldn't want Lilly to lose her job, she knew how hard it was to make sure the bills were paid. "My apologies, I shouldn't have asked," she said humbly. "It's just I'm imagining all sorts about this Sasha woman…"

"Sasha woman?" Lilly suddenly sat up a little straighter with interest.

"That's who texted my umm, 'friend', saying she was the host?" She replied.

Lilly stayed quiet for a few minutes whilst she thought it through. One of the tables had finished their course and Lilly knew she would have to get back to work, so time was limited. "Liv, you have always been so kind to me; you looked after me when I started here. You've always watched out for me. I'm afraid I can't tell you what happens at the club…"

"I shouldn't have asked, I am sorry." Liv looked crestfallen and raised her hands in protest.

"Wait, I can't tell you but I can show you," Lilly whispered, not wanting to be overheard.

"Really?" Liv didn't know what else to say except, "Thank you."

"Give me your number and I will text you on Saturday," Lilly said seriously, pulling her phone from her apron pocket. Liv reeled off her number, just as Carlo, one of the many waiters, called her to help serve at the busy tables. "Wear those clothes and you will hopefully go under the radar until Saturday then." Lilly smiled meekly and slid off the seat, returning to her customers. Liv sat in the booth for a few minutes collecting her scattered thoughts. She was expecting a brief outline of what actually happens at the club, not an invitation to see it for herself. Maybe it was literally just a posh gentleman's drinking hole and she had the complete wrong impression. Her parents always told her she had an overactive imagination.

A glance at her watch gave her a kick up the bum to get moving. She left the main restaurant and made her way up the side stairs to the apartment. As she walked down the spacious hall, she saw Bella leaving Lucas' bedroom. "Hi, Liv, how are you?" Bella faltered taking in Liv's baggy black tracksuit and baseball cap. The look on her face said it all and Liv burst out laughing. Bella looked like she had just left a fashion shoot, black tailored capri trousers, a black and white stripey silk blouse and a white fitted blazer. She was wearing ridiculously high stilettos, accessorised with a Gucci clutch bag and large Gucci sunglasses were perched on the top of her head. Her jet-black pixie cut looked immaculate.

Along with perfectly applied make-up, Bella Ricci looked amazing. A little alarmed that Liv thought she had said something funny, they still hugged each other warmly. Bella was Angelo's sister and was always dropping in to see

Stacey, Luca, and her big brother. "Excuse the outfit, I've been at the institute all day," Liv said by way of her appearance.

"You look pretty in anything, Liv, but it just doesn't look like you," she sounded concerned.

"I hear you've had quite an adventure in the Maldives?" Liv asked.

Bella rolled her eyes. "I have a lot to fill you in on but we will need wine…I am free next Friday." Now it was Liv's turn to be taken aback. They got on really well but they were not very close friends; Bella was a lot older than her and had a close click of friends.

"Umm…" Liv couldn't think of what to say when Bella took her hands in hers.

"I've met someone," she said excitedly, her face glowing with sheer joy. "But I can't talk to my close friends as they are all busy and Stacey is exhausted, sooo…" She trailed off.

"I've met someone too," Liv said smiling and Bella squealed with delight. "It's a bit complicated." Liv frowned and suddenly, the idea of chatting to a friend about it all seemed a bloody good idea.

"I can do complicated. I need to fill you in on my leg injury as well."

Liv automatically looked down at Bella's legs and then back to her face. "They look okay," Liv said politely.

"Oh, believe me, I have a lot to fill you in on." Bella winked. People seemed to be doing that a lot today.

"Can I let you know?" Liv said smiling.

Bella smiled broadly. "Sure, I'm free next Friday, so text me," she said clapping her hands. "I can tell you how I was pushed off a billionaire's yacht into shark-infested waters." Bella winked again as Liv's mouth hung open in shock.

"Oh, we will definitely need wine." She laughed as Bella hugged her again and said her goodbyes. Liv made her way into Luca's room. The curtains were closed and he was lying on the floor looking at the ceiling. He had a special lamp that projected the stars, he could name every formation. "Hello, Luca," she said smiling. "Hi, Stacey," she said turning to Luca's bed, where a blooming Stacey was rubbing her tummy with both hands.

"Hi, Liv, I'm so happy to see you. He's tired and very grumpy today and he wanted his stars on after nursery." Stacey filled her in and covered her mouth to stifle a yawn.

"Go and have a lie-down and I will wake you before I go," Liv replied.

Stacey staggered to her feet, she looked exhausted. "Thank you," she said as she gently kissed Liv on the cheek. She really didn't know how they would cope without Liv. She helped out with Luca and in the restaurant, she was a true blessing to her and her family. Liv sent a quick text to Hallie and Jay asking one of them to visit Pong as she wouldn't have a chance to go herself tonight. It had already seemed like a really long day. Liv lay on the floor next to Luca and he immediately climbed on top of her, giving her a huge hug.

She pointed at a star formation. "That's the chicken dipper, isn't it?" Her rouge worked and Luca corrected her.

"That is the big dipper!" He said looking at the ceiling and frowning. He then continued to name other formations with facts about each that she had heard many times before. After an hour had passed and the formations had all been discussed, Liv asked Luca if he was hungry. "Yep," was his simple reply, along with a huge smile. She stood up and walked out of his room towards the kitchen, he followed her and climbed up onto the bar stool at the breakfast bar. He watched with interest as Liv heated up a pan of Bolognese. She buttered some thick, crusty bread and spooned some of the hot mixture into a bright green pasta bowl.

"What is the magic word?" Liv gently prompted.

"Please." The little boy grinned, picking up some bread and dipping it into his Bolognese. He loved Bolognese and Liv knew he would eat the lot. She poured them both some orange juice and sat opposite to him whilst he ate. When he had finished, he climbed down from the high stool and lifted his empty dish, carrying it over to the sink and placing it in the washing-up bowl.

"Thank you, Luca. Now do you want a bath?" Liv asked.

"Woo hoo!" He squealed and ran to the bathroom, where he sat on the floor and started emptying his bath toy box. Once Liv had bathed and dressed him in his cute dinosaur pyjamas, she tucked him into bed. After several bedtime stories, Luca fell asleep. He was so cute; she really did love him.

After making Stacey a milky hot chocolate and leaving it on her bedside table, she went down to the kitchen. "Angelo, you need to go and wake Stacey," she said to the good-looking Italian chef.

"She's asleep?" He questioned.

"She was tired and Luca has had a bad day, so what do you think?" Liv smiled. Angelo and Stacey were one of those couples who truly loved each other and were genuinely happy together. "Luca had his tea, a bath, and is fast asleep too. I know you are really busy but maybe you could spend an hour with Stacey?" Liv was trying to be helpful and Angelo knew she was right.

"Hey, Vince, take over, I'm going to make food for my lovely wife," he called across the hectic kitchen. Vince wolf whistled and the whole kitchen team laughed and joined in. Angelo hugged Liv tightly and kissed the top of her head. She always felt uncomfortable with hugs, unless they were from her siblings. "Thanks, kid," he said, grateful for all of her support. "Vince, do a few bags of specials for Liv," he shouted and before Liv could object, he winked (must be catching) and left the kitchen.

Pedalling home, she shivered as the freezing evening air assaulted her body. As she wearily locked up her bike, she was grateful for the warmth as she walked through the front door. She was carrying two huge brown bags of Amores food and was greeted by both Burt and Ernie, mewing for food and attention. "Hi!" She shouted up the stairs. It was after seven o'clock and Hal and Jay must be starving.

"We're in the kitchen, Liv!" Hal shouted back. Liv locked the front door and trying not to step on her fur babies, who were skimming around her feet, she walked into the kitchen. Hallie was sat at the kitchen table with Guy. The handsome French teen stood and nodded seriously.

"Bonsoir, Olivia."

Chapter 20

Liv's expression was one of shock. She had completely forgotten that Guy was coming around. He was so lovely and she felt terrible to have lied to him for so long, especially after what he had said this afternoon. He stared at her solemnly, until Hallie jumped up and slapped him on his shoulder. "Pack it in." She scowled at him and then laughed, turning to her big sister. "You do realise he just called you Olivia?" She questioned. Liv's mouth dropped open again but no words came out. Hal grabbed the bags from her and took them to the breakfast bar, calling Jay at the same time.

Guy stepped away from the table and took Liv's hand, kissing it gently. "'allie 'as explained it all," he said smiling.

"All?" She queried her eyes widening as she snatched a look at her sister.

"Relax, sis, he knows everything," Hallie said beaming.

Jay came running in, singing, "Food, food, food, food!"

"Liv brought us Amores." Hallie's whole face had lit up and Jay cheered as he fetched four plates and cutlery. The three youngsters took their seats at the table, Liv just stood there staring. They were chatting like they had been friends for years and Jay was asking Guy to check out the new FIFA game after they had eaten. "Liv?" Hallie turned to her sister as Jay dished out the containers, still surprisingly hot.

"You might need to heat those up." Liv managed to find her voice.

"Naaa, we can eat it quicker now, more time for gaming." Jay winked at Guy. What was it with all the winking today?

"Come and eat, Liv." Hallie nodded at the delicious-looking food, but once again, Liv's appetite had left the building.

"I'm just going to shower and change, then I will be down," Liv said, still a little bewildered. Hal, Jay, and Guy all smiled at her and continued their conversation about which gaming platform was the best. Liv ran up the two flights of stairs, entering her bathroom in a trance. What a weird day. Guy knew her name, possibly that she was twenty and not sixteen, and that she had fraudulently become a student at the institute. Fuck. She was in the shower when without warning, it entered her head that Hal may have mentioned Pip.

No, surely not. Surely, her little sister wouldn't have mentioned the fact that the professor had visited their home. Double fuck. With her stomach churning, she made her way back to the kitchen. She was now wearing long pyjamas and her kimono dressing gown. She had tied her hair up in a loose bun. Her appetite still escaped her, so she poured herself a glass of red wine and took her seat at the table, where the others were all deep in conversation but now about their favourite artists. As she observed her younger siblings, she noticed Hal was very animated, she kept looking at Guy with wide, sparkling eyes. Guy was looking at Hal in the same way, all smiles and endearment.

Jay was oblivious to the hearts flying around the room and between mouthfuls of the delicious food, he was again thoroughly enjoying having another male in the house. Guy turned to Liv, who was deep in thought about what had been said without her present. "You okay, Cherrie?" He asked, his long eyelashes fluttering.

Liv decided, as usual, the best thing to do was be honest. "How much do you know?" She asked quietly, both Hallie and Jay stopped eating and waited for Guy to respond.

"I know everything," he answered with yet another wink. "Your secrets are safe wiz me," he finished with a small smile and Liv felt the breath she had been holding gently blow out of her pursed lips.

"I am so sorry I couldn't tell you, I just loved being at the institute. I should have been honest from the start," Liv said quietly. Guy tilted his head and his smile grew even bigger.

"I have made a talented new friend," he said sincerely. "…and now I have met your beautiful family, I understand completely." He glanced at Hallie when he said the word beautiful and she blushed from ear to ear. Liv turned to look at Jay and he was grinning with a mouth full of food, filling his cheeks. He looked like a happy hamster. Liv could not help but return the smile and raised her wine glass to the three of them.

"Cheers," she said as she lifted her glass and they in turn lifted their glasses of Pepsi Max, all chinking together.

It had been a lovely evening; Jay and Guy had played FIFA and Hal had cheered them both on. When it got to nine-thirty, Liv was shattered. She had tidied the kitchen, finished two loads of washing, fed the cats, and done the lunches for the next day. She shouted up to Jay and told him to switch off the game and get ready for bed. Jay realised he had had more extra time playing than usual, so didn't push his luck. He gave Guy a firm handshake and thanked him for staying for a few games. Hallie said she would see Guy to the door and Jay rolled his eyes at her. "Yeah right…bet you're gonna snog him," he said laughing heartily as he left the games room.

Hallie was mortified. Her cheeks flushed a rosy pink and Guy was officially smitten. He grabbed her hand and they walked down the stairs to the front door. Liv heard them chatting from the kitchen and just as she turned the corner into the hallway, she saw her little sister and the suave French student in a clinch, kissing softly. She edged back into the kitchen and smiled. Guy was lovely, very kind, and just the type of man that she would want for Hallie. Hallie was young but knew her own mind. The Whitmores were all strong, independent thinkers and this was Hal's first relationship. Liv closed her eyes and thought of the conversations she would have to now have.

They were very close and Hal told Liv everything. She knew that Liv would answer any questions she had, without any judgement or embarrassment. She had had sex talks with both of her siblings and felt it was her duty to ensure they had enough knowledge should they start dating and then get into a relationship. Later that night, Jay fell asleep dreaming of becoming FIFA Champion of the world. Hallie dreamt of Guy and the romantic good-night kiss she had that night. Liv had a restless night, her mind not shutting down. She was an honest person, so how could she go on lying to the institute? She had cheated some worthy teenager of a place. That, plus all that had happened with Professor Denton, led to very little sleep.

The week passed quickly, Pip had been texting desperate to see Liv, but between them both and their hectic work schedules, it had meant they could not get together until the weekend. The flirty texts of Pip left Liv in a huge love bubble and even with her grandad's constant calls and visits, work and sorting her own home and siblings, Liv felt happy. One slight issue caused a little shadow over the latest events and that was the text from the Oyster Club. She had pushed it to the back of her mind, but as the week drew to an end, she could not help her brain exploring what she thought lay behind the exclusive gentlemen's club doors.

She had worked over Friday night at Amores, starting off looking after Luca and then assisting in the bustling restaurant, serving and preparing food. She had left the institute as soon as the end bell had trilled, racing home on her bike and swapping it for her car as she knew it would be a late night. Amores had a large Christmas party booked and it would be Sunday morning before she would be able to get to bed. Pip had watched her run towards the bicycle stand from the windows of Studio Two. He had been inundated with meetings as Professor Millward had arrived a week early and sent the faculty into a whirlwind of conferences and meetings after the usual teaching sessions.

He had missed Liv and was itching to hold her in his arms and do unspeakable things to her lithe body. He was also well aware of how hard she worked and the fact that she had looked tired when he had managed to glimpse her in Studio One. He knew she needed sleep more than she needed to see him and so any late-night rendezvous were not going to happen, as much as he wanted them to. After an exhausting day, Liv managed to get into bed around three am. Even though she was exhausted, she again had a restless sleep. Angelo had given her the Saturday off as she was one of the last to leave the restaurant in the early hours. For once, she did not have an alarm.

At seven am, she was wide awake and decided to go down and feed the cats. Liv had tossed and turned so much, that she had given herself a headache. Burt and Ernie were meowing loudly at her feet as she dished out their breakfast in their ceramic cat bowls, each with their names painted on. As her fur babies scoffed their food, Liv changed their water bowls and put the kettle on. She made a strong cup of coffee and chose two chocolate biscuits for her breakfast. She switched the plasma screen on and it flickered to life. It brightened the kitchen, which until now had been lit only by the under-counter lights and a lamp by the settee. Liv curled up on the settee, pulling the grey teddy throw over her legs.

She was quickly joined by Burt, who snuggled up on her lap, purring loudly. Ernie had gone out into the dark, cold morning, on the hunt for any birds, or neighbourhood cats that dared to stray into his garden. By nine o'clock, Liv had caught up on the world news, emptied the dishwasher, and put yet another load of washing on. It always amazed her that the washing baskets were never empty. The morning sun was shining into the kitchen and as she was just wondering what time her family would actually be getting up, when her phone pinged; it was a message from Lilly.

It read: 'Are we still on for tonight? I have spoken to Gary, who is one of the security team. I told him that you are thinking of working at the Oyster and I wanted to sneak you in just to look around. He is quite nice and flirts with me all the time, so he said he would get you in the side door. You will have half an hour to look around and then you will have to leave. Liv, whatever you see, you must not say a word to anyone…ok? I will meet you at eight-forty-five on the corner of Pear Street. Hugs, Lilly.'

Liv's eyes widened in alarm. Oh my god, she was actually going to get inside the Oyster Club. What did Lilly mean when she said Liv couldn't tell anyone what she had seen? What on earth was happening there? She would be finding out later that day and to be honest, she was nervous now. Liv washed and dressed quickly and left a note for Hallie and Jay. She went to the local shop to get Pong a few bits of shopping, including toffees and mints. She spent a few hours with him, cleaning his apartment, sorting his washing out, and making his dinner. She avoided Pip's messages, just sending one text saying she was busy working and would catch up later.

By the early evening, Liv had looked after her grandad, washed and dried her sibling's school uniforms, and dusted and vacuumed the whole house. Jay had gone over to Tom's and was staying there the night. Hallie and Mazz had gone to a friend's birthday sleepover, armed with more chocolate than Cadbury World. She changed into her student outfit of a baggy black tracksuit, black baseball cap, and Converse trainers. She wasn't sure what she should wear at first but decided that the understated look was best. Promptly, at eight-forty-five, Liv met Lilly on the corner of Pear Street, just a short walk from the Oyster Club.

It was still early for the club; however, a range of expensive cars were parked in the well-lit private car park. Liv pictured Pip's car parked alongside them and felt a bit sick. Lilly hadn't said much and Liv could see she was nervous too. This was a big favour she was doing and Lilly could lose her job by sneaking her friend in and that was the last thing Liv wanted. At the side of the fenced-off site was a well-lit path. Liv followed Lilly in silence as she typed in a key code at a large gate. It swung open automatically and Liv found herself holding her breath. Lilly made her way to a fire exit door that was ajar. She turned to Liv and smiled.

"He's done it," she whispered. "He left it open for us." Lilly was excited by this and she beamed at her friend. Liv returned her smile but it did not reach her eyes. They weaved their way down several passages and up two flights of stairs. The place was enormous. They were now walking down a huge corridor. It was plush with thick dark, grey carpet, and beautiful paintings and ornate mirrors aligned the walls. On each side, double doors were evenly spaced out and individually named. Lilly stopped at the third one on the right. A beautifully designed plaque had the words 'The Perowne Suite' in a fanciful font.

Lilly turned and whispered, "This is it, Liv. You have thirty minutes and then you have to leave. Please don't mention my name if anyone stops you." Her brow was furrowed and she looked genuinely concerned as she pleaded with her friend.

"Of course, I won't, Lilly." Liv was even more nervous now and fiercely hugged her friend. Lily turned and made her way quickly down the ornate corridor and through the double glass doors at the end. Liv took a deep breath and without knocking, opened the suite doors.

Chapter 21

As Liv stepped in, she couldn't see much except the plush cream carpet on the floor in front of her. She closed the door gently but it made an unnerving clunk as it shut tight. The large room was dimly lit, except to her far right-hand side where there was a ceiling spotlight. It was shedding light on an artist's table and stool, much like the ones they used in the institute. Frowning at the weird scene, Liv tiptoed her way around the left-hand side of the huge room, staying in the darkest shadows. As her eyes started to adjust, she could make out large pieces of furniture, including a four-poster bed and a large smoking chair, facing the illuminated artist's table.

She was just wondering what the hell was going on when a door opened on the far right of the room. Liv clasped her hand over her mouth to stop any sound coming out as she took in a figure dressed exactly the same as her. A female in a dark Loose fitting tracksuit, black baseball cap, and sunglasses entered the room silently, with her head facing downwards, so Liv could not see her face. As the narrow door closed, Liv watched, eyes wide in alarm, as her identical twin took a seat on the artist's stool. Liv noticed that this imposter also had a mousey brown ponytail sticking out of the back of the baseball cap and she was even wearing a pair of Converse.

As her senses slowly recovered from the shock, Liv also realised that the radio station playing softly in the background was actually Professor Maggie Harpers' favourite station. What the fuck? She could only see the back of this woman as Liv watched her remove her sunglasses and put them on the desk in front of her. She then picked up a pencil and started drawing on the large piece of paper, which was waiting for her on the angled desk. Liv watched on from the shadows, not daring to move, waiting for something else to happen. After a few minutes, Liv un-cupped her hand from her mouth and shook her head.

What on earth was happening? Why would Pip come and watch this? It made no sense. Liv weighed up her options. Quietly, make a run for the door and get out of the club as fast as her legs would carry her, or stay and face the music. Should she ask what was going on and maybe find out the truth about the Oyster Club and Pip? She chose the latter and after taking a deep breath, Liv opened her mouth and said the only thing she could think of. "Excuse me," she said louder and braver than she felt. The artist froze and then dashed to the wall behind the illuminated desk. "Hello, I am sorry to bother you…" Liv's voice trailed off.

She was sure this imposter was pressing a panic button and sending for reinforcements. *I bet Gary will come crashing through the doors at any moment and cart me off to prison,* Liv thought wildly. Suddenly, the whole room lit up and Liv blinked at the light that flooded the suite. It was like a luxury hotel. Liv could see clearly now and there were large wooden drawers, mirrors, and a huge four-poster bed. In front of the bed was a large leather smoking chair. Next to the chair, an elegant side table stood, holding a crystal decanter, half full of amber liquid. Next to the decanter was a single crystal tumbler and a small glass vase, containing a single red rose.

At the back right-hand corner of the room were a mirrored cocktail bar and two comfortable-looking leather settees. As Liv took in the suite, her identical twin made her way from behind the artist's table and now stood in the middle of the suite, sizing up the intruder. Liv realised she was being stared at and bravely met the woman's eyes. She looked nothing like Liv. Angular features and a much slimmer face, Liv was relieved to see that she wasn't a mirror image of herself at all. "Professor Denton no come theez evening?" Her thick Russian accent and low tone made Liv feel like she had walked into a Bond film.

"Umm…no," she answered truthfully.

"Huh." She looked entertained. Smiling, she showed off her gloriously white teeth and thin lips. She had no make-up on but still looked like a Bond girl. "Come sit, ve drink," she said firmly, with a nod of her head. This was not an invitation but a demand. The Bond girl made her way to the mirrored bar and Liv walked quietly to one of the large leather Settee's and nervously took a seat. The Bond girl thrust a crystal tumbler, half full of clear liquid, into Liv's hand and raised another in her own hand. Liv gratefully accepted the water and knocked it back, her throat was ridiculously dry.

She coughed and spluttered as the clear liquid burnt her throat. "Oh, darling, iz not vater." The imposter laughed and placed her own glass on the coffee table. She walked back to the bar and returned with a litre bottle of Smirnoff vodka. Refilling Liv's glass, which was still in her shaking hand, the Russian sat down beside her. Placing the bottle on the table and retrieving her glass, she raised it in the air and said loudly, "Na Zdorovie." With that, she took a large slug.

Liv felt obliged to do the same, raising her glass in her trembling hand, she nodded and took a small sip. This time, the liquid was a welcome relief, as she knew it was alcohol and not water that she was being offered. "So, start at ze beginning, darling. I love good story." The Bond girl then whipped off her baseball cap, revealing cropped silver hair in a neat pixie cut. She was really stunning and as Liv looked down at the cap now on the cushion in front of her, she burst out laughing. As Sasha took in this pretty young intruder, she was slightly envious. She was obviously in her late teens and even without a stitch of make-up, she was naturally beautiful.

Liv picked up the item of amusement, the black baseball cap with a mousey, brown long ponytail, sewn into the closure. Sasha joined in the laughter and the ice was officially broken. Once they had both calmed down and Liv had taken another sip of vodka, she explained why she had snuck into the Oyster Club. She told her that it was she who answered Pip's text and that she had deleted them so he would not know about it. Liv explained that she had fallen in love with him but was scared of what she would find here. Sasha liked this young girl and was impressed by how ballsy she had been to break in to the club.

She decided to help her and told Liv all about the private gentleman's club and how it hosted an array of wealthy, well-to-do men. Downstairs, there was a large cocktail bar with beautiful waitresses who would serve drinks and snacks to the rich men, who wanted nothing more than a quiet drink. There was also a restaurant where, again, beautiful women would accompany the gentleman who wanted an evening of sparkling champagne and scintillating conversation, along with some harmless flirtation. "We also 'ave nightclub…and then theze exclusive suites," she said, eyeing her new guest, watching her reaction.

"I am ze exclusive 'ostess and I will do vhatever zeir heart desires," she finished and waited for this information to sink in.

Liv tried not to be judgemental but could not help but ask, "Are you sleeping with Pip?" Her voice was as shaky as her hand and once again, she found herself holding her breath.

"Pip?" Sasha questioned.

"I mean Professor Denton." Liv stumbled over the words; she felt sick asking.

"Hell, no," Sasha gave a simple reply and Liv blew out the air she had sucked in to her lungs.

"Drink," Sasha instructed, nodding at Liv's glass and Liv picked it up and took a large slug. "I vill explain…" She was now staring straight at her and there was no escape. "I did no fuck Professor Denton…Drink!" She demanded as Liv thought she was going to pass out. She took another huge gulp of alcohol to try and quell her fears. "He come and ve talk, ve dance, ve eat, but ve no fuck. Zat was few months ago, now theez…" she said pointing at the easel and stool scene. It was Sasha's turn to pick up the cap she had been wearing which Liv had placed back on the table.

Sasha examined it closely and then looked at this young beauty before her. "Ven you meet professor?" She was serious now and her eyes were like slits as she measured Liv's response.

"I started at the institute on the fourth of September…but nothing happened until last week."

She looked so vulnerable, Sasha nearly hugged her but that would break her façade of being a Russian bitch who would stand no nonsense. Sasha smiled politely. "Iz okay, darling girl, iz good dates." Liv did not understand and her frown returned.

"What does that mean?" She asked, completely at a loss.

"Ze professor, ee lonely, no want relationship…no complications, so ee come here, ee come to me." Liv looked pale; the thought of Pip spending time with this Russian Bond woman was depressing. "Eet vas end of summer when ee ask for zis," again she pointed to the easel. "Eez strange, no? Ee get vat ee vant, of course. I like drawing now, eet relax me, iz good."

"Are you telling me that he hasn't slept with you, ever?" Liv couldn't bear to say 'fucked' and she was more than dubious that he had not been having it off with this goddess in front of her.

"Eez true, darling. Professor eez my biggest money. I get paid a ridiculous amount for pretending to draw and dress like zis." She laughed. "It eez best job in world…Drink," she instructed Liv again, seeing that her new friend was looking a very odd colour. Liv finished the warming liquid in her glass and Sasha quickly filled it. "All eez good, angel; zee professor as not visited in tree veeks…eez why I text. I feel zorry taking money and ee not be here," she said simply.

"You still get paid? Even if he doesn't turn up?" Liv was feeling braver now, with the liquid courage coursing around her body. Sasha nodded her answer.

Liv couldn't help herself. "How much? How much does he pay per umm…session?" She struggled to put a name on it but the session seemed to fit.

The beautiful Russian tilted her head and tapped her perfectly manicured finger to her lips, deep in thought. Finally, she nodded again. "Between you and me…" She looked sternly at Liv, who was now vigorously nodding like a loon. "Eez tree," she said knocking back her vodka, instantly refilling her glass.

"Three? Three hundred pounds for this?" Liv looked at the empty stool and easel, contemplating changing jobs.

Sasha laughed again. "No, darling…tree tousand." A gobsmacked Liv had no reaction to this, she didn't know what to say. Three grand per session. Was he mad? He must have more money than sense. After Sasha had reassured Liv that Pip had definitely not had any form of sex with her, Liv felt a little more comfortable.

"I wonder who he was having sex with?" Liv said her fears out loud.

Sasha replied quickly, "Iz 'and."

"Oh my god, who is Izand?" Liv looked like she was about to throw up. Was there another Bond woman about to join them?

"No, No, eez 'and!" Sasha spoke slowly and tried to annunciate, along with a hand gesture to help Liv understand.

Liv frowned and then it clicked. "His Hand!" She shouted out and sat with her mouth open in shock. Both women burst into laughter again.

Five hours later, and copious amounts of vodka, the two women had shared life stories and many laughs. Sasha had told Liv how her family had moved to England when she was a teenager. She realised her looks could make her money and became a high-class escort in London. The owner of the Oyster Club had met her at an exclusive bar on Regent Street and made her an offer she could not refuse. She loved her body and loved sex, so why not make as much as she can now, a nest egg for her future? She owned a six-bedroom barn conversion on the outskirts of Worcester. Her boyfriend was a bouncer at the local nightclub, Tramps.

They had discussed her job on their first date and although he wasn't delighted, he respected her and her choices. They had decided to work and earn as much as they could, so that when they had enough in the pot, they could marry, have lots of children, and not worry about paying the bills. Liv was not surprised to hear that Sasha and her partner had saved almost four hundred thousand pounds and that she and Craig Is it Tramps or Craig? we're hoping to give up work in the new year. She owned several acres of land with their property and went into great detail about her pet alpacas, of which she had four.

Liv was enthralled by her story and thought her own was pretty dull in comparison. She told Sasha she worked at Amores and she had clapped her hands in recognition; apparently, it was her and Craig's favourite restaurant. She touched upon her parent's death and that she cares for her younger sister and brother. Liv also talked fondly about Pong and it turned out Sasha's nanna was also living with dementia. After a few hours, the unlikely friends decided to call it a night, or rather morning. Sasha used her posh mobile phone to call the Oyster Club's exclusive car service as she did not like the idea of Liv walking through the city on her own at that time in the morning. Liv said she would walk as she didn't live far away, but her new Russian Bond friend insisted.

Ten minutes later, Sasha escorted Liv out of the suite and down the luxurious corridor. Once through the double doors, there was an open hallway. On the right and straight ahead, there were glass doors leading to other long corridors. On the left-hand side were two sets of lift doors. Sasha put her hand over the plasma pad on the wall and a gentle ping showed them that her palm had been accepted and the lift was on its way. They were both giggling as they stepped into the lift. The mirrored walls gave an optical illusion, showing images of them both going on forever into the distance. Liv's head started spinning and she was glad when the lift doors reopened.

On the ground floor, there was a lot more activity. Sasha threaded her arm through Liv's and with her head gestured to the right, she said, "Zat eez bar…and zat is restaurant," she said indicating to her left. "Nightclub eez at back," she said with a smile. She loved to dance the night away and if the suite wasn't booked, that is where she would have been. A handsome gentleman in his fifties walked in front of them. "Good morning, ladies." He smiled and continued on into the open bar, which was busy for this ungodly hour. As they walked through the lobby, there were a number of gents milling around, most stood waiting to check-in.

The ladies drew much attention, even though they were dressed in identical tracksuits. Mortimer was waiting outside, holding open the rear passenger door of a black, sleek limo. "Good morning, Ma'am," he said to Sasha.

"Morty, I vant you to ensure my friend gits home zafely." Morty smiled warmly as the two women hugged each other tightly.

Liv ignored the open door and made her way to the front passenger seat. "Morty, do you mind if I sit in the front, please?" Liv asked politely. Although her head was spinning from all the vodka, she managed to get into the car like a lady without falling over.

Chapter 22

After sleeping away most of Sunday, Liv had been a little disappointed to hear that Pip had been dragged up to Edinburgh for a gallery opening that Professor Millward wanted to attend. She had an influx of texts and voicemails from Pip, full of apologies, as he had had different ideas of how he wanted to spend his weekend, and they of course included Liv. She was actually grateful that he wasn't around, so she could mull over the Sasha situation. To her utter astonishment, Liv had actually liked the gorgeous Bond woman. Although it had crossed her mind how on earth could she compete with a Russian sex siren?

She had never been out to a posh restaurant with a man, never really danced with a man, so compared to Sasha, she was a complete novice. The thought was depressing. Liv busied herself with household chores and although she had caught up on some missed sleep during the day, she had yet another restless night.

Monday morning seemed to go in a blur. Liv arrived just in time for the start of her art lesson at nine o'clock. She had been engrossed in her latest drawing when she realised for the first time in a few hours, she hadn't actually checked her mobile phone. She had been drawing in her own studio during the early hours and then cleaned the fridge at six am for something to occupy her overstimulated mind. Forgetting to check her mobile, she had ridden her bike to the institute in a brain fog. Now glaring at her mobile, Liv had somehow missed several missed calls and texts from Tina asking her to call her back urgently.

She caught Maggie's eye and they both nodded at one another, Maggie understanding that Liv had to make a call. She slipped out of class and waved at Mrs Bushell as she ran past. "Morning," she called but didn't wait to hear the response. Liv ran to the bike shelter, where her cold fingers pressed the redial button on her phone. After a brief conversation with Tina, she undid her bicycle lock and sped off in the direction of the Waterside Village. On her arrival at Pong's apartment, she found Tina in tears. Two solemn-looking female paramedics were kneeling on the floor, where her beloved grandad was lying, grey and still. "No," Liv whispered.

"He's gone," Tina blurted out between sobs as she flung her arms around Liv's slim frame. Once she had finished crying and let go of a shaking Liv, she offered her and the paramedics a cup of tea for the shock. Liv shook her head but the paramedics both gratefully accepted. Tina made them large mugs of tea and insisted Liv sit down, handing her a large glass of brandy, which Pong always had a good supply of. "It's for the shock, my love," she said kindly. Stifling another sobbing outburst, Tina excused herself. She had to notify the management team of Pong's death and fill in the necessary paperwork.

One of the paramedics introduced herself. "My name is Ruby and this is Angie," she said walking over to where Liv was sitting. Ruby joined Liv on the settee, whilst her colleague discreetly covered the body with a blanket. Ruby covered Liv's shaking hand with her own. "Tina said you are Gerald's granddaughter?" She queried politely. Liv couldn't speak, she just stared at her grandad's body lying on the floor. Ruby continued patiently, "We are so sorry for your loss. We did everything we could but he had already passed away when we arrived." Liv said nothing. "It looks like he suffered a massive heart attack; there was nothing anyone could have done," she said softly, rubbing Liv's cold hands.

"We have some paperwork to do," Angie spoke now, as she stood and sipped her tea. "Would you mind if we stayed here with you? We can fill out all the forms here." She was a slim lady with a pretty, friendly face. Her mousey hair was loosely tied up in a ponytail. Liv tried to smile but her mouth was set in a grim line. She turned to Ruby who was sitting next to her. She was an Asian beauty. Her long, black shiny hair, was tied up in a neat bun. She was also slim and naturally pretty.

"What happens now?" Liv asked, her own voice sounding strange in her head.

"We will complete the paperwork and arrange for your grandad to be taken to a funeral director. After that, they will be in touch with you in regards to the funeral, although Tina said your grandad had already organised it?" Angie's voice was very soothing and Liv guessed that both ladies were used to sitting with shocked and distressed relatives.

This was all so surreal. Pong had been the only senior family member left after her parents died and she was left to care for Hallie and Jay. He had helped as much as he could, however, the dementia had made things difficult for him and as the years progressed, she had also taken responsibility for his care and well-being. Now he was gone and the same lonely feeling overwhelmed her, just like it had the day she was informed of her parent's tragic deaths. She was truly an orphan and solely responsible for her siblings. She had been for years now, but just having Pong in their lives had been incredibly reassuring and important to her. Now he was gone, gone forever.

"Have some of that drink, honey." Ruby placed her arm around Liv's shoulders and then gently rubbed her back. Angie sat herself down in the armchair and began flicking the screen on her computer. Liv took a slug of brandy and felt the liquid warm her as it made its way down her throat. She felt chilled to the bone. After what seemed like an eternity, the paramedics said their goodbyes, both hugging Liv hard, before making their way to their next emergency.

Liv managed to say a quiet thank you as they left and whilst sitting there alone, with Pong's body still covered on the floor, she took her phone from her pocket. Checking the time, she realised it was only one o'clock in the afternoon and decided not to disturb Hal and Jay in school. She would wait until they were all together at home before she broke the news to them. Her memory returned her to the day she had to tell them that mum and dad were not coming home and she took another slug of brandy to try a quell the heartbreak she was feeling. She sent a text to Maggie, apologising for missing the afternoon session and explained that she wasn't well and had gone home to bed.

She messaged the same thing to Stacey, informing her that she would not be going to the restaurant that afternoon or the next day. She had several missed calls from Pip; she replied saying she had a stomach bug and was home in bed. For some unknown reason, she did not want any of them to know the truth. Tina came to join her just after two o'clock as she had officially finished her shift. She refused to leave Liv's side until Pong's body had been removed. They both drank brandy and talked about the funny things Pong used to do, the same stories he would tell over and over, and the way he was a real charmer with the ladies.

Eventually, there was a knock on the door and two stoic gents entered. Paying their respects with curt bows, they informed Liv and Tina that they were going to take Gerald to Fervers and Sons Funeral parlour, just as Pong had planned. He had arranged and paid for his own funeral years before the dementia had taken his mind and logic. It was on his 'Respect' form, which noted his wishes should he need care and also his funeral plan, as and when the time came. When they had left the apartment, which had always been full of life and warmth, it quickly became gloomy and icy cold. Liv wondered if she would ever feel warm and safe again.

Chapter 23

Liv pushed her bicycle through the quiet streets and contemplated how best to tell her siblings that their beloved Grandad Pong was gone. She smiled as she remembered how he had been bestowed the title of Pong. It all started when Hallie was a toddler and she couldn't say the word grandad. He was always playing Ping Pong at his house and would love to play with Liv's parents. He was teaching Liv how to play and Hallie was desperate to join in, even though she was just a baby and could barely walk at the time. She would sit on the Ping Pong table and take great delight in trying to hit the small ball with her hand.

She had started saying the word Pong whenever she saw her grandad and the name had just stuck. Hallie had always been sporty and her love for all sports, especially football, had grown with her. Now Pong had gone forever. They had all adored him, even though his memories had faded and he hadn't recognised his own grandchildren for a while. They would go and visit as much as they could, although with his behaviour changing, they had found it increasingly difficult. The dementia had taken most of his memory from him but had also made him very angry and frustrated at times.

As she closed the front door to her home, Liv decided to bake some brownies and cookies. Anything to kill time before her sister and brother came home and she would have to break the news.

Just before midnight, an exhausted Liv was just turning the lights off in the kitchen when there was a sharp knock at the door. Jay and Hal were in their rooms, their best friends, Tom and Mazz, had come round to offer their condolences to the grieving family. They had all been devastated when they heard the news that Pong had sadly died. Liv was the only one not shedding a tear as she was keeping it together for the youngsters. Her siblings were now ensconced in their bedrooms.

Liv had discussed it with both Tom's and Mazz's parents and they had all agreed that the youngsters could miss a day off school, due to the bereavement.

Their own children had looked at Pong as a grandfather figure and were also terribly upset by the news. Liv had already put off a visit from Pip, saying they all had stomach bugs now and that he should stay away from the house. He was not happy but said he understood. Again, due to Millwards' whirlwind schedule, he was incredibly busy himself. She hadn't mentioned her grandad's demise.

Wearily, she opened the front door. There was a waft of strong, flowery perfume that overwhelmed her nostrils as the cold night air filtered onto her warm skin. Liv took in the tall frame of a stick-thin woman; supporting the fakest-looking boobs she had ever seen. The stranger was wearing towering neon green heels and a long, shocking pink Mac, with a matching trilby-style hat. Liv almost laughed. It was a bit early for a Christmas-o-gram and shouldn't she be dressed as an elf or something festive? The woman looked Liv up and down and sneered through her veneers. Her bleached white teeth looked odd against her tanned skin. "Hallie Whitmore?" She said pursing her lips together and tilting her head.

Her American accent was strange and Liv had no idea who this woman was. She was also in no mood for messing about and it was freezing cold, so she just nodded silently. There was no way she was going to disturb her little sister at this hour of the night. The woman suddenly looked very intimidating, her eyes mere slants and her nose now high in the air. She looked like she had stepped in something nasty. "I am only going to tell you this once, child, stay away from my fiancé, or there will be consequences." She sneered, her overfilled lips looked like they had been stung by a bee.

Liv's mouth hung open and her eyes were wide with shock. There was no way Hal was seeing anybody other than Guy and surely this woman was too old to be his fiancé. And Guy wouldn't string Hallie along if he was actually engaged to another woman, would he? The thought repulsed her. "I think there has been a mistake…" Liv began carefully, trying to keep her cool.

The neon stick talked over her. "There is no mistake. You're sixteen and fucking my fiancé, so this is what you are going to do." Her English/American accent made her sound even more snide. "You are going to stay away from him, or you will pay," she finished with a look that could turn liquid to stone.

Liv was still gobsmacked and stood shaking her head in disbelief. "I assure you I am not sleeping with your fiancé and you definitely have the wrong person…" She was about to stand up for her sister when the nasty woman said through gritted teeth.

"I am Alexia Millward and I own the institute and I own Philip Denton." A smug look crossed her face and then she pouted, tilting her head slightly, still observing this plain, pale-looking child before her.

Liv felt the bile rise in her throat. "Philip Denton?" She questioned in a small voice.

"Professor Denton to you. The man is engaged to me…you hear!" Her voice was sharper and higher than before and Liv felt vulnerable stood there in her pjs and kimono dressing gown. She continued to shake her head in disbelief as the neon menace turned on her heels and clicked her way down the driveway to a waiting car. A gorilla-sized man in a dark-fitted suit was holding the car door open for her and as she stepped into the rear of the vehicle, she called out, "Stay away from him or there will be consequences!"

With that, the burly man closed the door and turned to look at Liv. He was built like a brick shit house and Liv bit her bottom lip as she considered what he was going to do next. He simply nodded at her and with a grimace, he turned to get into the driving seat of the sleek-looking vehicle. The engine hummed to life as Liv stood in the doorway, frozen in shock.

After a few minutes, the cold night started filtering through into the cosy hallway. Burt mewled at her feet and rubbed his soft, furry body around her legs. It brought her back to her senses and she quickly scooped him up and closed and locked the door. She walked up the first staircase, deciding not to bother her brother and sister. She could hear the boys watching a film as she could hear the sounds of revving cars and fast-paced music blaring out. The girls were talking quietly behind closed doors, and so, Liv continued up the second flight of stairs, cuddling Burt in her arms.

When she arrived at her bedroom, she gently placed Burt on her bed and went into her en-suite bathroom. She switched the shower on and undressed. The frigid night air had chilled her to the bone and she was shaking from the cold. Liv stepped into the stream of water and then sat on the floor, under the hot, powerful jets. She folded her arms around her legs and rested her head on the top of her knees. There in the security of her own bathroom, she started to cry. For the first time in years, she let go. Floods of never-ending tears came in waves as she reflected on her day.

Pong was dead and Pip was engaged. She was completely grief-stricken and heartbroken. Why had she let Pip into her already complicated life? Liv let the tears fall as she huddled under the protection of the streaming hot water, trying to get warm. It seemed like hours later, she regained control. Switching off the shower and wrapping herself in a huge towel, she made her way into her bedroom, where Burt was already snoring softly. She flumped down on the bed and wrapped the covers around her body. She closed her eyes in an attempt to shut the world out but it didn't work, she was in too much pain.

The night seemed endless and she was physically and emotionally exhausted. Unfortunately, her beloved Pong, and then Pip, appeared clear as day in her mind, not letting her sleep or get any rest. For the umpteenth time, she checked her alarm clock; it was just after three am. She gave up on sleep and donning a warm, navy lounge suit, she made her way downstairs to crack open yet another bottle of Shiraz.

The rest of that week was a blur as she dealt with Hallie and Jay's grief and organised her grandad's affairs. Pong had been strong-willed and wanted a no-fuss funeral. He had already arranged and paid for a 'Pay and take me away' funeral package, as he called it. He would be cremated and in a few weeks' time, his ashes would be sent to Liv. She knew he wanted them scattered in the Cathedral Garden, under his favourite tree, where his beloved wife, Hazel's, ashes were scattered. Hallie and Jay both returned to school after their one day off, deciding they were better off there as it would keep their minds off things. However, when at home, they were both sullen and tearful.

Liv had a day clearing Pong's apartment. Her dear friend and Pong's wonderful carer, Tina, stayed over after her shift to help Liv sort through his belongings. All of his clothes and furniture were modern and in great condition, and so Liv decided to donate them to the home. There were elderly people less fortunate than Pong who needed not only clothes but furniture too. They were grateful for a bed and mattress, or table and chairs, etc. Sidney (affectionately known by them all as TCP Sid due to the fact he washed in TCP and the odour was always strong on his skin) popped in to give Liv a hug and pass on his condolences.

Tina smiled as Liv held her breath, being closer to Sid than she really wanted to be. He was ninety-seven and had no family. Pong had been one of his drinking partners and he would miss him greatly. Tina escorted him back to his flat, loaded with bin bags full of Pong's smart clothes and a few items to remember Pong by, including two bottles of brandy and a poker game. Liv looked around the bare apartment and her heavy heart sank lower. She would no longer have to constantly check her phone, or constantly pretend to be her mum in order to placate her dear grandad. No more visits at all hours of the day and night, sorting his shopping, washing and cooking for him; it was all over.

Another life gone, their little family now consisted of three; well, five as she had to include Burt and Ernie. Between them, Liv, Tina, and a number of staff had moved all the furniture required to other apartments in the building. The only thing left was the carpets and curtains. An elderly lady was due to move in soon and Liv knew there was a waiting list for the apartments as the site was the best in Worcester. The carers actually cared, although Tina was the absolute best and outshone them all. Liv had cleaned every room, although they were not dirty. She wanted the new lady to be able to walk in and not have to worry about anything. She had also left a card, welcoming the newest resident to their new home.

Liv had presented Tina with a bottle of Advocaat (her favourite), a huge bunch of flowers, and a card. A tearful Tina said she would open the card when she got home as she did not want to break down completely. They hugged each other and promised to stay in touch. With that, Liv walked away from Waterside Village for the last time. Her car was loaded with a few boxes of Pong's photographs, her paintings, and a few keepsakes, including his war medals, which she would keep safe for Jay until he was older. A huge lump formed in her throat as she turned back and took in the sign for the last time.

Chapter 24

Visiting the Edinburgh Art Exhibition had been a distraction that Pip could have lived without. Although he enjoyed James' company and the artwork was magnificent, he would have preferred to be with Liv, holding her naked body close to his. Instead, he and James had a whistle-stop visit to Scotland to attend a new art exhibit and see the fine piece of art that James wanted to procure for his collection. Whilst inspecting the painting, Professor Millward had a message from a friend in Italy, saying that a major piece of artwork had just become available to purchase. His excitement was obvious, although his travelling companion did not seem to share his joy.

"What is wrong with you, dear boy?" James asked with concern. "You do not seem to be yourself?" He questioned.

Pip smirked; he loved the old man and realised his brooding over Liv had meant he had neglected his friend. "I've met someone," Pip replied quietly.

James' face lit up with a large smile. "Good for you, Son," he said patting Pip's back and shaking his hand at the same time. "It's about time," he laughed heartily. Pip was smiling too, although he hadn't long received the message that Liv had a stomach bug and all he wanted to do was get on a plane and be at her side, comforting her. He had frowned absentmindedly and James tilted his head, taking in the expression. "What is it?" He asked his young prodigy.

Pip decided to tell him the truth. He told him the whole story over a few large scotches. He began with how he had first seen Liv (although he thought her name was Hallie) and then continued with the unfolding story which led them today. The fact that he couldn't stop thinking about her was driving him mad. "Ahhh, so you're homesick for your sweetie pie?" James chuckled.

"You're not concerned about her being at the institute under false pretences?" Pip asked with concern.

The old man smiled. "I think we can overlook that fact, as not only are you in love with her but her artwork is exquisite." He chuckled again and Pip wasn't sure if it was the scotch or the sound of the old man's reverberating laugh that warmed his soul. "Well, I hate to do this to ya, kid, I know what it's like to be away from the woman you love…" Pip raised his eyebrows and James smiled. Had he fallen for someone too? "However, this painting in Venice is a must-see, so how would you like a short trip overseas? I have a few people I would like you to meet and of course, I value your opinion on the painting."

Pip looked sullen. To be fair, Liv had a stomach bug and hadn't been replying to his messages. She wouldn't be happy if he just rolled up and demanded to look after her. "How long would this 'trip' take?" He asked his mentor, a serious expression on his face.

"Well, let's think about this." His brow furrowed as he thought through a plan of action. "We could fly to Venice tomorrow, relax for the rest of the day, see the painting Wednesday, then meet acquaintances and business contacts Thursday and Friday." It was Pip's turn to frown. James ignored him. "Then fly back Saturday morning, in time for the Christmas Ball," he finished with a broad smile. The thought of returning to his own sweetheart made him happier than he ever thought he could be.

"This was supposed to be a few nights away and now you're saying we are going to be away for a whole week?" Pip questioned sullenly; he too wanted to get back to the woman who had captured his heart. Being away from her whilst they were in Scotland was bad enough, but now flying off to Venice and not being able to hold her in his arms until Saturday was depressing.

"Come on, son, you have to give her a chance to miss you." James was still smiling, enjoying the fact that his young friend was obviously completely smitten.

Pip knew that Liv was inexperienced when it came to relationships and the fact she was poorly made him think. Maybe a few days' break is what she needed. Give her some time and space to process what had happened between them and think things through. She must be so overwhelmed with the institute, looking after her family, and of course, having a sexual relationship with her professor. "You're right, James. It might be a good thing to give her a chance to breathe, a chance to realise that I am serious about her," he finished.

Both he and James were smiling broadly, chinking their crystal tumblers together. Having both agreed, all that was left to do, to let the women folk in on their plan. James' companion was not amused as she was hoping to spend some quality time with her handsome man. Liv did not respond to Pip's text; maybe she was still asleep. He shrugged and tried not to let it bug him. This evening was going to be full of drinking, so maybe the alcohol would numb these feelings of want for her.

Liv looked at her phone as it beeped and lit up. Another message from Pip. She felt sick. Still grieving for the loss of her grandad, she was also struggling with what to say to say to him. She had found out that he had been visiting with Sasha at the exclusive Oyster Club. The fact that he had paid for her company was disturbing and Liv could not get her head around it. He was handsome, seemed well-off, and had a good job, so why would he feel the need to pay a woman to spend time with him? It made no sense. Then there was the way that he had asked Sasha to dress. Identical to Liv. Surely that is just weird? What was she supposed to make of that?

Then there was that woman, Alexia Millward. He had also been sleeping with her and she said they were engaged. Liv ran to the bathroom and hung her head over the toilet. Her face was pale and her whole body was clammy. She wretched and brought nothing up. There was nothing in her stomach to bring up. She hadn't eaten properly since Pong had passed away and then all this with Pip's women. *Omg, Pip's women!* She retched again. Liv felt a furry friend at her hip and turned to see Burt rubbing his chubby chin against her and giving her affection. She held back the tears as she scooped him up into her arms and turned so he was cradled on her lap like a furry baby.

Burt purred loudly, loving the attention. She rubbed his thick furry tummy. He felt so soft and his purring was like ointment to her soul. Hallie and Jay were on their last few days at school before the Christmas break. They were both cheered by the upcoming Christmas Ball at the institute and they had not stopped talking about it for the last few days. Both Tom and Mazz were attending too, so the girls were gushing about how they were having their hair and what shoes they would match their stunning dresses. The boys, however, were more interested in the fantastic food that would be on offer and spent hours perusing the high-class menu online.

Liv did not have the heart to tell them she would not be attending but was just going to send them off in a taxi and say she would meet them there later. She had pre-booked a taxi for both journeys, so when the youngsters were ready, they could just call and get picked up. Hallie and Mazz had been obsessed with the gorgeous French student, Guy. Hallie was besotted and Mazz was so excited to hear all about Hal's boyfriend. They had also looked through the institute's site but at a different menu. They had been looking at the male students who had paintings showing in the huge gallery on the day of the gala. A true smorgasbord of handsome, rich young men from around the globe.

Liv sighed. Life was so complicated, she thought to herself as she cuddled up to Burt. The devastation she felt at Pip's lies was immense. She had felt the pain of loss when her parents were killed and now on the death of her grandad. They loved her and were taken from her; they had no choice. Pip, on the other hand, had professed his love for her, she had trusted him with her body, she had fallen in love with him, and all this time, he had been sleeping with another woman. Not just sleeping but engaged to an American woman, who looked twice Liv's age. Then there was Sasha and the messed-up stuff going on at the Oyster Club. How could he lie to her like that? She had trusted him.

With Burt securely in her arms, she made her way back to her bed. She lay Burt down by a sleeping Ernie and got into bed. She pulled the sumptuous duvet over her clammy body and closed her eyes. Her head was pounding and she desperately needed some rest. Once again, she was in for a night of broken sleep and nightmares.

Liv was consumed with her latest portrait. Having once again given up on getting some sleep, she had spent the last four hours holed up in the studio. Burt and Ernie were cuddled up on the corner settee, never wanting to be far away from their precious human. It was as if they sensed she needed the extra support. Liv was deep in thought, adding dashes of white paint, which suddenly changed the subject from a flat image to a human being, who could have literally stepped off the canvas and into her arms. She gulped and shook her head at the thought of the painting being real.

Liv jumped as she heard the doorbell, 'We wish you a merry Christmas' chiming loudly through the quiet house. Returning to the present, Liv looked up at the clock, it was after three in the morning. Both cats stretched and yawned, hoping that their human would soon retire to the comfort of the bedroom. Thank goodness Hallie and Jay were stopping at their friends as the bell would have disturbed the whole house. Liv made her way to the door. Before she looked through the peephole, she realised that the late-night visitor could be Pip.

She had asked him not to message her as she still had a stomach bug, hoping this would deter the onslaught of texts and missed calls. She had actually found out that Pip was away abroad with Professor Millward and was due back on the morning of the gala. It was, in fact, now Saturday morning, so was it him?

Coming straight from the airport to rip her head off for not answering his messages. She held her breath as she peered through the peephole. She took in the quiet cul-de-sac. The street lights were illuminating the snowflakes falling gently from the sky. There was no one outside the door and for a second she questioned if she had actually heard the bell or imagined it.

As she went to unlock the door, she saw a black envelope on the floor. She picked it up and turned it over, her name was written in intricate calligraphy in a fine silver pen. Confusion overtook the sleep exhaustion as she wondered why anyone would post a Christmas card at three o'clock in the morning and then ring the bell. She opened the envelope and produced a large square invitation a black matt card with the same silver writing came out, inviting Liv to the Christmas Ball. It had the time, date, and address on it and Liv felt that she had wasted someone's time and effort as she was not attending. Turning over the card, she found a message which read:

Olivia,
 Please meet me in my office at eight tonight.
 I need to see you; we need to talk.
Forever yours
Pip

Without thinking, she yanked open the door, the cold air assaulting her warm skin. There were footprints in the snow-covered drive leading up to and away from her front door. She strained her eyes to try and see up the road but there was no sound or movement. Apart from the falling snow, all was quiet. Pip had been within touching distance and now he was gone. Her stomach turned as she thought about him. All of these days and nights in turmoil, utterly devastated by his lies. He had told her he loved her and she had believed every word. But he had lied. The whole time he was making love to Liv, he had been fucking his finance and god knows who else.

She had tried to forget him, ignored his constant calls and texts, even blocked his number, yet now he was back. He had been at her door but instead of confronting her, he had left this card. A handwritten invitation to the gala and on the reverse, a plea for her to meet him in his office. She stood in the doorway, snowflakes softly falling and melting on her flushed skin. Maybe he's left her. Maybe he ended the engagement because he had finally realised he loved Liv.

Suddenly, there was a small chance. A slight possibility that Liv's broken heart might be fixed.

As if in a trance, she closed and locked the door. She walked back into the brightly lit studio and stared at her painting. Pip's handsome yet serious face stared back. Liv knew she had to meet him, she had to find out how he really felt about her. She had to know.

Chapter 25

By late afternoon, the siblings and their friends had returned to the Whitmore home and an excited household was getting ready for the ball later that evening. Hallie had been worried about her big sister. Liv had lost so much weight over the last few weeks and had to cope with Pong's death and all that had been involved. Liv looked pale and exhausted and both Hallie and Jay knew she was struggling with Pong's loss. They hadn't seen Pip for a while and they knew something was up, but Liv had asked them both not to talk about him as she did not want to discuss it.

However, when Hallie and Mazz arrived home, Liv welcomed them both with a huge hug and an upbeat energy. She asked the girls if they would help her with her hair and make-up in preparation for the prestigious evening and the girls squealed in delight. Jay and Tom had also arrived overly excited. It had been snowing and they had had a morning of sledging and snowball fights. Returning home, they had found a mound of warm chocolate chip cookies that Liv had prepared. They had a few hours to play FIFA before they had to shower and get into their posh tuxedos, something they were eagerly awaiting to do. They had been practising their James Bond phrases and poses all week.

Everyone was in the kitchen/diner and Liv had just fed Burt and Ernie, who were noisily scoffing their meals. The TV was suddenly muted and the humdrum chatting and laughing stopped. Liv was drying her hands at the sink when she turned to see her siblings and their friends all grinning like idiots. They were all standing on the other side of the breakfast bar, on top of which was a large black box tied in a large, beautiful black satin bow. Liv placed the hand towel on the counter and looked at them all with confusion. "What's this?" She asked, taking in the large gift box. Jay pushed the box over to Liv's side of the counter, still grinning like the Cheshire cat.

"Open it, Liv," squealed Hallie; the others nodded their heads in unison. Liv smiled, their excitement was contagious. She gently undid the bow and slid the lid off the large box. The was an envelope and then black tissue paper guarding something beneath. Liv couldn't help but smile as she took in the youngsters' faces, all watching her impatiently. She opened the small black envelope to reveal a bright pink card. She opened the card and deciphering the scrawled writing, she read out:

My darling girl,
  This belongs to you. Your beautiful mother would be so proud. Live your life!
  With affection
Edie
X

Liv was speechless. The words soothed her bruised heart. With a shaky hand, she placed the card at the side of the box. She dared not look at the young faces that were still staring at her. She did not want to cry. Slowly lifting the tissue paper, she revealed a silky turquoise material. Liv held her breath as she gently lifted the material and there in her hands was the stunning peacock dress from the boutique. The tiny beads and gems glistened magnificently in the spotlights of the kitchen. Liv looked up in awe. "Edie gave it to Hal when she collected her dress," Jay said practically bouncing on the spot.

"She said there was no one else who could do it justice and she wanted you to have it for the ball," Mazz said breathlessly.

"You're going to look ace in it, Liv," Tom gave his opinion, just as excited as Jay.

"She has also sent you a gorgeous pair of shoes," Hal interjected. "And we have brought you these." Hallie was super excited about a second, much smaller box, which she now slid across the counter towards her sister. Liv placed the dress gently onto the tissue paper and picked up the smaller black box. It too was tied with a black satin bow. As she pulled the bow and opened the box, she found a stunning peacock hairpin, an emerald bracelet, and drop emerald earrings. They held identical emerald stones linked with a dainty gold chain.

"You brought these for me?" Liv asked, slightly choked. They all nodded gleefully as Liv took in their happy faces.

"We all put together and brought it for you," Jay said proudly.

"When she said she wanted you to have the dress and shoes, we had to get you these, Liv." Hallie's eyes were now brimming with tears. "We are so proud of you, but we weren't sure if you were going to attend tonight's ball. Otherwise, we would have given it to you before." Tears were now rolling down Hal and Mazz's cheeks, the lads just looked uncomfortable. Liv just started laughing. She hadn't even thought about what she was going to wear and now she had been given these beautiful gifts. How kind were the people who loved her? "And mum had that gorgeous peacock clutch bag in her collection. We thought it would match perfectly," Hal managed to say between sobs.

Liv placed the box carefully on the countertop and walked around to the youngsters, where they had a huge group hug. Jay and Tom broke away first and grabbing a handful of cookies each, they disappeared upstairs to the games room, leaving the girls talking about up-doos and eyeliners. The lads enjoyed a few hours gaming whilst the ladies showered, primped and preened in much anticipation of the Christmas Ball. By six-thirty, Jay and Tom were standing at the front door impatiently waiting for their taxi. They looked so grown up in their black tuxedos and Jay reminded Liv of their handsome dad.

Many selfies had been taken and now the girls had joined them, Liv was bursting with pride. Liv was still in her kimono as after having her own hair and make-up done, she had helped Hal and Max get ready. They looked stunning and much older than their sixteen years. A car horn sounded from the road and the four bustled out into the cold, snowy night. Liv smiled at the excited chatter and waited in the chilled evening air until the taxi had safely driven away.

She practically ran up to her room where she picked up and reread Pip's invitation. She looked up into her wall-length mirror and took in her appearance. Thanks to the girl's make-up artistry, the dark skin under her eyes, from the endless sleepless nights, was hidden. A soft blush on her pale cheeks had lifted her skin. She had gone for a natural look, with beige and brown eye shadow, finished with a dark brown liquid liner which lifted into a small flick at the end of her eyelids. A rich, chocolate brown mascara had lifted and separated her long lashes. Along with plum-coloured lipstick which plumped her full lips, an identical varnish had polished her finger and toenails.

Her hair had been piled into a sleek French pleat, adorned with the dazzling diamante peacock feather hairpin. Even in the soft light of the bedroom, the pin was glinting in all its glory. Liv nervously put her delicate earrings in and fumbled with the small clasp on the identical bracelet. She sat on the bed and absentmindedly stroked Burt and Ernie, who were both purring loudly. Checking the bedside table clock, she realised she had to put her dress and shoes on. To be honest, she had been putting off trying on the dress, as she knew it was at least two sizes too small for her. She would be gutted if it was too tight but had other dresses that would do, so she was trying not to worry.

In the dressing room, she removed her kimono, revealing sexy, teal lace pants. She was going braless as the dress had a plunging back. Carefully lifting the dress over her head, she felt the soft, silk material glide over her warm skin. Closing her eyes tightly, she waited for the dress to catch. It would probably stick on her bum, stomach or boobs. Hearing the beaded feather-like trail hitting the floor, she blinked her eyes open and stared in disbelief. There, looking back at her, a reflection of someone she didn't know. It reminded her of her parents who used to attend balls and galas all of the time.

With immaculately executed hair and make-up and a stunning dress, her mum always looked incredible, and Liv used to be able to stay up late to wave them off. Today was Liv's turn. The dress fitted perfectly and was actually loose enough that should she wish to eat anything this evening, there was room to expand. Although the thought of food made her stomach churn, she knew at some point she would need to eat something. She really had lost a lot of weight. She was excited as she put her new shoes on. A stunning pair of Manolo Blahnik's in a deep turquoise silk edged in shiny sparkling gems. They were gorgeous.

Liv became nervous as she grabbed her handwritten invitation and her mum's long cloak and clutch bag. The cloak was a floor length, black velour number, with a silk effect lined hood. Her mother's go-to for the winter balls. She had also found the clutch bag from her mum's beautiful selection of evening bags. It had peacock feathers depicted in tiny beads and it was beautiful. With one last look in the mirror, she ushered Burt and Ernie downstairs into the laundry room, where they happily accepted a handful of treats. Once the cats were safe, she donned the cloak and grabbed a gift bag she had prepared on the counter, along with the peacock clutch bag, her invitation, and her keys. After securing the front door, Liv made her way to the awaiting taxi.

As the car slowly navigated the snowy roads, Liv's mind raced about what was going to be said between her and the man she loved. Would he kiss her? Or more…? Her stomach churned again as she took in the snow-laden streets of the city she loved.

Chapter 26

When Liv arrived at the art institute, the snow had begun falling heavily. There was a larger number of security guards around the site itself, especially at the main reception entrance. Liv prepared to show her invitation when one of the guards stepped forward. "Miss Whitmore?" His broad American accent echoed slightly in the entrance gallery.

"Yes," she replied in a timid voice, slightly taken aback.

"Follow me," he said sternly. Liv heard a whimper from behind Mrs Bushell's desk. With everything going on her head, she had nearly forgotten about the bag of Christmas gifts. Placing her clutch bag and invitation on the reception desk, she moved around to the left-hand side and opened the desk's half door. She was greeted with a very excited spaniel, whose tail was wagging so much, Liv thought he was going to take off. She had been bringing Freddie treats since she had heard him whining during her first few weeks at the institute.

Liv had to duck out of a lesson to calm down an emotional Pong. Mrs Bushell had been called away from her desk and Liv had heard a whining noise. Once she had ended her call, she looked over the desk to see the handsome face of a tan-brown spaniel. He had a thin streak of white fur on his head and a white chest. If ever there was a dog handsome enough to be a model, it was him. She had sneaked around and petted him. He was so friendly and just wanted attention. He had a red collar with a bone-shaped identity pendant, it read 'FREDDIE' on one side and on the other, 'Mrs Bushell's Fur Baby' and a phone number.

Since that day, Liv had snuck him treats and toys and he recognised her perfume and the sound of her voice. Placing the gift bag onto the worksurface, she produced an unwrapped present from it. A soft, fluffy reindeer dog toy. Freddie was delighted and grabbed it in his mouth. The security guard coughed to gain her attention and Liv stood up and stared at him. She reached for the ceramic jar on Mrs Bushell's desk and retrieved a bone-shaped dog biscuit.

Freddie dropped his new toy and sat obediently looking up at Liv with his huge blue eyes.

She smiled down at him and rewarded his patience with the delicious treat. With a final pat on his head, she turned and walked back around to the front of the desk. Picking up her peacock clutch bag and invitation, she nodded politely at the mean-looking guard. He turned and she followed him through the entrance gallery and past the spiral staircase that led to Studio Two. She resisted the urge to stare at the stairs that led to Pip's domain. Silently, they walked through one of the large doors to Studio One. Liv thought it was strange that tonight's guests would be led through the studio and not taken via the more direct tunnel straight to the great halls' reception area.

She followed the guard down the Studio One mile tunnel, which brought them out into the eerily empty seating area. It was dark and as they walked, the ceiling lights sprang to life. She could hear the jazz band playing music in the Main Gallery and the rumble of chatter. They must be using the rooms on the other side of the vast hall for toilets and a respite from the bustle of the ball. Liv started to feel uncomfortable as the lights continued to flicker to life. She followed the security guard as they walked the length of the deserted area.

As they passed Maggie's office, the light illuminated the area outside Pip's office. It also lit up the huge bulking figure of another guard. It was the one she had seen before. The night Pip's so-called fiancé had visited her house, he had been the hulk who was protecting her. The guard leading her abruptly stopped in front of this huge beast of a man. He was the brick shit house. He looked Liv up and down, still wrapped in her thick cloak, with the hood down. He walked towards Pip's office door and silently gestured to her with his hand. She walked towards him as if in a trance. He knocked on the door loudly, making Liv jump.

Without waiting for Pip to reply, he opened the door and again gestured for Liv to walk through. She walked into Pip's office, her mind reeling and wondering how she was going to start the conversation. His huge chair was facing the opposite direction when she entered. The door closed with a sharp click, again making her jump. She was a nervous wreck. Just as the lurid smell of over sprayed floral perfume hit her senses, the chair spun around to reveal none other than…Alexia Millward. The look of disdain on her face said it all. "I thought I told you to stay away from my fiancé," she said, her botoxed face not allowing for much movement.

"He invited me here," Liv said bravely, throwing the handwritten invitation onto the desk.

Alexia laughed, a high-pitched fake cackle. Liv wondered if she was actually a witch and if so, if had she put Pip under her vile spell. "You listen to me, bitch…" Alexia began, literally spitting out each word. "This is the last time you will ever enter this building; I will have security notified that you are no longer part of the institute's art programme." Alexia's nasty smile faded quickly as Liv stood staring at her with no response. Little did Miss Awful America know that Liv had already had a meeting with Maggie weeks ago. She had agreed to discreetly finish and leave at the end of this term.

Not getting the rise she had expected from this little British brat, Alexia stood up, her fists banged heavily on the desk. Liv took a step back. "He loves me!" She screamed, again banging on the desk. Alexia suddenly stopped shouting and with another snide cackle, she stood up, holding her trim stomach.

"I wanted you to be the first to know, I am pregnant." She smirked maliciously. "Philip is going to be a daddy; I am telling him tonight," she finished, watching her enemy pale. Liv felt her legs turn to jelly. She thought Pip had changed his mind and picked her. She had been sent his handwritten invite and had stupidly thought that he had realised he loved her and not this American witch. "Now, if you stay away from him, he will have everything…me, a baby, a career." Alexia counted each one off on her bony fingers. "And of course, money. But if you dare to go near him again, he will lose everything."

Once again, she used her witch-like fingers to count off each punishment. "If you see him again, I will know. I will abort his baby." She actually smiled as she spoke. Liv felt faint. "I will take him for every dime he has. He will lose his job and have no career. I will make sure his life is over." Her eyes tightened and her lips pursed together. "He loves me but he has cheated before. He always comes crawling back. I will tell my daddy what a shit he has been to me and his whole future will go down the pan," she finished, staring at her opponent.

Liv put her hands up in the air. "Please…please you have said enough." Liv's voice was quiet and shaky compared to her nemesis. "Don't hurt him, please don't hurt him," she begged, feeling useless. Alexia was pregnant with Pip's baby and Liv couldn't bear the thought of him losing the person he loves, losing his unborn child, and even his career. Her heart would break even more. Liv was in love with Professor Philip Denton, and even though he had cheated and lied to her, she still loved him. She did not want to hurt him; she certainly didn't want him to suffer at the hands of Alexia. Liv took a step back and shook her head.

She felt as though her heart had literally been ripped from her chest and torn into a billion pieces. She had never felt pain or loss like this. Alexia smiled menacingly; she knew she had won, this little English girl was no match for her. She made her way around the desk, her huge purple taffeta ball gown making her look larger than she was, or maybe it was her pregnancy showing, Liv thought miserably. She walked right up to Liv's face. "Wait ten minutes, then leave the same way that you came in," she sneered nastily. Not waiting for a response, her and her ghastly dress left the room.

Liv stood stock still and tried to slow her rapid breathing down. Her body felt as though she had just had a physical fight. Suddenly, it felt as if someone had tipped a bucket of scalding hot water over her head. The heat spread down her body and she found herself gasping for breath. Unclasping her cloak, she let it fall to the floor. She leant onto the sturdy oak desk in front of her. She kicked off her impressive heels and felt the need to run. She looked out of the patio doors to her right at the heavy snow. It had already covered the grounds.

She knew that opening those doors would set off the alarms but couldn't face sneaking out the way she had come in, in case she bumped into Pip. Her heart simply wouldn't cope. She looked down in despair and noticed something on the desk that might help. Without thinking, she grabbed it and ran barefoot from the office.

Chapter 27

As Alexia entered the grand hall, she was ebulliently smug. The meek English girl had been defeated and Alexia was still the queen. Philip had been on her radar for years and there was no way she was going to let some pale-faced teenager take him away from her. As she glided into the Great Gallery, all taffeta and fake smiles, she didn't notice that all was quiet. The jazz band had stopped playing and the chatter was no more. Her father, Philip, and a small group of others she didn't recognise were huddled in front of the temporary stage. "Daddy?" She called out and still didn't realise her voice had resounded loudly around the vast hall.

Her mind still cheering her on as she had won her latest battle, but the penny still hadn't dropped. Her focus was on the handsome professor, who had turned to her with a thunderous look on his handsome face. God, he was hot. The hag who worked with him seemed to be restraining him as her father walked towards her, his face grave. "Daddy?" She said again, this time realising that the huge space was silent except for her own resonating voice. She looked confused as her father addressed her.

"Alexia, I have never been more ashamed and disappointed in you," he spoke quietly, however, his words also seemed to carry around the huge gallery. She was about to demand a reason for this outburst from him when he turned and addressed her security guard. The huge brut had been stood on her right-hand side. "Please arrange for my daughter to be escorted from the institute immediately," he said determinedly, "I will deal with her later."

The guard nodded but Alexia was going nowhere. "What the fuck is happening?" Her voice was shrill and again seemed to fill the room.

"Where is she?" Professor Denton was now at Millward's side. "Where's Liv?" He demanded. Maggie and the other people she didn't know had now joined them.

Mrs Bushell stepped forward from James' side and without warning, slapped Alexia hard across her overly made-up cheek. "How dare you upset your dad like this and how dare you talk to Olivia the way you did, you horrible bum hole," she finished angrily. Alexia was in shock; no one had ever dared lay a finger on her, let alone talk to her like that.

"Daddy, you saw that…she just assaulted me, I will sue your old ass, you bitch!" She shrieked. Her father stepped in front of Joyce Bushell, protecting the woman he loved. Without words, he nodded at the burley guard who stepped forward and guided Alexia away with his huge frame.

"No, wait…" Pip rushed forward and grabbed Alexia's arm. "Where is she?" He demanded again, his face full of fury. The guard then roughly pulled a wire from Alexia's battery pack on the back of the taffeta creation. A loud tone emanated from the sound system and everything went quiet again. Alexia looked at the wire in his hand and it slowly dawned on her that her whole conversation in the office had been heard by everyone at the ball. Glaring around the room, she took in the onlookers' faces as they sat uncomfortably at their elegant tables.

As her mind rallied as to a way to excuse what she had said, the guard leant into Professor Denton and whispered something in his ear. He then turned and practically dragged Alexia from the gallery. Her mouth was gaping like a fish, but for once, not one nasty word escaped. Earlier that evening, she had demanded to be the one who would present the art awards later that evening. She loved being the centre of attention. The old hag who worked with Denton had fitted a mic and battery pack to her dress, just before Alexia had been informed that Miss Whitmore had arrived on site.

Maggie was suspicious of Alexia and thought she was up to something. She decided to flick the switch to the microphone and battery pack so that she could hear any conversation that the minx might have. What Maggie hadn't realised was that the mic had already been linked to the main stage speakers and as soon as Alexia addressed Olivia, in what she thought to be a private conversation, the Great Gallery had filled with their whole drama.

"Liv's in my office," Pip spoke as he turned and ran towards the other side of the Great Gallery. He was closely followed by James Millward, Hallie, and Guy. Maggie took control of the ball and with her arms around the visibly shaken Jay, Tom and Mazz, she instructed the band to begin playing again and shouted to the guests to all have a drink and enjoy what was left of the evening. The chatter erupted with much to gossip about. Joyce helped seat the teenagers down at their table and then went to check on Freddie, in much need of her fur baby's love to calm her down. For the first time in years, she was absolutely seething.

Pip burst through his office door, his mind working overtime. What must Liv be thinking? How long had Alexia been threatening her? Is this why Liv has not returned his calls this week? He felt sick. How could Alexia sink so low? He was relieved that she had been escorted from the building, as for the first time in his life, he had wanted to actually punch a woman in the face. His office was empty, apart from a cloak in a heap on the floor and a pair of heeled shoes which had been left beside it. He picked up the cloak and instantly smelt the scent of Liv's perfume, Olympia.

The others had followed him in and a distraught Hallie went straight to the desk and picked up Liv's peacock clutch bag which was abandoned on the desk. "She was here, this is hers," she whimpered as Guy placed a reassuring arm around her shoulders. Placing the cloak on his desk, Pip noticed the invitation and picked it up with his hand shaking in anger. Alexia had been a ruthless liar and he could only imagine what was going through Liv's mind. He had to find her. His eyes scanned the room and he made his way to the patio doors, pushing the emergency exit bar down, he shoved the doors open.

The snow made the doors hard to push and an alarm bell tolled, the sound echoing around the building. There were no footprints in the deep snow, so she could not have left this way. Another member of the security team entered the office and spoke quietly to James. "What is it?" Pip questioned harshly.

"The security team have advised me that Miss Whitmore has not left the building via the main entrance." Pip scanned his office again. What was he missing? Where would Liv have gone?

"Come on, Freddie my beauty, find our friend," Joyce Bushell's Black Country accent filled the room as she entered with a handsome-looking dog on the end of a lead. Freddie's nose was twitching as he bounded straight to Liv's shoes. He sniffed enthusiastically and his tail started wagging. "Good boy, find Liv," Mrs Bushell said excitedly. Freddie turned and practically pulled his owner out of the office. The others followed their faces creased with confusion and worry. Freddie took a sharp right from the office door and galloped towards the archives lift, Joyce being dragged behind him. He stopped abruptly, and with his nose pressed against the closed doors, he started barking.

"Good boy, you are so clever." Joyce was patting his head in praise.

Pip came to a halt beside the dog and turned to James. "She's gone to my studio," he said gravely. "I told her once it was my one place I felt safe," he finished grimly, his mind racing with what she must be thinking right now. James pulled out his ID badge and flashed it at the small camera on the wall. The lift doors slid open and they all made as if to enter. "No." Pip turned to face them all. "I need to see her on my own." He was so wound up with Alexia's lies, that he needed to put things right; he needed to make Liv see the truth.

They stared back at him, each one nodding in agreement. He entered the lift, scanned his hand onto the screen and then selected the Correct floor. The lift doors closed smoothly and there was a small jolt as the mechanism that moved the lift to the lower levels kicked in. As the door gently pinged open, he took in the scene. Kiwi, one of the security guards, was asleep with his feet up on the desk. He was hugging a half-drunk bottle of whiskey and wearing a chunky blue knitted hat and scarf. His cheeks were rosy and he was snoring loudly.

The computer screen was showing clips of football highlights and he was totally oblivious to the fact he had a visitor. Pip walked quickly to his left and again scanned his hand to open a secure door which led to the private studios.

Chapter 28

Liv had made her escape out of the office and down the corridor to the archive lifts. Using the ID badge she had found on Pip's desk, she scanned access for the lift doors to open. She was debating what to say to the security guard that she knew would be on duty on the lower floor. However, when the doors pinged softly open, she saw the guard was fast asleep. He was the happy Liverpudlian gent who always said hello with a smile and liked to tell a joke. She remembered he had mentioned he was retiring soon. Today must have been his last shift as he was cuddling a bottle of whiskey and his desk was covered in cards and gifts. He was wearing a chunky blue knitted hat and scarf and his cheeks were flushed; he must be so cosy.

Along with the insulation, he had had a few slugs of whiskey and fallen fast asleep. The computer screen was showing a football game but the noise was drowned out by the sound of his snoring. Grateful for not having to give an excuse for hiding down here, Liv quickly made her way to the left-hand door and used the stolen pass again to scan access to the private studios. As she stepped into the dark corridor, the first set of lights sprang into action illuminating the floor in front of her. As she walked forward, another section of lights lit up the next part of the corridor. She felt as if she was in a horror movie and a shiver ran down her spine.

The next light illuminated large wooden double doors on her right, with a sign saying 'Prof. P. Denton: Studio'. She opened the door, relieved to find safety and, tiptoed in. Immediately, the room was lit with what seemed like bright sunlight. She had heard Maggie speak of the incredible lighting available at the institute and how with modern technology, artists could have bright natural-looking light to aid them when working. Liv was blown away by the light in here; it literally felt as if she were outside on a beautiful summer's day.

Unfortunately, with a lack of shoes and suitable attire, she felt cold. Her temperature plummeted even more when she looked around the large studio, taking in the pictures that adorned almost every wall. They were all of her. Sketches of her sat at her desk in Studio One, and drawings of her sat in the crowded auditorium, trying to hide under her baseball cap. Simple sketches of her eyes, face and hands were everywhere. A large pencil sketch was framed and hung on the right-hand side of the studio. It depicted Liv in her baggy jumper and tracksuit bottoms, her small hands holding a mobile phone. She was wearing her baseball cap and all you could see was her chin and mouth.

It was a snapshot of her studying her phone. A lonely, stark picture and although you cannot see her eyes, the artwork exudes sadness. She drew in a large breath and walked further into the room. In the middle of the studio was a stool and desk, Identical to the ones they used in Studio One. Her mind flitted to the Oyster Club in an unwelcome memory, which she quickly shook out of her head. Moving forward, she approached the desk which was at a ninety-degree angle, with a brilliant white cotton sheet covering the artwork beneath. With intrepid fingers, she gently pulled the material so it fell to the floor, revealing the painting below.

Liv stepped back as she took in a depiction of herself. This was nothing like the sketch on the wall. This was a skilfully painted image of herself. Her hair was piled up on top of her head, tied up in a loose bun, with tendrils framing her happy, smiling face. She was wearing her favourite butterfly kimono and was holding a bottle of red wine. He had captured her perfectly and Liv was taken aback by the accomplished artistry. She knew Pip was an expert in landscapes but she had never seen any of his portraits. The painting was breathtaking.

It looked like she was turning back to look at her admirer, her beautiful face lit up and her body relaxed. She was barefooted and wearing nothing but the silk kimono. Liv studied the painting for a few minutes, the wide smile looking back at her not seeming right for the way she felt now. She caught a glimpse of something moving to her left but it was just her reflection in a huge, ornate mirror.

She glared at her reflection. She was wearing the most beautiful peacock gown, the teal silk changing colour as the material caught the light. It looked bluer in the studio's exceptional natural effect light. The beaded peacock feather detail that splayed out behind her, glinted and shone, along with the diamante pin that was holding her hair up in an elegant French pleat. The outfit was simply stunning but Liv was staring at her face. The woman looking back at her looked pale and gaunt, with a haunted expression on her drawn face.

After a few minutes, she turned to her right to examine the pencil sketch. It must have been when she had first started at the institute and was juggling caring for her siblings, her grandad, work, and the institute's schedule. She had the weight of the world on her shoulders. She turned back to the mirror on her left. The reflection showed loss. Loss of Pong, loss of weight, loss of the institute placement, and the most heartbreaking of all, the loss of love. She wanted to throw something at the mirror and destroy the image she was staring at, but the last thing she wanted was seven years of more bad luck.

She turned her head again, so she could take in the painting in front of her. The image exuded joy. It was when she had been the happiest she had ever been. Her sister and brother were doing well, Pong was safe and ok, and she enjoyed her work. The institute placement meant she could spend hours drawing and painting and of course, she had fallen in love. Pip had changed her world and made her feel safe and loved. Her joyous smile on the canvas was contagious and she reached out her hand to touch it, trying to capture some of that happiness back.

Just as her finger touched the canvas, she heard a gentle click and then, "Liv?" Her hand dropped to her side and she took an involuntary step back. "Olivia?" It was a question, not a statement and she felt as if a bucket of ice had been tipped over her head. Pip was here in the studio with her. She started shaking, wrapping her slender arms around her body for some warmth. He was standing by the door trying to calm his breathing down after the frantic search for the woman he loved. If it wasn't for the peacock dress, he would not have recognised her. The gem-encrusted clutch bag that had been left on his desk matched the dress perfectly.

Nonetheless, the frame of the woman standing in front of his painting looked nothing like Liv. The female's body was almost skeletal and pale. He had said her name twice and the figure had not spoken. Maybe it wasn't her? "Olivia Whitmore?" He said determinedly. The figure suddenly fell to her knees. He ran to the shaking fragile woman and knelt down at her side. After shaking off his tux jacket, he wrapped it around the woman's shoulders. As he did so, his warm hands touched her cool skin, making her flinch and look up at his concerned face. "Oh my god, Liv," he whispered. "What have I done to you?" He grabbed her in both arms and hugged her tightly.

That was too much for her to bear and tears started rolling down her pale cheeks. "I am so sorry; I had no idea…" His words were lost on her as he heard her quietly sobbing. His own eyes were full of unshed tears. He had fallen in love with this young woman, who had bravely coped with the loss of her parents and had managed to raise her siblings into two happy, wonderful individuals. She looked after her grandad who had dementia and she had worked god knows how many hours to make sure her family had what they needed. He had turned her world upside down and she had trusted him. His grip grew tighter on her slim frame. He would never forgive Alexia for this.

Adjusting his arm to support her weight, he lifted Liv with ease. His stomach churned at how light she felt; she had lost so much weight and it sickened him. He strode over to the far corner of the studio and placed her gently on the large comfortable settee. He grabbed a throw from off the arm and wrapped it around her shuddering body. She was sobbing into her hands and he felt as if his heart was literally breaking. She felt his arms move from around her as she was placed on the seat and felt even colder than before.

Why would he want to stick around with her having a mini breakdown? She felt the blanket being placed around her and then nothing. The tears continued; she couldn't stop them. All these months of hurt and upset had taken their toll. She felt lonely, cold and heartbroken as she sat curled up on the settee on her own. Suddenly, a warm arm enveloped her and she felt his body sit close to hers, pulling her onto his lap. He sat there not saying a word, holding her tightly and letting her cry.

When she opened her eyes, Liv felt her headache and rubbed her forehead to try and relieve the pain. "Is your head hurting?" A quiet voice spoke near to her face. Keeping her eyes closed, she nodded gently. After leaving her briefly, he returned and held her in his arms again. A cool, wet piece of cloth was placed on her forehead and she felt instant relief, letting out a long breath. Opening one eye, she saw Pip's face only a few inches from hers. He was taut and anxious, his piercing gaze causing her to recoil. She closed her eye and raised her hands to cover her face. "Don't," he demanded as he pulled her hands down.

Shaking her head, she knew she had to face him. She didn't want to hear about the engagement or the fact he was soon to be a dad but she knew she couldn't put it off. Slowly she opened her tired, swollen eyes and gazed directly into his. He was so handsome, even though his glare was serious and she knew he meant business. "I guess I'm happy for you," she said unconvincingly, breaking eye contact, dropping her gaze and focusing on his neatly tied bow tie.

"For fuck's sake…" It was almost a growl and she made eye contact immediately. "Liv, seriously? Alexia has been lying to you…about everything." He paused to make sure she was keeping up with what he was saying. "I have never dated, slept with, or proposed to her, and she is certainly not pregnant by me." His tone was angry and she closed her eyes as she assessed the words.

Alexia had lied to her. Her eyes were still closed when she answered, "But why?" Her head felt like a washing machine, everything tumbling around and getting mixed up. Why would Alexia Millward lie to her? She felt a warm hand cup her cool cheek.

"Look at me." His tone had softened and when she opened her eyes, he let out a long breath. "You scared me tonight," he said honestly.

"I scared you?" She said making to sit up but her pounding head prevented that and she stilled. His expression instantly darkened. "Please don't be mad at me," she said quietly, taking in his solemn look. His hand was still cupping her face and his finger moved to trace her full lips.

"I am not mad at you," he said quietly. "I am mad at Alexia Millward for lying, but most of all, I am mad at myself. I should have realised something was going on. When I was in Scotland and Italy, I couldn't understand why you weren't replying…but now I Now know Alexia had spread her poison," he finished with a melancholy look, which Liv hadn't seen before.

With her head pounding, she just raised her hand and cupped his cheek. "I love you, Philip Denton," she whispered as an overwhelming tiredness hit her. Her hand dropped back to her side and her heavy lids gave in to complete exhaustion and closed.

Hours later, Liv awoke from a deep sleep to the comforting sounds of Ernie's purring and Burt's snoring. She smiled as she recognised her fur babies were near and slowly opened her eyes. Hal was lying on the bed next to her, stroking a relaxed Ernie's tummy. Burt was cuddled up next to Liv and grumbled as she stretched and turned to face Hal. "Hello, sleepyhead," she said as she greeted her drowsy big sister. "How are you feeling? You've slept for hours." Hal and Jay had been so worried last night. "That bitch has a lot to answer for," she said seriously.

"Bitch?" Liv questioned, still half asleep.

"Alexia Millward!" Hal answered quickly. "The bitch who lied to you about seeing Pip." Suddenly, yesterday's events came flooding back and Liv sat up, her head feeling heavy and foggy. A disgruntled Burt refused to move and adjusted himself accordingly, with a look of utter disgust at being disturbed.

"She was lying," Liv said to herself.

"Why didn't you talk to me? I'm your sister, you can tell me anything." Hallie had grown up and Liv realised in that moment just how much. "Liv, you don't have to do everything on your own. Jay and I can share some of the load now, we are all older and we are a team."

Liv smiled at the word team, as their dad used to say they were the best team in the world. Liv took Hal's hand and squeezed it. "I know, Hal, I am sorry. It just seemed like so much was going on, I just…" Words failed her and Hal grabbed her sister in a huge hug.

"Am I interrupting?" Pip's sexy voice came from the doorway. He was carrying a large wooden tray with coffee and fresh croissants. The smell of which was delicious.

Hal smiled and kissed Liv on her forehead. "I will leave you to it," she said brightly springing off the bed, earning another grumble from Burt and a startled look from Ernie. As she passed Pip, Hal turned around and mouthed the word 'Hot' to her big sister, making them both laugh. Pip also looked amused even though, he wasn't in on the joke. He placed the tray down on the bed and climbed on gently, so he didn't disturb the cats.

"You look brighter," he said happily. He looked like a model in dark grey Adidas bottoms and a matching t-shirt.

"I was so tired," she answered honestly. "So much has happened," she finished, absentmindedly stroking Burt's super soft fur.

"We need to talk and clear all this mess up. Starting with Alexia Millward." Liv bit her bottom lip, even the woman's name disturbed her. "She lied about everything," he said solemnly. "Her dad is furious with her. She's been shipped back to America this morning, so she can't hurt us again." He was watching Liv for any reaction, no matter how small.

She felt numb. Alexia had caused a lot of issues but there were other problems that needed addressing. Liv was always honest and decided to broach the subject she had been avoiding. "I have something to tell you," she said shifting uncomfortably in the bed.

He had picked up a mug of coffee but placed it back on the tray. "Okay," he said seriously, his mind reeling.

"It wasn't just what Alexia said and did that messed with my head." She bit her lip again, not sure how to continue with this conversation; she knew he would have a dickie fit.

"Go on," he said encouragingly, wanting everything out in the open.

"I know about the Oyster Club," she said quietly. His mouth opened as if to speak but he closed it again before any words came out. Shit, did this mean he was too angry at her to even speak? Bravely, she decided to carry on. "I know about Sasha." His eyebrows were raised and his expression was one of shock, but still, he didn't speak. Taking a deep breath, Liv decided to tell him everything. "I went to the club and met her…actually. I thought she was lovely."

"You went to the Oyster Club?" He said surprised.

"Yes," she answered.

"So, you got into the most private, high security gentlemen's club in England?" He queried again, his face showing complete disbelief.

"Yes," she said simply.

"How on earth did you get in?" He was dumbfounded.

Not wanting to get anyone in trouble, or worse sacked, she replied as honestly as she could. "A friend of a friend snuck me in." She felt embarrassed now.

"And you saw Sasha?" He questioned.

"Yes," she answered again.

"And she spoke to you?" He was astounded.

"Yes…and we had a few drinks…"

"You drank with her?" He interrupted again in shock.

Oh god, is he about to blow up?

"And you got out how?" He questioned.

"I walked out the front door." Again, an honest answer. He did not speak, so she decided to go on (Maggie's expression, in for a penny, in for pound, sprung to mind). "It was the early hours of the morning and Morty, one of the club's chauffeurs, kindly dropped me home." Again, she finished, staring at Pip's shocked face. She was just waiting for him to start shouting when he shook his head and started laughing. Real belly laughing, which confused the hell out of her. He took in her confused face and tried to take deep breaths to stop the laughter.

With a huge smile on his face, he began. "So, you broke into a high security gentlemen's club, not only met with and got on with the top mistress, drank with her, walked out of the front door, and finally, got a lift home with one of the club's chauffeurs?" He said in disbelief. This was it; he was about to go ballistic.

"Yes," she said, waiting for the explosion.

He crawled nearer to her and lifted Burt over to the empty side of the bed. Turning to look directly into her eyes, he cupped both of her cheeks in his hands, and said, "I love you."

His broad smile took her breath away. "You're not mad?" She questioned, shocked at his reaction.

"How can I be mad at you? You are the most incredible woman I have ever met and I love you." With that, he kissed her fiercely. She responded by wrapping her slender arms around his neck and kissing him back with such ferocity that one thing naturally led to another.

Almost twelve months later, Olivia Whitmore was stepping into the most stunning taffeta red ball gown she had ever seen. It had a fitted strapless bodice and a full, floor length skirt. Naturally, she had found a stunning black beaded, heart-shaped hand bag amongst her mum's treasured collection. As she adjusted the gown, she thought back on how fast the year had gone. Both Hallie and Jay were doing well at school. Her inheritance had become hers after midnight on Christmas Eve, so life was not so much of a struggle. Burt and Ernie were sprawled out on the chaise long, admiring their owner in her new frock.

Tonight, was the institute's Christmas Ball. It had been a year since she last attended and it hadn't gone well. Although, since that awful day, her life had been like a fairy tale. Pip had practically moved in and she couldn't be happier or more in love. Professor James Millward had also taken her under his wing and had made Liv an honorary professor of art, teaching at the institute two days a week. She still worked at La Amores as and when they needed a hand. As she slipped on her black patent heels, she called out to the bathroom, "You nearly ready? I don't want to be late." She smiled as she thought of her own artwork hanging in the reception's reception area and the Main Gallery.

She was so excited. "I'm coming, beautiful," he shouted back. "I wouldn't miss tonight for all the world," he finished, a huge smile on his excited face as he quickly tucked the small Tiffany box in the inside pocket of his tuxedo.

The End